NEW MEMORIES

NEW MEMORIES

NEW MEMORIES

S.E. SHEPHERD

This edition produced in Great Britain in 2024

by Hobeck Books Limited, Unit 14, Sugnall Business Centre, Sugnall, Stafford, Staffordshire, ST21 6NF

www.hobeck.net

A CIP catalogue for this book is available from the British Library.

ISBN 978-1-915-817-51-8 (pbk)

ISBN 978-1-915-793-52-5 (ebook)

Cover design by Jayne Mapp Design

Printed and bound in Great Britain

ARE YOU A THRILLER SEEKER?

Hobeck Books is an independent publisher of crime, thrillers and suspense fiction and we have one aim – to bring you the books you want to read.

For more details about our books, our authors and our plans, plus the chance to download free novellas, sign up for our newsletter at **www.hobeck.net**.

You can also find us on Twitter **@hobeckbooks** or on Facebook **www.facebook.com/hobeckbooks10**.

This book is dedicated to all the wonderful women I get to call my friends.

Real friends are the ones you can count on no matter what. The ones who go into the forest to find you and bring you home.

Mindy Kaling

PROLOGUE

SUSAN, MAY 1992

MARTIN STILL WASN'T HOME when Susan returned. Retrieving the key to her lockable box, she made her way over to the tea chests in the corner of the lounge and dug deep. Unlocking the box, she took the top diary from the pile, turned to the next blank page and wrote the date. Susan knew she ought to jot down the day's events, in particular the conversation that still had her head spinning, but one single sentence bounced around her brain, demanding to be written. So she wrote it: *I've told him everything!* At that moment, there was a knock at the front door. Shoving the diary back into the box, she locked it and hid it under the baby blankets in the tea chest. With no time to put the key in its usual place, she popped it in her pocket. As she made her way down the hall, the knock came again, louder and more insistent this time.

HANNAH, MARCH 2023

WITH HER SPIKY, bleached hair and assortment of ear piercings, Hannah knew she was no Jessica Fletcher. But from the easy smile on her face, down to her comfortable, ever-present biker boots, Hannah Sandlin PI still radiated cordiality. Her aim was always to make her clients feel as comfortable as possible. She had learnt that the best way to get anyone to talk was to allow them to relax and give them time. Whilst she waited for this particular client to feel ready to speak, she attempted to suss her out.

Liv Farnley sat opposite Hannah, fidgeting and sipping cautiously from a mug of near scalding, black coffee. She had come to Hannah via Dave, Hannah's employee. He had brought in a couple of clients last year, too, and it was helpful to have his input. However, Dave said that as he'd met Liv at an AA meeting, on this occasion it might be better if Hannah conducted the initial consultation alone.

The café Liv had chosen to meet in was not one that Hannah had previously frequented. Personally, she would've preferred her and Lottie's favourite café, the one by the clocktower, or maybe Costa Coffee. She'd walked past this place often and had never felt the slightest inclination to enter. But this was a familiar place for her client, and that was the most important thing right now.

Hannah glanced around, taking in what little ambiance there was. The tables were white Formica; the walls a faded seaside blue. There were no personal touches as such. No flowers, no paintings, not one quirky, inspirational quote on the wall. It could be described as basic or functional, if you were being polite, spartan if you were not.

Straightening her back and trying to remain upright on the slippery plastic bench, Hannah indicated she was ready to talk business.

'So, why don't you tell me what Sandlin Private Investigation can do for you?'

She wished the lighting was a little more subtle. Perhaps a couple of those oversized bulbs with an amber filament. But no, this café had 1970s' fluorescent strips, which gave the impression her poor client was under interrogation. Hannah smiled in an attempt to assure her she was not.

Liv shuffled in her seat. It was clear that despite Hannah's approachability, Liv was still unsure. If she wasn't repeatedly tucking her dark hair behind her ears, she was fiddling with one of the many thick, silver bands on her fingers and thumbs, or chewing on her stubby nails.

Hannah waited patiently. She knew Liv wouldn't tell her anything until she was ready.

Eventually, Liv spoke. 'Dave gave me your number yesterday; he said you could help me.'

'Yes, I'm sure I can.'

Liv took a few more tentative sips from her mug. Her eyes were constantly darting from the door to the only other customer in the café.

'Listen,' Hannah said. 'I'm not charging you for this meeting.

It's just us. You can talk to me about whatever you like. And I won't involve Dave if you'd rather not.'

Liv instantly replied, 'I don't mind. He seems like an all-right bloke.'

'He is. But, if you don't want him to know why you need help, I have other people I can call on.'

Liv reached for her aged, leather, satchel-style bag and began rummaging. Hannah caught a glimpse of empty tobacco pouches, loose change, old forgotten packets of throat sweets – the usual detritus of a well-used bag. Pulling out two old photographs, Liv held one in each hand. After a short pause, she said, 'This man killed Susan Farnley. She was my mother.'

She carefully placed the photograph from her left hand onto the table, in between their mugs.

Hannah remained silent, sensing there was more to come.

She wasn't wrong. Placing the photograph from her right hand onto the table with equal precision, Liv continued, 'And this man ... was convicted of the murder.'

She sat back in her seat, clearly awaiting the obvious remark.

Hannah didn't disappoint. 'Surely ... it's the same man!'

Shaking her head, Liv said, 'But it's not. *You* look at those photographs and you see the same man. *I* see my dad, Martin.' She gently tapped the photograph she had previously held in her right hand. 'And I see his shit of a brother, Ray.'

She tapped the other photograph, far less affectionately.

Secretly delighted that this case had just got a hundred times more interesting than anything she could've predicted, Hannah replied, 'That's fascinating. I have to admit, I've often wondered what it must be like to be related to an identical twin. But I'm going to need a lot more detail. I mean ... I understand that to you this is a clear-cut case. You obviously have no doubts about who's to blame. But, if your mother was killed, there must've been police involvement, a court case, evidence!'

Hannah waved her hands in the air to suggest that so much must've already been investigated. She couldn't help thinking that people didn't end up getting convicted of murder willy nilly.

'There *was* a court case. But sometimes people get it wrong. You can't say no one's ever been wrongly convicted of a crime, or that the police haven't made mistakes.'

Liv took a swig of her coffee, which seemed to have finally cooled down.

Picking up her mug, Hannah did the same. It wasn't a great latte. Disappointed, she placed it back on the table. 'I told you on the phone yesterday that I'm an ex-police officer, didn't I?' she asked.

Liv nodded.

'So, I'm clearly not in the habit of accusing the police of mistakes.'

'But even you must know it does happen.' Liv bit down gently on her thumbnail, then asked, 'Do you smoke?'

Hannah shook her head.

'Shame. We could've carried this on outside.'

'I'm happy to talk wherever you're most comfortable,' Hannah said. 'Would you prefer to head over to the park? It looks like the sun's trying to make an appearance.'

'Yeah. If you don't mind. I really need a smoke.'

They took a couple of gulps, and then abandoned their drinks and shrugged on their jackets.

Hannah went to the counter to pay the bill. Liv stuffed the photographs back into her satchel and swiftly rolled a tiny cigarette.

As soon as they left the café, Hannah asked, 'When did this happen?'

Lighting up, Liv replied, 'Over thirty years ago now. I was fourteen when my mum was killed.'

She smoked ferociously, taking drag after drag. Barely stopping for air.

'I'm sorry to hear that.' There was genuine compassion in Hannah's voice. What an awful thing to go through at that age. At *any* age. 'Was your dad arrested soon after? I mean ... was he the obvious suspect?'

'Yes. The police picked him up within hours. We lost them both that night.'

'We?'

'My older sister, Annie, and my little brother, Toby. We all went to live with my grandma. We never lived back in our house. Some other family eventually made it their home.'

They walked in silence for a minute or two, before reaching the small, well-kept park.

'It's hard to believe it all happened. Even now, it still surprises me. How stupid.' Liv dropped her cigarette on the grass, stubbing it out with her converse trainer.

Hannah was desperate to ask her to put it in a bin, but also aware that she didn't want to ruin the flow of the confessional moment. Instead, she asked, 'How long did your dad get?'

'He didn't get a chance to complete his sentence. He didn't even get time to put together an appeal.'

'Right.'

Hannah waited, with more than an inkling of what Liv was about to say.

'My dad died in prison. He died with the label of a guilty man, and he never got the chance to prove he wasn't.'

'Do you mind me asking how he died?'

'Of course not.' Liv turned her head and looked Hannah dead in the eye. 'I want this sorted.'

'Okay. So ...?'

7

'He was stabbed in prison. A crappy little shank some useless bastard cobbled together. It wasn't a bad injury; he was stitched up and sent back to his cell. But a few days later he started to feel ill. They thought he had the flu. They left him in his cell to get over it.'

Liv made her way over to a bench, signalling that Hannah should join her. No sooner had she sat down than she rummaged in her bag again and began rolling another cigarette.

Hannah lowered herself onto the cold, metal bench next to her client, not bothered by how hard and uncomfortable it was. She'd done many a stakeout and suffered far worse seating arrangements in the last few years.

'Surely they would've looked in on him. Frequently. The staff wouldn't leave a fresh wound unchecked.'

'I don't know what they did, how often they checked, or how thorough they were. All I know is that they missed what was really going on.' Liv's voice took on a belligerent tone.

'Was it sepsis?' Hannah asked.

'Yeah. Although, I think they called it blood poisoning back then.'

'So, what do you want me to do? You want me to prove it was your uncle who killed your mum, is that it? Because, if you know something, you should speak to the police. You really ought to have spoken to them years ago.'

'I didn't know years ago.' Liv lit up her cigarette. 'Anyway, I did try to tell them. I went to the cop shop yesterday. They weren't interested.'

Hannah took out her phone and typed a few lines into notes, suggesting with a nod that Liv should continue.

'They took one look at me, and clearly thought I was just an ex-junkie who was wasting their time.'

Hannah concluded that Liv felt the same way about the police as she did about the prison guards. Understandably, she didn't appear to have much trust in people of authority. That made sense given the childhood traumas she'd experienced.

'I'm sorry,' Hannah said.

'Don't be. It's not *your* fault.'

'Answer me something, please? You say you didn't know years ago. How come you do now? What's happened to make you so sure your dad didn't do it, and to make you believe that your uncle *did*?'

Liv chewed on the inside of her cheek for a second, then said, 'Recently ... I've started to remember stuff. Like, all kinds of stuff. Some of it's about that night.'

'Recently?' Hannah asked gently, hoping to get more details on this miraculous memory retrieval.

'Yeah. Recently!'

Liv inhaled deeply on her cigarette.

Hannah took note of the expression on her face and decided not to push it. She had plenty to be getting on with for now.

2

LIV, FEBRUARY 2023

LIV FARNLEY gently ran her index finger over the indented letters on the wet, brass plaque. This was it then. Were the answers to her questions inside this building? With one last glance at the plaque, *Stephen Lawson-Ewart, Psychotherapist and Hypnotherapist PsyD*, she pushed the door and climbed the steep stairs.

At the top, she found herself in a modest reception area. It contained only a desk and an office chair, behind which was a row of coat hooks. A soft, leather jacket hung on one of the hooks. A door to her left opened and a man appeared. He looked to be a little over six feet tall, with an athletic body. Liv guessed he was in his thirties. Whereas she had spent the last three decades forcing all number of legal and illegal drugs into her body, as well as eating an embarrassing amount of unpalatable food, this man appeared to have been taking care of himself. He had a pleasant, tanned face. Not so good looking you couldn't take him seriously, but nice enough that your eyes wanted to linger. He had a tidy beard and an obviously expensive haircut. She was immediately drawn to his handsome face.

Liv wasn't sure if he was the receptionist. But as he walked towards her with his hand outstretched, it became obvious that he was in fact the psychotherapist. Shaking her hand, he wished her good morning, and introduced himself by his full name, but asked her to call him Stephen.

It didn't feel natural. She felt she ought to refer to him as Doctor or Sir. At the very least, Mr Lawson-Ewart. But she did as he asked.

'Good morning, Stephen.'

———

After Liv's black, denim jacket had joined his leather one on the coat hooks, Stephen collected some paperwork, a clipboard and a pen from the desk and led her into his room: the inner sanctum. She couldn't say what she'd been expecting, but this was most definitely not it. The room was so beautifully and tastefully decorated, Liv could've wept. Grey panelling covered the bottom half of the walls, apart from one, which she assumed was what people were referring to on those lifestyle TV shows when they talked about a feature wall. It was covered in a dark grey wallpaper, decorated every so often with hand painted birds. She spotted a puffin, a blackbird, a swan and many more, all wonderfully recreated. Never in her life had she seen such exquisite wallpaper. The room was split in two by a free-standing curtain. The half of the room they were currently in contained only a sofa. It was also beautiful. Again, it was a dark grey, and it was made of what appeared to be extremely plush velvet. *Jeez, no wonder this guy charges the earth.*

Walking towards the sofa, Stephen encouraged her to join him. Once they had sat down, he handed her a blank form, the pen and the clipboard, and instructed her to fill in the form, requesting as much detail as possible.

Once she had done this, he asked her to give him a moment's silence, whilst he quickly read through the section regarding what she hoped to gain from the sessions. She kept quiet for a few minutes and focused on the certificates on the feature wall.

'We'll move over to the therapy area shortly, but I want to explain what's going to happen first,' he said.

'Okay.' Liv's heart hammered in her chest; she prayed her jeans were clean. Imagine if she left a mark on the luxury sofa!

'I don't want you to be nervous.'

Too late!

Stephen continued to speak in his calm, even voice. 'I find it works best if there are no surprises. That's why I take the time to explain everything to my clients first.'

'Okay.'

'Behind that curtain, there's a bed and my chair. In a little while, when you're ready, you will remove your shoes and we'll get you settled on the bed. There will be an electric blanket underneath you, and I will place a throw over you. Okay, so far?'

'Y ... yeah.' Liv really wasn't okay. Her stomach was churning, and she was desperate for a smoke. She had not expected to be asked to lie down. This whole thing was becoming more than a little uncomfortable. Was he going to tell her to remove her clothes, as well as her shoes? Should she refuse? Was she allowed?

As if reading her mind, Stephen said, 'It's all above board, I can assure you. The reason for the electric blanket is, my clients used to say that despite having a blanket over them, they were still a little chilly when they came round. So I added the electric blanket underneath and I'm told it's a most pleasant feeling. Like being in the womb, apparently.'

Liv wanted to ask how his other patients knew what being in the womb felt like, but she didn't. Instead, she gave a tight smile.

'So, as I say, you just need to remove your shoes and lie on the bed, and I will cover you and get you comfortable. After that, I'll take a few minutes to put you into a very relaxed state. From there, you'll slowly drift into what we call a receptive trance. All right?'

'I … umm. Yeah.'

'Once in that trance we will simply begin talking.'

'Will I know what I'm saying? Like, will I be able to hear myself?'

'Yes, Ms Farnley.'

'Call me Liv.'

'Okay. Let me assure you, Liv, you will know where you are and what you're saying. This is not like a stage show where I make you cluck like a chicken.' He gave a gentle laugh. 'However, there is a chance you might not process everything you say. So I offer all my clients a transcript of the conversations we have, in case there's anything you don't remember once you come around. It's all going to come from your subconscious.' He tapped the side of his head. 'We're simply going to delve into the deeper part of your mind. Once you're under, I'll take you back to various points in your life, and we'll see if we can help you to unlock some of the memories you think you may have been suppressing.'

She tried to nod to show that she understood but found her head wouldn't move.

He continued, 'Now, if you're happy to proceed, let's get those shoes off and pop you onto the bed.'

Initially, she didn't move. She was still weighing it all up. Once she was on the bed, there was no turning back.

Stephen waited patiently, giving the air of a man in no rush at all.

Liv recalled the conversation she'd had with her brother, just before Christmas.

———

She'd told Toby that she didn't feel right using his money to pay for the therapy. It was just too much. He'd said it was fine, he could afford it, and he wanted to pay for it. She'd begun listing all the things he'd already paid for: rehab, the bills, her food … But he'd been adamant – she was more important than money, he wanted to help. Liv had felt her insides twist. She hated to be beholden to her little brother. It was embarrassing. She was supposed to take care of him, not the other way around. She'd sighed and said that she just wished that she didn't need the treatment and she wanted nothing more than to be able to remember it all, then move on. He'd said that they both knew why it had hit her harder than it did him and Annie. He just wanted to try to fix things for her.

She was going to interrupt him, to say for the millionth time that it wasn't his job to pick up the pieces of her shit life, but he left no gap for her pathetic words. He simply said that if she thought a psychotherapist could help her, that was good enough for him.

She knew Toby had felt guilty ever since that night. He wished he'd been awake, too, or that Annie could've been home; she might have seen something. Toby had always hated that it all came down to Liv.

He'd told her to just go once and see what it was all about. If the guy turned out to be a total fraud, she didn't have to go back. She would've lost nothing. Liv tried to point out that maybe *she* had nothing to lose, but Toby would have lost a load of money. But he'd simply said that if it worked it'd be worth every penny.

———

So, thanks to her brother's insistence, and his money, here she was.

Making the decision to continue, Liv pulled off her sodden

converse trainers. As she placed them to the side, she felt ashamed. What a stupid choice of footwear after all the rain they'd been having. Poor choice aside, they in no way belonged in the vicinity of such a fine-looking sofa. Leaving her humiliating shoes behind, she shuffled, in her mismatched socks, over to the other side of the room, where Stephen had pulled back the magic curtain.

The bed was not a narrow fold-out table such as the skinny, blonde beautician had used the one time Liv had grudgingly been for a facial – a treat from Annie for her twenty-first birthday. Nor was it a clunky A&E hospital bed, like the one she'd spent a couple of hours lying on many years ago. No, it was a single mattress on a base. The mattress was covered in a crisp, pale grey sheet and there was a matching pillowcase. The bed linen smelt clean and fresh, as if it had been line-dried in a wildflower garden.

Next to the bed there was an upright brown leather armchair that looked comfortable and just a little worn. Next to this was a small glass-fronted fridge, which displayed two rows of artesian spring water. Everything about the place suggested class and decorum, especially Stephen.

Liv gently sat on the bed. It was a great mattress. It gave way just enough to tell her it was not going to be hard and orthopaedic, but likewise, it in no way sagged, like the rehab beds used to. She let out a sigh.

'Comfy, isn't it?' Stephen smiled.

'Uh huh.'

'My wife chose it. She chose all the furnishings. She loves to shop.'

Liv smiled back, noticing for the first time the thick gold band on his ring finger. *He has a wife. He's not going to do anything odd to me whilst I'm asleep. He has a wife, who loves to shop and who has impeccable taste. Why would he want to molest a useless, waste of skin, recovering addict like me when he has an amazing, stylish wife?* Swinging her legs up onto the bed and resting her head down onto the pillow, she instantly felt better. *Let's do this.*

3

SUSAN, AUGUST 1970

Susan Davies was doing the food shopping. Just the usual stuff for her and her flatmate, Jenny. They were on a strict budget, so she never varied the menu. Jenny wasn't the slightest bit interested in cooking. If it was left to her to feed them, they would live off her classic dish of packet mash and grated cheese, followed by tinned fruit and evaporated milk. So it worked out best that Susan cooked.

Walking past WH Smiths, she stopped to read the front-page news on the stand outside. God, it was truly shocking to see actual photographs of the basement. Those poor kids!

Susan was still thinking about the kids when she stumbled into Safeway. And who should she see leaning into a freezer, trying to pick up a box of fish fingers? None other than her boyfriend, Martin. Fish fingers must've been a popular choice with shoppers, because there were only a few boxes left, and they were at the very bottom of a large, open freezer.

She and Martin had been going out with each other for a few months now, so she thought she knew him well enough to creep up behind him and give him a tiny shove in the small of his back. She figured he would spin around, spot it was her and laugh.

Nothing could've prepared her for the actual response she got. He spun around all right. But then he gave her a totally blank stare, and demanded to know what the heck she thought she was doing. Susan was mortified. Shocked that he had somehow forgotten all about her, especially given that just two days ago they'd been doing some serious necking in his car. She stood gaping at him, wishing with all her heart that she'd simply walked past. He asked again why she'd pushed him. There was a flash of something behind his eyes. She'd never seen it before. It was frightening.

Blathering, nervously, Susan said, 'It w … w … was meant to be funny. I thought you would—'

'You thought I would what? Bash my head on the bottom of the freezer? Are you mad?'

His mouth was hard. There was not a hint of the usual smile that lit up his face and made her stomach turn somersaults whenever they met. Just this steely glare.

In that second, she thought she'd lost it all. The relationship that had previously been blossoming so well now lay in tatters at her feet.

'Martin, I'm sorry. It was a joke,' she whispered.

His eyebrows rose, and something akin to understanding flashed across his undeniably handsome face. 'Martin?' he asked.

'Yes?'

'Try Ray.'

'I don't understand.'

He began to laugh, and his face finally softened. 'Martin's my brother. My twin brother,' he volunteered.

'Your twin?'

'Yeah. We're identical. But you don't need *me* to tell you that.'

He laughed. His voice sounded so much like Martin's. She could find nothing to differentiate it.

'So you're …?' It was such a bizarre moment. Like meeting someone you already know, but for the first time all over again.

'Ray Farnley.'

He held out his hand. Susan shook it.

'Sorry about the whole …' He mimed being pushed into the freezer and spinning around angrily. 'I thought you were a lunatic.'

'It's me who should apologise.'

She squirmed, realising how odd the whole thing must've been from his perspective.

'Oh, what the hell. Let's both apologise and then say no more about it.' Ray took a step back and looked her up and down intently. 'Sneaky old Martin, hey!' he laughed.

'He never mentioned he—'

'Had a brother? That doesn't surprise me. He wanted to keep you all to himself.' There was a glint in his eye.

Susan felt herself shiver. There was something a tiny bit dangerous about Ray and she couldn't be sure she liked it.

———

Later, back at the maisonette she shared with Jenny, Susan grabbed her diary. She was trying to write something every day. Today was an easy day; she wrote a few lines about the way she'd met Ray, and asked herself: how the hell has Martin kept that from me for so long?

4

HANNAH, MARCH 2023

HANNAH LET herself into the house and called out, 'Are you home?'

'Uh huh. We're in the kitchen!' Lottie shouted in return.

Hannah knew that when her friend said *we* she was including her little spaniel, Dixie. Joining them in the kitchen, she presented Lottie with one of the iced caramel lattes she'd bought from Costa Coffee.

'Thanks. I take it this means the meeting went well?'

Hannah did a cheers with the cups. 'Oh my God, you are not going to believe it.'

Smiling, Lottie said, 'Check out Hannah's cheeks, Dixie. All flushed.'

Dixie, dozing in her basket, chose not to comment.

'You may jest,' Hannah said. 'But your cheeks would be red, too.'

'Would they?'

'Let's just say ... identical twins!'

'Ohhhhh!' Lottie let out a squeal of delight. Like so many others, she had always been fascinated by the idea of two humans who were carbon copies of each other. 'How about we drink these quick, and then head out for some lunch? I'm starving. You can tell me everything. Or did you eat at the café with your client?'

'No. Just had rubbish coffee. Couldn't drink it. Hence why I got these for us on the way home. Anyway, yes, I'm hungry, too.' Hannah grinned.

———

They drove out towards Ayresworth, using a route that took them past Lullaby Woods. As the road dipped into the murky woodland area, the daylight disappeared for a second, and there was a sudden chill in the car. They stared out into the darkness. The woods passed by on either side. For a moment, the ease of their everyday chatter ceased, and they became silent and a little pensive.

After a minute or two they left the woods behind, and both let out a small sigh.

Lottie asked, 'Heard anything from Eliza?'

Given their location, it was an obvious link to make. Neither one of them could drive past Lullaby Woods without thinking of Hannah's previous client, whose cousin, Ash, had caused a stir when she'd disappeared at just eighteen years of age.

'Not for a while. I ought to ring her and see how she is. We said we'd keep in touch.'

'Yeah, we did,' Lottie agreed.

———

The first pub they came to was The Fox and Hounds. They parked and made their way hastily inside, impatient for food.

'I haven't been here for ages. Years, actually. I used to hate this place when I was younger,' Lottie remarked, holding the door open for her friend.

'Thanks. Why?' Hannah asked.

'The name, the whole hunt theme. Back then there were some horrible paintings on the walls of mutilated foxes.'

'Bloody hell,' Hannah said.

'I swear, Han.'

'Well, I think it's all changed now. No more hunting memorabilia.'

'Thank goodness. That kind of stuff always reminds me of my dad.'

The pub had received several makeovers since Lottie's childhood. Each one, an upgrade on the last. The fox hunting artwork had been replaced, and only one or two paintings following the equine theme remained.

Now, it boasted crystal chandeliers, sage green wooden panelling, and French-style chairs, with elegantly carved legs and sumptuous seat coverings of rich emerald velvet.

'Wow. It's amazing,' Lottie said, as they grabbed a table for two in the bay window.

'That reminds me,' Hannah said, gesturing towards a painting of two galloping horses. 'Are you still thinking of getting another horse?'

'I'm keeping an ear out. Nothing suitable has come up, but, yeah, I still want to get one.'

'Nice.' Hannah smiled. 'You'll love getting back in the saddle.'

Lottie returned her smile, full of excitement.

'It's like the Mary Celeste, isn't it?' Hannah said, glancing around the pub.

'Well, it's still early.'

Checking the time on her phone, Hannah wondered, 'Maybe *too* early for food?'

'I'll get us a drink and find out,' Lottie said. 'What'll you have?'

'Just a latte for me.'

'You sure? That'll be your third coffee today!'

'I'm not counting the first one, it was dreadful. I told you, I hardly drank it. Anyway, would you rather I had a large wine and then drove you home?' Hannah waved her car keys in the air. 'Or maybe I could have a glass of awful, tasteless lemonade that comes out of a tap. Like TV static in a glass!'

'Sorry, you drew the short straw, didn't you?' Lottie blushed.

'No worries. I need to get working after this. That's why I offered to drive. The caffeine will help,' Hannah said with enthusiasm.

Lottie returned to the table with a glass of white wine for herself.

'She's bringing your coffee in a minute, Han.'

'Great. Any luck about the food?'

'She said the chef has a hospital appointment, but he'll be back in half an hour, we can order then.' Lottie picked up the specials' menu. 'Look, they do pan fried scallops. Yum!'

Hannah also perused the menu.

Sipping her wine, Lottie insisted they wait for the waitress to deliver the coffee before Hannah started her recount of the client meeting.

'Otherwise, she'll come over right as you get to a good bit.'

'All right. I'll wait,' Hannah agreed. 'Are you definitely having the scallops? I like the sound of the parmesan tagliatelle thing.'

The waitress arrived. Placing the coffee on the table, she asked, 'You all right to wait for food, lovies?'

Hannah nodded.

'So, if the news at the hospital is good, we could get our food in about forty-five minutes? But if it's bad ...' She laughed.

'Oh it's nothing like that,' the waitress said, with a straight face. 'He goes for a regular appointment; he's up the hospital all the time. It never takes more than half an hour. Some special ultraviolet lamp thingy ...'

'Uh huh.'

Hannah wasn't sure what to say. She hadn't meant to pry. Damn her dad's genes and his stupid sense of humour.

The waitress completed her sentence. 'It's for his psoriasis. Poor sod gets it really bad.'

Hannah and Lottie smiled politely.

'I'll come and take your order once he's back,' the woman said, totally oblivious. She would've created less carnage had she thrown a grenade into the middle of their table.

They waited until she had returned to her post behind the bar and begun talking to an elderly man who clearly spent much of his life propping it up before their eyes met. Clenching their mouths shut, they tried incredibly hard to keep straight faces. But eventually, silent tears of laughter began streaming down their faces, and Hannah thought she might choke to death if she didn't let it out.

'Oh my God!'

'I know. TMI! I don't fancy the scallops anymore,' Lottie said, wiping mascara smudges from under her eyes.

'Well, I definitely don't want fucking parmesan!'

They finished their drinks, said a cheerful but determined goodbye to the waitress and headed for the door.

'Chef won't be long now,' she called after them.

They lied that they were just going to see what else was around, but they'd probably pop back.

———

They laughed all the way to the next pub, then found a similar table by a not-so-beautiful window, surrounded by not-so-magnificent décor, and checked out the not-so-adventurous menu.

'This'll do,' Hannah said. 'And Lottie, for goodness' sake, please don't enquire after the chef's health.'

They ordered their food with the pleasant, and thankfully tactful, young waitress.

'Right. I want to know *everything*!' Lottie said.

'I'm finally allowed to speak about it then?' Hannah grinned.

'Uh huh ... go!' Lottie instructed.

Hannah explained Liv Farnley's situation, making sure to include a dramatisation of her placing the photographs on the Formica table as if revealing her hand at poker. She never felt bad about sharing confidential information with Lottie. After all, Lottie had made a generous investment in her PI company, and she was a (somewhat) silent partner.

Their food arrived and they tucked in eagerly.

'And you really couldn't tell them apart?' Lottie asked, forking pasta alla norma into her mouth. 'This is lovely, by the way.'

'Good. Mine, too.' Hannah gestured towards her chicken pie. 'Well, obviously I only looked for a second, and the photographs were old. Maybe if I'd had the chance to meet them in real life ...' She shrugged.

'So, what's first?'

'I spoke to Paul, only briefly. I called him from the car. He's going to let me have any info from the station.'

'Good old Paul,' Lottie said. 'Your man on the inside.'

'He's rewarded for his trouble. Don't you worry about that,' Hannah said, thinking of all the rib-eye steaks and bottles of wine she'd had to treat him to of late, not to mention the back-handers in cash.

'Uh huh. I know he is. Then what?'

'My next task is to track down Liv's uncle. He lost touch with the family years ago. She said he went off travelling and eventually he stopped making contact altogether, not even with his mother.'

'Rude!'

'I'm going to have to check he isn't dead himself. I mean, it's been three decades since all this happened. If he is dead, then there's no way Liv's going to bring him to justice, so not much point in pursuing it.'

'But if he's alive?' Lottie queried. 'Are you going to try to find him?'

'I am,' Hannah said with a grin.

'It's Vincent Rocchino all over again.'

'Similar, yes. We always seem to come back to the hunt for your wicked stepdad, don't we?'

'We do.'

They both put down their cutlery and stopped eating for a moment, clearly recalling the case that had cemented their friendship.

'Seems like a long time ago now,' Lottie said.

'Mmm,' Hannah agreed. 'Finding that yacht, though. What a rush.' She gave a little laugh, then said, 'D'you know when Chen's flying back?' Seamlessly shifting topics, as they always did.

Her friend's face lit up at the mention of the young man who had played a large part in what they often referred to as *Lottie's awakening*. Without Vincenzo providing her with the low down on her dad, she would never have known what a total monster he was. Hannah knew, sadly, that the connection with her dad meant Lottie thought they could only ever be friends. But the more time he'd spent away, the more Lottie had hinted she wished there could be something special for them.

With a grin, Lottie replied, 'He's home at the end of next month!' She picked up her fork and resumed eating.

Hannah knew that grin; she'd seen it every time Chen came up in conversation recently.

'Well, I hope you get what you want from him when he swans back from his trip, all tanned and muscley.'

Lottie gave a little wiggle in her seat.

'You make him sound very appealing. But I can't—'

26

Hannah cut her off, 'Give it a go. See if anything develops. You'll regret it if you don't.' Her face fell.

'Aww, Han. I'm sorry, I know you're still raw about Mandy. I wish she'd given you more of a chance.'

Hannah shook away the comment.

'We both know I was fighting a losing battle the minute her parents were told about me. Expecting her to choose me over her family, her culture, everything she knew; it was futile. She couldn't bring herself to let her parents down. I have to respect that.'

'Well, they're idiots.' Lottie pulled a face. 'Mandy was lucky to have you, and they ought to have seen that.'

'Forget about it. *I* have.'

They both knew that wasn't true. Just as they both knew that all the matches she'd made on Tinder, and all the first dates she'd managed to squeeze in between work commitments, were pointless. Hannah was no more over Mandy than Lottie was able to see Chen as just a mate.'

By the end of their lunch, Hannah was in a reasonable mood. Her sadness regarding Mandy was always there, under the surface, but this new case was definitely going to take her mind off her relationship woes for the foreseeable.

5

LIV, FEBRUARY 2023

LIV DECIDED Stephen's other patients, or *clients* as he preferred to call them, were correct. It *was* like being in the womb. Obviously, it was a guess rather than a memory; they hadn't even begun the regression yet. But lying there, feeling the warmth begin to radiate up from beneath her, into her poor, sorry body, was like nothing else she'd ever known. *I took an assortment of drugs in the past to try to reach my own nirvana, and all the time I just needed a fucking electric blanket!*

Stephen asked her to begin counting down from two hundred. She quietly obliged. He told her that her eyes were so heavy she could no longer open them, and as if by magic, he was right. He told her that her muscles were like warm wax sinking into the restful mattress, and again he was correct. He took his time, speaking slowly and surely. Telling her that there was no rush. For the first time in as long as she could remember, her hands were still. They simply lay by her sides, too heavy to lift. There was no need to fiddle with the blanket, knot her fingers, or pull at the hard skin around her nails. All sense of time had left her. She had no idea how long she'd been on this bed, under

Stephen's wife's well-chosen cashmere throw. All she knew was that she never wanted to leave.

Stephen continued to gently tell her that her muscles were relaxed, her nerve endings calm, and her breathing deep.

Liv was reminded of the countless times she and her ex had smoked weed in an effort to fall asleep and escape their torturous lives. With Radiohead playing in the background, they'd lain side by side on sullied sheets, smoking joints and slowly drifting away. Liv would find herself inside vivid dreams, each one playing out to the backdrop of Thom Yorke's distinct voice. This was similar to one of those dreams, only this time, it was Stephen's words that invaded her mind.

He told her she was almost under. She continued to count, drifting further and further away, until she was detached from both the street noise outside the window and Stephen. She no longer counted, she no longer thought anything, she simply breathed deeply.

A comfortable silence continued for a few minutes. Then, suddenly, he asked, 'What did you have for breakfast this morning?'

Liv was bone tired. She felt her mouth open and close.

After a pause, he said, 'You can tell me. Whatever the answer is to all my questions you'll always be able to tell me. I know you're tired, but I promise you, if you try to speak it will come easily. The correct answer will just come into your head immediately.'

'Okay.'

'What did you have for breakfast this morning?' he repeated.

'A black coffee and a packet of cheese and onion crisps.'

'What time did you leave your home to get here?'

'It was late, like, gone ten.'

'Did you leave late because you were nervous? Were you putting it off?'

'Yes, I was.'

'That's okay. I understand. Now, Liv, I want you to tell me your earliest memory of your dad. You won't have to go back through all your childhood memories like a filing system and find the oldest. It will be easier than that. Let it come into your head.'

'The wooden slide.'

'Okay. Can you tell me about it, please?' Stephen asked.

———

'It was hot and sunny. We were in the garden. Annie was hogging the swing. She always did.'

'What were *you* doing?' Stephen asked.

'At first, I was hanging around by the swing, begging my sister to get off and let me have a go. Then, when she wouldn't budge, I was in the paddling pool. Sitting on my bottom, the cool water soaked into my green, flowery swimming costume.'

'You mentioned Annie, your sister, on the form. You mentioned a brother, too. Where was he?'

'Toby wasn't even born then.'

'I see. So, how old were you?' His voice remained calm with just a hint of enquiry.

'I was about three. Annie would've been seven-ish. If she'd just got off the swing, I wouldn't have gone down the slide.'

'But she didn't get off the swing?'

'No. She said I was too small, and I'd fall off,' Liv said.

'She may have been right, if it wasn't one of the swings especially for little children.'

'I'd been on it before. I would've been fine. She just didn't want to get off.'

Stephen encouraged Liv to move on. 'I'm guessing you went down the slide instead?'

'Yes.'

'Tell me about the slide.'

'It was old … made of wood. Not like the slides you see today. Not plastic.'

'And what happened?'

She flinched. Her face screwed up tight.

'You can tell me.'

'It's just that … I remember, it really hurt.'

Stephen reassured her. 'You can describe the event to me without feeling the pain. I promise. Go ahead. Try it.'

Liv continued. 'I climbed up the rungs. My feet were still wet. They slipped off a couple of times. But I kept going, because if I wasn't going to swing, then I sure as hell was going to slide.'

'So, what happened?'

'I slid down the slide. I didn't go smooth like usual. I kind of juddered. I guess it was because I was wet. About halfway down, I felt this pain in my thigh, like something was slicing me up. Like a red-hot blade. I got to the bottom and I jumped up. I was screaming. Annie jumped off the swing and came over to me. I think she could tell from my screams this was no joke.'

'What had happened?'

'A splinter. A huge one. It was right under my skin. I could feel it, but I couldn't get to it. My mum came running; she'd seen it all from the kitchen window. Next came my dad; he'd been gardening or something. He swooped me up in his arms and took me into the house. It was cool inside. He shouted to my mum to grab some ice. Then he laid me on the sofa on my belly and tried to freeze my leg with all the little cubes. My mum struggled to pop them out of the tray. After a while, I cried because my leg was so cold. I told him I couldn't feel it. He said that was good. Then he tried to get a hold of the end of the splinter with my mum's tweezers. That thing was stuck so far into my leg, it was awful. Every time Dad got hold of the very tip, the only piece that was sticking out, he'd pull it and try to get a decent grip. But I would scream and wriggle. I made so much noise that Doris, the lady next door, came knocking on the front door, and my mum had to send her away. Eventually, I think my screams broke my poor dad's heart. He gave up. He scooped me up into his arms again, grabbed a towel to wrap me in because I was still damp from the paddling pool, and put me in the car. He drove to A&E, with me screaming the whole way.'

'Were they able to fix it there?'

'Oh, yes. They froze it properly. No little ice cube trays for them. Once my leg was good and frozen, they told me to keep my eyes focused on my dad's face. I lay there on my front, looking at my dad. He was pulling funny faces to keep me distracted. I even managed to giggle. Then, as quick as you like, the doctor said it was all sorted. My dad asked to see the splinter, and he whistled. *Jesus, that's a big one!* We left without the splinter. My leg healed up fine.'

'And the slide?'

'A ceremonial bonfire a week later.'

'Thank you, Liv. That was really helpful,' Stephen said. 'Now I want you to just breathe deeply and relax.'

After an indistinguishable amount of time, Stephen gave a gentle cough.

'Right, I think that's enough for your first session, Liv. I'm going to bring you gently round now. I'll count to ten, and then I'll tap you on the shoulder. When you feel the tap, your eyes will open, and you'll feel refreshed and ready to continue with your day. Do you understand?'

'Yes.'

'One, two, three ...'

Gradually, Stephen added energy to his voice. By the time he got to ten, he was decidedly upbeat. He touched Liv's shoulder and her eyes opened.

'Okay?' he asked.

'Yes. I umm ... I feel good actually.'

Stephen took a bottle of Voss water from the fridge and handed it to Liv.

'Please sip this,' he said.

Liv twisted the lid on the bottle and did as he instructed.

'Your father sounds like a nice man.'

Liv nodded. 'I can't imagine how awful it must've been to keep joking whilst a doctor pulled that splinter out of his little girl's leg.'

'All part of being a parent.'

'I wouldn't know.'

'No. But you do know how well your dad did. There's a reason why it's your earliest memory of him. We often recall the traumatic times.'

'You say that, but I've forgotten the most traumatic time of all.'

'Well, yes,' Stephen said. 'But there's traumatic and then there's *catastrophic*. I think your mother being murdered would most definitely fall into the second category.'

'Why didn't you just order me to tell you about it?'

'Steady on. These things take time. It's currently locked away; I can't simply tell you to remember it today.'

'When then?'

'When I think you're ready.' Stephen nodded towards the bottle of water. 'Drink some more. We're done for today.'

6

SUSAN, AUGUST 1972

ONE MORE NIGHT until Susan Davies became Susan Farnley. She couldn't wait to be married! The weather forecast on TV wasn't good. When they'd chosen August, it was because she'd wanted to be married in the sunshine. Now she was just crossing her fingers for a dry day. But, if she was honest, it really didn't matter either way. Nothing could ruin her day. She wrote in her diary: *I'm getting married tomorrow. I'm so excited!!!*

That night, Martin had gone out for drinks with a couple of his friends and his brother. Susan had begged him to have an early night and *no* alcohol. But unfortunately, Ray overruled her. He'd insisted no brother of his was going to get married without a good drink inside him the night before.

In contrast, Susan was in bed by nine, sober as a judge. She got out of bed approximately fourteen times to stare at her wedding dress, which hung on a padded coat hanger in the hall-way. It was a long white satin gown covered with lace; it had billowing sleeves, which ended in tight lace cuffs at the wrists. Susan loved it. Eventually, against the odds, she managed to stop getting out of bed and dropped off to sleep.

When she first heard the noise, she assumed it was an animal outside in the garden. Only as she came to and awoke properly did she realise it was someone tapping on her bedroom window. Jenny had moved out, and Martin was all set to move in as soon as they returned from their honeymoon in Lynton. But, for now, Susan was alone in a ground floor maisonette, and she felt a little vulnerable.

Clambering out of bed, still groggy, she made her way over to the window. Throwing back the curtains, she saw Martin in the shadows. She opened the window.

'What are you doing here?' she shouted in a stage whisper. 'Go back to your mum's. You don't live here yet.'

He laughed. It was clear he was very drunk.

'I mean it. You're not coming in. I'm not that kind of girl,' she added with a giggle.

Again, he just laughed.

Susan beckoned to him. 'Come and give me a kiss before you go though.' She just couldn't resist him.

He stepped out of the shadows and gave her one of his gorgeous smiles. Her stomach flipped. He was so handsome. *How did I get so lucky?*

He stepped towards her with a slight stagger to the left.

Their faces met, the window frame between them. He reached in and cupped her face with his hands.

'I love you, you drunken fool,' she said, closing her eyes and awaiting a kiss.

Their mouths touched and he kissed her passionately. Moving his hands around behind her head, he began pulling her towards him. At one point, she thought she was going to fall out of the window.

Eventually, with some effort, she pulled away, surprised by his display of passion. Usually when he was that drunk, he could think of nothing but sleep.

'Go on now. Get yourself home.' She patted down her hair where his hands had ruffled it. 'I'll see you at the registry office.

Don't be late!' she instructed, giving him a gentle push to send him on his way.

He turned and began staggering back down the garden, still leaning to the left. A second before he was immersed in shadow, once again, he spun around. There was something about his expression. Susan couldn't put her finger on it, but he was different.

'Just as I'd imagined it would be,' he called out, wiping his mouth with the back of his hand.

Recoiling back into the bedroom, Susan wondered what on earth he was talking about. She thought about it late into the night, and there was only one explanation for what the man in her garden had said, and she decided it was best not to think about it.

———

The next day, at the wedding, Martin made no mention of coming to visit her after his stag do, and neither did she.

HANNAH, MARCH 2023

'HE'S DEFINITELY NOT DEAD THEN?' Dave asked.

'Not according to the public records.' Hannah gestured to her coffee. 'This is good. You're learning.' What good were employees if you couldn't tease them?

'It ought to be good, it cost enough.' Dave made a grumpy face, before adding, 'So, if we're trusting the public records, and Ray Farnley really is alive, what's the plan to find him?'

'I *am* trusting them. Plus, I checked for any random obituaries, just in case. Fortunately, the surname is an unusual one, so I'm confident he's out there, still pink and breathing. The thing is, I can find him all I like, but this whole thing is based on an assortment of memories that have been stuck inside Olivia Farnley's head for years. Despite her insistence that her dad is innocent, it's all conjecture at this point.'

'Absolutely.' Dave nodded his agreement. 'It's odd. Obviously, she's talked about her addictions at a couple of meetings, I know she goes to NA as well. She's got a lot going on, poor cow. But she's never spoken about her family. Not a single reference to all this stuff.'

'I get that though,' Hannah said. 'Let's be honest, I'll bet you don't say much about Noah, do you?'

Dave considered the question. 'Not by name, but I have acknowledged that I have a son. Especially the fact he was my main reason for getting sober.'

'Has she not said anything about her brother, Toby?' Hannah asked. 'She seems close to him. On the phone, she mentioned he'll be funding the investigation.'

He screwed up his eyes for a second.

'Umm ... yeah, maybe.' He seemed distracted. 'It's hard to be sure, people come and go at the meetings. But I reckon I would've remembered a friggin' murder.'

Hannah finished her coffee and waved her empty mug in his direction, questioningly.

Refilling it, Dave continued, 'I guess I never realised she had all this in her past. It was only when she was bad mouthing the police, saying they wouldn't help her, and they were all useless bastards, that I decided to take her to one side and tell her what I do, and about you being my boss. I suppose it was serendipitous that she happened to mention it at a meeting I was at.'

Hannah nearly spat out her newly refreshed coffee. '*Serendipitous!* Dave, what the absolute fuck? Where did you get a word like that from?'

'Don't laugh at me,' Dave said, irritably.

'I'm not. I'm ... smiling loudly,' Hannah replied.

'Right, well ...' Dave shrugged. 'Shelley used to say it all the time. About us meeting. Us conceiving Noah. Loads of stuff. Anyway, I did have an education, you know.'

Hannah tilted her head to one side and raised her eyebrows. 'You sure about that?'

Giving her a gentle swipe, he nearly spilt her coffee.

Steadying her mug, she apologised.

'Just joking, mate. Jesus, you're tetchy today. You okay?'

He shrugged again, then asked, 'When are you meeting Liv

again? I'd like to be there next time. You did say she doesn't mind.'

'In a couple of days. At that charmless café. She's promised to go through the details of the night her mum was killed. I know it's not going to be easy for her. But, before, it was all, *I've remembered recently*, but no concrete details, and no proper explanation. Well, that ends next time she meets with me. I need some facts. I'm not going on a wild goose chase, and I don't expect you to, either.'

'What about Paul? What did he say? Surely, he could give you some facts.'

'He gave me what he could over the phone. He's going to dig into the archives and find out a bit more. He cursed me,' she laughed. 'He said, *Why are you always interested in stuff from bloody years ago? First that little Italian bloke, then the missing teenager. Now this! Thirty years is a long time, Han!*'

Hannah was surprised to hear Dave scoff. 'Let him earn his fucking keep. He's lucky to be a copper. He was a right twat to me back when I—'

'*Stop it!*' she instructed. 'Everyone was angry at you, *at us*, and we know why. They had every right. Paul's a good man. We would've been exactly the same if he'd done what we did to Dawn.'

Dave rose from the sofa and paced the tiny lounge, taking deep breaths, rubbing his forehead.

'Seriously. What is eating you?' Hannah asked.

He blew all the air out of his cheeks. 'I think I need a meeting.'

'Okay. We can pick this up some other time.' Hannah began gathering up her phone and jacket.

'Sorry. I really want to help with this case. It sounds bloody interesting. I umm ... I dreamt about her last night. I should've told you as soon as you got here. I thought I could keep the wolves at bay. Stupid, isn't it? When will I learn? As if that day is ever going to leave me alone.'

Hannah dropped her stuff and, grabbing him by the arm, led him back to the sofa. 'It's shit you dreamt about Dawn, but good you've recognised the need for a meeting. It's better like this.' Hesitantly, she asked, 'Do you want to talk about the dream?'

'There's nothing new to tell. I was giving her CPR and there was fucking claret ... everywhere! She was bleeding out, and I was shouting, *let me try again.* You know how it goes. I'm sure you've thought it, dreamt it, too.'

Hannah nodded silently. It was always there; they could be having the most innocuous conversation. Discussing a completely unrelated case. But, somehow, Dawn Barton's death, and their unintentional involvement in it, had a tendency to sneak in.

After a moment, Dave took out his phone and checked the internet.

'There's a meeting this evening. It's not my usual one. But I'll go.' Catching Hannah's expression, he said again, '*I'll go,* I promise!'

'Good.' She gave his arm a reassuring rub. 'Do you need to call your sponsor?'

'No. The meeting will sort me out,' Dave said. 'Anyway, where were we? Oh yeah, Paul, he's going to give you the low down. What can I do to help?'

'When you're ready, can you find out any information there is on the death of Martin Farnley? He was in Crow's Wall prison when he died.'

'Sure.'

'Shall I stay until the meeting?' Hannah asked.

'No. I'm okay. I'll grab a shower first.'

'Right. Well, I'm not staying for that.' She laughed, hastily picking up her stuff.

'You sure I can't persuade you?' he joked.

'Abso-bloody-lutely!'

'Right you are then. I'll speak to you soon.'

They made their way down the small hallway.

At the front door, Hannah said, 'You're right, this *is* going to be an interesting case. I need you to be fully with me, or not involved at all. You understand?'

'Yes, boss!'

'Good.' Hannah gave him a hug. She knew him now. He needed tough love. Threatening to take a murder and an unjust imprisonment away from him if he drank was probably the best way to keep him off the booze.

8

LIV, FEBRUARY 2023

ONCE AGAIN, Liv felt the electric blanket beneath her and the cashmere throw on top. She quickly began to relax. Stephen's voice was calm and smooth. She heard him ask if she was ready to proceed and pondered the question. What would he ask this week? Last week's session had brought memories to the forefront of her mind that had lain way at the back for decades. She had known she'd had a large splinter removed from her leg when she was a small child. Her grandma had mentioned it and she had always had a vague recollection of the pain. But since she'd talked about it to Stephen and read the transcript he had kindly emailed the next day, the memories had become clearer. The details were vivid: the way the garden had looked, Doris coming round, Annie's worried face. So many things had come into focus and, even weirder, they had remained. She could still see the wooden slide memory clearly. What if he asked her something today that brought back some more vivid memories? She wanted to remember exactly what happened to her mum, but the thought of seeing it all again made her heart race in her chest and her ears buzz.

'I said, can you count down from two hundred, please?' Stephen gently repeated.

'Y ... yes.'

'Okay.'

Liv began counting, and Stephen carried out his process of putting her into a receptive trance. As before, it was an unhurried process, during which her muscles relaxed and her breathing deepened.

When Stephen asked, 'What did you have for breakfast today?' Liv replied automatically, without thought or reason.

'Toast and marmite.'

He instantly hit her with the next question: 'Tell me, Liv, what annoys you most?'

'I hate it when people pity me.'

'Who does that?'

'Strangers, Annie ... everyone.'

'You think your sister pities you?'

'Yes.'

He continued, 'Can you give me an example of a stranger's pity?'

'Like, yesterday, in the shop. Some horse-faced woman with a screaming toddler in a buggy offered to buy my food for me.'

'That sounds like a kind gesture.'

'You think? You'd like someone to assume you couldn't afford a fucking ready meal?'

'I don't know. Tell me what happened, please?'

'I'd left my bag at home, but I figured it would be okay because I always have my phone on me, and I'd pay with that. I picked up an energy drink and one of those fake Italian things.'

'Fake Italian?' Stephen asked.

'It's just pasta in a tomato sauce. They put it in green, white and red packaging and call it the Italian selection.' She tutted.

'And ...?'

'I got to the self-checkout thing, I scanned the two items and

I pulled my phone out of my back pocket. It was dead. I'd forgotten to charge it. It can happen to anyone.'

'Of course it can. It's happened to me. So, what did you do?'

'I swore a bit. Waved my arms about. Said something like, *Great. Now I have to go home with nothing.* Anyway, the woman at the self-checkout next to me asked if I'd like her to get the items for me.'

'Kind.'

'Yes, very kind.'

'You don't think she was being kind?'

'Maybe she was. But when I said, *No thanks, I'll come back later with my card,* she looked at me as if I was lying. As if I had no card and I couldn't afford an energy drink and a crappy ready meal.'

'You think she was looking down on you?'

'*Yes!* Like everyone always does.'

'Everyone?'

'Yes.'

'Do *I* look down on you?' Stephen asked.

'No. But you're paid not to.'

'Well, I guess we'll have to disagree about my motives. Anyway, continue, you told her you would come back with your card, and she didn't believe you had a card.'

'She kind of insisted. She was all like, *Come on, hun, let me and Otto pay for you.*'

'Otto?'

'I think that was the kid.'

Stephen nodded. 'I see.'

'She said I needed feeding up.'

'And ... do you?'

'I'm just naturally thin. I always have been. Even before I ... you know.'

'Did you let her buy you the goods?'

'Yeah. So she got to act all superior and like she'd paid it forward.'

'You think that's why she offered?'

'I think she was on Facebook within the hour, saying how good she felt about herself.'

'But *you* didn't feel good?'

'No!'

Stephen's voice remained calm, even when hers did not. 'What happened after that?'

'I went home, and I ordered a bloody great Indian takeaway. I stuffed my face with food until I was sick.'

'Why?'

'Because I'm not poor. I'll never be poor. Not as long as I have Toby's money sliding into my bank account to cover my every need.'

'You don't like being beholden to your brother for money?'

'Who would? People like to pay for themselves, don't they?'

'Does it bother you even more that it's Toby? That it's your *little* brother?'

'When we got to Grandma's house, the night my dad was arrested and my mum died, Toby was terrified. He clung to me like a limpet. I had to go to the toilet with him waiting just the other side of the door because he would not leave me. Yes, we had Grandma, but Toby only wanted me. The first few weeks, he slept in my bed with me every night.'

'How old was he?'

'He was eight. He barely spoke, he hardly ate a thing and he never let go of me. I think a part of him was touching a part of me almost every second of the day and night.'

'And Annie?'

'What you have to understand is...' Liv paused.

'You can say anything. You can answer all the questions I ask you,' Stephen reminded her.

'She was ... still is ...' Liv sighed. 'You know the expression, three's a crowd? Well, Annie is the crowd.'

He sounded surprised. 'I don't imagine you to be someone who leaves others out.'

'I didn't!'

'So ...?'

'Annie left herself out. She chose not to be a part of *us*. She was older, nearly eighteen when Mum died. She was out with her boyfriend. She told me once that she was shagging him in his car when it happened. I thought she'd feel awful about that. I thought she'd be wracked with guilt. I would be!'

'She wasn't?'

'No. She just told me as a matter of fact.'

'Why do you think she removed herself from the family in the way you describe? Why did she make herself the crowd, as you put it?'

'I don't know. She didn't like living at Grandma's. As soon as she could, she got herself out of there. She rented a place with her boyfriend and a couple of other friends. A horrible, poky little two-bedroom flat out the other side of Ayresworth. She hardly ever came to see us. She told me that Toby and I had each other and we didn't need her.'

'Do you think you needed her?'

'*Yes*. But my sister only visited on high days and holidays: popping in with a present for a birthday or Christmas. She never stopped long, because there was always a man on the scene somewhere waiting for her. The longest time we spent together was a spa day for the two of us on my twenty-first.'

'So, you would've liked more from your sister. More contact. More love, even?'

'Yes. I wish I'd mattered more to her.'

'Did *she* matter to *you*?'

'Yes. Always.'

'And Toby, did *he* give you lots of love back then?'

'Toby is the person I love most.'

'That's interesting. Do you remember him being born?'

'Yes. Of course.'

'Can you tell me about the first time you met him, please?'

———

Within a second, Liv began to tell Stephen the story of Toby's birth.

'Apparently, only a very small percentage of babies arrive on their due date. Well, I can tell you this, Toby was one of them. He was due on December 25th and both Annie and I were worried he would ruin our Christmas. We thought he would arrive in the middle of dinner. Or worse, before we'd even had the chance to open our presents. But our parents insisted babies never come when they're due. My mum said she didn't feel like the baby was ready; she was sure it would wait until at least Boxing Day.'

'But he didn't wait?'

'No, he did not! It was about eight o'clock in the evening, and we were playing with the new game I'd got in my stocking. Jenga. Mum got up to pop to the loo. She was gone a while, and when she came back, she said she needed to speak to Dad in the kitchen. I honestly thought she had a cunning plan to win at Jenga and she wanted to talk to him about it. Just goes to show how focused you can be as a kid when you're playing a game. They returned from the kitchen, and Dad was kind of pale and clammy. Which was odd, because it was a cold winter's night. He told us Grandma was coming over to look after us. He was going to collect her.'

'Did she live far?'

'Fifteen minutes or so in the car. I was confused. We'd been over to Grandma's for tea earlier. Like we always did. I thought

47

she'd be tucked up asleep. She was only in her sixties, but that seemed very old to me at the time.'

'Our perception of our elders adjusts as we ourselves age,' Stephen suggested.

'Yes, I suppose it does.'

'Your dad went to fetch her so she could take care of you both?'

'Yes. Although my mum wasn't keen. She said there wasn't time, and they should ask Doris from next door. But Dad insisted they couldn't bother her on Christmas Day and that it should be Grandma. But in the short time he was gone, Mum began to behave strangely. She was pacing the floor, checking the time, and every so often her breathing went kind of funny.'

'She was in labour,' Stephen said.

'Yes. By the time Dad got back with Grandma, Mum was clutching the back of the sofa. Kind of doubled over. She said in a high-pitched voice that it was too late to go to the bloody hospital. Dad was mumbling that she mustn't say that, and it couldn't be true. Grandma suggested that she and Mum needed to go upstairs. She told Dad to call the midwife, an ambulance, a doctor, anything. Just get help. Annie and I were instructed to stay in the lounge. Up the stairs Mum and Grandma went, and Dad began frantically hunting through the address book for a phone number.'

'Your mum must've been glad to have her mother-in-law there,' Stephen said.

Liv replied, 'I'm not so sure. They were never that close.'

He pressed on with the questions. 'So, Toby was born at home?'

'Yes. Annie and I stayed in the lounge, playing Jenga. After a while, a woman arrived who turned out to be a midwife. I went upstairs to the bathroom to use the toilet at one point, and there were sheets in the bath, they had blood on them. I was petrified. I thought Mum had died and they weren't going to tell us. I did a quick wee and crept back downstairs to the lounge. I was too scared to search for Mum, terrified of what I might see. I didn't even tell Annie about the sheets. More Jenga followed. Then, finally, the sound of a baby crying came from upstairs. We stood, motionless. Did that mean everything was over? A moment later, Dad rushed into the lounge, sending the final Jenga pieces flying off the coffee table. He shouted *Annie-Panny, Livvy-Lou, it's a boy!'*

'Livvy-Lou?' Stephen said with a chuckle.

'Yeah. He sometimes used those silly names for us.' Liv smiled. 'We charged up the stairs behind him and crept into our parents' room. Towels had replaced the sheets. They were also bloodied. But it wasn't so scary, because there was Mum, and she was alive, and she was smiling. She gestured for us to join her on the bed, and, in her arms, wrapped in a blanket, was a baby. Not just any baby. The cutest baby I'd ever seen. She asked if we knew his name. I said something like *Have you called him Jesus?* I thought it made sense. Mum laughed, and said he wasn't Jesus, he was Toby. It was the name she planned to call both Annie and me, if we'd been boys. I stared at my brother, and he stared back at me. He had dark, wavy hair that was stuck to his little, damp head, and big eyes, and he was absolutely the most fantastic thing I'd ever seen. I vowed then that I would do everything in my power to protect that boy, everything to keep him safe and make his life perfect.'

Unbeknown to Liv tears were creeping down her face.

Stephen stepped in. 'It's okay. You don't have to be upset.'

'He was just such a beautiful baby.'

'It's a lovely story. But I'm going to wake you up now. Is that okay?' Stephen asked.

'Yes.'

Slowly and surely, Stephen brought Liv out of the receptive trance, until eventually she felt him tap her on the shoulder. Her eyes opened and Stephen came back into view.

As before, he handed her a bottle of cold water and told her to take a drink. 'Water's really good for you, Liv. Especially after hypnosis.'

'Thank you.'

'Do you feel okay? You're not upset.'

'No. I feel fine.' As Liv took a drink, her hand brushed against her cheek. Her face was wet. 'Have I been crying?'

'Just a little, when you thought about Toby as a baby.'

'Oh yes. I vowed to protect him, didn't I?'

'That's what you said.'

'I didn't protect him though. I didn't keep him safe. He still ended up an orphan by his tenth birthday.'

'That wasn't your fault.'

'But I said I was going to look after him, and all the poor sod had to do as soon as he earnt a quid or two was look after me.'

'You're making great progress,' Stephen assured her. 'Now take another sip.'

Liv did as he asked.

9

SUSAN, DECEMBER 1972

SUSAN'S first Christmas spent as Mrs Farnley did not go well. She insisted they had lunch on their own, in their little maisonette. Martin was desperate to see his mum and his brother, but she wanted them to be alone. He eventually agreed, but only on the understanding that they went over to his mum's straight after they'd eaten.

Susan worked hard on the lunch. She had made chestnut stuffing the night before, from scratch. Her nails were broken and torn from peeling the damn things. She also made four different kinds of veg, two other kinds of stuffing: pork, and sage and onion, and of course there was a turkey, big enough for four people. They finished the meal with a Marks & Spencer's special pudding with brandy butter and cream. Susan was totally exhausted, but she was happy. Yes, she was uncomfortably full, and yes, Martin had eaten the food in such a way as to suggest he was trying to clear his plate, rather than savour the taste. But it didn't matter; they were married, and it was their first Christmas as Mr and Mrs Farnley. Martin had proposed a toast, to them, to the Queen, and to anything else he could think of. He'd been drinking since 11am. She allowed herself only a couple of glasses of Liebfraumilch because she was driving over to her mother-in-law's. They finished with a cracker each and laughed at the tacky gifts inside them. Placing a tiny plastic fish on their palms, they watched as it predicted their mood.

Rising from the table, Susan began to clear up. She was hoping Martin would offer to help. She'd been cooking, stuffing and scraping veg since way too early. But he didn't offer. Instead, rubbing his belly, he said a cursory thank you and made his way to the lounge, where he promptly fell asleep. She was washing up for a good hour. Slightly miffed, and more than a little ready for a rest herself, she joined him and flopped exhausted into her chair. Her eyes began to close, and she figured a little nap might be exactly what was needed. To be perfectly honest, she wasn't one bit in the mood to see Ray or her mother-in-law, Shirley. She could've done without the trip over there altogether. Besides, Martin was snoring gently in his chair, so she'd be mad to wake him.

———

Susan was awoken abruptly by Martin. He was faffing and waving his arms about, shouting that it was getting dark. She checked her watch – it was almost four. The way he was going on you'd think it was closer to midnight. She told him to calm down; they still had plenty of time to see his mum. But he was beyond grumpy. The plastic fish had not predicted this! He kept moaning about missing the Queen's speech and demanding to know why she hadn't woken him as soon as she'd finished washing up. Susan felt her heckles rise. He was usually such an easy-going man. Today, he was being lazy and rude. She ranted back, telling him in no uncertain terms that if he'd helped her with the washing up, she wouldn't have been so fucking knackered. He asked her not to swear, and said it wasn't ladylike. Susan said she didn't give a damn; he was acting like a prick, and she wasn't having it. She stood to face him. There was a moment of confrontation. She had defied his wishes and sworn again. Her hands were shaking, but she couldn't be sure if it was rage, or if she was afraid. He'd never before given her cause to fear him. He took a slow step towards her and looked down into her eyes.

Her breathing became shallow. There was a horrible coldness in her stomach.

'Don't call me that,' he instructed rather than asked. 'Never call me a prick again.'

'I'm ... I'm sorry. But you're being unreasonable,' she mumbled in reply.

'How do you figure that?' he asked. 'I'm merely upset you didn't wake me so we could go and see my brother and my mother straight after lunch, as agreed.'

Susan paused, mulling over what he'd said.

'You've had the part you wanted. Now it's my turn to have the Christmas I wanted. Or do we only do what you want now?' he asked.

Susan thought about it. He'd spent every Christmas of his life with his mum thus far. All he was asking was for them to go to her as soon as possible. And she'd messed it up for him by nodding off in the chair. She looked outside. It *was* getting dark. He was right. Closing the gap between them, her voice softened.

'Sorry. You're right. You must be desperate to see your mum.'

He took her in his arms. 'Darling, I've loved our first little Christmas together. But since our dad died, Ray and I have always rallied around Mum. That's all it is.'

She closed her eyes, nodded, and said, 'I'm sorry I called you a prick.'

He gave a slight wince.

'That's all right. You can make it up to me later.'

Shirley was not too impressed with their arrival. She made a point of saying that she'd been expecting them before three. Susan wondered what their obsession with the Queen's speech was all about. She tried to explain that there had been a lot of washing up to do, but Shirley insisted that between them it shouldn't have taken long. Far be it from her to tell Shirley that her son had not offered to help.

What followed was a huge supper: sausage rolls, quiche, pigs in blankets, coleslaw, and what Shirley referred to as cold cuts, which was basically all the food left over from her Christmas lunch with Ray. There was way too much for Susan, who only managed to nibble on a sausage roll. She allowed herself one snowball to drink because Martin was once again tucking into the beer, and she knew one of them was going to have to drive home. Besides, her head was already a little dizzy. After supper, Martin rose and accompanied his mum to the kitchen to help her clear up. Of course he did! This left Susan alone with Ray. They watched *Morecombe and Wise* in silence.

Eventually, Ray spoke.

'Have you enjoyed your first Christmas as my brother's wife?' he asked.

'Yes.'

She smiled. But the smile was fake, and she knew he saw that.

'You do surprise me,' he replied, with a smirk.

———————

Her diary entry that night was brief. It focused on the good parts of the day. The amazing meal she'd cooked all by herself for the first time, and the bracelet Martin had bought her. She decided not to write that her husband had been a bit of a prick.

NANCY, OCTOBER 1969

NANCY GREENWOOD AWOKE to the sound of her sister coughing. One of them always seemed to have a cold or a cough. Their noses were always running. Nancy was embarrassed about the snot smears on her face. Maybe it was because it was so damp and smelly in their room. They used to live upstairs in the house. They'd had a lovely room, with pink bedspreads and flowery walls. She could still picture the wallpaper – tiny white flowers on a pale pink background. Nancy looked around their current room. The walls were just bricks, like the outside of houses, and the floor was hard and grey. She hated the floor; it was so cold. If only they had slippers or socks. Patty coughed again, a deep chesty sound that shook her small frame. Nancy wanted to ask if she was okay, but she knew the answer. Neither of them was ever okay these days.

The key turned in the lock and the door opened at the top of the steps. Derek stood in the doorway.

'Quit making so much fucking noise. One of those nosey neighbours will hear you.'

'Sorry,' Patty whispered. 'It's just ... this cough is—'

'When I want to know about your health, I'll ask,' Derek snapped.

Nancy was only six, but she was sure some of the words her brother used were bad. It was the way he said them. He kind of spat them out between his teeth. *Fucking* was one of the words he said a lot.

Patty stopped talking and tried to stifle the coughs.

'Your food is here. Come and get it after I've left,' Derek said, gruffly. 'And shut your fucking mouth.'

He slammed the door and turned the key.

'I'll go,' Nancy said. She made her way carefully up the five steps. They were dirty, and she hated how they felt under her bare feet. They were kind of gritty, and often small stones would get stuck into the flesh on the soles of her feet or between her tiny toes.

Bringing the two bowls back down the steps, Nancy placed one on Patty's mattress.

Grabbing the two plastic beakers, she turned the tap on at the large aluminium sink and poured them both a cup of water.

'Thanks.'

Patty grabbed the bowl and began spooning porridge into her mouth.

'Is it …?'

'No, it's cold,' Patty said, woefully.

Sometimes Derek brought their food a bit earlier, and then the porridge was still warm. Not today though. Today it was stone cold. Maybe he'd come a little later than normal. They had no way of knowing what time it was. Even if there had been a clock, at six years old, Nancy had no idea how to tell the time. Patty was ten. She said she vaguely remembered learning how to tell the time before, but she'd forgotten now.

After the porridge was consumed, they took it in turns to pee in the toilet. It was old and smelly. It had no door, so they never looked when each other was on it. Nancy always tried to hold her breath when she used it because of the overpowering smell of urine. It was impossible to do so when she was doing a poo though. It took too long. She'd tried holding her breath once during a poo and had nearly passed out. The cubicle that housed the toilet was in the corner of their room. It was full of spiders, too, which made it an even worse place to be. Neither of them flushed the toilet, in case they disturbed the neighbours. They were only allowed to flush it once a day. It was mostly Patty's job because she was taller and stronger. The old chain needed a good yank to get it to work, and it made quite a racket when you pulled it. Patty wasn't stronger today though; the coughing was making her weak.

The sisters quickly completed their three jigsaw puzzles. They'd done them so many times, they could practically do them with their eyes shut. Then, they played Happy Families and Old Maid. The cards were very old. The sisters often wondered if Derek knew they had them. They doubted it. They always made sure to hide them when he came, just in case he took them away. Sometimes Patty would tell Nancy stories about Mr Bun the baker or Master Brick the builder's son. Nancy enjoyed those stories.

All was quiet upstairs. Derek must've gone out. Somewhere in the distance a dog barked, and a car started up. Nancy wondered what the neighbours were like. Did their children live downstairs too, or did they have rooms like the girls used to?

'Can you tell me another story?' Nancy asked her sister.

'What about?' Patty asked, with a cough.

'*Before* ... of course,' Nancy replied.

Patty looked a little sad.

'I don't like remembering them, it makes me feel a bit sick in my tummy.'

'Please!' Nancy begged. 'You remember them better than I do.'

She waited, hoping that her sister would agree and would tell her a few things about their parents.

'Oh, all right.'

Patty moved up her mattress and patted it to show that Nancy should join her.

Nancy did so, and Patty put her arms around her little sister, pulling her close. This was how they always sat when they talked about *before*.

11

HANNAH, MARCH 2023

'You're sure you're okay to work on all this now?' Hannah asked Dave.

'Yep. One hundred percent,' he replied. 'I had a day out with Noah yesterday, took him to Lynton Haven. He loves the boats, and we managed a bit of crabbing. Plus, the meeting the other night was good, lots of anonymous faces. Sometimes it's easier that way.'

Hannah never asked what went on at the AA meetings. It was up to him how much of his past he shared with other people. But she could tell from his manner that the dark clouds that were gathering the other day had cleared. Albeit temporarily. Sadly, they would return. Such was the nature of his life.

'So did you manage to find anything out about Martin Farnley's death?'

'Yeah. I've pieced together information from various "find my past" and "ancestry" websites, along with government public records.'

'Well done.'

'I also dug deep online and managed to find a fatal incident report. It doesn't name any names, but it's got to be him, the details are too similar.'

Hannah dunked a chocolate chip cookie into her coffee, bit it in half and awaited the story. A simple Google search had led her down similar rabbit holes many times before.

'October 3rd 1993,' Dave said. 'Crow's Wall Prison. Approximately 8am. An inmate aged forty-six, clearly Farnley, was found on the floor of the bathroom. As well as some sizeable bruises, he had a nasty cut to his arm. Its position suggested a defence wound. It was fairly deep, and he was bleeding. He refused to say how he'd been hurt. The wound was stitched and dressed. The report says it appeared to have been made with a jagged edge. Later supposition went with a makeshift implement, something like a toothbrush filed to a sharp edge.

Hannah winced. 'Crow's Wall was a tough old place back then. I think they've done a lot to improve it in recent years. But in the nineties, it was rough. Fancy putting him in there.'

Dave shrugged. 'Category B. Makes sense given the charge.'

'Bit of a trek to Kent for the family.'

'Uh huh. But, Han, he was a convicted murderer. They had to send him where they had the space. Anyway ...' Dave raised his eyebrows to ask if she was ready for him to complete the report.

She nodded.

'He spent the rest of the day and one night in the infirmary and was then returned to his cell. They had single cells at that point. Tiny, but I'm guessing Farnley would've preferred it that way. Three days after he received the wound, he began to complain to the staff that he felt ill. The nature of his ailments – aching limbs, a raised temperature, and disorientation – suggested a virus. His mother, having heard about the injuries, asked to visit, and was told he had the flu and was not well enough to make it to the visitors' room. She requested they give him Lucozade.'

'Bloody hell. Poor woman!' Hannah pushed the packet of

cookies into the middle of the table. She had lost her appetite.

'Despite the usual medical care, the wound wouldn't heal, and Farnley was eventually moved back to the infirmary where he presented with a mottled grey skin that was freezing to the touch. Apparently, as he had received bruising to the face a few days before, it hadn't been obvious to anyone that the unfortunate bastard had turned grey! Antibiotics were given, but it was all too little, too late. He died.'

The atmosphere in the room was gloomy. 'So, pretty much as Liv described. Good work, Dave,' Hannah said. 'So what are we thinking? Martin simply got himself in the wrong place at the wrong time. Or was it an attempt to seriously harm him? Or even kill him. Maybe the assailant was interrupted?'

'Hard to say. As you've already mentioned, prisons were tougher places back then. Especially Crow's Wall. I'm not sure inmates were cared for as well as they are today. He was in there for killing his *wife*. People have some strong opinions on shit like that. You can get the meanest, toughest blokes – geezers who'd think nothing of slicing up a rival gang member. But mention putting an end to your mother, your kid or your wife and they get very judgy.' Dave shook his head. 'I've seen it before.'

'True,' Hannah agreed. 'But Martin Farnley must've been a model prisoner. He would've kept his head down, minded his own business. He was hoping to go to appeal. He pleaded not guilty, for God's sake.'

'Well, perhaps your other theory's right then,' Dave said. 'Rather than a targeted attack on him, he might've walked in on something. Saw a drug deal take place. Witnessed a beating. Or worse! As you say, he could've simply been in the wrong place. He didn't seem to have much luck.'

'He certainly didn't. From what you say, the wound was by no means fatal. If he hadn't got the infection that led to his death, he'd have been back on his feet in no time. Who knows, he might even have won his appeal. If Liv is correct, then he didn't do it, and he would've been able to prove it.'

'That would've led to a far better life for his children,' Dave mused. 'Perhaps Liv wouldn't have finished up an addict.'

'It's truly one of those *what if* moments.'

Hannah felt a lump in her throat. Purely from meeting Liv and talking to her for a short time, she already hoped Martin Farnley had not been a bad man.

'So ...' Dave sighed. It was clear he was feeling a little down-hearted, too. What a pair they were. 'Tomorrow's the day you meet up with her and get the whole story?'

'Yes. She's texted me to confirm. We've agreed on the park, so she can smoke. Unless it's raining. Then I suppose it'll have to be that awful café.'

'And you're still okay for me to come, too?'

'Yeah, sure.'

'Two heads are better than one,' Dave said.

'Unless you're thinking of going into modelling,' Hannah quipped. 'I'm going to start cautiously. But I do want to cover the night her mum was killed in full. I know it must be hard for her to speak about it, and that's why I didn't push it the first time.'

'Absolutely,' he agreed. 'But she can't just say, *I know it was my uncle* and not back it up with some facts.'

'I might ask if I can record our conversation. What do you think?' Hannah asked. 'I find making notes on my phone can distract people. They tend to think I'm not listening.'

'I get you.' Dave nodded. 'It's like you're playing *Candy Crush* or checking out your socials.'

'Which of course I am not!' Hannah said, indignantly.

'I know that, boss.'

'Yeah,' Hannah said. 'I'm definitely going to record it.'

She experienced a little spike of adrenalin. She couldn't wait to get to the heart of this case.

12

LIV, FEBRUARY 2023

As the Uber carried her ever closer to Stephen's office, Liv considered what they would discuss today. He seemed to be skirting around the subject of her mum's death, but she assumed there was a reason for that. He had said right at the beginning, that very first time she'd ventured into his beautiful room, that his methods might seem a little odd and she was not to worry if he appeared to be meandering through her life. That was fine for him to say; he wasn't in any rush. As long as Toby kept paying his bill! Liv gave herself a shake. She mustn't think like that. Stephen was amazing. He'd reminded her of so much already. If he was holding off talking about her mum, then there had to be a good reason for it. *Trust the process*, she repeated to herself. As she did before every AA or NA meeting. Once Stephen decided she was ready to relive her mum's death, all would come clear to her, and then she would know once and for all what had happened. Toby was still apologising for being asleep. He was convinced that if he'd seen something, too, Liv wouldn't be forced to keep trying to remember. He'd carried that burden around for far too long. She hated to think of him upset.

As always, she told him that that was simply how it had happened. He had been eight for goodness' sake, of course he'd fallen asleep! He mustn't blame himself for the state of her life and her fractured mental health. She'd assured him that once she found out what really happened, things would be better. Oddly, he'd said that perhaps it would *actually* be better if she just left the past alone now. But she'd told him that the past was all she had. Surely, he knew that?

After that conversation, Liv had cried herself to sleep, sobbing for the people she'd lost so unfairly, so abruptly, and for the sorry state of her own paltry life.

———

Refocusing her attention on the street outside the steamy taxi window, Liv noted they were almost there. Not long now. Her heart gave a little flutter. She was surprised to realise that she was excited. Excitement had not been a part of her life for quite a few years. When she had been drinking and snorting copious amounts of coke up her nose, she'd thought life was exciting. How stupid! In actual fact, every drink, and every drug, had simply been a way of blotting out that night. Now, thanks to Stephen, she was fast approaching the truth. Her heart gave another little flutter, and she gathered up her bag, ready to leave the car.

———

Being here in Stephen's soft grey room, under the blanket, letting herself go, had swiftly become the highlight of Liv's week. She gave him the answer to his usual first question.

'A chicken and mushroom pot noodle and an energy drink.'

His next question was a little different.

'How did you feel about coming here today?'

'Not anxious. I didn't stress about it.'

'That's good. How did you get here?'

'I grabbed an Uber.'

'Were you running late?'

'No. I couldn't be arsed to walk. It's just a little bit too far, and it's so wet today.'

'True.'

'Besides, it's all Toby's money. So ...'

'We're going to talk about your mum today, Liv. Is that okay?'

'Yes.'

'Your mum was called Susan.'

'Yes.'

'She died in 1992?'

'Yes. She did.'

'To be precise,' Stephen's voice rose slightly, 'she was killed, wasn't she?'

'Yes.'

'That must've had a big impact on your life. I mean, it's something that follows you, surely?' he asked.

'Yes. It's like everyone knows *that* thing about you, sometimes before they've even met you.'

'I'm sorry.'

'My dad was also killed. In prison.'

'Yes. I know. You mentioned it on the form. We're not going to talk about him today though.'

'Okay.'

'We're not going to talk about your mum's death yet either, Liv. But I would like to hear more about her. Is that all right?'

'Yes.'

'What was Susan Farnley like?'

'She was a kind soul. One of those people who puts others first. She smelt of flowers and something else. Something sweet.

Like vanilla. She was … soft. Her hair, her skin, everything was soft.'

'Is it painful for you to think about her?' Stephen asked.

'Sometimes.'

'But you're okay to talk now?'

'Yes.'

'Tell me about the last time you saw your mum. Not when she was killed. The last time before that. Do you understand?'

'I do,' Liv said. 'I was fourteen. I was in my bedroom.'

'What was your room like back then?'

'The Pasadenas were playing. There was a messy pile of *Just Seventeen* magazines on the floor next to my bed. The geometric bedding clashed with the flowery wallpaper – a sign that my bedding had moved on from childhood, but my walls hadn't.' Liv smiled. 'There was a gentle knock on my bedroom door. My mum asked if she could come in.'

She paused.

'Tell me what happened next, please,' Stephen asked. 'Describe it for me.'

'My mum came in the room. She looked like she'd been crying. I wasn't really worried though.'

'Why not?'

'I was too preoccupied thinking about Alan, a boy from school. I cared so much about what he thought of me.'

'Teenagers!' Stephen said with a wry smile. 'Carry on. Your mum had been crying.'

'Her eyes were a bit red, and her voice was … kind of jagged. She was sniffing. She said she had an errand to run, and she wouldn't be gone long. Anyway, Dad would probably be home soon.'

'You didn't ask for more information?'

'No. I was distracted – by Alan.'

'And then …?'

'Annie appeared behind Mum. Her face was covered in

makeup. I expected Mum to demand that she *go and wash that muck off your face*. But Mum didn't say a word. Annie said she was going out and she'd be back later. Mum didn't challenge her about timings or even ask who she was going out with. Annie was nearly eighteen and she had a habit of reminding our parents in a shrill voice that she was almost an adult and could do as she pleased. Mum said she would prefer it if Annie stayed home until she had had time to run her errand, but Annie argued that at fourteen I was legally allowed to babysit other people's kids, so I could definitely babysit my own brother. So, Mum asked me if I'd be okay to look after Toby. I said yes, and told her that I wasn't a baby.'

'Did you mind being in charge of Toby?' Stephen asked.

'Not really ... I just wanted to get back to reading my magazines and thinking about Alan, to be honest.'

'What was Toby doing?'

'Probably playing Sonic.'

'So, your mum went out?'

'Yes.'

'And ... Annie?'

'Uh huh. She went, too.'

'What happened after they left?'

'I lost track of time. I was reading about snogging and ... imagining it was me and Alan.'

'So, moving forward in time, who came home first, your dad or your mum?' Stephen asked.

'The front door banged, and there were footsteps in the wooden hallway. It was definitely Mum. You could always tell straight away if it was her because of her heels.'

'Where was Toby?'

'In his room. He'd fallen asleep. I glanced at the clock next to my bed. It was pink and white. A remnant of my youth, along with the walls. It was nearly 9.30pm.'

'Your mum didn't come upstairs to check on you, or Toby?'

'No. She probably thought we were both asleep. She was moving about downstairs, backwards and forwards; I could hear the floorboards creaking. She was rummaging through boxes and stuff.'

'Rummaging through boxes?'

'Yes.'

'Cardboard boxes?'

'No, kind of like old wooden tea chests. They used to be in the corner of the lounge.'

'Oh, right. What was in them?'

'Videos and books, I think.'

Liv shook her head, and began twiddling the ring on her left thumb, around and around in agitated circles.

Stephen spoke carefully. 'Is this it? Is this when she dies?'

'Almost!' Liv said. 'I went downstairs to see what she was doing. There was no hall light on. Only a small table lamp. I waited on the stairs. I was crouching in the darkness and—'

Stephen interrupted her. 'We're not going to talk about this anymore today.'

Suddenly, Liv shouted, 'There's the knock!'

'I'm going to wake you up now.'

Stephen began counting.

'When I get to ten, I will tap you on the shoulder, and you will wake up feeling refreshed and in good spirits.'

'Don't open the door, Mum!'

Stephen reached ten a little quicker than usual and tapped Liv gently on the shoulder.

Her eyes opened.

'Do you feel all right?' Stephen asked, handing her a bottle of cold water.

'Yes. Was I upset?'

'No,' Stephen replied.

'Good.'

'Do you remember what we were discussing?'

'Yes,' Liv replied. 'My mum went to the front door.'

'Your life was about to change dramatically, wasn't it?'

Liv nodded.

'I knew she wasn't herself; something wasn't right. For God's sake, I couldn't even tell you Alan's surname now. Not even if you held a gun to my head. And yet, he was more important that night than my own mother.'

'Try not to blame yourself. You couldn't have known what was going to happen. You did well today.'

'Thank you.'

Liv twisted the lid off her water bottle and took a long swig. Best drink it all. She'd Googled it; this stuff wasn't cheap. It was also, according to the internet, suitable for vegetarians. What a crazy world!

13

SUSAN, JULY 1974

SUSAN'S first baby was due on the fifteenth of July. Despite her concerns, Martin arranged a business trip out of town on the ninth, insisting he had time to get everything done before the baby arrived. Unfortunately for him, the baby was early, and he, several hours' drive away, was unable to get back. He was beside himself with remorse once he did arrive and vowed that if they were blessed with any more children, he would ensure he was right by her side for the delivery.

Susan secretly wondered if he'd arranged that trip on purpose. She knew men were slightly put off by all that child-birth entailed, and he had mentioned on more than one occasion that he had a delicate stomach for such things.

He arrived at the hospital a full two hours after their daughter made her way into the world. Susan couldn't lie – she had been shocked by the birth. She hadn't anticipated the raw agony. She'd been telling herself for weeks that women had given birth for centuries, and one way or another, their child would make it safely into the world. The truth was that it had been incredibly difficult. Annie was larger than expected – a little over eight and a half pounds. Given that Susan had always been described as petite, the baby had felt enormous. The pushing stage had seemed to go on forever. Every time she'd asked if her husband had arrived, she had been told not to worry about him, and to get on with the task in hand. But she hadn't been worrying about him. She'd been worrying about herself. She'd been seriously doubting that she'd ever get the baby out, and she had wanted Martin there. Not so much because she'd needed comfort from him, but because she'd wanted him to see how hard it was for her. She'd needed him to know this was incredibly difficult.

Annie had been a surprise pregnancy. They'd thought they were being careful. Martin had constantly said that they needed a good five years of married life before they would be ready for children. But Annie had come along whether they were ready or not.

Once home from the hospital, Susan dug out her diary. Out of interest, in case Annie ever asked her, she jotted down the news from the papers on her birth date. The local paper had an interview with the neighbour of the little Greenwood girls. Susan wished the press would leave it alone now. *Why didn't the bloody neighbour do something about it at the time?* And the Nationals went with a bomb that had gone off at the Tower of London.

Later, when she thought about it, Susan realised that neither of those stories was very pleasant, and they were not really suitable for sharing with her beautiful baby girl, now or in the future.

14

HANNAH, MARCH 2023

HANNAH TAPPED the Formica table impatiently as she waited for Dave to pick up the phone. After a couple more rings, she heard him clear his throat.

'Dave?'

'Yeah. What's up?'

'Wherever you are, don't bother coming.'

'What? I'm nearly there.' Dave sounded annoyed.

'Don't bother. She's cancelled.'

'Liv?'

'No. Taylor Swift. We're all very disappointed here in the café.'

'Ha ha. Seriously, I thought you only spoke to her late last night.'

'I did. I told her the forecast said heavy rain and she agreed to switch from the park to this fucking café.' Hannah lowered her voice for the tail end of the sentence.

'So, when did she cancel?'

'Literally two minutes ago. She rang and said she's ill. Woke up with it this morning, apparently.'

Dave's disbelief was clear by his tone. 'What exactly is she claiming to have woken up with?'

'She's not sure. She's saying Covid. But she's got no tests. I think she's merely saying that to put us off going round to hers to talk there.'

'Did she sound hungover?'

'Hard to say.'

'Just thinking, possibly knowing she was going to have to talk about some sensitive stuff today led her to start drinking last night. I've done it myself.'

'Well, either way, cold feet, Covid or a hangover, we're not going to get any answers today. I even offered to do a FaceTime call, but she was all *I can't, I look awful!*'

'What about a good old fashioned phone call then?'

'No. I want to *see* her when she's telling the story. You know how important body language is.'

'So, what now? She's out of the picture for what … a week?' Dave asked.

'S'pose so. If she's going to stick to the Covid story.'

'Are you going to shelve the whole case or …?'

'I'm going to go home for a decent coffee,' Hannah whispered. 'And then I'm going to see if I can locate Ray Farnley. You've got other stuff to be getting on with, haven't you?'

'Sure. I'll work through the jobs you emailed me.'

'Thanks, Dave. Speak soon.' Hannah hung up and asked for the bill, leaving most of the disappointing bacon butty she'd been reckless enough to order.

———

An hour later, Hannah called Dave again. 'I think I've found him.'

'Ray! Where is he?'

'He's on my laptop. Facebook to be precise.'

'So, you've got an address for him?'

'Well, this is the thing. I haven't actually found *Ray*, but I've found a guy called *Jake* Farnley and he has a sister called Emily Farnley.'

'Uh huh.'

'Jake's in his late twenties, and his sister looks a few years younger. So I figure they could be about the right age to be Ray's kids. He could've had them after he lost touch with his family.'

'Definitely.'

'Anyway, as per usual, this Jake fella has set his privacy settings to *show any old stranger my entire life*. So, I had a good nose through his photos, and who did I spot?'

'You spotted Ray!'

'Yes, I did. In the background of a group photo from about a year ago. He's not tagged because he's not on Facebook. But it sure as hell looks like a grey version of the men in the photographs Liv showed me.'

'Excellent. So, where do they all live?'

'That's the fun part. You remember I said I needed to find out if he was still pink and breathing?'

'Uh huh?' Dave answered, in a kind of *Where the hell is this going?* tone.

'Well, he's more of a chestnut brown. They live in Puerto Banús, Marbella.'

'Spain?'

'Yes. That's the one. You weren't lying about that education,' Hannah laughed.

'Nice.'

'Yes. So, anyway, I was thinking ...'

'You were thinking of combining a little holiday with a stakeout.'

'It couldn't do any harm,' Hannah said. 'Fancy coming along? He lives in the posh part. They call it the Golden Mile, so Google tells me.'

Dave paused. 'I wish I could. But it's Easter break in three days. I've got all kinds of plans with Noah. I can't let him down.'

'Of course not. I'd forgotten. When you don't have kids you kind of lose touch with the school holidays.'

'I'm sorry, boss. If it was any other time, I'd be packing my budgie smugglers.'

Hannah gave her head a shake. The image of Dave's pale body in tiny swimwear was going to take some shifting.

'No worries. I can go on my own or ...' She had a sudden thought. 'I'll ask Lottie if she wants to come.'

'Good idea.'

At the sound of Dixie's little claws on the laminate flooring in the hall, Hannah announced, 'Talk of the devil, that's her now. I'll hang up. I'll let you know how it goes in Marbella.'

'You'd bloody better,' Dave said.

————

Lottie's answer was a resounding yes. Within five minutes she'd made a call to Hannah's mum, Jacqui, to ask if she could look after Dixie.

'I'll pay for all of it, Han. I've been desperate for a holiday for ages.'

'Have you forgotten Portugal, you idiot? That wasn't very long ago.'

'No, I haven't. But ... when I was poor, I had no holidays. Barely even a day out at the seaside. It was so bleak. I just want to make up for those awful days.'

'I understand,' Hannah said. 'But I can't let you pay. I'll pay for some, and bung as much on expenses as possible. I mean, if we find Ray and solve the case for Liv, I'm sure she won't mind paying.'

'It's not even her money, anyway, is it?' Lottie asked.

'No. Like I said before, it's her brother's. He's made a lot of money trading. One of those young bucks who seems to know exactly where to invest.'

'Unlike my evil stepfather.'

'Yes, Vincent wouldn't recognise a hot tip if you poked him up the arse with it.'

Lottie giggled. 'Oh, I wish he was still here so I could.'

'Anyway,' Hannah continued, keen not to dwell on the subject of Vincent Rocchino, 'you never know, you might meet a tasty Mediterranean man to take your mind off Chen.'

Tilting her head to one side, Lottie said, 'Anything's possible, I suppose.'

'Right, let's check out flights from Southampton then.'

Hannah's fingers flew over the keyboard. A minute later, she said, 'Typical, we can only fly to Malaga from Southampton on weekends. The next flight leaves on Saturday April 1st.'

'Well, we'd be foolish not to be on it!' Lottie laughed.

15

LIV, MARCH 2023

LIV HAD BEEN EXPECTING Stephen to ask her more about her mum. After reading through the transcript of last week's session, she naturally assumed this was the week they would finally address the murder. So, she was a little irritated when he indicated she should get on the bed and said, 'I'm going to begin the relaxation process now. We'll be talking about something different today. Your past relationships.'

'Oh ... okay.' She tried to hide her disappointment.

'Are you all right?'

'Yes. I just thought ... you know, we would've got around to my mum's murder by now. It's what I need to remember.'

'Do you think I'm delaying you?'

'A bit.'

Liv was cautious; the last thing she wanted to do was piss Stephen off. But, yes, she did think he was delaying her. Toby's money was paying for this, and surely to God, he could've moved onto the most important subject by now.

'Have you noticed ...' Stephen placed the cashmere throw on top of Liv and took his seat in the armchair next to the bed.

'Every time we meet, you go into a deeper trance. Each memory is clearer.'

'Is it?'

'Most definitely. It may not seem obvious to you, but I can hear it. Are you thinking about the memories after you leave here?'

'Yes.'

'And you're reading the transcripts?'

'Yes, as soon as you email them.'

'Have you noticed they're much more detailed now?'

'Erm … yes. I suppose so. Well, they help fill in the gaps, not that there are many.'

'If you're finding yourself thinking about the memories during the week that follows, that means it's working.'

'Oh yes, I am. The details stay with me for a long time. I keep going over the memories, and the transcripts.'

'Exactly!'

'So, you're not just delaying for the sake of it?' Liv asked.

'Far from it. By the time we get to your mother's death, I expect that the images you'll see will be sharp and clear. You'll be able to tell me every little nuance. You will get the answers you need.'

'That would be amazing.'

'We'll get there. You need to trust me,' Stephen said.

'I do. I promise.'

Liv gave herself over to the by now familiar relaxation process, any concerns about Toby's money banished.

————

'Have you ever been in love?' Stephen asked, after they had established her breakfast choice of the day.

'I'm not sure.'

'Does that question surprise you?' he asked.

'A bit. It's like something a friend might've asked me when we were fifteen and having a sleepover.'

'Is it?'

'Yes. Although, I didn't really have sleepovers, because at fifteen, most of my time was taken up by Toby. He was still sneaking into my bed most nights, after he'd had a nightmare.'

'Poor Toby,' Stephen said, before confirming, 'So, Liv, you're not sure if you've been in love.'

'I thought I was once. But, looking back, I know I was just infatuated.'

'That's very interesting,' Stephen said, 'the fact you can now see it for what it was.'

'Oh, trust me, I am under no illusions now. It's like a take-away burger from one of those awful shacks that are open at three in the morning. A *dirty* burger. The whole time you're eating it, you think it's great. You crave the next bite, and if anyone tells you it's bad for you, you ignore them. But then, when it's finished, and you have time to reflect, you realise how shit it was, and you feel ashamed of yourself for ever liking it so much.'

Stephen gave a hearty laugh.

'Perfectly put. You've really thought about this, haven't you?'

'I suppose I have, yes.'

'So then, tell me about this dirty burger of a man who wasn't good for you.'

Liv instantly launched into a story. A story that she had played over and over in her mind for years. The story of the only man who ever came close to being her significant other.

'I was twenty-five when I met Sy.'

'Sy?' Stephen asked.

'Simon to his parents. But only to them, and … more recently, the authorities.'

'I see,' he added, nodding. 'Continue, please?'

'It sounds like a huge bag of clichés, but Sy wasn't like

anyone else I'd met before. He was older than me and I was quite naive at that point. Toby had just left for uni, and I think it was the first time I felt able to fully exhale. My brother had mates, and lecturers, and all kinds of pastoral care; I could finally concentrate on me. I met Sy in a pub. I thought he was good looking and confident. He was thirty-two and he came across as someone who figured they knew it all. Sadly, I agreed with him.'

'Uh huh.' Stephen encouraged her on.

'It was one of those whirlwind things. I moved in with him within weeks. Actually, I was declaring my love for him within days. But he never … he wasn't able to …'

'Love you back?' Stephen suggested.

'Yeah.' She gave a cynical laugh. 'It's that fucking Meatloaf song, isn't it? He said he liked me and all that, and he liked having me around. But there was this girl before me, and he loved her and … you get the picture.'

'But you stayed anyway.'

'Oh, yeah; I stayed for years. Hoping he would change his mind. But …' She shook her head.

'What was so special about the other woman?'

'She was expecting his baby. They had this whole thing about calling the baby Bump. He never once told me the other woman's name; he called her Bump's mum. I tried to find it out. I searched his stuff when I was alone in his flat. I read private letters; things he'd hidden in the back of drawers. But I couldn't find any reference to her. She was my nemesis, and I never knew her name.'

'Why weren't they together anymore?'

'Oh, she died. So did Bump,' Liv said, casually.

This terrible disclosure was old news to her and therefore needed no reverent pause.

'Shi …' Stephen stopped himself and regained his professional demeanour. 'That's awful.'

'Yeah. Awful for them, and awful for me. It's impossible to compete with the dead. Trust me, I've tried.'

'So, you say you realised Simon wasn't good for you after you split up. When was that, please?' Stephen asked.

'Ten years later.'

'You were together for ten years!'

'Give or take. I clearly don't learn quick.'

'Was it simply the fact he couldn't love you that told you he was no good for you?'

'Well, that was a big part of it. But mainly it was because he was the one who got me seriously into drinking and drugs. He was always trying to heal his pain. He was a stubborn man who refused to go to counselling or to get any help for his grief. Instead, he created an outer shell, the confident man I first met. People thought that was him; that Sy had it all together. They didn't see him sobbing all night, mourning the loss of Bump and Bump's mum. They didn't know about the demons that took over when the sun went down. He'd been dabbling since their deaths. At first it was drinking until he passed out, then a bit of weed or the odd pill. I joined him for a couple of joints or a bottle of wine. It relaxed me. It also helped me to ignore my own memories. Let's face it, I had a truck load of shit in my past, too.'

'So, Sy was the one who pushed for more?'

'Yeah. I would've been happy to leave it at the drink and weed. He was the one who needed more. He wanted to block everything out, and it was only a matter of time before he moved on. I know what you're thinking – why did I move on, too? Why wasn't I strong enough to get him help, or at the very least to get myself the hell out of there?'

'Well, why *did* you move on too?' Stephen asked.

'I refer you back to my previous comment – *infatuation*. For me, Sy was the drug. I needed to have him, and if the only way I was going to keep him in my life was to continue blindly along the yellow brick road, moving through the list of recreational drugs he had in mind, then I was going to do it. What I hadn't bargained for was the fact I would get hooked, too. When I was high, I no longer felt the need to go over and over the night we were all taken by the police to Grandma's. Before I knew it, I was chasing oblivion right along with him.'

'Trauma victims are often drawn to each other. But it's not always best for either party,' Stephen said.

'No shit!' Liv agreed.

16

SUSAN, FEBRUARY 1989

NOT LONG AFTER Susan's son Toby's fifth birthday he began to complain of pains in his legs. He was constantly pale and had lost all his enthusiasm for life. He'd started school a few months before and the doctor said he was probably tired. He said it was tough, a long day, filled with much activity. He was sure Toby would soon adjust. But if anything, the pains in his legs increased. He seemed to have a new bruise every day, even when he'd been nowhere and only played quietly in his room. Susan watched as the tiredness got worse for her baby. He began missing days at school. She simply couldn't wake him, and it felt mean to insist he attend school when he was clearly exhausted. What was he going to miss that was so important at that age anyway?

Martin said Susan was mollycoddling him. He figured she didn't want to let their little boy grow up. They'd agreed that three children was enough. Susan had to admit, it was awful knowing she would never again have a baby at home all day with her. But she was not fabricating Toby's problems. Far from it. If anything, she was trying to make light of it because she knew Martin didn't agree.

Finally, she couldn't bear it any longer and demanded he have some tests. The doctor reluctantly agreed. It annoyed Susan how he made eye contact with Martin, who had insisted on coming along for the appointment; probably because he thought Susan was going to embarrass herself. As she rose from her chair, she spotted a look between them, a *Women – what are they like?* kind of look.

———

A week later, neither of them expected to hear the three words that changed their lives – acute lymphoblastic leukaemia. Everything Susan had known and assumed to be normal was taken from her that day. And so began the most horrific time of their lives.

They clung to each other at night, her face forced into the pillow, to muffle the sound of her tears. She blamed herself constantly, going over and over the things she'd done in the past that could be the reason for this awful abhorrent situation that her poor darling Toby found himself in. Oddly, in a strange way it brought her and Martin closer. Their need to support each other, whilst simultaneously playing it all down for the children, somehow led them to become stronger together. They were Team Farnley. Toby was only ever allowed to see a smiling face and feel a supportive hug.

17

HANNAH, MARCH 2023

THE DAY before they flew to Malaga, Hannah needed to tie up some loose ends for work. On her way back from a meeting, she popped into Costa Coffee for lunch. She usually preferred to work from the car or at home. But on this occasion, her laptop needed charging, and she decided to make use of Costa's electricity at the same time as indulging in a large maple hazel latte and a cheese toastie. Firing off emails and ticking boxes in her head, she kept herself busy. With her air pods in, her music drowned out the chatter of the room. She was confident that what work there would be left could easily be handled by Dave, in between his days out with Noah, whilst *she* was looking forward to doing some serious undercover work in Spain.

Taking Lottie with her had been a stroke of genius. If she wanted to attract the attention of this Jake Farnley guy, who better to accompany her than an exceptionally beautiful young woman, who never failed to turn heads? At the exact moment that she had this thought, another beautiful woman walked in the door. Her ex, Mandy! Hannah felt her stomach pitch. She dropped her toastie back onto the plate and glanced up again, allowing herself a proper stare. Mandeep Khan was stunning.

Hannah had thought it the first time she'd seen her. The day she'd stepped back in her biker boots and trodden onto Mandy's delicate foot in this exact coffee shop. Her long dark hair had shimmered. Her brown eyes had been the biggest and the most soulful Hannah had ever seen. Even Dixie the spaniel couldn't compete.

Hannah didn't know what she was hoping for. Did she want Mandy to glance over and spot her? Did she want her to join her at the table? Or did she want Mandy to buy her usual beverage, turn, and make her way out of the café?

Ultimately, it didn't matter what *she* wanted. Mandy would do whatever she chose, and Hannah could do nothing but sit bolt upright, with a fake smile on her face, waiting to see which scenario would play out.

Mandy left. Not a backwards glance. Hannah convinced herself Mandy hadn't seen her. It hurt too much to think she might have caught sight of her out of the corner of her eye and had still chosen to leave without acknowledgment.

There was a time, a few months ago, when Mandy would've rushed over to be with her. They would both have worn the cheesiest of grins. Hannah would've held onto Mandy's delicate hands and the rest of the coffee shop would've disappeared. But that was before. Before the day Mandeep's family found out about her love affair with a woman. They had put their collective feet down hard. Not just the parents; aunts, uncles, and so many brothers! Mandeep had not known what to do for the best. In the end, all Hannah's attempts to persuade her to stay had failed.

———

They'd managed to date in secret for a good few months, and Hannah had stupidly allowed herself to think they could have a future. They'd kept things on the quieter side, occasionally going to the pub with Lottie, as well as the odd trip out just the two of them. Mostly, they'd indulged in takeaway meals and movie nights at Hannah's home. Lottie had been a good egg, often going out and leaving them alone, allowing them the lounge to themselves. To Hannah, it hadn't mattered what film was playing in the background or what food Mandy had arrived with. The main event had always been Mandy. Hannah had had to pinch herself sometimes to believe that a woman like Mandy had wanted her in the same way. Hannah had had her fair share of girlfriends; she was experienced and adventurous. In her younger days she'd loved to use all the toys on offer and wasn't afraid to try anything. But Mandy had been different. She'd confessed early on that she was a bit of a novice. Her trust in Hannah had been the biggest turn on. She had put herself in Hannah's hands absolutely and asked to be taught. Hannah had known right then that the games she'd played in her youth were not for Mandy.

The first time they'd been alone together in the lounge, Hannah had slowly removed Mandy's clothes, her eyes widening with each glimpse of her body. Once they had both been naked, she had selflessly lavished attention on Mandy. Expertly using her fingertips, she had watched as the goosebumps had risen on Mandy's penny brown skin. As she'd circled Mandy's flat stomach with her tongue, her breathing had all but stopped. Hannah had waited for a second, drinking in the sight of this exquisite woman, alive with anticipation. Then, when she'd known Mandy couldn't bear it any longer, she had lowered her head. Kissing the most intimate part of her girlfriend, she'd brought her to a juddering orgasm. Afterwards, Mandy had cried, and Hannah had asked her why.

Her response had sent a jolt of joy to Hannah's heart. 'I've never felt so free. Every other woman I've been with has tried to help me relax. But no one has ever made me truly believe that what we were doing was right. What you did then, it was ... it was so perfect!'

After that first night, they'd just fitted together, like two palms touching in prayer. Mandy had grown in confidence, and on so many occasions she'd used her soft hands to bring Hannah to equally amazing orgasms.

———

Hannah realised she was practically drooling. Why torture herself by thinking about how much Mandy had meant to her?

Stupidly, it was a simple afternoon out that had brought their love affair crashing down around them. Mandy's eldest brother, Saleem, had seen them coming out of the cinema. It would've been okay if they had walked out like two female friends who'd been to see a movie together. But as bad luck would have it, the film they'd watched was a slushy romance – Mandy's choice. So they had stumbled into the daylight, blinking, holding hands and sharing romantic pecks on the lips. Any other day it wouldn't have mattered a bit, but on this occasion, it ruined everything.

———

Hannah scrolled through her messages until she found the last one she'd received from Mandy. How many times had she read this text? A hundred? A thousand? She'd received it a month after they had finally, tearfully agreed to call it a day. Neither of them wanting to, but both of them knowing it was the only way forward.

The message simply read: *I was more alive with you than ever before. I will never be so alive again. X*

What had Mandy intended her to do with that information? If she'd thought it was an invitation to fight for her, then she would've done so. If she had even the vaguest notion it would get Mandy back in her arms, she would've fought like the third chimp on the way to the Ark. But the message had not come across that way. It was simply a statement of fact, a fact that broke Hannah's heart at the unfairness of it all. If truth be told, she hadn't felt fully alive since she'd lost Mandy either. And, sadly, listening to Dean Lewis' 'Be Alright' on a permanent loop wasn't helping.

Swiping out her air pods and putting her phone in her pocket, she unplugged the laptop and shoved it roughly back into its holder. Sitting here mumbling *I know you love her, but it's over, mate* wasn't doing her any good at all. She needed to get home and pack.

18

LIV, MARCH 2023

ANOTHER APPOINTMENT WITH STEPHEN, and Liv's heart sank a little when he told her they were going to discuss her Uncle Ray. She couldn't see the point. He'd been around when she was young, and as a small child she had found it funny that there was a man who looked so much like her daddy. But he hadn't been important.

'Why do you want to hear about *him?*' she asked.

'Because he's a part of your story, a member of your family.'

'Barely.'

'You wrote his name on the form. You obviously thought he was worth mentioning to me.'

'Your form asked me to list *all* my relatives. I did as you requested.'

'You said he was your dad's identical twin; that alone makes him interesting, surely?'

'If you say so.'

'Okay. Well, humour me, Liv, let's talk about him.'

Liv felt she had to put her trust in him, and allowed Stephen to put her into the relaxed state, and from there into a receptive trance.

After she had told him that she'd eaten a BLT meal deal before jumping into the Uber that morning, Stephen asked, 'When were you first able to tell your dad and uncle apart, simply from a glance?'

With a shrug, Liv replied, 'From a *glance*? I'm not sure I can say.'

'Roughly?'

'They were *very* identical, if that's, like, even a thing.'

'They didn't choose to dress differently or change their hair?'

'Not noticeably. Not that I recall.'

'But they behaved differently towards you and your siblings?'

'Absolutely. That's how I knew who was who. My dad looked at me differently. There was a bond between us; it showed in his smile.'

'Ray didn't have much to do with you?'

'Not really. We got gifts from him at Christmas when we were young. But he worked a lot. He was sometimes there when we went to Grandma's house, but not always.'

'How did that go?'

'What?'

'The times when he was at your grandma's house.'

'I guess I wasn't keen on the way Grandma seemed to run around after him, making his favourite food or getting him endless cups of tea. That seemed odd. Surely he was a grown man; he ought to get his own drinks.'

'So, he was controlling?'

'No. Not that exactly.'

'What about after your mum died and your dad was taken away, how did he behave towards you then?'

'He was a bit wary of us kids, I suppose.'

'Wary?'

'Yeah. He wasn't living at Grandma's by then, he had his

own place. But it was like he still thought of it as his home. I don't think he liked us all being there when he visited Grandma.'

'He looked down on you?'

'A bit.'

'Pitied you all?'

'Kind of,' she sighed. 'I don't know exactly.'

Stephen considered for a moment, and then said, 'Maybe he simply didn't know much about children. I mean, he was what age by then?'

'Late thirties.'

'Yes, and no kids of his own. Either he didn't know how to be around you, or you brought home to him what he had missed out on.'

'Who knows?' Liv said in a frustrated tone. 'Like I say, I didn't know him well enough to work him out back then. He'd had plenty of time to get to know what we were all about before the night that changed everything. He never bothered. Always too busy working or going out. He struck me as a selfish man. Besides, he could've gone on to have kids of his own. He could have had them after he left.'

'He left?' Stephen asked.

'Yes. He went travelling,' Liv replied.

'I see.'

'I think he should've stayed, that's all. I mean, his brother was in prison, for fuck's sake. His mum wasn't young, and she was trying to hold everything together, and his sister-in-law was dead. What did he do? He buggered off to start a new life. Travelling God knows where.'

'You mentioned that your dad died in prison.'

'Yes.'

'So, you're saying Ray left when Martin was still alive?' Stephen seemed surprised.

She nodded.

'He went abroad and abandoned his brother? Left him in prison to cope alone?'

'Yep. A thoughtless fucker,' she fumed.

'Hmm ... more than just thoughtless, wouldn't you say?'

'Cruel, selfish ...?'

Stephen cleared his throat. 'Doesn't it seem odd to you?'

'Odd?' she asked.

'Yes. I mean – why go when his brother needed him the most?'

'I don't know. I was kind of preoccupied with my own concerns back then.' There was impatience in Liv's voice. 'Look, Ray was a shitty brother to my dad, and a shitty son to my grandma. It's a waste of my time and Toby's money to talk about a man who left his family and had nothing to do with anything.'

After a moment, Stephen replied in a calm voice, 'I apologise if I'm annoying you.'

'You're not.'

'You want to get on to finding out who killed your mum?'

'Of course I do. I want to know who knocked at the door that night, and exactly what happened when my mum opened it and immediately disappeared out into the night. It simply can't have been my dad. It must've been some violent stranger. That's the only explanation, and I need you to help me to see it in detail.'

'I will, I promise. But I think it's important to cover every possibility.'

'Fine,' she snapped.

He stopped talking for a second, rubbing his chin. 'I guess you can't see it. Because you lived through it, and you were too young at the time.'

'Can't see what?'

'Maybe, because you'd already been left by so many people, it felt like the natural next step. I think you were possibly blind to it.'

'Blind to what?' she demanded.

'The fact is, Liv, your uncle choosing to leave at the time he did was not simply him being a very unsupportive brother, I'd say it was highly suspicious.'

19

SUSAN, OCTOBER 1989

THE DAY they were told Toby had beaten leukaemia was the most glorious day of Susan's life. Throughout the preceding months she had made so many bargains with God. She had agreed that if it had to end in a death, then it simply must be hers. She had promised everything for the sake of her son. And it had worked. He was saved. Susan and Martin cried again, this time tears of joy. They told the girls their brother was going to be fine. Now, they could settle down to live the rest of their lives together.

Susan made a promise to herself that nothing would ever convince her to take even the slightest of steps off the path that she had promised to walk along.

In her diary, she wrote: *My gorgeous boy is cured. I can't stop smiling. God is good.*

20

NANCY, OCTOBER 1969

NANCY LEANT into Patty as she began to speak. 'When Mummy met Daddy, she was very young and very beautiful. Daddy was very handsome. He had a little boy, called Derek, who was only six.'

'Like me!' Nancy said.

'Yes, like you are now. Mummy and Daddy got married and Mummy loved the little boy. When Derek was twelve, Mummy had a little girl.'

'You!' Nancy said, with a smile.

'Yes, me.' Patty smiled back. 'Then, later they had another baby girl. She was small and ugly.'

Nancy laughed. 'Oy!' She gave her big sister a nudge.

'Only kidding. She was actually very cute.' Patty paused to cough, then continued the story. 'They all moved to a place called Airy Woods.'

'Are you sure?'

'It's something like that.'

'Okay.'

'Their house was big, with lots of rooms. The girls' bedroom was pretty and pink. They had toys and dolls. Derek had a room with cars on the walls. Mummy and Daddy had a big bed, and sometimes, on Sunday mornings, they would all sit in the bed together, laughing and talking.'

Nancy began to experience that sick feeling in her belly. Patty was right; it was lovely to think about them, but sometimes a memory would come along that would make her feel so wretched she thought she might sick up her porridge.

Patty was still talking. 'And they were all happy and—'

Nancy interrupted. 'But we weren't all happy, were we? Derek wasn't happy.'

Patty stopped for a second. Then, shaking her head, she said, 'No. Derek wasn't. He didn't like sharing his daddy with us. He said it was better when it was just the two of them.'

'Remember when I hurt myself in the garden?' Nancy said. 'I fell into those stinging nettles, and Derek just laughed at me.'

'Yes. He did,' Patty agreed.

'But Mummy and Daddy didn't see it,' Nancy said.

'No. There were lots of things they didn't see.'

'Why did they leave us?' Nancy felt tears begin to prick at her eyes, and before she knew it, they were falling down her face.

Patty pulled her close. 'This is why I said I didn't want to tell you stories about them. This is what always happens, Nancy.'

'Sorry.' Nancy wiped the tears across her face, where they mixed with the endless supply of snot.

'I don't know why they had to leave us. I don't know why Derek moved us out of our room and decided we should live down here. I don't understand why he never liked us. And I don't know why he won't let us out!' Patty banged her clenched fist on the mattress, sending little dust clouds into the air.

'I'm sorry. I'm sorry. I won't ask again,' Nancy said, hugging her sister close. But she knew, deep down, that she would. Because she always asked. Thinking about Mummy and Daddy was the only thing that made her feel something in her heart. Even at the tender age of six, she knew she ought to feel *some-*

thing. She knew living in this new bedroom was horrible. She knew being given small amounts of boring food by Derek was wrong. And she knew, even though he was her brother, she really hated Derek.

Later, the key turned again, and Derek appeared at the top of the steps. Nancy briefly thought about making a run for it by charging up the steps and swerving past him. But she recalled the time Patty had tried the same thing. Derek had pushed her back down the steps. Poor Patty's arms and legs were black and blue for weeks afterwards, and Derek had changed the rules so that he would not leave the food unless they stayed on their mattresses.

Nancy caught a waft of Derek's aftershave. That meant he was going out later. Even though they didn't like him being home, because he could appear at any time and shout at them to shut up, it was worse when he went out. They would be alone in a big dark house; they had no lights in their room. Every gust of wind would cause the tree branches to blow against the grimy window. Those branches sounded like claws. Every animal's howl would sound like a wild beast.

It seemed like it was becoming dark earlier and earlier at the moment. It was like it was getting close to winter outside. Nancy and Patty often needed their threadbare blankets during the day. But a few months ago, it'd been warmer, hot even; the whole room had felt stuffy, and they could see all the dust hanging in the air when the sun shone in through the dirty window. It was so confusing not knowing the time or the day. How would she and Patty know when their birthdays had passed? Was she already seven?

'Come and get your food,' Derek said.

Nancy began to rise slightly from her mattress.

'After I'm gone! You know the rules, you little shit,' he added.

Nancy dropped back onto the mattress. *Shit* was another bad word Derek used, another one he spat out frequently. She waited until she heard the key turn again, and then headed up the steps. There were two plates, which had not been washed up well from their last meal. On the plates there was some tinned spaghetti and a piece of bread and butter.

Patty got the water beakers this time, and the girls sat down on their mattresses to eat their meal. Nancy didn't mind spaghetti. But she remembered a different kind of spaghetti that her mummy used to make. It came with something called bolly nice. Thinking about it made Nancy hungry and upset all at the same time.

After their meal, they both used the toilet, neither wanting to be in there in the dark. Then they lay down and tried to fall asleep.

'Patty, I'm cold,' Nancy said.

Patty shifted over to one side of her slim mattress.

'Come on. Bring your blanket.'

This is what they did when it was cold; doubled up on the covers.

————

Later, by the light of the moon, Nancy lay on her side, watching a beetle cross the floor and make its way up the steps. It might be lucky enough to fit under the door. It would probably escape. But how were she and Patty ever supposed to escape?

21

HANNAH, APRIL 2023

HANNAH AND LOTTIE found their seats on the plane. To say they were squashed would be an understatement.

'I told you to let me pay for something a bit more comfortable,' Lottie said, trying to tuck her hand luggage under her seat.

'Don't be daft. This is fine. We're not going to bloody Australia in the thing. We'll be off it in a couple of hours.'

'Still. It's a bit ... crap.'

'You'll be okay, princess,' Hannah said.

'I know what you're thinking. You're thinking that I'm going back to my old ways.'

'Well ... aren't you?'

'No. It's just ... travelling economy is dead. It's as dead as a dado rail.' Lottie winked.

'Idiot!' Hannah laughed.

Most of the flight was taken up with an ongoing argument of a similar ilk. Nothing too disagreeable, just their usual banter and difference of opinion. Hannah had been prepared to book a cheap hotel or an apartment in Malaga. Despite Liv's brother clearly having the money to pay Liv's expenses, she thought it wasn't fair to charge too much for the accommodation, and anyway, Jake seemed to spend a lot of time in the bars of Malaga. Lottie, on the other hand, was keen to make a proper holiday of it in Marbella. Offering to pay the bulk of the accommodation bill, she had persuaded Hannah to choose a classy hotel that she claimed was conveniently placed halfway between Jake's home in Puerto Banús and his preferred drinking venues in Malaga. The trip had also somehow gone from a quick jaunt to a fourteen-night holiday.

Now, as Lottie took a sandwich from the good-looking male flight attendant, and Hannah declined one, the discussion continued.

'It's not the money, Lottie. I know you'll cover it. It's just … I don't want it to appear like I'm off having a jolly, when Liv needs me.'

Pulling apart the soft, white bread to further investigate exactly what the caterers considered to be coronation chicken, Lottie replied, 'She doesn't need you. According to her she has Covid, and she won't allow you near her until she's over it.'

'I know. But a two-week holiday, Lottie! You've turned this into a full-on spa break.'

After a tentative bite of the dubious sandwich, Lottie tossed it to one side.

'Yuck. That does not taste like coronation chicken.'

'I need to work,' Hannah continued. 'I need to find Ray Farnley.'

'What makes you think I don't know that?'

'Because you spent the whole Uber ride to the airport talking about the hotel pool and facilities.'

'Yes. Because *I* want to use them. No one said *you* have to.'

Pointing at the discarded sandwich, Hannah asked, 'You not eating that?'

Lottie shrugged. 'No.'

'Bit wasteful, precious.' Hannah rolled her eyes, before asking, 'Am I mad to leave Dave in charge?'

'No. He's all right. He won't let you down.'

Hannah couldn't help thinking about the Dave she'd first met. The man who tried every trick in the book to get out of work. The man who claimed filling in a single form was a total ball ache. The man who ...' She mustn't think about all that now. He'd changed. So had she. End of discussion. 'I know. You're right. He practically saved my life last year, didn't he? And he's great at all the everyday bread-and-butter side of things.'

'Whilst you get to go jetting off to chase baddies.' Lottie grinned.

'Is Ray a baddy though?' Hannah turned to face her friend. 'I mean, seriously, we only have Liv's word for it, and who knows if she's right?'

'She said he killed her mum.'

'I know, but ...'

'When you told me about this case, you said she put his photograph down on the table and she was definite,' Lottie said.

'She was,' Hannah agreed.

'So, he's a baddy. But it's odd, I'll give you that,' Lottie said. 'The fact she reckons she's only just remembered it was him. How does that work?'

'She's promised to explain everything when we meet. It had better be good. I'll be pissed off if we're on a wild goose chase.'

'A wild goose chase with an indoor pool, a spa and a jacuzzi.'

'The pool again,' Hannah sighed. 'I can't believe I let you talk me into booking for two weeks. You really are a persuasive little minx.' She picked up the coronation chicken sandwich and took a bite. Waste not want not.

———

The hotel seemed to be everything Lottie had hoped for. It was clear from her face that this was the kind of luxury she'd been used to for the first part of her life. Hannah knew how hard things had been when Vincent tricked her out of everything, so she allowed her this little moment of indulgence.

'Look, Han, we have a connecting door as well.'

'Great!' Hannah drawled. 'We can spy on each other.'

Lottie gave her a shove.

'Stop it. You know full well you'll be popping in and out. Just like at home.'

'This is merely a place to lay my head. I plan to be out scouring the streets as much as possible.'

Throwing herself onto her bed, Lottie said, 'Please yourself, madam. I plan to enjoy every second of this hotel, and not even your grumpy, ex-copper face can stop me.'

Hannah laughed. 'Fair enough. But you are coming out with me tonight, aren't you?'

'Absolutely. Where are we heading?'

'Well, Jake's been posting on his Facebook page a lot over the last couple of weeks, and he seems to be hanging out in a few bars in Malaga. So I figured we'd head over there, go for a meal at one of his favourite restaurants, and then maybe bar hop for a while.'

'How far is it?' Lottie asked.

'About half an hour by car. A bit of a trek, but you would insist on staying here,' Hannah said. 'Luckily, Liv's brother will be paying for the Uber.'

'Sounds like a plan. Have I got time for a swim first?' Lottie asked, already searching through her suitcase.

'If you like. You swim. I'm going to check in with Dave.'

———

The Uber dropped them off by Malaga Park and they followed the crowd down to the waterfront restaurants and shops.

Hannah was fascinated by the Malaga pedestrian crossings: the way they counted you down to the time when it was safe to cross. But she was a little unnerved by the way they also counted you back up to when the cars could go. So many people would skip across with only two seconds left.

'I'm not sure whether I think these crossings are a brilliant idea or an invitation to an RTC.'

From a law enforcement point of view, she hoped it was the former.

'I think he's cute,' Lottie said.

'Who?'

She pointed. 'The little green man who's running for his life.'

Once they were past the shops and Lottie had bought a new pair of sunglasses, they found one of the restaurants Jake had posted selfies at the week before. There were numerous tables outside, and a smiling man ushered them over. Without asking their nationality, he began explaining in perfect English that the restaurant did a wide selection of foods. They offered Indian, Italian, burgers … It was hardly the intimate tapas menu Hannah and Lottie would've preferred, but they were there to look for Jake Farnley, not to enjoy the local cuisine.

As the man who had seated them left to heartily recruit more diners, Hannah whispered, 'We must look very British.'

'I know. I was so tempted to speak in French. To show him he ought not to judge a book by its cover.'

'He seemed nice enough,' Hannah said. 'Can't blame him for working out we're English, when we're so pale. We haven't seen much sun yet this year.'

'True.' Lottie glanced around the rest of the tables. 'Is your guy here?'

'No. But it's still early. He could turn up any minute. What do you fancy to eat?'

They both chose a steak with all the trimmings and ordered a bottle of red wine. Lottie insisted it was her treat, and Hannah, too tired to argue, gracefully accepted.

The meal was good. More than good. It was delicious, and Hannah found herself perking up a bit.

'You look better now, more awake,' Lottie noticed.

'Yeah. Don't let me have any more wine though. One glass is enough. I might have to wander the streets until the wee hours.'

'I'm happy to finish it.' Lottie poured more of the wine into her enormous fishbowl glass. 'What was up before? I mean, it wasn't jetlag, was it?'

'No!' Hannah smiled, sadly. 'I can handle a short flight. I just didn't ...' She paused. 'I didn't sleep well last night. In fact, I think I only got about two hours tops. And even *I* need more than that.'

'How come?'

Hannah explained about seeing Mandy in Costa the day before.

'You should've said something. There are cookies in the fridge, and I'd have made you hot chocolate.'

'I know. I know.' Hannah placed her hand over Lottie's and gave it a squeeze. 'But it's such old news. Why the hell am I still lying awake thinking about her? Arggh!' She gave herself a shake. 'I thought I'd moved on.'

'Seeing her must've been hard, Han. Don't beat yourself up.'

'Thanks.' Hannah gave another weak smile.

A waiter appeared with a menu. 'Dessert, girls?'

Hannah curtailed the desire to say, *We prefer the term women,* and accepted the menu. She noticed a small smile from Lottie, who knew exactly what she was thinking.

––––––

After a cocktail for Lottie, and a lemon sorbet and several glances at Mandy's last text for Hannah, they were thinking about making a move.

'I'm going to head back into town to try a few bars. Are you up for it?' Hannah asked.

'Yes. I love a bit of undercover work. What's our cover story?'

'I was thinking we could be two mates on holiday. What do you think?' Hannah asked, sarcastically.

'Bit boring. You sure you don't want to marry me?' Lottie, now slightly drunk, asked, a little on the loud side.

Hannah glanced around fearfully.

'Keep your voice down, you bloody pisshead. Someone might think you're proposing. The last thing we need is all the friggin' waiters making a fuss.'

'Why?'

'Because, dopey, if Jake was here, we'd then have to stick to that story for two weeks.'

Lottie nodded, enthusiastically, 'Okay. I'll keep it down,' she giggled.

22
LIV, MARCH 2023

LIV HAD READ through every transcript Stephen had emailed. They brought the happy memories flooding back: her dad nursing her after the wooden slide incident, her little brother being born, to name a couple. But they also reminded her of unhappy occasions, such as the horse-faced woman in the shop, and the many times with Sy when she'd passed out on filthy sheets, next to a man who was perpetually seconds away from choking on his own vomit. The most recent transcript unnerved her and made her think perhaps her uncle had been more than just a waste of space.

Her reason for re-reading the emails from Stephen was her total belief that today was the day they would finally talk about the most important memory of all.

———

Stephen was his usual smart self and Liv was pleased to see him. 'Hi, what are we going to talk about today?' She took off her shoes, chucked them to the side, and jumped up onto the bed.

'I thought I'd give you the choice. Would you like to talk some more about Ray?'

Liv instantly replied, 'No, definitely not. I've already thought about him nonstop since I received the transcript.'

'It was interesting, don't you think?'

'It made my blood boil.'

'Which part?'

'The fact he left my poor dad to die in jail, and my grandma to cope alone. And that he *never* came back to check on his own nephew and nieces.'

'Yes, it definitely seemed to bring certain things to the forefront of your mind that you had previously not considered.'

'A hundred percent. I'd never fully appreciated the atrocious timing of his departure. I swear he was the straw that broke the camel's back when it came to my grandma. She didn't live for many years after that. Who could blame her? He was a total arsehole.'

'So it would seem. You'd say he was worth discussing after all, then?' Stephen asked with a slightly smug smile.

Liv agreed. 'Yes, all right. You got me. It was worth talking about him.'

'Good. So, today, how about we talk about your sister?'

'Annie!' She considered for a moment. 'What is there to say?'

'You tell me. That's the point of these sessions.'

'I honestly don't think we could do a whole session on her. She isn't a big part of my life.'

'You're not in touch with each other at all?'

'We text occasionally. We call even less.' Liv shrugged.

'You think she prefers it that way?'

'Why else would she drop out of my life? She has her own stuff going on, and I can't think what you and I would find to say if we were trying to fill a whole session about her.'

'But you said it wasn't worth talking about Ray, and that proved fruitful.'

'I know. But ...' Liv clenched her jaw. Twiddling her rings around her fingers, she tried to stop herself from shouting out that she couldn't bear the suspense any longer and she just wanted them to go over the night her mum was killed.

Thankfully, Stephen seemed to pick up on her mood. 'Okay. I won't force you.'

Relief flooded her veins. She wasn't sure she could've coped with another session spent talking about anything other than her mum's death.

'So, that leaves us with the last choice.'

'Which is?' She held her breath.

He cleared his throat dramatically. 'Would you like to talk about the night your mum was killed?'

'Oh, yes!' There was an odd juxtaposition between the question and the elation in her reply. She heard it, and tried to rein it in. 'I mean, yes, I'm ready to do that.'

'Okay, if you feel able. I think now might be a good time.' Stephen stood and tucked the cashmere throw around her, before seating himself and instructing, 'Please count down from two hundred, Liv.'

———

Stephen tapped her on the shoulder, the street noises became clearer, and Liv found herself coming to. Her eyes sprang open, and she was greeted once again by Stephen's elegant office.

'What the ...?'

'Quite an eye-opener, hey!' Stephen said.

Liv was confused. 'Why did you wake me?'

'We'd finished. There was nothing more to say.'

'Finished!' she shouted. 'We hadn't even begun.'

His brow creased. 'I asked if you'd like to wake up, and you replied with a resounding yes. There was nothing more to discuss. What were you hoping to hear?'

'All of it. What did I see after Mum went to the door?'

'But …?' Stephen appeared confused.

'I thought we were going to talk about my mum's murder.'

'We did! We covered the whole thing.' He paused, his confusion clearly increasing. Then he asked, 'What can you remember about our discussion today, Liv?'

'The stuff you do at the beginning, the counting, the relaxing, and the breakfast bollocks.' She knew she was being rude, but she couldn't help herself. Her heart was racing. What was he trying to tell her? That she'd said it all and didn't remember? *Surely not!*

He didn't appear to take offence. 'That's all you can recollect? The routine to get you into a receptive trance and the first question.'

'Yes!'

Giving a sigh, Stephen said, 'I *have* seen this before, but only once.'

'Seen what?'

'When a memory is very traumatic, the client is able to recount it under hypnosis, but, upon waking, they find that the pathway to that memory is still blocked for their conscious mind. It would appear,' his tone became remorseful, 'that in actual fact you were *not* ready after all, and despite describing in detail to me what happened that night, you are still unable to recollect it for yourself once awake.'

'Well … put me back under. *Just fucking ask me again!*'

'I totally understand your frustration. But that is unlikely to help.'

Liv knew she should apologise for her language, but, shit, this was too frustrating. 'So, what *can* you do?' she asked.

'It's all recorded. I'll transcribe it as usual and let you have it tomorrow.'

'Tomorrow!'

'It's the best I can do.'

Baffled, she asked, 'If it's recorded, why can't I listen now?' She tried to rise from the bed, as if intent on finding the recording mechanism.

'Because,' Stephen placed a steadying hand on her, gently encouraging her back onto the bed, 'it's not ethical to do so.'

'What? Why not?'

'There are many other voices on the device. The client who was here before you, for example. If I were to press play and I accidently played you even a second of their consultation, I could be struck off.'

'I won't tell anyone. I promise.' Liv clutched desperately at his hand, which still rested gently on her torso. Her stomach was churning, little beads of sweat gathering on her forehead.

'It's not that simple, I'm afraid.'

'Okay, so … tell me then. Who did it?'

'You really can't remember what you said?'

'No!' God, this was an absolute nightmare. He had to tell her.

Stephen appeared to be considering his options. His eyes rolled towards the ceiling, and he tapped his chin rhythmically.

She waited, afraid to draw breath. The silence in the room cocooned her like an avalanche. She wanted to wrestle her way out and gasp for air.

After what felt like a small lifetime, but in reality was maybe ten or fifteen seconds, Stephen cleared his throat.

'I think the transcript would be the best way to enlighten you.'

Liv opened her mouth to speak, unsure what to say. Frightened that a horrified scream might escape.

He gave her no time to beseech him further, saying in a decisive tone, 'I'm sorry. But that's my final ruling. I'll send it tomorrow morning, as usual.' Stephen rose from his chair and made his way back towards the door, adding, 'Take a bottle of Voss, and pop your shoes on. I'll get your jacket.'

23

SUSAN, DECEMBER 1991

THE EUPHORIA CREATED by Toby's remission carried Susan for
over two years. Much changed during that time. They even had
a new Prime Minister, which was good; Martin wasn't keen on
Maggie and was often vocal about his dislike of her. Susan's
friend Jenny thought it was a shame they'd gone back to having
a man.

In the time since the good news about her son, Susan had
been a model wife. Even if Martin said something she didn't
agree with, or that concerned her, she never answered back. She
had been the wife he wanted, and the wife he expected. But
Christmas Day changed that!

———

It drove Susan to distraction that, for Martin, Christmas was
still about his mother. Even though it was their son's birthday as
well, and Susan wanted to make it an extra special occasion
for him.

However, for Martin, every part of the day always seemed to
be a terrible rush to get to Shirley's house. Despite being more

than capable of cooking a Sunday roast, not once had Shirley invited them to have their Christmas lunch with her and her precious Ray. Instead, she always chose to eat with Ray and then invite Martin and his family to join them in time for the Queen's bloody speech.

Today, like their first Christmas and all the others in between, Susan was expected to slave over a hot stove all morning, clear up the debris caused by five people eating an enormous meal, and then jump in the car to drive them all to Shirley's. It was not in the slightest bit relaxing for her. She had wanted to linger over the presents with the children. Toby was particularly enamoured with his teenage mutant ninja turtles, which, as always, they'd made a point of saying was an extra present to all the others. This was specifically his eighth birthday present. But typically, there wasn't enough time to dwell on the gifts, not for Susan anyway. For her, it was straight onto peeling potatoes, whereas Martin allowed himself the time to sit surrounded by children, used wrapping paper and a mountain of toys, whilst watching Noel Edmonds do his thing on the television. Like he always did!

Susan let it go and held it in for the sake of the family. But by the time they got to Shirley's, she was in a foul mood. They went through the usual charade at Shirley's house: Shirley praising Martin and saying what a wonderful help he was around the house. *Yes, Shirley, he always is for you!* No one noticed Susan's disposition. Not even the children. They were just delighted to receive more gifts from their grandma and uncle.

———

Later, as the children and Martin merrily recounted all the items on the *Generation Games'* conveyor belt, and Shirley snoozed in her chair, for all the world appearing to catch flies, her painted pink mouth slack and ugly, Susan took the opportunity to leave the stuffy lounge and step out into the back garden.

The freezing air hit her; it was a particularly cold Christmas. She wrapped her arms around herself, rubbing briskly. Despite the adverse temperature, she wanted to remain. It was so quiet and peaceful.

Until ...

'You'll catch your death out here without a coat.'

She heard Martin's voice, and felt him place her new C&A woollen coat gently around her shoulders from behind. It was the nicest coat she'd ever owned. He gave her a gentle squeeze. She was delighted at his concern.

Leaning into him with a sigh, she said, 'Thank you, darling.' She turned her face to him, hoping to forget the bad feelings of earlier and rekindle the love.

He smiled.

She spotted the slight beard on his chin. Martin was clean shaven, whereas Ray had a couple of weeks off work and had allowed his facial hair to go slightly rogue.

'Ray?'

'At your service.'

'Sorry. I ...' Her head snapped back, her gaze no longer on him.

'No worries. You can call me darling any time you like.'

'I only did it because—'

'Don't spoil it.' He reached around, placing a finger to her ice-cold lips. 'Don't say you only spoke softly to me and leant yourself into me so seductively because you thought I was your husband.'

'But ... its true.'

'So ... why are you still leaning?'

'Because ... erm ...' Susan couldn't think of an answer.

Ninety percent of the time she disliked Ray. It was irritating how he had Shirley wrapped around his little finger. Not that

Susan cared much. He could use Shirley as an unpaid house-keeper as much as he liked; it didn't affect her. But she also objected to the way he had a different woman on the go every time they saw him. With no apparent plans to settle down and dedicate himself to someone special, he was like the opposite of Martin. What Martin might've been if he hadn't married her. She wasn't a prude, but she found his inability to commit both immature and selfish. For some reason it just really irked her.

Then there was the other ten percent. Those moments when he looked at her and there was a flash behind his eyes. A sexi-ness that Martin simply couldn't muster. There was a naughti-ness to him. He was like riding the highest rollercoaster in the park. He was frightening and dangerous, but the anticipation as you queued was like nothing else. After years of marriage, all the initial excitement with Martin had settled to a more realistic level. If Ray was a rollercoaster, then Martin was a carousel. There was no comparison.

Most times, the ninety percent won, and Susan looked at Ray with the disdain he deserved. But occasionally, the ten percent reared its head, and she couldn't hide her attraction. Tonight, in Shirley's frosty garden, he caught her off guard.

Wordlessly, she turned around. Taking his face between her frozen fingers, she pulled him towards her and found his lips. Their mouths opened and greeted each other, like old friends. He slipped his hands inside her coat, and she felt them climb up her back, pulling her closer. There was no gap between them. No partition of cold air. Just his body touching hers. They kissed with a fuel, a passion, a need. Their eyes met, and the question was asked and answered in an instant. Stumbling around the corner, they made their way to the little shed that Ray ostentatiously referred to as his workshop. Silently, and without adding any light to the situation, they slipped into the shed and closed the door behind them. Susan wouldn't say they *made love* in there. It was too cold, and too crowded with tools to enjoy each other with any finesse. But they did have sex. A quick, animalistic coupling that was accompanied by frantic groans and desperate pleas to hurry. The finale was exquisite. An avalanche of orgasms for Susan, each shudder stronger than the last. He also came. With a loud shout, which she feared would penetrate the walls of the house and wake the sleeping Shirley.

————

Within minutes they had rearranged their clothing and were ready to head back inside the house. Susan's thoughts instantly turned to her children; had they noticed she was missing? Had Martin? A silent fear gripped her. How would they explain their absence? What had she done?

'Quick, we need to get back inside. I don't want my family to—'

Again, he pressed his finger to her lips, which were warmer now. 'It'll be fine. They won't even know we've been gone.'

God, she hoped he was right. They made their way back towards the kitchen door.

Gesturing to the shed, she tried to think of something to say. Something that would explain why she'd done what she had.

'Ray, we ... I ... don't know ...'

'It's okay,' he said, placing his hand on her back to guide her into the kitchen. 'Just ... let's not leave it so long next time.'

24

HANNAH, APRIL 2023

THEY HAD TRIED three different bars before they got a hit. Hannah was delighted. Realistically, she hadn't expected to find any of the Farnley family on the first night. But there he was, Jake Farnley. As she had expected when she'd searched his Facebook photos, he was surrounded by a bevy of beautiful people. They were drinking in a large Irish pub in one of the many town squares.

Hannah and Lottie positioned themselves at a table across the way. The plan was to watch and wait, possibly eavesdrop into a couple of Jake's conversations, and generally adopt the observational stance. But Hannah hadn't bargained on Lottie's good looks, or her drink-induced, louder than usual voice. Within five minutes of sitting at the adjacent table, she had most definitely caught the eye of an equally sloshed Jake. He stood and, with a swagger, made his way over with a broad grin.

'You girls are new around here. Arrived today, did you?'

Again, the urge to correct his vocabulary choice was very strong. But Hannah let it go. Instead, she gave a welcoming smile and allowed Lottie to take it away.

And take it away she did.

With several hair flicks and a bat of her recently acquired holiday eyelashes, she got them an invite to join Jake and his crowd. Hannah watched as before her eyes, Lottie became a giggling, excitable Malibu Barbie. Unsure whether this was an undercover act or if this was how she always was when full of alcohol and faced with an attractive man, Hannah concluded it didn't matter. Her only thought was, if this was how Lottie behaved around men, she really must be sure to make herself scarce when Chen returned from travelling.

Lottie told Jake they were on holiday. Hannah heard her explain she had a renovation business back home, implying Hannah was one of her many employees. Jake seemed to lap it all up, not only impressed with her gorgeous features, but also with her nicely spoken Hampshire accent.

The rest of the evening was spent drinking wine and the occasional shot, all paid for by Jake. Hannah did her best to remain sober, whilst still appearing to join in with the fun. Somehow, she found herself sitting at the end of the table with some of Jake's female friends, who introduced themselves as Thalia, Zoe and Claudia. As with everyone within a fifty-foot radius, these three were very well groomed. Thalia, in particular, was stunning. Hannah couldn't help comparing her to Mandy. Thalia was from Greece. She explained she was on a year's travel experience. Hannah vaguely wondered if England was on her bucket list. Thalia's black hair shone, and her skin glowed a stunning cappuccino brown. How did these women manage to look so amazing? Hannah tugged at her spiky bleached hair and tried to imagine for one minute how long it took Thalia to get ready for a night out. Not only was she stunning on the outside, but Hannah's first impression of Thalia was that she was rather lovely on the inside, too. Her voice was soft and alluring. She reminded Hannah of the flower fairy transfers her mum had put on her bedroom walls when she was little. They had long ago been painted over with crisp white paint, but still remained somewhere in the back of her mind. Thalia wore a flowing skirt, which was embellished with jewels and tie dyed into a rainbow pattern. There was a moment in which Hannah pondered if the rainbow was a good sign for her; could this gorgeous creature possibly be gay? But no. Within minutes, Thalia was talking about how sexy Jake was when he smiled and leaning down the table trying to involve herself in his conversation. Jake seemed to give no regard to the attention of Thalia, which was an awful waste. Hannah concluded either he simply had so many choices he was planning to get to her on some other occasion, or worse, he had already slept with and discarded Thalia in the past.

Zoe was pale with bobbed blonde hair. Also good looking, but without the *je ne sais quoi* and exotic air of Thalia, her face often wore a blank, lost expression. She remained silent, and mostly appeared to focus on her drink.

Being new to Jake, Lottie managed to not only get a seat in the much-coveted middle of the table, but she also monopolised his time. He was clearly charmed by her, and Hannah spotted them swapping Instagram details within half an hour. *Perfect, Lottie!*

Hannah noticed that Claudia tutted whenever Lottie and Jake shared a joke or laughed a little too loudly. Claudia wasn't an unattractive woman, far from it, but her features were on the coarse side. She was possibly a little older than the others; Hannah estimated her to be in her forties. But, thanks to Botox and a fancy-arsed catsuit, she managed to blend in. She'd also clearly had some fillers. These had left her with what some might refer to as blow job lips. Sneaking the occasional sideways peak at her, Hannah noted she often switched from resting bitch face to a face that said *I'm simply having the best night of my life*, whenever she thought Jake was looking her way.

Hannah might be completely biased, but she could see Lottie was way more beautiful than the other women vying for Jake's attention. Especially Claudia, whose boobs gave the impression they might deflate like cheap armbands if they collided with a corner. The others must all be cursing Lottie's arrival in the bar.

Sure enough, within five minutes, Claudia asked Hannah, 'Is she with you?'

Hannah nodded. 'Yeah. We … work together.'

Claudia's eyes darted up and down, taking in every aspect of Hannah's appearance in a second.

'Hmm … must be tough for you?'

'What?'

'Being the plain friend.'

Hannah wanted to laugh; it took more than a bitchy comment to take her down. Instead, she said, 'Oh, I'm used to it. Besides, we're attracted to very different people.'

'Meaning?'

I don't fall for good looking players, who spout shit and mindlessly kiss-arse to beautiful women, Hannah thought. But she simply said, 'I'm not attracted to people like him.' She pointed at Jake.

'Jake's all right, if you take the time to get to know him. Like *I* have,' Claudia said.

'If you say so.'

At that point, Lottie gave a ridiculously loud giggle as she tossed back another tequila rose shot, and Claudia remarked in the cattiest tone Hannah had heard for some time, 'Dear Jake. He does love a new plaything.'

Hannah moved seats to position herself between Thalia and Zoe. People like Claudia simply sucked the fun out of everything, and she could do without spending the rest of the evening with her by her side. Once she moved, she discovered Zoe was deaf, and what had previously appeared to be aloofness was actually concentration. Zoe was trying to follow several conversations at once, using only her lip-reading skills. Hannah was immensely impressed. She'd used lip-reading on a couple of occasions to work out what was being said during a stakeout, most memorably when she had the appalling Charlie Bradbury under surveillance for Mr Wilson. She could honestly say it was incredibly hard to keep up. With her embarrassingly rudimental knowledge of sign language, which she'd taught herself via YouTube before she joined the police, Hannah managed to have a pleasant, but fairly basic chat with Zoe. She often had to resort to spelling out entire words, and, bless her, Zoe was very patient. Hannah established that Zoe was British, but her family lived in Spain for much of the year. She enjoyed being with the glamorous people for a while, but was more at home having a girls' night in with her sisters, watching re-runs of *Friends* on Spanish TV. Hannah liked her for that. She was a real person in a sea of phonies. When you have a lack of one sense, you often develop a sixth. Zoe most definitely had a sixth sense regarding Jake. She wasn't a hanger on, and she wasn't spellbound; she was there for a few drinks and a night out, but she'd be back in her PJs doing impressions of Monica and Rachel soon enough.

———

The evening finished with a shared Uber with Jake and a couple of others who were heading towards Marbella. There was an awkward moment when it appeared Lottie might be considering going on to Jake's home, instead of coming back to the hotel. Hannah thought her friend was most definitely going above and beyond for the sake of the assignment. Thankfully, at the last minute, Lottie seemed to come to her senses, and they jumped out of the Uber at their hotel, leaving Jake to pay the full fare on his account. He was clearly okay with this, explaining he often got Ubers to and from Malaga, and it was his dad's account anyway.

With a drunken cry of, 'That's nice of him. Can't wait to meet the rest of your family soon!' Lottie fell out of the car.

Hannah followed on, making sure they both got to their rooms safely.

Not even stopping to carry out her usual cleansing routine, Lottie crashed out on her bed.

'Blimey, for a sleeping partner, you sure put in the work tonight.' Hannah smiled, pulling a sheet over her already snoring friend.

25

LIV, MARCH 2023

LIV HAD READ through the transcript of her latest session with Stephen several times, and still struggled to take it all in. How the hell had she repressed that? Why hadn't it occurred to her sooner that Ray leaving when he did was so suspicious? She'd accepted the fact he'd gone travelling, and, apart from seeing her grandma tear up whenever her uncle was mentioned, she had not given him another thought. Now it made sense. He'd left because he was guilty, and he needed to put as much distance between himself and his poor brother as he possibly could. Her dad had always been the fall guy; she knew it, she'd felt it for years. But now she had the whole story.

Well, he wasn't going to get away with it. Not for a second longer. She'd decided to go to the police. She'd tell them exactly what she saw that night and they'd drag Ray back from wherever the bastard was hiding out. Her dad's name would finally be cleared.

She had hoped that Toby would be as excited as she was to finally get to the truth. But he had been strangely quiet on the subject. Whatever. She would worry about that later. For now, she was off to the police station. Not a favourite hangout of hers. She'd been there a few times to collect Sy, and she'd been interviewed twice there herself. This time, however, things would be different. She had some news for them that was going to change everything.

———

The police station in Kingshurst was a joyless place. From the outside it could well be mistaken for a local council building or something equally dull. Liv walked past the front door, turned, walked back the other way and, finally, turned again and approached the door. It wasn't a building with happy memories, and she wasn't the least bit keen to actually enter it. But she knew that the other option was to go home and forget what Uncle Ray had done. That would leave her dad eternally in the role of the killer, and she couldn't have that. She'd waited too long for the memories to resurface; now they had, she owed it to her dad to share them with the police. Finally halting in front of the heavy-duty door, she pressed the button to her right. Clearly, she was being viewed by someone on the inside, because a moment later the door gave a loud buzz and juddered open. Liv pushed it and stepped into the police station.

She was immediately hit by the smell of disinfectant, and vaguely thought perhaps a drunk had thrown up in the waiting area. But then, maybe it simply always smelt this way. Approaching the officer behind the desk, she wondered how anyone could work here.

'How can I help you?' the fresh faced woman asked from behind a thick glass screen.

'I …' Liv coughed. 'I need to speak to someone. I have something important to tell them.'

———

So, Miss Farnley, I'm told you have some information for me?'

'Yes.' Liv chewed the skin on her knuckles.

'Does this relate to drugs?'

'No!'

The police officer, young enough to be her son, nodded slowly. 'O … kay.'

'You shouldn't assume,' Liv said. 'You know what it does to you and me?'

'I do, yes, Miss Farnley.'

She could tell he was bored. He had already made up his mind that she was wasting his time. She wanted to tell him to go screw himself. Every nerve in her body was tingling, telling her to get up and walk out. This was not the place for her. But what if she did? How would her dad get the justice he deserved? If she walked out now, Ray would continue to get away with the terrible thing he'd done, and her dad would remain a murderer to everyone who had known him. She took a deep breath and tried to change her tone to one that the officer might find more cordial.

'What I have to tell you is important. It's to do with an old case.'

'How old?'

'Thirty-one years.'

'We have officers who deal exclusively with cold cases, Miss Farnley.'

'Good. Can I speak to one, please?'

'What case are you referring to?'

'My mum was murdered in 1992.'

'I'm sorry to hear that.'

'Thank you.'

'So … what can you tell us that might solve the case?'

'I've remembered who killed her,' Liv said, with confidence.

'Do you mind me asking why now? After all these years.'

'It's kind of difficult to explain.'

'Try me.' The officer gave a barely audible sigh.

'At the time, my dad was accused of the murder, but it wasn't him.'

The officer shuffled in his chair slightly.

'Can I confirm, Miss Farnley, was he accused or charged?'

Liv's stomach dropped, and she sensed a change in the young officer's manner.

'He was charged.'

'And convicted?'

'Yes, but—'

He interrupted her. 'A cold case is an unsolved case. My apologies, I mistook what you were saying.'

'Does it matter?'

'Yes. Very much so.'

'Why?'

'Because ...' He shuffled again. 'If your father was convicted of the murder of your mother thirty-one years ago, and he served time, you cannot simply say today that it was someone else who did the crime.'

'Why not?'

'In the eyes of the law, the case is complete. A sentence would have been given and the case closed.'

'But he was going to appeal. I know he didn't do it.'

'Why didn't he go ahead with the appeal?'

'Because some fucker killed him in prison. Look it up. Crow's Wall Prison – Martin Farnley.'

The officer made a note on his pad. 'I don't personally know of any cases where a criminal was pardoned posthumously, but it is a possibility.' He pushed his chair back from the table. 'Can you give me a moment, please? I need to speak to a senior officer.'

'Yes. Right. You do that.' Adrenalin was pumping around Liv's body. This was it.

26

SUSAN, FEBRUARY 1992

MAKING her way down to the kitchen to begin the busy process of preparing breakfast for five, Susan spotted a red envelope on the hall mat. She picked it up, turned it over, and read the front. *To My Valentine.* There was no stamp. It had obviously just been dropped there. She was excited. She'd never had a card from Martin on Valentine's Day before. In fact, she'd never had one from anyone. Unless you counted the ones her children made for her at school, or the equally handcrafted versions the boys in her class gave her when they were all about ten years old. This one was the real deal. Whilst the writing didn't resemble Martin's at all, she simply convinced herself that he'd gone to some lengths to disguise it.

Ripping the envelope cleanly across the top, she placed her eager hand inside and pulled out the card. It was fairly generic; a single red rose on the cover, with some mushy words printed on the inside. Handwritten at the bottom was the word *from* and a large question mark. This was followed by some kisses. Susan had no idea what had inspired Martin to send it, or why he'd decided to be so cheesy with his choice of card. But she was touched, and, having never received a Valentine before, flattered.

———

When Martin returned from work in the evening, he found the children had finished their dinner and were all in their rooms. Susan had even persuaded Annie to stay out of sight. *Top of the Pops* could be heard blasting from her bedroom.

In the kitchen, Susan served a delicious meal: duck à l'orange with croquet potatoes and long stem broccoli. Martin seemed delighted with the meal and pleased at the alone time. Afterwards, she suggested they ought to head to bed early. Again, she saw delight on his face, but also a little confusion.

'What have I done to deserve all this, Susan?'

She smiled, hoping it came across as sexy, as opposed to the annoying lopsided grin she always seemed to do in photos.

'Stop acting like you don't know,' she said.

'I …' He rubbed his chin, quizzically. 'I know it's not my birthday.'

She leant across the small table and gave him a gentle push. 'It's Valentine's Day, you dopey sod.'

'Is it?'

'You know it is.' She got up from the table and nipped over to the work surface to grab the card that she'd slid next to the toaster earlier. 'You sent me this.'

Martin snatched the card from her.

The smile, sexy or not, froze on her face as his eyes scanned it.

'I did not!'

'You … didn't send it?'

'No! But I'd like to know who did.'

He stood up, all four of his chair legs scraping across the lino floor with a horrible screech that made her wince. With one quick motion he tore the card in two and thrust both halves into the depths of the kitchen bin.

'But ... if it wasn't you, then I don't know who it was.' She shook her head, desperately trying to suggest her innocence.

'You're sure about that, are you?'

'Umm ...' She hesitated for a fraction too long. A tiny voice in the back of her head asked, *could Ray really be that senseless?*

The slap, when it came, confused the hell out of her. It was so sudden and so unexpected that she honestly thought she'd been hit by some unknown flying object. She looked up, expecting to see that the ceiling had fallen in, and rubble had flown at her. But no, the ceiling was intact. The flying object that had hit her had been the flat of her husband's hand.

Her own hands rushed to her cheek. In an effort to calm the throbbing pain, she placed them both gently onto her flesh and held them there for comfort. They felt cool. Never before had Martin been violent. Short tempered? Yes. Frustratingly stubborn? Again, yes. But this! Her brain frantically tried to make sense of his actions. All the time, in the back of her mind, she cursed Ray for his stupidity.

'Why are you being sent a Valentine's card by another man?' Martin shouted.

Dreading that the children would hear, she tried to calm the situation. 'I don't know. I just thought it was you.' Susan took a step towards him, her hand outstretched. 'It's probably a joke or something.'

'Now I get why you made me flammin' French stuff. You're feeling guilty, aren't you?'

'No.' Her heart was pounding, and she feared what was to come. But she had to convince him, so she stepped even closer.

Less than six inches from him, she stopped. Trying her hardest to smile, and with a quiver in her voice, she lied, 'There's only ever been you. Since the day we met.'

He looked down at her, and for a second, she questioned if he was going to hit her again. She knew she mustn't flinch.

'You promise?' he asked, the anger beginning to leave his voice.

'Yes,' she lied again. Placing her hand on his arm, she forced herself to say, 'Now, what about that early night?'

———

For longer than she cared to admit, Susan's love for Martin had been like a string vest of good memories and feelings held loosely together. Every time he lost his temper or was infuriatingly stubborn, he created yet another hole in the garment.

Tonight was the only time in her life that Susan made love when she absolutely one hundred percent did not want to. Prior to this, she thought women who had sex with their husbands when they weren't in the mood were idiots. She always wondered why they didn't just say no. Why use sex as some kind of tool? But tonight, she used it. She used it to diffuse a potentially explosive situation. She used it to keep her children from hearing or seeing something that might upset them.

Susan made sure to write exactly how she felt about Martin in her diary that night.

27

HANNAH, APRIL 2023

SHORTLY AFTER NINE the next morning, Lottie received a message from Jake inviting them over to his dad's villa for brunch. It was perfect. Lottie accepted immediately and got the address from Jake. Hannah punched the air, dying to get a look at Ray.

———

Jake welcomed them at the front door and said, 'I know you mentioned something last night about meeting the fam, Lottie. But Dad had to go out.'

Hannah tried to hide her disappointment.

'If you're really desperate ... my sister, Emily's here somewhere,' he laughed.

Hannah wasn't sure it was a joke.

'Make yourselves at home and use the pool and stuff,' Jake added. Interestingly, there was no mention of his mother.

Lottie thanked Jake, and they followed him into the villa.

On the way over they'd been speculating as to why Jake still lived with his parents. They figured he might have asked his dad for the money for a little place of his own. But now, seeing the villa, it all became clear. This place was enormous. There were so many rooms it would've been quite possible for four people to live in it with ease and never lay eyes on each other. Hannah let out a whistle when they moved from a large reception room, through some sliding patio doors out onto a terrace. There before them was an enormous, crystal clear, infinity pool. She didn't need to look at Lottie to know what expression she would be wearing.

Jake saw their faces.

'Pretty decent, isn't it?'

'Stop! It's gorgeous,' Lottie enthused.

'Did you bring your bikini, like I said?' Jake asked, his eyes fixed on Lottie.

She pulled down the shoulder of her sundress to expose the red spaghetti strap of one of the many bikinis she'd bought for their trip to Portugal a couple of years ago.

'Nice.' Jake seemed suitably pleased. Clearly not interested in seeing Hannah's bikini straps, he turned towards a table in the shade, which was groaning with all kinds of breakfast goodies, and said, 'Help yourself to food if you like.'

Hannah and Lottie occasionally liked to have what they referred to as an Agatha Christie breakfast. It was basically an array of all the things one might find in a full English breakfast laid out on a table, buffet style. Here, whoever had prepared this smorgasbord of foods had gone for the continental version. Hannah spied croissants, cheeses, hams, smoked salmon, pastries, pancakes; you name it, it was there. In the middle of the table was an impressive display of tropical fruits. Did they eat like this every day?

The question must've been an obvious one, because Jake said, 'It's Emily's birthday, so we're having a kind of open house thing. Anyone can pop in. Like I said, she's around somewhere.'

He opened the patio doors, stuck his head inside, and called out, 'Oy, Emily, don't be so rude. We've got guests.'

'I'm sorry. We had no idea,' Hannah said. 'Are we gate-crashing something?'

'Nah! Don't worry. It's just gonna be family, friends, and some of her snowflake mates. All sitting around being fucking aware of the world.' Jake rolled his eyes, adding, 'Not a bikini between 'em.' His gaze returned to Lottie for a second. 'She had one friend last summer ... a body made for sin.' He grinned. 'Sadly, a head made for Sainsbury's checkout. But she seems to have given up coming round. Emily's wokeness probably pissed her off.'

Hannah was sorry to see that this comment didn't turn Lottie's stomach in the way it turned hers. She got the impression Jake was old school, a man's man. To him, women were *birds* who brightened his day just by looking good. Marvellous. She was going to have to keep a very close eye on her friend. The last thing she needed was for her to get obsessed with this guy. Granted, he was a looker. He had striking hazel eyes and well-cut, thick, brown hair, and, judging by his physique, there was one hell of a gym somewhere in this vast villa. He was the very definition of tall, dark and handsome. But it was clear from his manner last night and his derogatory comment about Emily and her friends today that he was of the opinion that men were the superior gender. This made Hannah even more pissed off that Ray had gone out. She would love to know if the ideals and morals Jake displayed had been handed down by his father.

———

After they'd eaten a delicious brunch, they moved out of the shade and lay, enjoying the Spanish sun, on the loungers by the pool. They watched as more people began arriving for Emily's birthday celebration. Hannah recognised Thalia and the notorious Claudia, plus a few others from the night before.

By lunchtime, when the sun was at its strongest and Hannah had insisted Lottie get under the parasol, there was quite a crowd in and around the pool. Everyone was gorgeous. Everyone was glamorous. The women wore bikinis that, although miniscule, were obviously expensive. The men wore small shorts and continually flexed their muscles.

Leaning towards Lottie, Hannah whispered, 'I feel like I'm in that stupid *Love Island* thing you watch.'

'Would all islanders please gather by the firepit,' Lottie whispered back, pointing over to the seating area, where there was indeed a large firepit.

The only people Hannah could see who didn't conform to the uniform of *wear as little as possible* were a group of older men who, sensibly, stood up on the terrace in the shade. They all wore smart-casual clothing, blazers, white trousers, loafer shoes. There were several Rolexes on show, and it was evident these men had money.

And then there was Jake's little sister, Emily, and her crowd. Hannah studied them for a while. She could see the family resemblance between Liv and Emily, although Emily was younger, and life had not been so cruel to her. There was definitely something similar about them. Jake was right; neither Emily nor any of her friends wore a bikini. Instead, they swam in an assortment of swimming costumes, t-shirts, and in some cases even shorts. They were not here to show off their bodies. They were here for their friend, to celebrate her turning twenty-four, and nothing else. Hannah was proud of them all. Sadly, she was wearing one of Lottie's little bikinis. This had been agreed that morning when Lottie had insisted it was simply an under-cover outfit. 'You want to fit in, don't you?'

Hannah constantly had to stop herself fidgeting; she had never been a fan of the G-string. But Lottie was right. She was simply playing a part. If Ray did return to the villa, she wanted to observe him unnoticed, and this was the best way to blend in. Her usual air force blue, all-in-one swimsuit lay rejected on her bed at the hotel. It would not do under these circumstances.

———

It wasn't until almost four o'clock that Hannah finally got to lay eyes on Ray Farnley. She was dozing on a lounger, facing the terrace, and occasionally glancing over to admire the ethereal Thalia. Lottie was in the pool with Jake. Hannah could hear her squeals as he threw her into the water. Scooping her up again and again, he took the opportunity to show off his muscles and his broad, hairless chest.

Then, a little flurry of activity on the terrace told her someone new had arrived. And there he was. As she had expected, Ray was considerably older than the picture Liv had shown her. But it was definitely him. Hannah had expected an out of shape, elderly man, but Ray had taken care of himself. By her maths, she worked him out to be in his mid-seventies, and yet he had a look of a man at least ten years younger. If she'd thought he lived in Spain to finish out his musty years in peace and avoid the cold English winters, she was wrong. He was clearly someone to be reckoned with. Again, she decided there must be a gym in this place. Instantly joining the group of men on the terrace, he began a loud discussion about the money markets.

She watched him as he repeatedly swirled a tumbler of whisky; he appeared almost entranced by the golden liquid. Occasionally sipping from his glass, he spoke with enthusiasm, and heartily clapped the other men on the back when they made what he obviously thought were valid points. These men were clearly friends as well as business associates. Hannah heard a comment about Ray handing another man his arse during a recent game of squash, and another about how someone had drunk him under the table during a card game. This open house thing really did include all sorts. She noticed there was a woman trailing along by Ray's side, who seemed to follow him from group to group, but said nothing. She was attractive, but very timid, failing to make eye contact with a single one of Ray's old boys' club. Where had she appeared from? She had a look of Emily and, despite being well kept, it was clear she was somewhere around her late fifties. Hannah concluded she must be Jake and Emily's mum.

Hannah waited a while before nonchalantly climbing off her lounger. Leaving Lottie, who she noted was now taking numerous selfies with Jake, she put her shorts and t-shirt back on top of the torturous bikini and made her way slowly up to the terrace. She hung around, close to the *smart casuals*, as she had nicknamed them, and waited for a way into the discussion.

But none came. They weren't interested in asking her opinion on the current market volatility or what she thought of the going rate for the Euro or the US dollar. Neither was she invited to contribute to their poker discussions. To them, she was invisible. Calling them all tossers in her head, Hannah moved on and headed inside the villa.

28

LIV, MARCH 2023

Liv waited, alone in the small room. There was nothing to focus on but the Formica table and the now vacant, black plastic seat opposite her. The room was airless, and soulless. Liv wondered how many people had sat in this room awaiting their fate. Poor bastards. The isolation did nothing to calm her nerves. That bloody child of a copper had to believe her. He had to sort this. She was so sure it was Ray who had killed her mum. She could see it all now. After a few minutes, a middle-aged woman came in and asked if she would like a hot drink. She was nondescript and dull, like all coppers. Liv figured she was probably in admin or something equally boring. She then returned five minutes later with a cup of decidedly tepid black coffee. Liv waited some more, sipping what the woman had laughingly referred to as her *beverage*, willing the young copper to return with good news. Finally, fifteen long agonising minutes later, an older officer appeared. Liv instantly recognised him as the man who had questioned her when she'd been caught shoplifting several years earlier. It was before Toby's money had begun rescuing her. A time when both she and Sy were living in a world of desperation, simply hanging on for the next high. She had been pretty out of it, but if her rather splintered memory served her correctly, she had received a caution from this very man.

Attempting to hide the recognition on her face, whilst simultaneously spotting the same on his, as he took the seat opposite her, Liv asked, 'So ... what happens now?'

The older officer gave her a pitying look.

'Nothing will happen from here, Miss Farnley.'

His expression angered her. 'What?'

'I am familiar with your dad's case, and I've just done some more research. The conviction was a strong one.'

'No, it wasn't. My dad was innocent.'

'I know it's difficult, particularly as you say you've remembered something about the night in question, and you think it was in fact someone else who murdered your mum.'

'It *was* someone else.'

'Memories can play tricks on us, Miss.'

'I've always thought I saw something. I've known for years that it wasn't my dad. I just didn't know exactly who it was.'

'The evidence against him was good. He was seen by several neighbours fleeing the scene. He was picked up in the area within the hour.'

'I know all that!' Liv spluttered. 'But it wasn't him.'

'You're telling me those neighbours, who knew him well, and observed him in a well-lit street, all got it wrong?'

'Yes.'

'How?'

'It was his brother. They were identical.'

The officer shook his head. 'The defence would have looked into this as a hypothesis if that was the case. Nothing remotely similar was suggested at the time. I understand why you don't want it to be your dad. I know it must've been horrendous for you to lose both parents at such a young age. It's one of the reasons I was so lenient on you previously.'

Liv blushed at the mention of her past misdemeanours.

'Don't fucking pity me!' she insisted, curtly.

'I'm not. I'm simply trying to say that I understand why you're here today, but we can't help you.'

'Seriously?'

'Yes. The evidence against Martin Farnley was compelling. The trial was legally sound, and the verdict was guilty. He may have been planning to appeal, and we will never know how that would've gone. But, as it stands today, he was guilty.'

'But ... I'm telling you ... it was my uncle! I remember it all now.'

'May I ask how these new memories have come to you so late in the day, Miss?'

Liv hesitated. 'I was ... I was hypnotised and I—'

The officer snapped his notebook shut. Giving her no time to complete her sentence, he said, 'You must know we can't investigate something based on hypnosis. If we did, we'd have everyone who ever bought a ticket to see Derren Brown queuing around the block.'

'This was different.'

The officer was already standing. His expression had changed to one of irritation.

'I suggest, Miss Farnley, that you try to put all this behind you. I'm sure your parents wouldn't want you to still fret about it.'

'Fret?'

'Yes.'

'Fucking fret!'

'I'm simply saying – you've kept out of trouble and that's great. Now is the time to finally move on with your life and put the past where it belongs.'

'So, you're seriously not going to even question my uncle?'

'There really is no valid reason to do so.' The officer gestured towards the door.

All the way home in the Uber, Liv clenched and unclenched her fists. She'd hoped they would be interested. At the very least, she'd expected them to say they'd look into it. But no. *There's no valid reason*, he'd said. All that effort. The sessions with Stephen. He'd worked so hard. What was the point? She should never have told that idiot how she'd come to remember it all. Liv clenched her right fist again and repeatedly banged herself on the forehead with it, muttering, 'Next time you tell someone, don't mention the fucking hypnosis!'

29
SUSAN, MARCH 1992

RETRIEVING the key from its hiding place, Susan dug out the metal box from the very bottom of the tea chest. Martin was out with clients for drinks, so she knew she'd have plenty of time to write in her diary. All the time she'd lived with Jenny, she had left her diaries lying around; it really wouldn't have mattered if Jenny had read them. Back then, the entries were light-hearted. Mostly stuff she would readily have talked to Jenny about anyway. Then, when she'd married, she'd decided to keep writing, but had taken to putting the diaries in her bedside table. She figured that Martin wouldn't be interested, and besides, sometimes she was a bit grumpy when she wrote her diary, and the things she said about *him* weren't always favourable.

However, about eighteen months after they'd married, Susan did something shocking. Not only that, but she wrote about it in her diary. Maybe it had been cathartic, maybe she'd just written those few stark words so that she actually believed them herself. Whatever the reason, the next day, she began to question some of her earlier entries and realised that there was simply too much incriminating evidence in what had started out as an innocent diary. Susan was faced with two choices – she could throw them all away and stop keeping a diary altogether, or she could make them more secure. Not wanting to lose all the memories, she bought a large lockable metal box. This box now lived underneath some baby blankets in a tea chest in the lounge. The key was kept somewhere safe, in a place that no one would think to look.

Now, Susan wrote about the day's events. Not a lot to say. A nice lunch with Jenny, where they'd both tried beef stroganoff for the first time, and a slight argument with Martin before he'd gone out, which seemed to start with her not making a full-blown meal for dinner, because she was still full from lunch. She had offered to do him some cheese on toast, but he had considered that an insult.

Feeling disgruntled, Susan idly flicked back and read again her diary entry from last Christmas. She felt her face flush and a flood of pleasure rush to her crotch. Suddenly, from nowhere she remembered how those orgasms had hit her that night. How stupid to remember it all. They'd been in the bloody shed, for God's sake. Susan had barely seen Ray since that night, but she couldn't put on her C&A coat without remembering his hands gently placing it over her shoulders.

This was ridiculous. Susan stood and made her way over to the lockable box, ready to put the diary away. She needed to stop thinking about Ray, and she definitely needed to stop thinking about last Christmas.

But, as much as she knew what she *needed* to do, Susan found herself doing the opposite. Rummaging through the box, she found earlier incarnations of her diary. To be precise she found the diary that covered October 1973. Before she knew it, Susan was re-reading the event that had been the very reason she had needed the lockable box in the first place. Granted, it was a short entry, but there was more than enough to jog her memory.

Martin was working away for a few days. They'd been married for just over a year, and the honeymoon polish was beginning to wear off. They'd had a stupid row before he left. It had stemmed from a comment Susan had made about him not helping with the washing up. But, in all honesty, anything could've started it. At that time there was a lot in the news about feminism and equal rights. Jenny was really into it, and she'd made Susan aware of how old-fashioned Martin could sometimes be in his beliefs about women.

Martin hadn't phoned Susan since he'd left, and she was feeling rejected. She was particularly annoyed that he was off having a great time, staying in a hotel and pretending to slog his guts out at some sales thing, when she was at home, lonely and bored. Susan couldn't imagine ever being invited to a sales conference in a swanky hotel.

The knock on the door stirred her from a short, after dinner doze in the armchair. Rising from the chair, Susan checked her hair briefly in the hall mirror, and called out, 'Who is it?'

A familiar voice answered, 'Me.'

Her first thought was that Martin had cut the sales trip short and come home to make up with her. He was a terror for leaving his house key at home, and never took her advice to add it to his car key fob. He often knocked on the door, expecting her to open it instantly, so it could easily have been him. However, despite it only being one word, there was mischief in the way he said *me*, and it seemed incredible that Martin would be that way. He was a bit of a sulker, and always expected Susan to say sorry first. The chances of him coming all the way back to apologise to her were slim to non-existent.

So, it was with trepidation and almost an air of foresight that she slowly opened the door. Keeping her body in the gap, not welcoming, simply enquiring, she asked, 'Who's *me?*'

'*Me.*' He grinned.

Susan didn't recognise his jacket, and his hair was a tad shorter than Martin's had been when he'd left two days before. Plus, there was that mischief in his tone. This was not Martin.

'*Ray*, what do you want?'

'Charming!' He made as if to come in.

'Martin isn't here.' She kept her body in the doorway, surely an indication that she wasn't up for visitors.

'I know. He called me. He's on some boring sales thing.'

Susan scoffed. 'I'll bet it's not boring at all. I'll bet he's having a great time.'

Ray shrugged. Again, he tried to take a step.

'What's with the doorman routine? You not going to let me in?'

'I've got a bit of a headache. I was asleep.'

'Sorry to hear that. I figured ... you might want some company.'

It would be fair to say that in 1973, Ray still scared Susan a little. He was confident and commanding, and she wasn't sure she wanted to be alone with him. Also, stupidly, she still had that kiss in the back of her mind. She'd thought about it a lot. She used to sit in Shirley's lounge, drinking tea and listening to Shirley rattle on about how amazing her sons were, and how lucky Susan was to have married one of them. Susan would focus on Ray's mouth as he sipped from his mug, and she would wonder: *was it you who kissed me the night before my wedding?* And she would feel a horrible combination of guilt and excitement.

So, it was this frisson of fear that both made her initially say no to his request to come in, and ultimately caused her to change her mind. Stepping back, she held the door open.

He walked assertively into the maisonette; they didn't upgrade to a house until a few years later. Ray's grin widened as he finally made it over the threshold.

———

Ray helped himself to one of Martin's cans and promised to replace any he drank. He knew what Martin was like about his beers. Susan opened a bottle of white wine and asked that he replace that, too. Martin wouldn't have been happy about her drinking when he wasn't there.

They chatted and they drank, and before they knew it, all the beers were gone and so was the wine. Kneeling, Ray stuck his head inside the back of the cupboard where Martin liked to keep the *hard stuff*, as he called it. Pretending to bang his head, he swore jokily as he backed out of the cupboard. With a bottle in his hand, he gave a hearty laugh and asked, 'Fancy a whisky?'

Susan shook her head, recollecting the many occasions when Martin had poured himself a toddy and suggested she try it. The smell alone put her off. She'd given in once, a few months previously, when she'd had a stinking cold, and he had assured her it would help. Susan remembered the slight petrol taste that wouldn't leave her tongue. She definitely didn't want to help Ray drink it.

'No thanks. That stuff's vile.'

'Just pinch your nose and you won't taste it.' He laughed again.

'Seriously? You want me to take my medicine,' she giggled. Even to her own ears her voice sounded young and carefree.

'Yes. Come on. Be a good girl.'

Ray passed her a tumbler into which he'd poured a large measure of the foul liquid.

Holding her nose with one hand, she pressed the tumbler to

her lips with the other. Tipping it back, she swallowed the whisky down in one, and instantly felt her throat aflame.

'Ahhh, fucking hell. That's disgusting.' Her head shuddered involuntarily as she tried her hardest not to throw up.

'*Mrs Farnley.*' Ray was now howling with laughter. 'I didn't think your husband liked women to swear.'

'Screw him!' she shouted, feeling suddenly free and a little wild.

He swilled his whisky; the liquid skated around the inside of the glass. Then, rising from his seat, he replenished her glass, and once she was sure she was going to keep it down, she threw another large measure down her throat, using the now tried and tested *nose-pinch* method.

The more whisky she got down, the less the argument with Martin and the fact he'd gone off on a sales thing mattered.

Susan and Ray spent another hour talking and making each other laugh, and she realised she'd been crazy to be scared of him. He wasn't the hard-faced man she had him down as, he was funny and sweet, and the world was a warm, fuzzy place.

At what point it turned from laughter to kissing was a little vague. There must've been a moment when he made the suggestion, albeit a non-verbal gesture, and when she gave the go ahead. But it was hazy. All Susan remembered was watching his mouth as he talked and thinking how much she wanted to kiss it. Then, suddenly, she was. She was kissing him, and he was wrapping both his arms tightly around her, pulling her towards him. He pushed his groin forward, making it all too clear what he wanted.

She didn't mean to go the whole way. She was simply going to satisfy her curiosity regarding his mouth. But somehow the urge took over and the need was too strong. She had to have him. She had to know. They made love on the sofa. Susan didn't think it was right to take him into her marital bedroom. Undeniably it wasn't right to *take* him anywhere.

———

Afterwards, as they lay on the small sofa, their naked bodies contentedly squashed together as if they were oh so familiar, as if they had done this a thousand times before, he said he'd like to stay the night. He asked, and Susan refused. He promised to leave first thing. She told him the mere suggestion was preposterous. There was a sudden turning point.

As before, when they had swung from laughter to sex, this time they switched from intimacy to embarrassment, without a backwards glance. Susan found herself getting up from their embrace and searching the floor for her clothes. Her hands covered her private parts like a teenager as she untangled their clothes, just as readily as she had untangled their bodies. She couldn't believe what she'd done. She told him he ought to leave. Registering the now closed off expression on her face, he reluctantly agreed to call a cab.

———

The next day, Ray arrived back on her doorstep with the replacement beer and wine. Susan took it, thanked him politely and tried to close the door. He put his hand up and stopped her, asking, 'Can't I come in?'

'I don't think so.'

'About what happened last night—' he began.

Cutting him off, Susan said, 'Martin came back unexpectedly last night. We had a few drinks and made love on the sofa. He had to leave again. I heard his cab drive away.'

Ray's face took on a look of confusion.

'Why say that? You know it was me.'

'It was my *husband!*'

The next moment stayed with her for a long time. It was as if he reached into her soul and cut her open. 'That's what you're going to tell yourself, is it?' His voice was odd, like he was holding in a myriad of emotions, as if he dare not show her how invested he'd been a few seconds earlier. His eyes were those of a wounded animal.

Susan could barely breathe.

'Martin came back,' she whispered. She had to stick to her story. If she admitted even once how much she had enjoyed being with Ray, he would persuade her to let him in again, and God only knew where that would take them.

Ray removed his hand from the door and left without another word.

———

It took time, but eventually they were able to move on from the awful thing they'd done. If an image of Ray pulling her to him dared to creep its way into her mind, she would simply tell herself it was just one of numerous occasions when she had made love with Martin. For a few years, Ray was remote and unfriendly towards her and made every effort to have a young, attractive woman in tow every time Susan was forced to see him socially. But eventually they both got on with their lives. Susan had her family to think of, and he had his own ambitions and goals. She managed to put that night out of her head, and the atmosphere between them improved a little. She hoped he was able to put it behind him, too.

It was almost entirely forgotten until that frosty Christmas night, when Ray followed Susan into the garden and led her to the shed.

———

Susan closed up the old diary and placed it back in its correct place in the box. She locked the box up tight, buried it beneath the blankets, and hid the key.

'Stop this now, Susan,' she told herself with a dismissive shake of her head.

30
NANCY, JULY 1970

NANCY DECIDED it was definitely summer now. They couldn't be sure of the date, but it had become hot and sticky in their room. Nancy wished every day that they could open the window, but it was painted shut. She wished even more that Derek would let them go outside into the garden. Sometimes the sound of children playing in other gardens would float through the air, and their happy squeals and shouts of joy made her angry. She would clench her fists and bang them on the bricks that imprisoned them. Patty was angry, too, but she somehow managed to contain it. She always offered to hug Nancy when she banged on the walls. Taking her little fists in her hands, she would lead her to her mattress. They had both agreed they must be a year older by now. Therefore, Patty was now eleven, and she had begun to change. Her body was becoming a little curved, and Nancy loved to cuddle her. It was the closest thing she had to cuddling her mum.

———

Early on one of the many long, boring summer days, something happened that changed the Greenwood sisters' lives forever.

As usual, Derek unlocked their door and shouted for them to get on their mattresses. He placed two bowls of porridge on the top step and, without another word, closed the door behind him. As he did so there was a knock at the front door. People had come to the door before, but either Derek was out or he'd simply ignored them.

Derek opened the door to their room again and shouted in a stage whisper, 'Shut your fucking mouths.'

The girls sat silently on their mattresses, waiting for the visitor to leave.

Within a few seconds the knock was repeated, slightly louder this time.

The girls heard their brother mumble under his breath, 'Why don't you fuck off?'

But the person didn't; they called through the letterbox, in a powerful voice, 'Derek Greenwood. I need to speak to you.'

Derek sighed, then he opened their door one more time, and said again, 'Keep your mouths shut. Do you understand?' He then closed their door behind him and marched towards the front door, shouting, 'I'm coming.'

The girls waited a minute before they ventured off their mattresses and up the steps. Placing their ears to their door, they heard him reluctantly open the front door just a sliver.

The sisters had to strain to hear the conversation because the man's voice was muffled by the front door. But the gist of it seemed to be Derek saying that the man wasn't the police, and he had no right coming to the house.

The other man said, 'Mr Greenwood, I'm here because Patricia and Nancy have not attended school.'

Derek replied, 'I told that nosey, fat woman last year – they went to stay with their aunt.'

'You did say that, yes. But my firm have been in touch with your aunt, and she says the girls have not been there.'

Derek's tone turned nasty. 'She's not *my* aunt, she's *their* aunt. She's *their* mother's sister.'

'Fair enough. But the fact remains, Mr Greenwood, she hasn't seen your sisters since their parents died.'

'They are my *half*-sisters!' Derek said, unnecessarily.

After a pause, the man said again, 'She hasn't seen them.'

'She must be lying.'

'I don't believe she is.'

'Well, I don't know where they are. They're nothing to do with me.'

The other man's voice became angry. 'Mr Greenwood, I happen to know that the terms of your father's will are that the girls should remain in their home, and that you, as an adult, should care for them. It's why you inherited everything. I cannot simply accept that you do not know where they are.'

'Accept what you like. I want you to leave my property.'

The man stood his ground.

'This is important, Mr Greenwood!'

'What gives you the right to come here asking questions anyway?'

'I am the solicitor acting on behalf of your father. My daughter works at the girls' school, and she is adamant they have not been seen for quite some time.'

'Because they're not living here. Speak to their aunt.'

'If they were at their aunt's that would break the rules of the will, Mr Greenwood.'

'For fuck's sake, it's just temporary. They're on holiday.'

'Mr Greenwood, you can't keep changing your story.'

The argument continued, back and forth, like a game of tennis. Nancy and Patty remained silent at the top of the steps.

Suddenly, in a rage, Derek stepped out of the house, and the argument moved to the front garden.

Patty turned to Nancy and whispered, 'Did he lock our door?'

'What?' Nancy ensured her voice was at a similar volume.

'Derek. When he left. Did he lock *our* door?'

'I ... I don't know.'

'I don't remember him turning the key,' Patty said.

'Shall we try it?' Nancy asked.

'What! Open the door?'

Nancy nodded. 'Shall we?'

Patty paused. 'They're out the front.'

Nancy needed no further encouragement. She reached for the doorknob and turned it gently. Both girls drew in their breath as the door swung outwards into the hallway.

FORTUNATELY, Hannah managed to snoop around the villa undetected. As suspected, there were many rooms, including a massive, well-equipped gym. She found a bedroom that she assumed belonged to Emily. It was sizeable, with a separate dressing room and an ensuite. The villa had two wings, and on the other side she found Ray's office. A quick check inside confirmed that Ray was seriously security conscious. Every drawer was locked and there was not a single electronic device on show. Next to that was an extremely masculine room that was almost certainly Jake's. Hannah could smell him as soon as she stepped inside the door. He had a huge bed with a glass-topped bedside table, upon which lay a tell-tale little straw. The bed was covered with black satin sheets. 'Boom chick a wow wow,' she sang to herself. 'Bet you've filmed a few pornos on that bed, Jake my lad.' Her greatest fear upon seeing the bed was that at some point during this holiday, her fabulous but easily led friend Lottie might end up in it. Yes, Lottie had learnt the hard way not to trust people, but Hannah had seen how she'd looked at Jake when he tossed her in the air like a salad, and it worried her. 'Not on my watch, sonny,' she muttered to herself.

Leaving Jake's room as she'd found it, she took a left turn, hoping to find out something about Ray, all the while wondering how he'd made his money. As she walked down a wide corridor, she heard heavy footsteps coming. Opening the nearest door, she ducked into a room and pushed the door to behind her. She had stumbled upon a small room that held only a chaise longue and a bookcase. This was chock full of hard-back classics. Quite possibly known as something pretentious like the reading room, it was all very tastefully decorated. Hannah concluded any one of the novels on these shelves would cost a mint. Looking at the life the Farnleys had, she wondered if it was the sort of existence Lottie had known before Vincent.

She heard a ringtone, and the footsteps stopped almost directly outside the room she was in. The next thing she heard was Jake's voice answering the call with a grunt. What followed was a very short and heated discussion. Obviously, she only got Jake's side, but it seemed to consist mostly of him swearing and saying, 'Bro, I told you I would get you the fucking money, and I will.'

He hung up without a word of goodbye, and straight away made another call. This time Jake was the aggressor, shouting, 'Mate, if you want in on this deal, you'd better get the money to me today. No money – no gear.' After a second, he said, 'Don't bring my fucking dad into this. If you want in, you need to prove it.' He then hung up from the second call and stomped off down the corridor with even heavier footsteps. Hannah waited for a couple of minutes to ensure Jake was definitely gone. She then left the room and prepared to continue her impromptu tour.

Sadly, the next door she tried led to a reception room, within which she found several women, some of whom were seated on the sofas, drinking coffee and eating cake, and others who were standing in a circle, waving champagne flutes in the air as they talked loudly. Unable to back out, Hannah had no other choice than to brazen it out.

'Hi ... I was ...'

'Looking for the toilet?' a short woman with curly blonde hair asked.

'Yes.'

'There's one down the hall. Here, I'll show you.' The woman, who was one of the champagne wavers, carefully placed her glass on a coaster and joined Hannah at the door.

Hannah thanked her and took the opportunity to visit the loo as directed, hoping the woman would be gone by the time she came out and that she could continue to snoop.

Sadly, she wasn't. Standing in the hallway, once again holding her champagne glass, the woman asked, 'Better?'

'Erm ... yes, thanks,' Hannah said.

'Are you here for Emily's thing?'

'Not exactly. We met Jake last night in Malaga.'

The woman nodded. 'I get you. Jake's always out and about in the bars. He seems rather fond of it over there. Who's *we*, by the way? Husband?'

'No,' Hannah shook her head. 'Friend. Lottie, she's in the pool.'

'Ahhh. Yes, I heard the name mentioned earlier.'

Hannah began to question if in fact *this* woman was Jake and Emily's mum. Was there a likeness? Possibly. The eyes were a similar colour, although the hair wasn't a Farnley trait. She decided to keep with the chitchat and wait and see. 'He's talked about her?'

'Lottie this, Lottie that.' The woman waved her glass.

'She does have a way of making an impression.'

'And Jake is so easily impressed.' This was not said in a rude way. Hannah got the idea it was more of a slur on Jake than Lottie.

The woman smiled, and asked, 'Would you like to join us in the lounge?'

Deciding she might be able to do a bit of detective work in there, Hannah replied, 'That would be lovely. Thanks.'

'It's just a few of us more mature women. I popped out to the pool area before, but it's all youngsters baring their flesh, and the men have commandeered the terrace.' Leading Hannah back into the room where they had first met, the woman poured a glass of champagne and handed it to her.

Hannah spotted the nervous woman she'd seen when Ray had arrived. She was sitting on the sofa, holding a teacup to her lips, but not drinking. She merely stared off into the distance, apparently lost in a dream.

Obviously following Hannah's gaze, the other woman said, 'That's Beverley, Jake and Emily's mum.'

Mystery parentage solved. Hannah took a glug of her champagne, before asking, 'And ... how do you know the family?'

'Just a neighbour. I've not known you all long, have I, Bev?' The woman raised her voice to bring Beverley into the discussion.

Stirring slightly from her reverie, Beverley acknowledged the statement with a shake of her head. 'No. I suppose not.'

The woman continued, 'I've just rented a little place down the road. But I love it here in the Farnley villa.'

I'll bet you do, Hannah thought. *Who wouldn't love all the free food and booze?*

'They've made me very welcome. I'm like family already, aren't I, Bev?' The woman laughed, but Beverley gave no sign that she was still listening.

'Sorry, I forgot to say – I'm Toni,' the woman added, offering a small, bejewelled hand.

'Pleased to meet you. I'm Hannah.'

'I can't believe my baby is twenty-four,' Beverley muttered. Hannah figured she must be speaking to herself.

'She's a lovely girl.' Toni stepped towards Beverley and patted her pale hand.

Beverley continued to speak in a hushed voice. She was so quiet that Hannah had to strain her ears to catch the words. 'She's my greatest achievement.'

Hannah found it odd that Beverley totally disregarded her other achievement – the mighty Jake.

32
LIV, MARCH 2023

LIV PACED THE LOUNGE FLOOR. She needed a drink. All she could think of was that bloody copper and his condescending face. *Put the past where it belongs.* What the hell? Would he let it drop if he knew something as important as this? Again, she read the transcript of her session. She remembered it now. All of it. From the knock at the door to the final shocking seconds of her mum's life. It was so clear. She closed her eyes and saw it all again. Her hands shook. Why hadn't Toby given her his thoughts on it all? She needed his reassuring words and sensible suggestions. Thinking of Toby helped to calm her a little. She knew one thing for sure; he would hate her to have a drink. He would insist she get help. Grabbing her phone, she checked where the nearest AA meeting was.

33

SUSAN, MAY 1992

WHEN YOU'VE CARRIED a secret for years, and somehow, against the odds, you've managed to keep it within yourself, it gets to a point where you become convinced you're safe. You tell yourself if it didn't come out before, it will definitely not come out now. Sadly, that is exactly the point when fate strikes.

———

It was May Bank Holiday. On the Sunday morning, Martin played golf with his brother. He didn't particularly enjoy golf, but he did it because that's what salesmen were supposed to do. He went the whole hog; the ridiculous trousers, the cap. Susan couldn't take him seriously when he was all dressed up. Golf was one of the few things he and Ray had in common. They rarely met up anymore. Susan didn't mind them getting together. She knew she could trust Ray not to mention what they'd done the previous Christmas. He no more wanted to rock the boat than she did.

Martin returned from golf in a thoughtful mood. He seemed to be mulling something over. Susan wasn't overly concerned.

There had been a distance between them for weeks. An unacknowledged wall. They hadn't been close since Valentine's night. It felt as if the smack he'd given her had closed them off, and they couldn't get back. They were both broken by their own decisions.

———

Just before noon, Susan started preparing a roast lunch. Martin was sitting in the armchair, reading the paper, still wearing his stupid trousers.

Annie came in, slamming the front door behind her. It was so loud it made Susan jump all the way in the kitchen. But she said nothing. No doubt Annie had had another argument with her boyfriend, Trevor, and it was always best to keep out of one of those. Their arguments came and went, and they always made up afterwards.

Martin, of course, chose to comment. 'Oy, don't slam the door.'

Annie took the bait at once. With a sigh, she said 'Sorrrrry' in that tone only teenagers can achieve.

Martin snapped, 'It's shaken the ornamental plates on the wall.' He genuinely thought that was a valid point. Susan heard it from Annie's point of view. What seventeen-year-old gives a stuff about ornamental plates?

Annie laughed.

Martin said, 'Don't laugh at me, young lady.'

'I'm not. I'm laughing at your fucking plates.' There was a smirk in Annie's voice.

Susan drew in her breath. Martin couldn't abide swearing from her or the children.

Rising from his chair, he strode across the room at speed. Susan heard his newspaper splay out across the floor. 'Do not use bad language in this house.'

Susan's heart began to bang in her chest. She stood stock still in the kitchen. She wanted to warn her daughter. Annie didn't know the other side of him; she hadn't felt his hand on her face. But she was scared to intervene. Would that make it worse?

Annie replied, 'Fine. I won't be in this house then.'

'Good!' Martin shouted. Despite the wall between them, Susan knew his face would be red.

She heard Annie turn on her heels and make for the front door.

Martin called out, 'And mind those plates.'

Opening the door, Annie shouted, 'I don't care about your stupid plates,' and left.

Susan wasn't sure if the row was somehow going to transfer to her. Would she get the brunt of it? She suspected Martin would have a go at her for not taking his side. But there hadn't been time to take anyone's side really. It was over in seconds.

She was therefore surprised when, after picking up his paper, he joined her in the kitchen and began a conversation.

'Annie isn't like the other two.'

'She's older. That's all. They'll go through it as well.'

'No!' he maintained.

'What's the problem?' Susan asked.

He shook his head, sadly. 'She's trouble. She's nothing like Olivia or Toby. She doesn't belong here.'

'What on earth are you talking about?'

'She doesn't feel like a piece of me. In fact, if she didn't resemble my mother so much, I'd think she wasn't mine.'

Was he serious? They stood in silence.

'There's not the same connection,' he continued.

'She's nearly eighteen. That's what happens. Didn't you pull away from your parents a bit at that age?'

'It's not just now. It's always.'

'Nonsense,' Susan said. 'You two were so close when she was little.'

Martin turned to face her. Staring into her eyes, he asked, 'Is she mine, Susan?'

Her blood ran cold. So long. *Years.* She'd kept it from him. Surely it wasn't going to come out now. 'You just said how much like Shirley she is. She's got her features.'

'True.' He made a kind of *hmmm* sound, as if he was relieved. 'But she's still a cuckoo in the nest.'

'Please don't say that about our daughter,' Susan insisted.

'I will say it. I said it today, on the golf course with Ray. I told him the same thing. I said she looks like Mum, but she feels like she's not mine.'

Susan knew she could either crumple or fight. She chose to fight. Sucking in her breath, she summoned all her courage. 'I'd rather you didn't go around saying things like that about our daughter, Martin.' Her tone was purposely harsh. It was a risk, but a necessary one. She needed to shut this down. 'What you're suggesting is that I was unfaithful to you.'

'Ray knows I didn't mean it. It was just … talk.'

'Right, well, don't please. That's your wife's honour you're discussing.'

Thankfully, he saw her point. 'All right, don't get your knickers in a twist, woman. I wasn't accusing you. Like I say, it was just talk.' He returned to the lounge and flicked on the television.

Susan remained in the kitchen, on the pretence of finishing the potatoes. She was, in fact, taking deep breaths and trying not to throw up. She wondered what Ray would've made of that conversation on the golf course.

34

HANNAH, APRIL 2023

DURING BREAKFAST THE NEXT MORNING, Lottie shouted, 'I've got a text!' and grinned at Hannah.

'Is that from that bloody programme?'

Lottie laughed. 'Yes. But I really have got one, and it's great news.'

'Enlighten me, please?' Hannah asked, tearing off a piece of her pain au chocolat and dipping it into her coffee before popping it into her mouth.

'Jake has invited us out for tapas tonight.'

'Us?'

'Yes.'

'It's not a little date for two?'

'No, honestly.' She flashed the phone at Hannah: *Would you guys like to come for tapas with me and the others? Tonight. About 8.*

'Who d'you think the others are?' Hannah asked. 'Thalia, Zoe, the awful Claudia …?'

'Yes.' Lottie looked pained. 'And all the other hangers on.'

Hannah snorted. 'Why does he have such an entourage? It's not like he's famous.'

'He is charismatic though,' Lottie said.

'You think?'

'Yes. I mean, those eyes.'

'Nice, are they?' Hannah knew she was being obtuse.

'Mesmerising,' Lottie replied. 'Then there's his hair. It's so thick. Thalia says it used to be longer. God, I just want to run my fingers—'

'I thought you couldn't wait for Chen to come back so you could give it a go with him. You've been buzzing like an old fridge every time we talk about him!'

'I ... I *can't* wait.' Lottie sounded a little hurt at the tone of the interruption. 'Can't I admire a good-looking man now?'

'Yes, of course.' Hannah gave an apologetic smile. 'Sorry, sweetheart, it's just, I don't like Jake. He seems too far up his own arse for my liking, and I don't want you to get hurt or ... umm.'

'Swindled out of all my money. Is that what you're trying not to say?' Lottie asked, petulantly.

'No! Well ...'

'Han, I'm not that person anymore. I won't deny I fancy Jake, and I'm enjoying the little bit of luxury that comes with him. But I promise you, I've got the measure of him.'

'Good.'

'Besides, I thought you'd be pleased. Thanks to me, we're in with the Farnleys.'

'Yes, I know. And I am pleased. But I need to actually speak to Ray. I got stuck with all the women yesterday, and I didn't learn an awful lot. He'd done a bloody runner from the terrace by the time I escaped the lounge. I heard talk that he'd gone to his study to work. I never saw him again.'

'Well, he might be at the tapas,' Lottie suggested.

'I doubt it. It seems to me that Jake likes to go out and treat everyone using Daddy's money, but he doesn't appear to actually enjoy spending time with him.'

'Can I say yes to the text?'

'Go ahead. Jake's still my best chance to get closer to Ray.'

Within a second, Lottie had received a reply.

'He says the place we're going to does a delicious pork roll. It's his favourite. We should try it.'

'I don't eat pig,' Hannah said, tetchily.

'Yeah, right, unless it's a bacon butty.'

'Listen, if you promise not to fall head over heels for that bloody man-child, I promise to eat the pork roll. Deal?'

'Yes.' Lottie shook her friend's hand, adding, 'He says they do really good garlic prawns, too. You love them.'

'Forget the menu. Ask him if his dad will be there.'

'I can't; it'll sound odd.'

'We'll have to hope we get invited back to the villa afterwards then.'

'Uh huh,' Lottie agreed readily. 'What do you think of him? Ray, I mean.'

'He wasn't what I was expecting. I guess I thought he'd be a doughy old bloke, and he's so far from that.'

'Oh yeah. He's still fit. You can see where Jake gets it from.'

'I know Liv says he's a terrible man. But I can't see it,' Hannah said. 'He struck me as a hardworking, family man.'

'Well ...' Lottie paused, as if deciding on her opinion. Finally, she said, 'If I'm honest, I'm not keen.'

'Why?'

'He seems okay, but his wife is ...'

'A shrinking violet.'

'Absolutely,' Lottie agreed. 'And that raises some red flags for me. My mum was very shy. Just think about what she was covering up for my dad?'

'You think Ray's wife is timid because she's covering up for him?'

'Maybe.'

'Covering up what?'

'Who knows? All I know is when I meet a wife who never

speaks, and a daughter who's an introvert, like Emily, I wonder what the man is like to live with.'

————

After a day that involved a lot of flirty texts between Jake and Lottie, and some business texting backwards and forwards between Hannah and Dave, they were getting ready for the meal. Lottie was painting her nails, and Hannah was trying to control her bleached hair, which never responded well to chlorine and sunshine.

'Ahh, I see you're going for the shade *fuck-off red*,' Hannah commented.

'It's called *cherry smile*,' Lottie laughed. 'But yes, these nails mean business.'

'Don't forget our deal about the man-child,' Hannah reminded her.

'As if,' Lottie said. 'It was only this morning that we made it.'

'Good.'

'I just want to look *unreal*, as Jake says.'

'You always do, beautiful.'

'We could be rubbing shoulders with the elite of Marbella tonight.'

'Hmm …' Hannah pulled a face, 'It's not what your *shoulders* are going to be rubbing that I'm concerned about.'

'There's no harm in me looking attractive. You want me to get Jake's attention, don't you?'

'You've already got it.'

'I might be able to find out a few more things about his dad for you. Get you the intel.' Lottie winked.

Still trying to flatten her ridiculously fluffy hair, Hannah replied, 'Thanks.'

'But I can't do that if his eyes are wandering to everyone else, can I?'

'I just told you, Lottie. You've already got his attention. Why would he need to look anywhere else?'

'But he's so popular. All those women in the bar the other night, the people at the villa. Thalia definitely wants him, and she's gorgeous,' Lottie said.

'Yes, Thalia is gorgeous. But so are you. The others are possibly just interested in what his dad's money can buy. Anyway, so what if they do all want him?'

'I don't like it.' Lottie blew on her nails. 'He seems to make every straight female within a mile radius go weak at the knees. Claudia can't get enough of him.'

'You're not telling me you think she's serious competition, are you?' Hannah tutted.

'I don't know. I mean, she literally thinks she owns him. It's not just Claudia, everyone fancies him. I even saw him talking to some curly-haired, middle-aged woman at the villa, heads together in a corner. And she was old enough to be his mother.'

'That sounds like Toni. I've met her. She's just a neighbour. Or maybe,' Hannah teased, 'Jake simply likes older women!'

'Han, she had camel toes on the corners of her eyes.'

Dropping her brush, Hannah laughed. 'I think the term you're looking for is crow's feet.'

'Oh yeah. Those.' Lottie giggled.

Hannah retrieved her brush from under the dressing table and said, 'She's not *that* old. Besides, I spoke to her, and she seemed all right. But I don't think she'd want Jake in that way, any more than he would want her.'

Lottie began applying the sticky red varnish to her toenails.

'I hope you're right; I've got enough to worry about with flippin' Thalia and her sun-kissed skin.'

35
LIV, MARCH 2023

IT WAS FATE. Her slagging off the police at the meeting. That Dave bloke taking her to one side and telling her he worked for a firm of PIs. Thank God she'd gone. Liv clutched the business card he'd given her. On it was a phone number for Hannah Sandlin. From what Dave had said, this Hannah woman was good. Toby's money could once again be put to good use. Taking the plunge, Liv dialled the number. Hannah Sandlin answered within a couple of rings, and Liv introduced herself through dry lips.

They spoke for a few minutes, discussing fees and Hannah's credentials etc. Liv wasn't pleased to hear that Hannah was an ex-copper, like Dave, but she hoped maybe she would be one of the good ones. They arranged to meet in Liv's favourite café the next day. She was glad she'd been allowed to choose the location. The café was much better than going to some posh hotel lobby. She would've felt awkward somewhere like that.

Fishing around in the kitchen drawers, she managed to find a photograph of her dad and also one that she was reasonably sure was of her uncle. She would need them to explain exactly what had gone on. She wasn't going to mention the hypnosis.

She'd seen how it had gone down with the police. No, she'd tell this Hannah woman she knew it was her uncle because she'd recently remembered. But she would keep the details vague. If she was pushed, she'd have to give the full account, but not yet. Shoving the photographs into her old satchel, Liv took a swig of her black coffee, then rolled herself a ciggie.

36

SUSAN, MAY 1992

THE FALLOUT from Martin and Ray's golf game was swift.

On Bank Holiday Monday, when other families were out enjoying their extra day off, doing normal things together, like walking in Lullaby Woods or visiting the marina, Susan was home. Very early that morning, Martin had said he had some paperwork to catch up on in the office, and he had left Susan to entertain the kids. In truth, Annie was out all day with her friends, and Olivia was home, but distant. A typical fourteen-year-old girl. Susan could swear she spent more time mooning about the house than she did talking to her mother. Toby, as always, was her angel. They watched a video together, his favourite, *The Land Before Time*, and played a couple of games of *Guess Who*. He was never too busy to spend time with his mum. She supposed that at eight, she still had him for a few more years before puberty whisked him away.

The conversation with Martin about Annie played on a loop in her mind all day and she was dreading the next time she ran into Ray.

———

By the evening Susan was beginning to wonder where Martin was. He did sometimes work late into the night, but not usually on a bank holiday. When the phone rang shortly after 7pm, she fully expected it to be him letting her know he was leaving work. Sadly, although the voice was identical, it swiftly became obvious it was not her husband.

'I need to speak to you. I think you know why.'

'Ray?'

'Yes!'

'What's up?' She tried to keep her voice light.

'Surely you don't think we're going to do this over the phone!'

'Do what?'

'You know!'

'Listen, whatever Martin told you—'

Ray interrupted her. 'I need you to come and meet me. I've had all day to think about this, Susan, and I need an answer.'

'I can't—'

'Now!'

'Honestly, I can't. Martin isn't here. I can't leave the kids.'

'Where is he?'

'Working.'

'On a bank holiday?' Ray sounded dubious.

'Yes.'

'The kids will be fine. Annie's practically an adult, for Christ's sake.' Ray wasn't about to let her worm out of it that easily.

'She's getting ready to go out again. It's all back on with that boy.'

'I don't care who it's back on with. Stop her.'

'I can't. You know Annie.' There was a deathly silence as it dawned on Susan what she'd just said.

Ray gave a snort. 'Well, leave Olivia in charge. She's old enough.'

'Why the urgency? Can't we meet tomorrow?' Susan tried to stall.

Clearly struggling to keep his voice calm, Ray said, 'I need to talk to you. You choose; come and see me now, or we'll talk about this in front of my brother.'

'Okay, okay.' Susan gave in. 'I'll come. When and where?'

He explained where he was and told her to get there quickly.

Susan agreed. As soon as she hung up, the tears that had been waiting to spill gushed out. She heard herself sob, once, twice; she was in danger of losing it completely. An anguish she hadn't felt since Toby's diagnosis took over her. She tried to regain her composure. The kids mustn't see her like this. Grabbing a tissue, she blew her nose and dabbed at her eyes, knowing if she gave in to the overwhelming need to cry, she'd never stop.

So, the secret was out. Susan had kept quiet about Annie's conception for over eighteen years, but she couldn't lie any more. In some ways it was a relief. Knowing what she knew and keeping it from her family had been like a stone in the pit of her stomach. She had carried it everywhere. It never let up for a minute. It was always there, reminding her. A weight. An oppressor.

————

When she found out she was pregnant for the first time, Susan knew her child had been created the night she got drunk on whisky with Ray. There was no time when she had had sex with Martin that fitted the dates so well. Plus, Martin was way more careful. As soon as she knew, her fate was sealed. She and Martin were married; there was no way she could tell Ray what she so strongly suspected. For Susan, confessing was not an option. She had to do everything to convince Martin the baby was his. It was the only way forward. If she told the truth, it would drive a wedge through Martin's relationship with his brother. Not to mention what it would do to their marriage. So, she carried on as if Annie was Martin's child. But Annie wasn't early, of course she wasn't. She was bloody huge. The due date error was simply something Susan told Martin, to put him off the truth.

But Susan knew, when faced with Ray's question, that she would no longer be able to lie. She was going to have to tell him that Annie was almost definitely his, and that she had prevented him from being the father he'd had the right to be for all those years.

─────

As predicted, Annie refused to stay home and babysit. Susan wondered what she would say if she knew the reason for her mother's urgent departure from the house. She asked Olivia to keep an eye on Toby for her instead.

What a day for Martin to choose to work so late. Leaving to go and meet Ray, she told her children she wouldn't be long, and that it was just an errand. Her life was about to implode, and she was leaving them happily reading magazines and playing on a bloody Sega!

─────

Martin still wasn't home when Susan returned. Retrieving the key to her lockable box, she made her way over to the tea chests in the corner of the lounge and dug deep. Unlocking the box, she took the top diary from the pile, turned to the next blank page and wrote the date. Susan knew she ought to jot down the day's events, in particular the conversation that still had her head spinning, but one single sentence bounced around her brain, demanding to be written. So she wrote it: *I've told him everything!* At that moment, there was a knock at the front door.

Shoving the diary back into the box, she locked it and hid it under the baby blankets in the tea chest. With no time to put the key in its usual place, she popped it in her pocket. As she made her way down the hall, the knock came again, louder and more insistent this time.

37
HANNAH, APRIL 2023

HANNAH AND LOTTIE were surprised to discover that the entire restaurant had been hired out exclusively for the Farnley party. Joining Emily and some others at a large, round table in the centre of the room, they glanced around. Hannah was hoping to catch sight of Ray, but it was clear Lottie only had eyes for Jake.

Picking up a menu, Hannah asked Emily, 'What would you recommend?'

Emily smiled shyly. 'Hi, good to see you both again.' She glanced at the menu, although it was obvious she knew it by heart when she said, 'I love their aïoli with sweet potato fries, plus, if you don't mind doubling up on the carbs, there's patatas bravas, or you can't go wrong with a bit of stuffed aubergine.'

Hannah nodded. 'Sounds delicious.'

'I'm a vegetarian though, so you might prefer something else. Jake always raves about the pork thing. He eats here a lot. Mind you, he can't cook for toffee. He makes food like he isn't going to have to eat it afterwards.'

'Oh yes, I'd better try the pork roll,' Hannah said, thinking of her deal with Lottie. She added, 'But I'd love a bit of stuffed aubergine as well.'

'It's all tapas sized portions, so you can kind of order a few things and we'll all share.'

'Perfect.'

'What about you?' Emily asked Lottie.

'Sorry?' Still scanning the room, Lottie wasn't listening.

'Just wondered what you fancy, but I don't think I need to ask.' Emily sighed.

'Is Jake not here?' Lottie asked, seemingly oblivious to the exchange of knowing glances between Emily and Hannah.

'Not yet. Trust him to be late for his own celebration, after he made us all traipse over here.' Emily rolled her eyes.

'Huh?' Lottie asked, quizzically. 'What's he celebrating?'

'It's a birthday thing.'

'His birthday is the day after yours?' Hannah asked.

'No. Sorry,' Emily explained. 'He was on holiday in Greece for his actual birthday, so we thought we'd do something now. A couple of months behind schedule, but who cares? We eat out all the time, to be honest.' She shrugged.

'And what better way than to take over the whole place,' Hannah added.

Emily shrugged again, 'Thank my dad for that.'

'I will. Is he here?' Hannah asked, as casually as she could manage.

'No.'

'Is he planning to come?'

'Yeah. He's meant to be.'

Before they could continue the conversation further, a familiar face popped over to their table. 'Emily, you look lovely. What a pretty top.'

'Thanks, erm ... Toni.'

'So, where's the belated birthday boy?'

'God knows.'

'Well, he ought to get here. People have made an effort to come out,' Toni said.

Emily mumbled, 'Not that much of an effort. Besides, they're all getting a free meal and loads of drinks.'

'It's still disrespectful to make everyone wait,' Toni added with a frown.

Immediately, Claudia leant across Emily and snapped, 'Sorry, what's your name – Toni? What's it got to do with you? You're not his mother!'

'I'm fully aware of that, thank you. I'm not old enough for a start,' Toni said.

Claudia gave a cynical laugh. 'You keep telling yourself that!'

'Well ... I ...' Toni appeared lost for words.

'What are you anyway ... a neighbour? A friend of Beverley's? What are you even doing here?'

After an awkward pause, during which no one said a word, Toni turned and walked away. When she was a few steps from the table, Claudia called out, in a loud voice, 'You ought to have made a little more effort with your preparation. In the wrong light you'd give these hairy waiters a run for their money. You'll never get a man with a top lip like that, Magnum.'

Toni's cheeks flushed red, and her hand flew to her mouth. She tried to retaliate with 'I don't want one' but her response was a tad too slow and was delivered with shaky confidence. It was obvious Claudia's remark had hit home. Toni returned to her seat, continually running her finger along her top lip. Hannah guessed it wouldn't be long before she made her way to the toilet to check out her face in the mirror.

'That's her told,' Claudia sneered. 'I've got your back, Ems.'

'I don't need ...' Emily faltered.

'She shouldn't dis Jake like that,' Claudia continued. 'And, no offence, babe, but it's no wonder she likes your top, it's a little ... frumpy. Just because she's wearing a fucking roll neck jumper *in Spain* ... I mean, would it kill you to make an effort and show off a bit of flesh? You're not bloody ancient like her.'

Emily blushed.

There was so much Hannah wanted to say in Emily's defence. Why did Claudia think flashing one's flesh represented making an effort? And what gave her the right to criticise Emily anyway?

But, giving no time for a reply, and clearly not realising or not caring that what she had said was extremely offensive, Claudia pressed on, saying, 'We're only young once, hun,' before grabbing a passing waiter and asking for another bottle of Prosecco.

Brilliant, Hannah thought. Not only was she going to have to keep one eye on how Jake was treating Lottie, she was going to have to keep the other one on this judgmental bitch. Claudia, as her Grannie Annie would say, was meaner than a junk yard dog.

———

They gave Jake another half an hour, and then, because everyone was complaining they were hungry, people decided to order food.

Every dish on the menu was requested several times over, then they sat back and waited. The drinks continued to flow.

Fifteen minutes later, Hannah perked up as, to her delight, Ray arrived. *Now we're talking!*

He made apologies to the room for his wife, explaining she wasn't feeling well, and wouldn't be joining them. Emily jumped up from the table and made her way over to him. Taking her dad to one side, they had a short, whispered discussion, before Emily returned to her seat.

'Everything okay?' Hannah asked.

'Huh?'

'You were talking to your dad?'

'Oh, yeah. I was just checking on Mum.' Emily seemed distracted. 'He tried to persuade her to come, but …'

'He said she's not well.'

'Umm ... yes.'

'Is that all?'

'Emily looked up from her drink. Making full eye contact with Hannah, she said, 'My mum doesn't like social events. She's ... you know ... shy.'

'I get you.'

'Dad tries to get her to join in. He thinks it'll do her good. I don't know why. If she's not keen, she's not keen. But he doesn't get that. I'll bet he spent the last half hour badgering her to get changed and join us. She'll have hated it.' Emily sighed.

'I understand,' Hannah said.

'The problem is, Dad will keep trying. I don't know why. He knows the reason why she's how she is.'

'And what is the reason?' Hannah asked.

Emily closed her eyes for a second. Then, lowering her voice, she said, 'It's tricky. She ... she has bouts of—'

With a flurry, an array of waiters began noisily filing out of the kitchen, tiny dishes of food balanced up their arms. For a moment, the noise was deafening. The room became infused with the smell of a million different things, all of them mouth-watering.

'Now you can try the aubergine,' Emily shouted over the clatter, with a false smile.

'You were saying,' Hannah prompted. 'About your mum ...'

'She has depression. It's ... she's on medication, but ...' Emily's voice trailed off. After a pause, she said, 'Jake doesn't help. He's ...'

'What?'

'Nasty.'

'To his own mother?' Hannah pulled a face.

'Yeah. He just tells her to get over it. Listen, Hannah, Jake isn't what all this lot think he is. He's never taken the time to understand our mum. He laughs at her anxiety. He can be quite cruel. Basically, he's a ... dick.'

'Sorry to hear that.'

Before Hannah could say any more, Lottie leant over and asked Emily, 'Is Jake usually over an hour late?'

'Not usually. I guess he's off buying a little pick me up for later.'

'Coke?' Lottie asked.

'Uh huh.'

Hannah was reminded of the tiny straw in Jake's room, and the one-sided phone conversations she'd overheard.

'Well, there's going to be nothing left for him to eat soon,' she said, observing how the entire restaurant had begun tucking into the food with great gusto.

'I'll keep him some pork roll. He can eat it here,' Claudia butted in, making a point that the seat next to hers was free. 'It's his favourite.'

'Or he could have some of these,' Thalia said, placing a plate of prawns to one side.

Lottie couldn't wait to get involved. Patting the seat next to hers, she said, 'Luckily there are a few spaces.'

'Please don't fight over him.' Emily held up her hands. 'He's really not worth it.'

No one except Hannah seemed to take any notice of her comment. 'You're preaching to the choir with me,' she said.

'Sorry?' Emily looked confused, obviously too young to get the saying.

'It just means – I'm already convinced, you don't need to tell me.'

'Oh right. Preaching to the choir. Now I get it.'

'This lot seem to think he's charming.' Hannah waved her hand at the women around the table.

'About as charming as tooth ache,' Emily said. 'What they don't seem to get is the fact that he's just pretending. He's good at it. I guess you wouldn't know that his degree was in Psychology and Business Studies.'

'Wow, I did a GCSE in psychology. It was interesting.' Hannah tilted her head. 'Curious combo though!'

'The business part was on dad's insistence. He obviously funded the whole thing. The psychology, well, Jake just loves to get inside people's heads.' She shrugged. 'He works out what makes them tick, and he makes sure to be whatever they want him to be. None of them really know him. Everything they see is an act. *Fake Jake*, that's what I call him.' Emily returned her attention to dipping her sweet potato fries into the aïoli.

Hannah checked out the rest of the guests for a second. Her eyes settled on Toni, who was still struggling to gain her composure. She appeared visibly shaken. To Emily, Hannah said, 'Are you okay about what Claudia said?'

Noticing the direction of her gaze, Emily asked, 'You mean to that Toni woman? About her face?'

'No. Well, yeah. But I meant what she said to you really, about your clothes being frumpy. I'd have been tempted to tell her to fuck off if she told me to flash more flesh!'

Emily laughed. 'I *was* tempted.'

'Toni's been very quiet since.'

'Yeah. I don't get why Claudia picked on her. I didn't think she even knew her particularly.'

'She's your mum's friend, isn't she?' Hannah asked.

'Kind of. I think she lives down the road. I don't remember why she first started coming round, to be honest. She could've been one of Jake's bring backs.' Emily shrugged.

'Oh, right.' Hannah concluded that perhaps Jake *was* into older women. Maybe there was a chance for Claudia after all.

The women continued to glare at each other over the table. Hannah figured that each was hoping that when Jake came, he would choose the seat they had saved him to grace with the pressure of his admittedly tight little bum.

As if reading her mind, Emily repeated, 'They're all wasting their time. He's not what they think he is. I ought to know.'

38

ANNIE, MAY 2022

ANNIE FARNLEY COULDN'T BELIEVE it was thirty years since her mum had been killed. Where the hell had those years gone? Three decades without a mother. As she always did around this time of year, she tried to imagine what her mum would look like now. Dying at the age of forty-four meant that every image of Susan was of a young, vibrant woman. What would she be like at seventy-four?

Annie had decided to take the rest of the Bank Holiday week off work. She didn't need much of an excuse. She was bored with her job and longed for something else to come along. But nothing ever did. This week was going to be all about her mum.

On the Tuesday, she spent the afternoon retrieving the tea chests from the loft. This was no mean feat; they weren't that heavy, but they were awkward, and the loft hatch wasn't large. Plus, it was an uncharacteristically hot day for early May. Almost doing her back in in the process, Annie finally placed all three chests in the lounge. She threw herself into a chair, sweating and panting, hating the fact that there was no one to help her.

Resting for a while, and vaguely watching some nondescript comedy, Annie planned to go through the chests after dinner.

Later, she ate a quick meal, and washed up the plate and pan. *When did I last cook for someone else?* she wondered. *More importantly, when did someone last take me out to dinner?*

As the sun continued its journey towards the west, and the sky lost its glare, Annie decided to leave the windows open to let the evening breeze in. Her flat had been stuffy all day, and the tea chests gave off a slight damp loft aroma. The air was cool now, but it carried with it a taste of summer to come. She decided to make an event of this, and so opened a bottle of Chardonnay and poured herself a large glass of wine.

These chests used to live in the lounge of her parents' house. She could recall them sitting in the corner, and Susan gradually adding photographs, books etc. to them. Sometime after her mum died, they were moved to her grandma's loft, and there they remained for years, until her grandma died. Annie wasn't even sure how they'd ended up in her possession. She wondered why Olivia and Toby hadn't ganged up and insisted one of them should keep them. Let's be honest, it wouldn't be the first time they'd ganged up on her.

Sipping the rather good wine, Annie opened one of the chests at random and began to rummage. The first thing to come to hand was a photograph album. A generic image of a fluffy dog decorated the cover. She turned to the first page. Remembering all the albums she'd made up herself, she recalled you simply mustn't ever pull the sticky-back-plastic all the way off. If you did, you would never get it back in the same place and you'd get dreadful air bubbles in the pages. Her mum had clearly known this, too; the pages were smooth and bubble free.

She looked at the odd selection of photographs her mum had

chosen to adorn the pages. Every shot was important back then. There was none of this taking a few pictures and choosing your favourite, and absolutely no editing. You pointed the camera, and you clicked. Once you'd taken thirty-six shots, you took the film to the chemist and waited about a week to catch the first glimpse of your precious memories. It was clear Susan liked to choose pictures from different events, different seasons, different years even, and mixed them together in the albums. Each page was like a jumbled-up snapshot of life in the Farnley family. Annie looked down at the haphazard shots of life. Each one was so badly taken you'd almost think it was planned. The tops of heads cut off, the main feature of the shot off to the left or right, never in the middle, often almost out of the picture entirely, and blurred people, pets and buildings. She laughed. *God, Mum, what were you and Dad thinking? Did you even have your eyes open?*

It made her feel nostalgic to see her mum and dad wearing clothes that she vaguely recalled. There was her mum, with her big, bouncy hair, and that funny little smile she always did when you pointed a camera at her. It was always endearingly lopsided. On the fourth page she came across some photographs of her and her siblings. The first image was taken in 1985; Toby was less than two years old, and yet, already, he appeared to have chosen his allegiance. He was snuggled into Olivia, who in turn was snuggled into him. They sat on the old sofa Annie recognised from their childhood lounge. They'd had that sofa ever since they'd moved from the maisonette to the house, not long before Olivia was born. Annie looked at herself in the photo. Separate. She was sitting in an armchair a good few feet away from her brother and sister. So far in fact, part of the right-hand side of her body was cut off.

Annie's eyes moved down to the next photograph, the three siblings together in 1990. When Susan had taken this shot, she'd only had two more years left to live. She could never have guessed at such grave news. This one was taken on a family outing. The three kids were seated around a picnic bench, eating the classic packed lunch of the time: sandwiches, crisps and Dairylea triangles. Yet again, Toby and Olivia were on one side of the bench, and Annie was on the other. Of course, she could conclude that this was because she was sixteen at the time. She was the largest child, so simply from a balance perspective, she would need to sit opposite the other two. But Annie knew it had nothing to do with that. She remembered that day, spent at the zoo. She felt again the pain in her chest as she recollected asking Olivia to sit next to her, suggesting casually it would be nice for the girls to be together, and the blatant rejection of Olivia's reply, 'I'd better sit with Toby.' No more explanation than that. No reason why she'd *better sit with Toby*. Just the choice made. Annie hadn't even wanted to go to the zoo. She'd argued that at sixteen she was old enough to stay home alone. But Susan had insisted that as it was their dad's birthday, they would all do something together as a family.

As Annie flicked through the thick, yellowing pages of the photograph album, far too many images jumped out at her showing Toby and Olivia together, with her on the side-line. No matter how old they were, she was always excluded. Finally, she came to a shot of her and Olivia before 1983. When Toby simply hadn't existed. How did the sisters look then? Annie wondered. *Were we closer?* Yes, she concluded they'd been okay then. Something had happened when Toby was born. Some invisible link between him and Olivia. A link Annie couldn't fracture, and she could not compete with. She had felt it, always. No amount of effort on her behalf had been enough to break into and join their relationship. Toby's childhood illness had only served to make them stronger. After that, they simply knew, without words, what each other wanted. It was like they shared synapses. As soon as she had begun having boyfriends, Annie had finally discovered what it was to be needed. Maybe it was only sex, but it didn't matter; those boys had wanted her, and at last, she had been on the inside of something and not on the fringe. So boys had become her thing and her siblings had been set to one side. A failed project.

Annie took a large swig of wine. *Fuck you, Olivia*, she thought to herself. *I tried so hard.* Olivia's twenty-first was her last attempt to bond. She'd paid for a day out at a spa for the two of them. They'd had a facial together and she'd hoped it would bring them closer. But Olivia had claimed to find it all a bit odd. She hadn't appeared to enjoy having her face touched by a stranger, and, because she'd been on her period, she'd said she didn't fancy swimming or using the sauna afterwards. So Annie had agreed they could leave shortly after the unsuccessful facials. She'd gone back to her boyfriend at the time and sobbed, declaring she was done with trying to connect with a sister who clearly couldn't care less about her.

These days, she kept in touch with Olivia mostly by text, and very occasionally an actual phone call. She knew what Olivia had been through with her many addictions, and she felt bad not to support her more. But, over the years, rich brother Toby, Olivia's closest ally, made sure she was provided for, and the bond between them continued to leave no room whatsoever for Annie. Even now, after everything, it was still evident.

Tossing the albums aside, she stuck her hand back in the chest and found an assortment of old newspapers. Some had headlines that shouted about important world events, such as Charles and Diana's wedding. These were quite interesting, and Annie spent a few minutes reading through them. At the very bottom were some baby clothes and shoes, mostly Toby's.

———

Replenishing her wine, Annie decided to open the next chest. In this one she found exercise books from her schooldays. Reading through the maths equations and French verbs, she was amazed to realise she hadn't been as daft as she'd thought. She also found an old exercise book that Susan had used to keep on top of all Toby's hospital appointments. It was odd to read her mum's handwriting. All the appointments, notes about particular drugs, overnight hospital stays. It had all been recorded. Her poor mum. Annie could almost smell the despair.

39

HANNAH, APRIL 2023

HANNAH SAID, 'It can't have been fun growing up with Jake for a brother, if he's as bad as you say.'

'It was awful.' Emily nodded. 'Not so much when we were little. Back then he was just a mean older brother. A bit of a bully. But loads of my friends had those. I figured it was normal. But by the time he started studying psychology and getting inside people's heads, it was ...' She swallowed. 'I just hated it when he came home from uni.'

'D'you mind talking about it?' Hannah asked. 'I don't want to upset you.'

'It's okay. It's just ... as soon as I used to come through the front door, I knew Jake was back. Sometimes there was his suitcase in the hall, or a pile of washing in the laundry room. But even when there was no physical evidence that he was home – I just ... knew! The atmosphere at home always felt different. Whenever he came back for the summer or Christmas, something dark settled upon the place. It had always been so nice, so peaceful when he wasn't there. It was like someone turned a light off.'

Hannah gave an involuntary shudder but nodded for Emily to carry on.

'Dad didn't seem to notice. He was always busy working. He's a financial advisor. Anyway, his relationship with Jake wasn't good. But me and Mum always noticed when Jake was home. Mum would become even more reserved, and I always felt the need to check everything I said in front of him, in case I set him off on one of his misogynistic rants.'

'It sounds very stressful,' Hannah said, nibbling on one of the sweet potato fries and offering the rest to Emily.

She took one and continued, waving the chip in the air as she spoke. 'One summer, I guess it must be about seven years ago now, I came home, and I knew he was there. He never gave us the exact date; he just booked his flight through Dad's account. But like I said – I just knew. I called out, but there was no reply. Mum was in her room, probably sleeping. She sleeps a lot during the day, not so much at night. I went into the kitchen, convinced I was about to find him raiding the fridge. Nothing. Empty and spotless, as always. Mum has a real thing about keeping the kitchen clean. She often begins loading the dishwasher whilst people are still finishing their meals.'

'Jesus. I thought my mum was a neat freak.' Hannah smiled, in an effort to diffuse the tension.

Emily finally bit into the chip.

'I found Jake in the lounge. He'd drawn the curtains and pulled one of the armchairs up close to the TV on the wall. He was playing some shooting game on his Xbox. He had his headphones on. Next to him on one of Mum's little coffee tables were some crushed beer cans and another one that was clearly still full. Every few seconds Jake would swear loudly and shout a load of abuse through the mouthpiece. He always shouts at any poor unfortunate strangers who dare to try to annihilate him in a game.'

'Manchild,' Hannah said.

'Absolutely. I was really pissed off. Like ... why does he have to play those stupid games in the lounge? He's got his own room; plus, there's a smaller TV lounge. I knew if I said something it would be seen as antagonistic, but I was sick to death of the way he selfishly took over and changed things as soon as he came home. He made my parents' beautiful lounge look like a squat. So, anyway, I asked him if he could take the Xbox to his own room, so I could put the furniture back. I tried really hard to ask politely.'

'And ...?' Hannah asked, glancing up to keep one eye on Ray's whereabouts.

'He ignored me, so I tried again. This time I moved in front of him so he could see I was speaking to him, and I accidentally blocked his view of the screen.'

'Oh shit!' Hannah said.

'Yeah. He shouted for me to get the fuck out of the way and called me a twat or something. He had that look of total contempt on his face. The look he saves for me and Mum. You won't have seen it. But believe me, it's terrifying. I stepped to the side because I was upset. When he's angry there's a fierceness to his voice, and it can come out of nowhere.'

Hannah continued to listen, all the time vowing to keep Lottie as far away from Jake as possible.

'Anyway, a second later the screen filled with an image of blood; he was dead in the game. Well, he jumped out of the chair, flung off the headset and leapt towards me. He said something like, *you fucking little bitch. I had him. I was this close.* And he thrust his thumb and finger into my face to show me how close he'd been to killing the bloody unknown avatar.'

'I've not seen any of this behaviour from him yet,' Hannah said.

Emily looked a little downcast. 'I'm not lying.'

'Oh God, of course not. I wasn't saying that. I'm just ... look ... it's just that he lays on the charm so well.'

'I don't suppose that lot have ever had him shove his hand in their face or snarl at them.' Emily nodded in the direction of Claudia and Thalia.

'What happened after he got killed in the game? Did he move rooms?' Hannah asked.

'I apologised. I know it sounds weak, but he scared me when he shouted; he still does. So I said I was sorry, but I pointed out that he knew we all hated him playing those games in the main lounge. I told him that room was for all of us. He just shouted that I hadn't even been there. He said there was only Mum in when he got home, and she was hiding out like a bloody hermit, as per usual. I wanted to ask him not to be rude about Mum, but I could tell he was on a roll. Then, he said, *Christ, how that woman ever got up the energy to give birth, I'll never fucking know.* I ignored his remark about Mum and tried a bit of gentle persuasion. I said that Dad would be home soon, so ... I hoped he'd take the hint.'

'Let me guess ...' Hannah said with a roll of her eyes.

'Exactly,' Emily said. 'He just said that he wasn't going to fuck off out of the room just because I was threatening him with my daddy. I told him there were so many other rooms he could play his games in, but he insisted that the villa was still his home. He shouted that part into my face. A speck of spit touched my cheek, so I took a couple of steps backwards and bumped into the coffee table. I knocked his beers onto the floor.'

'What did he say?'

'Something like, *Yeah, you'd better back off.* He was laughing at me. He loved it when I was scared. I went to open the curtains. I hate how he always makes it dark. We're so lucky to live where we do. We have a massive window in the lounge. You've probably seen it. I just don't get why anyone would shut out the sun? But Jake barked for me to leave the curtains alone, then he started loading up another game on the Xbox.

'So he wasn't going to his room?'

'No,' Emily said. 'I gave up. I said, *Fine!* I turned my back on him. I thought I'd just go to my room or the kitchen. Get away from him. But he grabbed me from behind and spun me around; he held me by the wrist and asked me who I thought I was? I tried to shake him off. I told him to let go. But he was pinching my wrist really tight. He said as long as he was back home, me and Mum could stop thinking that we ruled the place. He said we'd get the villa back when he left, but whilst he was there, we'd better keep out of his way. I said I'd tell Dad that he'd hurt me, but he just said that Dad didn't care. All he was interested in was making money and trying to keep it all for himself. He said Dad had got a shell of a wife and a daughter who spent her life banging on about oppression of minorities. He figured Dad must be really disappointed in the pair of us. I told him Dad loved our mum very much. But he just said, *Well who wouldn't? I mean, she's so much fun!*'

'God that *is* below the belt.' Hannah wondered when she'd last disliked a man this much. She figured it was probably Lottie's stepdad, Vincent.

'I asked him why it mattered to him that I concerned myself with injustice or prejudice. He just said that I didn't get it. I lived in a fucking great villa, with my dad paying my private school fees. He said I wasn't really concerned about minorities. I was one of the people oppressing them.'

'What did you say?' Hannah asked.

'I said if *I* was, then so was *he.*'

'What did he make of that?'

'He just laughed and said the difference was that he didn't care who he oppressed. I tried to tell him that Dad was very proud of me and Mum. If anyone was letting him down it was Jake. I told him I wished he'd just stay at uni all year round. I hated the villa when he was there. He said he was sick of being made to feel unwelcome in his own home, and me and Mum had better watch ourselves.'

'God, Emily you poor thing.' Hannah took a sip of wine; she could feel her blood boiling. *What a fucking bully.* She wished he'd start on her instead of someone as sweet as Emily. She'd show him who should watch themselves.

Emily's voice interrupted her thoughts.

'I told him I wasn't scared of him. But I could hear my voice shaking. He just laughed again and moved his forehead close to mine, making out like he was going to head-butt me, you know? Just stopping short by a centimetre. Then he said, *Tell your face you're not scared!*'

'Did you think he was actually going to head-butt you?'

'I was sure of it,' Emily said. 'Right then, Mum came in the room and asked what all the commotion was about. I felt a tiny bit braver because she was there, so I said, *Jake's back from uni. You can guess the rest.* Mum looked from me to him and asked Jake what he was doing. He just unplugged his Xbox and said he wasn't doing anything. He told her she could stagger back to her bedroom; it must be time for her to take some more pills. I'll always remember him saying, *Well done, Mother, you've saved your precious daughter from the monster again.*'

'What a total bell end.'

'I had a mark on my wrist for a fortnight where he'd grabbed me so tight; it was like a Chinese burn. He gave me a few of them when I was a kid, too. Plus, I had that image stuck in my mind of him so nearly head-butting me. I've made sure to never be in a room alone with him since.'

'So, he really is a bully,' Hannah said.

'Yep.' Emily nodded.

'But ... he was at your birthday do, and he puts photos of you on Instagram ...?' Hannah said, shaking her head.

'That's all an act.' Emily sighed, 'Like I told you – *Fake Jake!*'

40

ANNIE, MAY 2022

THE NEXT MORNING Annie headed back to the lounge, this time with a mug of tea. She wasn't going to start drinking Chardonnay before noon; she wasn't Olivia.

She'd enjoyed flicking through all her school exercise books the day before but had chosen not to read Toby or Olivia's. Toby was so bright, a maths genius in fact. That's how he made so much money on the stock markets. There were many reasons why she didn't read all the glowing remarks from her brother's teachers about how amazing he was.

Today, she was going to open the third and last chest. Prising off the lid, she prayed there would be no more photographs of her siblings.

On the top were a few scrapbooks; these were filled with spring cleaning ideas, recipes and money saving tips, all cut from the *Reader's Digest*. Annie imagined her mum enthusiastically cutting out the chicken stew recipe that all the family would love. *Did we, Mum? Did we all love it?* In a second, her laughter turned to tears. Her poor mum had been so determined to keep a loving, family home going. She didn't deserve what happened to her. It had never made sense. Susan had barely made it into her forties, and yet she'd been cutting out articles on how to prepare for living off a pension.

Underneath the scrapbooks were some neatly folded, small white blankets. Annie presumed these must have been baby blankets used by her and her siblings. She lifted one to her nose and sniffed. Sadly, any baby smell had long since left; the blanket now smelt like everything else in the tea chests – dusty and old, like a forgotten property. Annie pulled the blankets out and placed them on the carpet next to her. There was nothing to suggest that there would be anything else in the chest, but, for whatever reason, Annie felt the need to check. She was rewarded for her diligence by the sight of an A4 lockable metal box at the bottom of the chest. A sticker on top of the metal box had obviously once borne the name of the manufacturer but it had rubbed off over time. Annie could just about make out the words *lockable* and *documents*. Sadly, there was no key.

Placing the box on the floor next to the blankets, Annie tried to lift the lid. Perhaps it was too much to hope that it would be unlocked and the lid would succumb to her touch. Indeed it was; the box was locked up tight. Annie now had two dilemmas; the first of course was how to get it open when the key was clearly nowhere in sight, and this was swiftly followed by the second: was it right to consider looking inside it? This box must've belonged to her mum, and whatever documents or papers were inside it, they were almost certainly private. Annie leant back on her heels and considered her situation. She could simply place it back in the tea chest and not give its contents another thought, or she could break into that bad boy and see what was so important that it needed to be placed under lock and key.

'Would you mind if I open it, Mum?' she asked the air around her. Her head turned from side to side, looking for a clue. A white feather, a butterfly, a robin on the window ledge, any of the apparent signs that a dearly departed loved one is close by. Nothing!

She decided to refresh her mug. Maybe she'd have a coffee this time. If there hadn't been a sign by the time the kettle had boiled, she would assume her mum was okay with her breaking the lock. Sure enough, five minutes later, Annie placed her mug of instant coffee on the table and surveyed the room. There was nothing to suggest her mum's disapproval. Annie switched the lights on; they didn't flicker. *I'll take that as a go ahead.* She smiled to herself.

She Googled how to break into a locked metal box and was soon intently watching a YouTube video. Finding the requisite two paperclips, Annie mused that the contents were no doubt simply going to be birth certificates or vaccination cards.

It wasn't as easy as the man on the video made it look. Firstly, she had no such thing as a pair of pliers and had to make do with some tiny nail scissors. It was frustrating, and more than once Annie felt like giving up. But eventually, her fumbling fingers worked their magic and the lock turned.

Inside the box was a pile of assorted exercise books. Flipping them out onto the floor, Annie wondered why her mum had decided to lock these particular books away when she had simply placed the other schoolbooks loose in a tea chest. Picking up the book that had been on the bottom of the pile, but was now upside down on the top, she noticed that it wasn't clear which child they belonged to, because there was no name on the front. As soon as she opened it, Annie recognised her mum's writing and assumed, incorrectly, that they were more notes on Toby's leukaemia. But no, the first entry was written in January 1970, long before Toby was born. These were not further notes on Toby's illness; these were her mum's diaries. Annie moved over to the sofa. Making herself comfy, she read her mum's words.

———

My twenty-first birthday! I've got the key to the door, never been twenty-one before. Now I'm officially an adult, I'm going to keep a diary. I think life is going to get more exciting. I must try hard to write it every day. The maisonette Jenny and I want to rent is all sorted, we can move in next week. It's going to be tricky to afford, but it's going to be so fab for us to have our own place. Met a man called Martin in Ryman's. He had amazing eyes. He looks a bit older than me. I told him where I work, and he said he might drop by. Fingers crossed; I hope I'll see him again. Went for drinks with Jenny at that new place by the bank. We had Pina Coladas. Delicious, and very sophisticated!

———

Annie was shocked. All the time she'd known her mum, admittedly not long enough, but still, she'd never imagined her to be someone who kept a diary. Clearly, judging by the number of exercise books, her mum had stuck at it. The books were all different colours and sizes, and, like the first, each one had no title on the front. Flicking through, Annie saw that they continued covering Susan's life, year after year. She didn't write every day, and some days would be a really short entry, but some were long and detailed.

Annie paused for a second; was it okay to read them? They *were* private after all. Would her mum prefer it if she simply threw them away? Or burnt them? She decided she would quickly flick through, ignoring the short entries, such as *Dentist at 4pm, filling, ouch!* She would read a couple of the long entries, to check how personal they got.

The first one to catch her eye was an entry where Susan discovered that Martin had a twin. She'd written that she'd made a fool of herself nearly pushing Ray into the freezer.

Laughing, Annie continued to flick her way through, picking out some of the more detailed entries, all the time finding out more about this young woman named Susan Farnley.

———

She stopped for a quick lunch, a simple cheese sandwich, before diving back into the diaries. She'd placed them in date order on the floor and had developed a routine of skimming through until she came to an interesting-looking entry. This method meant she had already made it into the 1980s. She'd laughed at some of her mum's crazy thoughts, and she'd cried at the description of her own birth, including her dad's absence from the hospital. She'd just finished reading about Toby's illness when she glanced up and saw it was dusk. *Bloody hell, where did the day go?* Tempted to keep the rest of the eighties and what little there was of the nineties until the next day, Annie wasn't sure what to do. These diaries were a precious gift. They could be read for the first time only once. She knew they ought to be savoured and that she would regret it if she binged them all in one day. But much like a favourite Netflix series, the urge was strong. She decided to take a break, stretch her legs and get some dinner. Then and only then would she decide when to read the rest.

On a whim, Annie decided to treat herself to her usual set meal for one from her local Chinese. She didn't do this often; money was tight. But what the hell, she was off work, and she was celebrating her mum's life.

When her phone beeped, she assumed it was a message from the takeaway place; they always texted when the delivery driver had left the shop.

But, checking her phone, she was surprised to see it was actually a text from her sister.

'Hi. How U doing? Have you remembered the date tomorrow?'

Had she remembered the date? Annie clenched her teeth. Olivia had a way of taking over their mum's death. Somehow, she owned it, like it was worse for her. *Why does she always assume she's remembered the date and everyone else hasn't?*

Annie was tempted to ignore the text. But then it might seem as if she really hadn't remembered. So, she sent a simple reply. 'I'm fine. How are you? Yes, of course, thirty years since Mum died.' After a second, she read it again and deleted, the *of course.* Why antagonise?

A moment later a reply came through. 'I wish I could remember more.'

Annie sighed. *Not this again!*

A text arrived from the Chinese; her meal had left the building. It would be with her in five minutes. She didn't want to get into a long text conversation with her sister. Worse, she didn't want Olivia to call her. She might feel obliged to tell her about the diaries, and, quite honestly, she didn't want to; they were hers to cherish. For fuck's sake! She just wanted to eat her Chinese and then finish reading the diaries. She texted, 'Don't worry about what you can't remember. It's all in the past. Sorry, I'm with someone, can't talk now.' She shut the conversation down and, just in case, shoved her phone down the side of the sofa.

Sure enough, five minutes later, Annie had her delicious takeaway in her hand. Serving it onto a plate, she ate as quickly as possible, eager to read more of the diaries. Who had she been trying to kid that she could wait?

41

HANNAH, APRIL 2023

BY TEN O'CLOCK everyone had had their fill of tapas. The waiters began to clear the food away, and Ray stood to announce that he'd paid the bill and placed a load of money behind the bar, and everyone should keep on enjoying themselves.

Hannah was surprised when he began marching purposefully towards her.

But, of course, it was Emily he was aiming for. Kissing his daughter on the forehead, he leant in and said, 'If Jake arrives, the kitchen will do him some food. I'm heading home to check on Mum.'

His jaw was set. It was clear he was not impressed with his son. Perhaps Jake had let people down before. Or maybe Ray also suspected Jake was out buying cocaine. Either way, the fact that he was leaving so soon was annoying. Again, Hannah hadn't had a chance to speak to him. She'd been biding her time. Waiting for him to get a few more drinks under his belt. Him leaving so early from his own son's celebration had not been factored into her plans.

Without thinking it through, she reached out a hand and

grabbed his arm as he passed. Standing, she asked, 'Ray, do you have a minute?'

His expression said he had no clue who she was, and why would he?

'What?' he asked abruptly.

She introduced herself. 'Sorry. I'm Hannah. A friend of Jake and Emily's. Do you have time to talk to me?'

'What about?'

Good question. She hadn't decided yet. She paused.

'Well?' He impatiently eyed her hand, which was still clutching at his arm.

'Financial advice,' Hannah heard herself say.

'Not now, sorry. I need to get back to my wife. She's not well. Call my firm if you want advice. Talk to Don or Mitch.'

She let him go. 'Okay. No problem.'

And just like that he left the restaurant and was gone. Another missed opportunity.

Lottie immediately made her way around the table and whispered into Hannah's ear, 'What the fuck was that?'

'I panicked. I need to talk to him. To get to know him. Who knew he'd leave this early?'

'You looked like you were accosting him,' Lottie laughed.

'I know.' Hannah laughed, too. 'I'm clearly not his type. He couldn't get away fast enough.'

———————

At eleven o'clock Hannah had to admit to herself that the evening was over for both of them. She was still fuming at her missed opportunity with Ray, and Lottie was deflated because Jake had failed to show up. She wasn't the only one. Several of the girls who'd been saving him a seat or food seemed disappointed, too.

'I think we're going to make a move,' Hannah told Emily.

'I don't blame you. Not much of a night, was it?'

Hannah gave a small smile. 'The food was lovely. And … it was great to see *you* again, and to get to know you better.'

'Thanks. It was good to talk to you, too. Thanks for letting me offload.'

'No worries.'

'But … honestly,' Emily said. 'It's a bit of a washout for the guests if the birthday boy and most of his family don't come.'

'Well, we're in Marbella for a good while yet,' Hannah said, fishing for another invitation to the villa.

'I expect Jake will text you to come over sometime. He seems to really like Lottie …' Emily paused, before adding, 'For now.'

Hannah nodded, glad that she had an ally in Emily.

'Thank you, by the way, for the warning about Jake. Lottie is a *very* good friend of mine.'

As they left, Hannah waved to Toni and Thalia, but avoided Claudia's eye.

———

In her ensuite bathroom, Lottie angrily swiped the make-up off her face and said, 'Fancy not turning up!'

'He probably got a better offer from some cocaine dealer.'

Hannah sat on Lottie's bed watching the familiar bedtime routine through the open bathroom door. When she was poor, Lottie hadn't been able to afford good skin care products, and Hannah had heard her say on many occasions that she would be forever making up for the damage.

'Hmmm,' Lottie mused, throwing a make-up pad into the bin with a flourish.

'Doesn't that put you off him?' Hannah asked, seriously.

'It's not great. I mean, you've seen where drugs took your client, Liv.'

'Exactly!'

'But,' Lottie continued, 'he could be a dabbler. I knew loads of those when I was part of the upper classes.'

'*Part of the upper classes.* Listen to you!' Hannah laughed.

'I just mean,' Lottie continued to wipe her face, now with toner, 'he might not have an actual coke habit. He might simply like a good time.'

'Good enough that it kept him from his own party.'

'Well, however we look at it, it was a shit night.' Lottie was finally onto the moisturising stage, rubbing it into her face and neck in well-rehearsed, circular movements. 'You didn't get to find out a single thing about Ray either.'

'I know,' Hannah agreed. 'That man is like the fucking Scarlet Pimpernel!' Her phone pinged to announce a text message. Checking it, she said, 'Ah ha. A text from a Farnley.'

'What?'

'Not him! Liv. She says she's better, and she'd like to meet me.'

'Does she know you're here?'

'No. I decided not to tell her until I had a better idea of who the real Ray Farnley is.'

'Which you sadly still don't,' Lottie said.

'Which I sadly still don't,' Hannah agreed in a sing-song voice, shaking her head slowly from side to side.

'So, what now?'

'I'm thinking – put Liv off for a couple of days, give myself time to finally talk to Ray, and then fly home and meet her.'

'No!' Lottie cried. 'I don't want to go home in a couple of days.'

'Not you, stupid. You can stay here if you like. Finish up the holiday. But, and I cannot stress this enough, do not let that fuck boy make a fool of you. I tried the bloody pork roll, which, by the way, was greasy, so you have to keep your side of the deal.'

'I won't even meet him without you there to chaperone if you like. I'll swim in the pool here and—'

Her promises were halted by the ping of Hannah's phone and the arrival of another text from Liv. 'Can we make it soon, please? I'm worried about something. I'll explain when we meet up.'

'Oh, bugger,' Hannah said. 'No flights to Southampton until Saturday. I can't wait that long; she clearly needs to talk to me. I'm going to have to fly into London tomorrow.'

'Can't you just phone her?' Lottie asked.

'No,' Hannah said. 'I need to—'

'You need to see the whites of her eyes,' Lottie volunteered.

'Exactly!' Hannah laughed. 'Seriously, this sounds important. I need to check in with her; this was never meant to be a long holiday. And I could do with seeing Dave, too.'

'Will you come back?'

'Probably. I guess it depends on what she has to say.' Hannah made her way through the connecting door into her own bedroom. After washing her face with Dove soap, her own, concise bedtime routine, which had stood her in good stead for over two decades, so didn't need revising, she began Googling flights for the next day.

42
ANNIE, MAY 2022

IT WAS GONE eleven when Annie read the entry in which her mother gave a very brief account of how she had had sex with Ray on Christmas night.

Annie was disgusted.

What had possessed her mum? God, no wonder she'd locked the diaries away. She remembered that Christmas. The year her mum got a new blue coat. *Jesus Christ, Mum!*

Annie couldn't understand what had made her do it. She closed her eyes, trying to figure out what in the world anyone could find attractive about Ray. He was a useless wanker. He'd left his own brother in prison and gone off to travel. She didn't share many opinions with Olivia, but one of the few things they did agree on was that Ray was an utter cunt, and neither of them used that word lightly. They were all better off without him. She'd never had the slightest thought to try to trace him. But now, knowing what he'd done to her mum, practically coercing her into the shed, she wanted to find him, and she wanted to kill him.

After pacing the floor and opening a bottle of Sauvignon

Blanc, to ring the changes, Annie sat down to read the next few entries.

———

It wasn't long before she was up and pacing again. This time the man she was fuming at was her dad. She'd always known he wasn't perfect. She'd seen and heard things that she had chosen not to discuss with her mum. But, bloody hell, Valentine's Day! She could remember asking her mum if a card had come for her. Susan had seemed kind of sad. Annie's boyfriend at the time, Tim? Tom? Terry? What the hell had his name been? Ahh yes, Trevor! Anyway, he'd asked her if she'd liked the card, and she'd said there hadn't been one. He was so insistent that he'd put it through the letterbox. She'd never believed him. Turns out he was telling the truth.

Annie wasn't sure what to think about the way her dad had reacted. Perhaps if they'd known then ... Oh, why torture herself? There was nothing to do but read on. But she was no longer enjoying the process. She wasn't giggling at the little comments. She was looking at the date and dreading what was to come. Now, like a person plunging their hand into a sink full of disgusting water to free the plug, she knew it was going to be horrible and it was going to turn her stomach, but she also knew it had to be done. May Bank Holiday 1992 was beckoning, and she was powerless to resist.

———

It was well after midnight when Annie reached the last entry. It was very cryptic. Just the words *I've told him everything.* Despite not understanding it, Annie cried as she read it, because it was the last words her mum had ever written.

Now, she felt a little sad that she'd rushed through the

diaries. She'd known there were a limited number of entries; why the hell had she binge read them in one day? In a quest to find out more about her mum, Annie decided to go back to the start. This time she decided to scan the short entries, too.

———

One of these seemingly innocent little entries was how she found out that her mum had already slept with Ray, years before that Christmas night. It was hidden amongst trivial accounts of everyday life. But there it was. A few words about Ray visiting when Martin was away, and a confession about sex on a sofa. Even in such a short record there was obvious regret.

———

After this, like a detective, Annie continued to search through the diaries, reading more thoroughly this time, looking for clues about her mum and Ray. And there, in a mere two-line entry, so short she'd previously disregarded it, was the fact that Susan had found out she was pregnant for the first time. Like her mum before her, Annie did the maths and came to the same hideous conclusion – Ray could be her father.

That realisation changed everything. Annie didn't want Ray to be her dad. It wasn't even that she wanted Martin to have fathered her; he had moved away from her as she'd grown older, and she had always felt that he loved the other two more than her. But to simply find out that biologically she could well be Ray's child was too much. It had taken her years to accept the facts surrounding her mum's death. She had made her peace with it, as much as was possible. Now this!

———

Eventually, Annie read the very last entry again.

So, when Susan had written that she'd *told him everything*, she could've been talking about Martin. But, even more likely, she could've been talking about Ray, maybe referring to the fact that Annie was his child. Had he been pleased to hear he could be her dad? Clearly not; he'd never claimed her as his. He'd left her with a dead mother and a father in prison. He'd gone travelling and never come back. Annie concluded he had most definitely not been pleased. She looked at the small, orange exercise book in her hand. This was the very last thing her mum had held. She had put it in the lockable box, no doubt intending to come back and write some more. It was safe to say that no one had touched it for thirty years. With her eyes tightly shut, Annie squeezed the book. It was the closest she could get to squeezing her mum's hand.

So, what now? What was she meant to do with this news? Part of her wanted to tell Olivia; even after all these years of distance and let downs, Annie still figured she had the right to know. But then she had another thought. *What even is Olivia to me now?* Maybe a half-sister? A cousin? It was confusing. A quick Google check seemed to say that identical twins shared pretty much the same DNA; only their fingerprints differed. So, if she and Olivia still shared the same DNA from their biological fathers, were they still sisters? She poured another glass of wine. This needed more thought.

———

The next morning, Annie was up early. She had barely slept. At some point during the night, she'd decided she needed to try to find out where Ray was. Was he even alive? There was a rage inside her that burnt like the worst Prosecco heartburn. She would find him, and she would confront him. How dare he take off knowing what he knew? Annie remembered her grandma crying. In the space of a year, she'd lost both her sons. Her home went from a warm refuge to a desperate, lonely house. Annie had moved out as soon as possible and had rarely gone back. What was there to go back for? A grandma who sat, staring through glassy eyes at photographs of her sons, and siblings who were so close you couldn't get a cigarette paper between them. It was a dreadful, cheerless place to be.

Annie rarely used Facebook; she couldn't abide the false lives people lived on there. 'Out with the family, what a lovely day,' followed by several staged shots of someone's kids pretending to enjoy a walk in the woods. Everyone knew the kids had done nothing but moan for the entirety of the walk, and the parents had cursed the day they'd had them. Then there were the endless Mother's Day and Father's Day posts. The 'we all got together for Christmas' posts. Each one rubbing salt into her wounds. Worse still were the looking for sympathy posts. 'Six years since my mum died. Struggling with anxiety. Finding life a little tough at the moment.' *Fuck off, all of you*, Annie would think. *You have no idea. You think your life stinks. Try mine!*

But today it was useful. Because today it helped her to find her uncle, who she supposed she might now need to think of as her dad. He wasn't on there himself. He was probably too old for the likes of social media. But there was a Jake Farnley, who lived in Marbella. He had a look of Toby about him. His younger sister, Emily, who was mentioned and pictured in a couple of posts, reminded Annie of Olivia. A sudden thought struck her – if they were Ray's kids, they could be her siblings. Yes, this was her brother and sister. Not Olivia and Toby. Suddenly it all made sense. It explained why they'd excluded her for all those years. Annie began to feel hope. Maybe these siblings would let her in. She scrutinised Jake's photos, searching for more family likenesses, and suddenly, there was Ray. In the background, his hair now silver. Annie began to cry. Not for him; he was still an arsehole. But, crazily, for her dad, Martin. He'd died with a full head of brown hair, and never got the chance to look like this.

So, if Ray was in the background of Jake Farnley's photos then she simply must have got the right family. The decision was made in an instant. She called work and told them there was a family crisis and she wanted to extend her leave. They seemed surprised she even *had* a family but agreed to another week off. If she needed longer, she'd cross that bridge when she came to it, as her grandma used to say. If she ended up getting the sack, so be it. Her family, her *real* family, lived in the Golden Mile in Marbella. They'd take care of her.

Within two days, Annie was on a flight to Malaga.

43

NANCY, JULY 1970

As the door swung into the hallway, Nancy wondered – did they dare leave? Turning to her sister for guidance, she asked, 'Can we go, Patty?'

'Where to?'

'Anywhere.'

'I ... I don't know.'

Nancy's eyes filled with tears.

'Please, Patty. I can't stay here. I want to go somewhere different.'

After a pause, Patty said, 'Okay. But I'll go first.'

They crept into the hallway, both pleased to hear Derek's voice out in the front garden. He was still protesting his innocence to the man who had come to visit.

They made their way through the kitchen, which was at the back of the house. It was very different to the place in which they used to bake fairy cakes with their mummy. It was now dirty. So horribly dirty it made Nancy cry some more. All the shelves that used to be full of clean plates and bowls were empty. The plates and bowls now lived next to the sink in a big stinky pile.

'Don't look,' Patty instructed. 'Try to think of it how it was.'

Nancy put her hands up to the sides of her face, making blinkers, like horses wore. Together the girls rushed through the kitchen and out of the back door. Once in the garden they stood for a moment, enjoying the heat of the sun on their faces. Nancy blinked. 'I can't see.'

Patty took her hand and led her through the garden.

'We need to wait until Derek goes back inside the house and then we can go and find that man.'

'The man who knocked on the front door?'

'Yes.'

'But he's a stranger.'

Patty gave her little sister a funny look.

'He's here to help us. He said so. He's Daddy's solisi-something.'

'But he's still a stranger.'

'I'd rather trust a stranger right now,' Patty said.

They passed a pile of shambolic logs, which Derek had clearly been chopping but had abandoned months ago in a colder climate.

'Do you remember the big fireplace in the lounge?' Nancy asked, wistfully.

'Shush. Not now,' Patty replied.

They made their way round the side of the house. Hiding themselves in a geranium bush, they watched Derek and the man continue their discussion in the front garden.

'Hurry up, Derek, go back inside,' Patty whispered.

They waited another couple of minutes. Nancy could hardly contain the excitement that soon they would be leaving Derek and the disgusting room they'd been living in, forever.

But Derek didn't go back inside. To their horror the girls saw the visitor get back in his car and drive away, leaving Derek swearing and shouting on the front doorstep.

What now? How were they going to get away? They needed a

grown up. Nancy's heart sank. She couldn't go back. She'd rather be dead like Mummy and Daddy. Why couldn't she have been in the car, too, her and Patty? They could have all died and no one would have to be with Derek.

They watched as Derek made his way back into the house, slamming the front door behind him. Patty stood surrounded by flowers, appearing too scared to move.

'He'll know, Patty. He'll know right away. We left our door wide open. Shall we run for it?' Nancy said.

'I ... no ... yes.' Patty seemed incapable of decision.

Before they had the chance to get the guts up to make a move, the front door once again opened.

'Patricia! Nancy! Where the fuck are you?' Derek shouted.

Patty gave Nancy a look that said, 'Stay still. Don't speak.' There was absolute terror in her eyes.

Nancy obeyed.

'How dare you leave your room?' Derek was so angry, he was spitting. Specks of his saliva were flying everywhere.

Nancy hoped one of the closer neighbours would hear him and come and save them. Poking her head out from the bush, she checked if there were any grownups around. It was a decision she would regret. Her eyes settled on Derek, as his eyes settled on her.

She gave a high-pitched scream. Patty, obviously aware they'd been spotted, grabbed her sister and began dragging her towards the back garden, as Derek made his way down the side of the house.

Both girls were sobbing as they ran. Twice, Nancy tripped, and had Patty not been holding on so tightly to her hand she would've fallen.

At the pile of logs, Patty pulled Nancy down behind them and placed her finger to her lips, saying, 'Shhhhh.'

Derek came around the corner, still swearing and shouting, his breath coming in short sharp bursts.

'Where the fuck ...?'

The girls held their breath.

Suddenly, Nancy felt a hand on her arm, and from the side of the log pile Derek yanked her out. She screamed, even louder than before, and tried to wriggle free.

'Let's get you girls back into the basement,' Derek said with an unpleasant grin.

'No!' Nancy tried to fight him off.

Derek picked her up under his arm and turned in the direction of the back door. Nancy couldn't bear it. She was going to be back in that stinking, hot room and Derek was never ever going to leave the door unlocked again. She wanted to die. She fought him as much as she was able, but he took her feeble attempts as nothing more than a joke. Laughing as she tried to kick out at him, he began walking towards the back door. Easily carrying her with just one arm, like a roll of lino, he called out, 'And you'd better fucking stay there, Patricia. I'll be back for you in a minute.'

IT WAS ODD, sitting here, looking at Liv, knowing what she now knew. She could see Jake in Liv's face. Emily, too. She could even spot Ray in there. She felt like she knew so much about Liv now, unlike before, when they'd been two strangers meeting for the first time over bad coffee. The urge to tell her she'd met her family was very strong, but she held back. Liv would find out soon enough when the case was over and she saw the expenses. For now, Hannah needed to get to the bottom of whatever Liv's dilemma was.

She stifled a yawn. What a day! It was hard to believe that just this morning she had been eating an amazing avocado and cheese omelette in the hotel with Lottie. Then, a dash to the airport in Malaga, a flight to Heathrow, and a dreadful, disrupted train ride back down south, which took longer than the flight from Spain. She'd showered, then quickly eaten a bowl of soup, longing for stuffed aubergine and perfectly cooked sweet potato fries, before texting Liv to ask if she could come straight over. Pleased to hear from her, Liv had given her the address.

Now, she assessed Liv's flat. It was larger than she'd imagined. Toby's money was evident everywhere. The flat itself couldn't have been cheap. Part of a converted building, it was wonderful. Almost definitely Grade II Listed. Imagine having a brother who bailed you out and paid for you to live in a place like this.

Liv returned from the kitchen with two black coffees.

'Sorry again about the milk situation. I've just not been out.'

'You should've texted; I'd have brought some with me,' Hannah said. 'And some food, if you needed it.'

'Oh, no, it's fine. I'll get some soon. I can go out again now, I'm sure I'm not contagious. She handed one of the coffees to Hannah and remarked, 'You've caught the sun a bit.'

'Have I?'

'Your face mostly.'

'Gardening,' Hannah lied.

'It's been lovely to finally have blue skies after the persistent rain, hasn't it?'

'Yeah.'

'You're lucky. I'd like a garden.'

'They're hard work,' Hannah lied again. She did nothing in the garden. Neither did Lottie, who simply paid for someone to cut the grass and do a little weeding in the summer.

Liv asked, 'You sure that's all you want? Just coffee? Not that I've got much, anyway. But I could maybe find a biscuit.'

'No. I'm good, thanks. I just need something to wake me up.'

'Have you been doing all-night surveillance or something?'

'Kind of,' Hannah said.

'Was it to do with my case?'

'No.' The lies kept coming. She didn't want the conversation to stray too far into what she'd been doing of late, or what she'd found out about Ray. Better to keep it focused on Liv.

'Oh, right.' Liv blew on her coffee.

'So, how are you feeling now?' Hannah asked.

'Better, thanks.'

'Did you get it bad?'

'Covid?' Liv shrugged. 'Not great. I was coughing most nights. I barely slept.'

Hannah wanted to suggest she cut back on the rollies, but she knew the reply would be something along the lines of *what's it got to do with you?* So instead, she asked, 'And ... why did you need to see me so urgently?' It was time to stop beating about the bush.

'I'll get to that in a minute.' Liv shuffled awkwardly in her seat, then said, hesitantly, 'Look ... I wasn't going to tell you why I only recently remembered all the stuff about Ray. I ... umm ... figured you'd think I was a crank.'

Hannah leant forward, intrigued. 'Right ...?'

'But I guess you need to know.'

'Yes, I do. And now seems like a good time.'

'Yeah. But I want you to hear me out before you decide I'm bat shit, okay?'

Hannah nodded.

Liv settled back in her seat, black coffee in hand. It was clearly more for comfort than sustenance, because she didn't appear in any rush to drink it.

'I've always thought I saw something the night my mum was killed. My brother was asleep, and my sister was out. If I didn't see anything, then ... no one did! So, I have to believe that I saw it.' She paused.

'Uh huh.'

'I remember my mum coming home and rummaging about in some boxes in the lounge. I know I crept down the stairs and sat at the bottom. I was worried about her. She wasn't herself that night. Then, someone knocked on the front door, and she shoved something into one of the boxes.'

'Why were there boxes in the lounge? Had you recently moved or something?' Hannah asked.

'No,' Liv said. 'I just have this vague recollection of boxes. Wooden, that kind of thing.'

'Have you ever gone through them to check what she put in there?' Hannah thought that seemed like a reasonable question.

'I have no idea where they are. They were probably in Grandma's loft for years. But now ...' Liv shrugged.

'Okay. So, she went to the door ...'

'Yes. And then there was this blank in my head. For years. Like a big smear of Tippex over a typed page. Do you remember that stuff?'

'I do.'

'I didn't know what happened next, but later, an hour, two hours, Christ knows, I remembered the police taking me and Toby to Grandma's, and then they picked up Annie and brought her there, too. But obviously something must have happened in between. Toby always told me to leave it. He said if my mind had blocked it out, then it was meant to be gone. He said I probably sat on the bottom stair and missed it all. But surely I would've got up and gone to see if she was okay, if she was screaming?'

'You were a child. It's highly possible you were too scared to move.'

Liv shook her head.

'No. I was fourteen! I would've gone to her. I saw something. I know it. I've always known it. It's like ... you know when you wake from a dream and you try to remember it, but ... it's gone. You get just a hint of it. It hovers in your peripheral vision and it's so close. It constantly feels like any second it will reveal itself.'

Hannah nodded; she got what Liv was trying to say.

'Anyway ...' Liv finally took a small sip of her coffee. 'Around Christmas time, last year, I decided to try to unlock the memories. I couldn't accept that I just sat there on the bottom stair like an idiot. I needed to know for definite if I got up and saw something. I read a leaflet about psychotherapy, and how this man had helped someone famous to unlock a chunk of their missing childhood, and I decided to spend Toby's money trying to remember.'

'Did Toby mind?'

'The money from Toby comes into my account on the first of every month. It's entirely up to me what I spend it on.'

'Okay.'

'I went to this guy, Stephen, and he started to hypnotise me every week. I know what you're thinking ...'

'Do you?'

'Yes. You're thinking I'm very naive.'

In reality, Hannah was thinking that this Stephen fella was probably no better than the Great Shazam, who she'd met at a garden fair and who had turned out to simply be Sharon, the cleaner. But she decided Liv didn't need that kind of negativity, so, instead, she said, 'I'm really curious to find out how it all went.'

'It went well. He didn't go straight to the night my mum was killed. He got me to talk about loads of stuff. Like: my family, my past relationships, what makes me angry, that kind of thing. And I can honestly say, I was hypnotised. I could feel it. I could see the memories as clear as I can see you. I saw my brother as a baby, honest, I swear it.'

'Intriguing. Out of interest, did you tell the police how you'd come to remember everything?'

Liv nodded. '*They* weren't intrigued at all.'

'Go on with the story, please,' Hannah instructed gently.

'Stephen sent me a transcript of each session, and when I read them, I could see it all again. Honestly, Hannah, it was brilliant.'

'Sounds like it.'

'But then, we finally got around to talking about the night my mum was killed, and it was different.'

'Different how?'

'I didn't remember it. He woke me up and I swear to God I thought we hadn't even started yet. Then he said that it was a very informative session and wasn't it great to finally find out what happened to my mum?'

'Right.' Hannah tried to hide her scepticism, but couldn't help thinking it all sounded a little too convenient.

'I was fuming. Like, how the hell could I have said stuff and not remembered what I said?'

'And the explanation?'

'He said sometimes, when it's a very traumatic memory, your brain doesn't allow you to see it, that kind of thing.'

Hannah kept her face dispassionate.

'But he said it was okay because he would send me the transcript, and I would be able to read it.'

'Which he did?'

'Yes. The next day, as always.'

'So, when you told me it was Ray who killed your mum, it was based on something a psychotherapist told you *you* had said to *him*.'

'Yes. You can see why I didn't want to tell you. I know how it sounds; I know exactly what you're thinking right now. But it's true. I've remembered it all now I've read it back. I remember going to the door. I know what I saw. The memories were just locked up.'

'Do you have the transcript to hand?' Hannah asked.

'Yes.'

'Would you mind if I read it?'

'I ... okay, fine. But ...' Liv sighed. 'You have to keep in mind that I've remembered it since. Okay? It's all true.'

'I'll keep everything you've told me in mind.'

Liv placed her mug on the small coffee table and walked over to the rather charming sideboard in the corner of the room. Hannah suspected it was a collector's piece and was sure Lottie would love to get a look at it.

'Here.' Liv placed a piece of A4 paper in Hannah's lap. 'I print them all out. I find it easier to read on paper.'

'Thanks.' Hannah took the single sheet.

Liv hovered next to her shoulder, clearly ready to reread the words she'd obviously already read many times before.

'Is there something else you can be getting on with?' Hannah asked.

'Erm ...yeah, sure, the dishwasher.'

'Great. I'd like to read through this alone, please.'

45

ANNIE, MAY 2022

ANNIE PERCHED ON A HIGH STOOD, her legs dangling as she took in the atmosphere. People bustled past, speaking untold languages. The sun shone in a cloudless, cornflower blue sky. Everyone seemed happy and relaxed as they strolled past or sat to enjoy a drink. Except Annie, who was far from relaxed. She was about to meet who she was pretty sure was her brother, Jake. She'd messaged him via Facebook. She figured it was best to merely mention that she thought they might be cousins and that she was in Spain. She'd said she'd love to meet him and Emily. Oddly, he had replied that he thought it was best if they met up first, just the two of them. Annie had agreed.

Now, he was ten minutes late and her stress levels were increasing by the second.

Annie swirled the ice in her drink, trying to give the appearance of any old tourist, not someone who was about to experience a life changing event.

Eventually, after twenty minutes and two large gins, she spotted Jake. He was striding confidently across the busy square, dodging tourists in a way that suggested he knew this place well. He anticipated where they would stop and knew the areas where small groups would gather. He was very much at home, and it was clear this was his turf. She clumsily jumped off her stool to greet him, not sure whether a handshake or a hug would be more appropriate.

As soon as he was by her side, he went for the hug. God, he was tall; she felt like a little squirt reaching up to get her arms around him. He wore a smart shirt and well-cut, navy Ralph Lauren shorts. The whiteness of his shirt highlighted his beautiful brown eyes. He smelt lovely.

'You must be Annie,' he said, offering no explanation or apology for his lateness.

'Yes, I am.' She couldn't think of anything else to say as she struggled back up onto her stool.

Supporting her elbow as she did so, he smiled at her.

'Drink? Is it vodka or gin?' He gestured to the remnants in her glass.

'Erm ... well, that was elderflower gin.'

'Uh huh. Tonic or lemonade?'

'Lemonade, please,' Annie requested.

Jake waved at the waiter, who clearly recognised him. Within a minute, another large glass of gin and lemonade appeared in front of her, and a bottled beer was handed to Jake. He pulled a card out of his back pocket and tapped it on the handheld device, nonchalantly.

She thanked him.

'No worries.'

'So ... you live here?' Annie asked, for want of a better conversation starter.

'Yeah. Not far from here.' Jake nodded. 'It's not a bad place to spend your time.'

'I can see that.' She gestured at the clear sky.

'How about you, where do you live?' Jake asked.

'Hampshire.'

'So, you're on holiday?'

'Yes.'

'Well, I can recommend a few places to visit. The cathedral's impressive, although, if you do the rooftop tour, the stairs can be a killer for ...'

Annie raised an eyebrow.

'Older people. Not us, obvs!' Jake laughed.

She laughed, too. 'I might give it a go.'

'The beach is good. But the waves sometimes come in hard. So ...'

'Be careful,' she added.

'All I'm saying is – I once saw a middle-aged woman almost lose her swimming costume out there. She finished up crawling back to shore on her hands and knees, with the rest of her family trying to get her up. Once that current's got you it's nearly impossible to get back on your feet.'

'I'll be sure to take care,' Annie said, adding, 'It's lucky I'm not middle aged, isn't it?'

Jake grinned. 'Sure is. So ... anyway, you think you might be my cousin or something.'

'Umm ...'

'Because I'm a bit confused. I mean, your surname's Farnley, but Dad doesn't have any siblings. So ...?' he shrugged. 'I'm guessing you've got the wrong person. Sorry.'

Annie shuffled on her stool; it wasn't the most comfortable of seats. He didn't know his dad had a brother; what on earth was that about? 'I have the right person, I'm sure of it,' she said.

'So ...?' Jake's eyebrows rose.

'I have something to tell you. Something important. But ...' She glanced around. 'I'd rather we were somewhere a bit more private.' Again, she eyed all the tourists, squashed in at high tables, some only inches away. 'Plus,' she added, 'these stools are bloody uncomfortable.'

'No worries,' Jake said. 'Drink that down, we'll go somewhere quieter.'

The next couple of minutes were spent in silence. She gulped her large, icy gin and lemonade down, and in her head, she went over and over the words she needed to say to Jake. This was going to be harder than she'd thought; it would seem he didn't even know about Martin.

———

Off a side street, away from the busy square, Jake led her to the back of a small bar. It was dark and the inside of the bar was virtually deserted. Of course it was; who would sit inside on such a beautiful day?

'This better for you?' he asked.

'Yes. Thanks. It was just ... I felt like everyone was listening.'

'I get you.'

'I don't know what your dad's told you, but clearly he's kept some things back.'

Jake checked she'd like the same again, then gave their order to a waitress, before replying, 'What kind of things?'

'He honestly never told you he had a brother?'

Jake seemed genuinely shocked.

'A brother?'

'Yes. An identical twin.'

'What the fuck!'

'Sorry. I thought you'd already know this part. I hadn't counted on being the one to tell you.'

Jake shook his head. 'Listen, you really *must* have the wrong man?'

Annie took an old photograph out of her bag. Martin and Ray, in their mid-twenties. She placed it on the table.

'What the hell?' Jake picked it up. 'You sure you didn't just photoshop a picture of my dad?'

She figured this was not a genuine question. The photograph was clearly an original print. 'I'm sure.' Reaching into her bag she found an even older one of the twins as children. This one was black and white. Handing it to Jake, she said, 'I promise you; all this is real.'

'But why?'

'Why?'

'Why keep it from me and Emily?'

'I think I might know the answer to that.'

Their drinks arrived and they sat back to allow the waitress to place them on the table. As soon as she was out of earshot, they leant back in, heads together. Jake asked, almost in a whisper. 'Go on then ... the answer?'

'There was a lot of terrible stuff in your dad's past. I mean *really* terrible.'

Jake leant even closer towards her, his handsome face now an inch away from hers.

'Like what?' he asked, with a morbid curiosity.

46
HANNAH, APRIL 2023

Hannah read with speed, but accuracy.

Transcript for client: Olivia Farnley

From: Stephen Lawson-Ewart, Psychotherapist and Hypnotherapist PsyD.

Date of session: 21/03/23

SLE: Do you feel ready to discuss the night your mother was killed?
OF: Yes.
SLE: Just to remind you, you won't be distressed by anything you see, and you will remain calm at all times. Happy to continue?
OF: Yes.
SLE: What did you have for breakfast, Liv?
OF: A cheese toastie and a coffee.
SLE: Do you remember previously telling me a bit about the night your mum was killed?

OF: Yes. We talked about me being left to look after my brother, Toby.

SLE: You mentioned that your mum returned from running an errand. You heard her footsteps on the wooden floor.

OF: Yes, I did tell you that.

SLE: Previously, we got to the point where you were sitting at the bottom of the stairs in the darkness, and your mother was rummaging through old tea chests.

OF: Mumbled words. (Playing with the rings on her fingers. Her breath quickening.)

SLE: You will remain calm, Liv. You're fine to talk to me about this. (A slight pause.) Are you all right to continue?

OF: Yes.

SLE: Can you remember sitting at the bottom of the stairs?

OF: Yes.

SLE: What happened next?

OF: My mum went to the front door.

SLE: What did you do at this point?

OF: I followed my mum down the hallway. It was really dark.

SLE: Did you see your mum open the front door?

OF: Yes.

SLE: You're doing really well, Liv. So, tell me, what happened next?

OF: My mum stepped out into the street. She pulled the front door to behind her, but she didn't close it shut.

SLE: Did you go over the threshold yourself?

OF: No. I just poked my head around the door.

SLE: What did you see?

OF: I saw my mum arguing in the street.

SLE: Who was she arguing with?

OF: It looked like it was my dad.

SLE: What were they saying?

OF: My mum was denying something. Shaking her head. Saying it wasn't what it seemed. He was really angry. My mum said she didn't want to stay outside on the doorstep. She wanted to go back inside.'

SLE: What did he say?

OF: He said she was ashamed. She kept insisting they go back inside, and he said no. He didn't want to talk about it in front of the kids. But she said – *please, Ray, I don't want to talk about it here.*

SLE: Wait. Stop a second. Are you sure that's what she said?

OF: Yes.

SLE: You heard your mum say the name Ray?

OF: Yes. I did.

SLE: What happened next?

OF: Uncle Ray was being aggressive, threatening all sorts. Mum just wanted to come back inside the house. Then she turned and tried to come back in.

SLE: What did you do?

OF: I ducked back inside for a second.

SLE: And then?

OF: I looked back out and I saw Uncle Ray stopping my mum from coming back into the house. He spun her around and put his hands around her throat.

SLE: Again, Liv, you're absolutely sure it was Ray?

OF: Yes.

SLE: How can you be sure? They were identical.

OF: I just know the difference. I can't explain it.

SLE: Where were you watching from?

OF: I was peeking around the doorframe.

SLE: Did either of them know you were there?

OF: No.

SLE: What happened next?

OF: Uncle Ray started putting pressure on her throat. He was squeezing.

SLE: Did you do anything? Did you move out to the street? Make them aware of you?

OF: No! I was too scared.

SLE: What happened to your mum?

OF: She was trying to fight him off. She whispered something like – please, I can't breathe. She was clawing at his hands around her neck. Then, her body went kind of limp. Like she couldn't hold herself up properly. She tried to get him to take his hands off her throat by slapping at his face.

SLE: Did that help?

OF: No. I think slapping him made him even angrier. He let go of my mum's throat, but then he pushed her back against the wall. She was screaming. Then, she fell backwards.

SLE: What happened next, Liv?

OF: She hit her head on the front wall of the house. She slumped to the ground. There was blood on the back of her head.

SLE: What did your Uncle Ray do?

OF: He just stood there, looking down at Mum. Front doors began to open, and our neighbours came out to investigate the commotion. Oh God, Doris was in her dressing gown!

SLE: Then what happened?

OF: Ray just ran away.

SLE: Liv, is there any doubt in your mind that the person who assaulted your mum was your Uncle Ray?

OF: No doubt whatsoever. I heard her use his name.

SLE: You've done really well, Liv. Now you know who killed your mum, would you like me to wake you up?

OF: Yes, I'm ready.

(SLE counted to ten and taped Liv on the shoulder, waking her from her receptive trance.)

End of transcript.

47
ANNIE, MAY 2022

The next few minutes were filled with Annie explaining to Jake about her mother's death, her father being charged with murder, and his own death in prison. She finished with Ray leaving his mother to cope alone before he went travelling. Throughout the story Jake simply muttered *fuck me* several times.

'So, he obviously finished up in Spain, and it would appear he's done very well for himself,' she concluded.

'You know he's a millionaire, don't you?'

'I suspected he may be.'

'Is that the real reason why you came? To ask for money?' Jake asked.

'No!' Annie tried to sound convincing, although, if she was honest, she wouldn't mind a piece of this evidently large pie. Suddenly, realisation hit. 'That's why you wanted to meet me alone. It's why Emily isn't here, isn't it? You thought I was a gold digger?'

Jake gave an *I'm not sorry* shoulder shrug. 'Like I say, my dad's a rich man; you wouldn't be the first person to try to get your hands on his money.'

'I suppose not. But I can assure you, I am *not* lying, and I'm not here to rinse you.'

'So, why then?' Jake asked, taking a swig of beer.

'Because there's one more thing I haven't told you yet. I only just found it out myself.'

'Right?'

Annie took a deep breath. 'I think Ray is my father. I found my mum's diaries from decades ago, and it's all there in her own handwriting. I think he was the one who got her pregnant with me, not Martin. I believe I'm your half-sister, Emily's too.'

Jake took a second to absorb the latest shocking information.

'I know how it must sound; I'm still getting used to it myself,' Annie said.

'Do you have any siblings? I mean *did* you? Or is it *do* you? Crap, you know what I mean.' Jake gave an almost manic laugh at his own, fumbling attempt to get his head around it all.

'Growing up, I thought Olivia was my sister and Toby was my brother. That's all I knew. They were my only siblings. If I'm right, I've literally just gained another brother and sister in the last week,' Annie said.

'Got any pictures? Like ... on your phone?'

Flicking through her camera reel, Annie wasn't expecting there to be many. But even she was surprised at how few she could find. Scrolling at speed with her thumb, she found one of Toby, taken years ago. She showed it to Jake, explaining that Toby was the brainy one at school.

'He went on to make a lot of money.'

'How?' Jake asked.

'Trading. Banks. I don't know what it all means.'

'Sounds similar to my dad,' Jake said. 'Taking other people's money and turning it into more.'

'Yeah, I guess so. So that's how Ray got rich?'

'Yeah.'

'Legit ... or ...?' Annie tilted her head.

'Probably not to start with. I reckon Dad hung out with some right pieces of shit in the old days, I've heard his stories, but, yeah, nowadays it's all legit. What about Toby?'

'Oh yeah, one hundred percent legal. He wouldn't have done it any other way.'

'Jake pinched the screen and zoomed in on the picture of Toby. 'Weird, isn't it?'

'Weird?'

'He looks a bit like me.'

'Yeah, he does.'

'Got any of your sister?' Jake asked.

Annie took back the phone and continued to scroll. 'Not many. She's ... not worn well.'

Jake laughed.

Annie didn't have the heart to tell him it wasn't a joke. Or to mention that her sister had been on a slow road to ruin since the day their mum had died. Eventually she came across one and handed the phone to Jake, saying, 'This is a photo of a photograph, if you get what I mean. This picture used to be in a frame in the hall at my grandma's. I don't know when I decided to take a shot of it with my phone, or even why, but ... this is Olivia and me.'

Jake glanced at the photo of two little brunettes, with bunches. Both had wonky home-cut fringes. They were standing in a well-kept garden. 'Cute. How old?' he asked.

'Really young. It's before Toby came along,' Annie said. 'We burnt that slide.'

She pointed to the slide in the background behind the two girls.

'Burnt it?'

'Yeah, it was wooden.'

'Why burn it though?'

'I have no idea.' She laughed. 'Something to do with my sister. I forget what though.'

Jake pulled a confused face and gave the phone back.

Annie thought it best to ask to see a photo of Emily, although the truth was of course that she'd already studied all of Jake's family back in her own flat, browsing through his Facebook photos to look for any family resemblances.

He began scrolling through his own camera reel. Eventually, he said, 'This is Emily,' and handed her his phone.

She took it and, as Jake had done before her, pinched the image. Zooming in, she pretended to scrutinise the young girl's face. Not wanting to freak him out, she kept her previous snooping to herself, and simply remarked, 'She's pretty.'

He didn't agree or disagree with her comment; he merely asked, 'Does she look like your sister ... erm, Olivia?'

'Hmmm ... maybe, yeah. Around the eyes,' Annie replied.

'Interesting. I always thought Emily took after our mum. That's her behind Emily in the photo. Her name's Beverley.'

Annie zoomed in on the woman in the background of the photo. She found herself looking at someone so pale she appeared ill. Her hair was insipid and flimsy, as if it was made of fine cotton. She was painfully thin and fragile. Staring off into the distance, she seemed distracted by something that clearly concerned her. Annie hadn't seen this woman before; there were no pictures of her on Jake's Facebook page. A shiver ran through her. If asked to put it into words, she would have to say that Jake's mum had an otherworldly look about her. It seemed a strange choice of photo to keep on your phone, and even stranger to show someone. But she decided that possibly Beverley looked like this in every shot ever taken of her. Besides, she was only in the background, and if your eye wasn't deliberately drawn to her, you could almost miss her. Jake didn't seem to find the photo odd or disturbing, he simply moved on to show her some shots of his dad. She found these images the most intriguing. There was no way of knowing what her own dad, Martin, would've looked like in his sixties or seventies, and she'd only managed to find a couple of shots of Ray on Jake's Facebook feed. But here he was, a much older version of Martin. Drinking by a pool, a rather amazing pool at that, eating in a nice restaurant, and standing proudly next to an extremely flashy car. It was the oddest thing to see what so easily could've been Martin, living another life. She felt tiny pinpricks of tears in her eyes, and quickly blinked them away.

Jake picked up on it. 'Sorry. Is this upsetting you?'

'No ... I ... umm ... I just never saw my dad grow older. Anyway, would you like a drink? It must be my turn,' Annie said. She knew she shouldn't have another gin. The doctor had told her to go easy, and her head was spinning, unpleasantly. But how often did something like this happen?

'Yeah, I'll get another one of these, please?' Jake said, raising his beer bottle in the air.

———

They sat back again to allow the waitress to put their fresh drinks on the table. Then, as if a thought had occurred to him, Jake said, 'Wait a minute. *Annie*. Hmmm.' He chewed the side of his cheek. 'You're not ... Antoinette, are you?'

She nodded.

'*You're* Antoinette Farnley.' He laughed out loud.

'Yes. But I hate my full name. I've never used it. Anyway, it's not that funny.'

'Sorry. It's not that. It's just ... all this time, I thought she was an aged great aunt or something.'

'Who?'

'*You*. Antoinette Farnley.'

'You knew about me?'

'Yeah. I guess I did.'

'How?'

'Because you're in my fucking dad's will.'

48

HANNAH, APRIL 2023

HANNAH READ the transcript document through twice, and then followed the sound of clattering in the kitchen to find Liv. As soon as she entered the room, Liv stopped what she was doing and said, 'See?'

'Mmmm.' Hannah made a noncommittal sound.

'I told you, didn't I? It was Ray.'

'And you remember it now?'

'Yes. I can see and hear it all.'

'Can we go back into the lounge, please?' Hannah said.

Nodding her head, Liv said, 'Yeah, sure. But … what's up?'

'Let's go in the lounge.'

'You don't believe me.'

'Says who?'

'*Says who? Says your face!*'

Hannah turned and made her way back to the chair she'd been sitting in in the lounge. She knew Liv would follow.

Once she'd sat down, she picked up the A4 sheet and scanned it for a third time. Sure enough Liv soon joined her. Hannah asked, 'You had no recollection of any of this when you awoke after this session on the twenty-first?'

'No. Because of the trauma!' Liv spoke as you would to a small child who was struggling to comprehend a very simple concept.

'But that's just another thing this Stephen told you.'

Liv folded her arms across her body. 'You think he made it all up?'

'Not necessarily. But you have to admit, you only thought the killer was Ray once Stephen told you it was.'

'But I've rem—'

'You've remembered it all since. Yes, I got that bit.'

'How would he know so much? Answer me that. How would he know about my mum's ... head hitting the wall?' Liv instantly became tearful.

Hannah felt absolutely shite for having to be the one to throw doubt onto her story.

'I don't know how he would know about your mum's ... injury. Perhaps it was reported at the time. Look, I don't want you to be upset. I can't begin to imagine how terrible all this must be for you.' A horrific image of her own mum being throttled on the front doorstep popped into her head. 'There's no denying you've been through it. But, Liv, you came to me because you wanted me to substantiate that your Uncle Ray was the one who killed your mum. To do that I'm going to need evidence. The burden is on us to prove this; it's not on him to disprove it. Besides, I want to be sure you're not being played by some charlatan.'

'*Played!* For what reason?' Liv asked.

'I don't know yet.'

'Stephen knew everything. He knew Ray ran away, he knew about Mum screaming, the neighbours coming out. That was true; the neighbours did apparently come out because they heard screaming. He knew our neighbour's name, for Christ's sake. He knew *everything*. How could he know if I didn't tell him?' Liv's left leg jiggled repeatedly. It was quite off putting, and very distracting.

'I get you. I really do. But ...' Hannah paused. She knew if she continued to doubt Liv's word, she could simply lose a client. That wasn't going to do either of them any good. She gently rested her hand on Liv's leg to cease the anxious movement. 'He might have researched the case. I'll bet the part about the neighbours was in the papers.'

'Not Doris's dressing gown! For Christ's sake, he knew *everything*, Hannah.'

'Can you honestly say when you think about it now, you see Ray, not Martin?'

'Yes.'

'But ... they were identical.'

'It wasn't my dad. Okay?' Liv said, resolutely. 'It was Ray.'

'Right.' Hannah took a deep breath. 'I'm not saying you're an idiot or anything ...'

'Great start!'

Hannah laughed, embarrassed.

'Sorry. Listen, I did psychology at school. I'm far from an expert, but ... have you ever heard of false memories?'

'No.' Liv shook her head and stuck her chin in the air, defiantly. 'But I suspect you're going to tell me about them.'

'False memories can be placed into your mind. A clever hypnotist can make you think you're remembering something, when in fact they're implanting things into your head that didn't happen.'

'Stephen didn't do that,' Liv snapped. 'He's a professional. He helped that famous person.'

'Which famous person was it, by the way?'

'I can't recall their name. But they were *very* famous.'

'So famous you can't name them,' Hannah said. Reaching for the A4 sheet of paper, she added, 'I need to check Stephen's full name.'

'Why?'

'I'm going to Google him. You must've done the same.'

'No.'

'What? You didn't research him?' Hannah asked, incredulously.

'No.'

'Did you Google *me*?'

'No.'

'Jesus, Liv, you're way too trusting.'

'Why would I Google him when he helped a—'

'Enough about the bloody famous person!' Hannah raised her voice slightly. She got out her phone and typed Stephen's full name into Google. Approximately one second later, she turned her phone around and showed Liv the results on the screen. 'Nothing!'

'You probably spelled it wrong.'

Hannah carefully checked the spelling, before confirming, 'Like I said, *nothing*.'

'But ...' Liv snatched up her own phone and searched Stephen's name. 'What the hell?'

Hannah then typed *false memories* into Google. Again, she turned her screen around and showed the result.

'So what? So some people can remember things that didn't happen. It doesn't mean it's true in my case. Besides, it wasn't false. We both know my mum died.'

Hannah then changed the search to *implanting false memories* and read aloud, 'Studies have shown that it's easy to make people falsely recall small details about events ...'

'*Small details?*'

'Yes. I think somehow, Stephen knew most of what happened to your mum. Possibly some of it from things you told him in your previous sessions, and the rest from goodness knows where. But ... I think it's highly possible that he changed something – the part about the man being Ray. He took details that

were familiar to you, and in them, he embedded a lie.' Waving
the transcript at Liv, Hannah said, 'I don't think *you* actually said
any of this.'

'What?'

'Occam's razor,' Hannah said. 'The simplest explanation for
why you didn't remember saying it when you woke up, was that
you didn't say it!'

'But ... *why?*' Liv asked, her cheeks flushed.

'Who knows?' Hannah threw up her hands. 'Bloody hell, I
wish you'd told me all this at the beginning, before I—'

'Before you what?'

'Before I began investigating.'

'So, what have you detected so far?'

You'd be surprised, Hannah thought. However, she decided to
ignore the question, and simply asked, 'Can you give me this
guy's number, please? I'd love to have a little chat with him.'

Liv blushed further.

'What? You're not going to tell me you never had his number
either? For God's sake, how did you get in touch with him?
Semaphore?' Hannah was seriously beginning to wish she'd
questioned Liv more thoroughly. Covid or not, she ought to
have interrogated her before she flew to Malaga.

'Of course I had his number.'

'Had?'

'Have. I *have* his number. It's just ...'

Placing her hands either side of her head, Hannah gave it a
shake. 'Go on. You might as well say it.'

'That was why I needed to speak to you urgently. I was
thinking about all this yesterday. I was thinking it might be
worth going back to the nick and being more insistent. I was
like ninety-nine percent sure I remembered it, but I wanted to
be really sure. So I figured I'd call Stephen and ask if he could
take me back there. I thought if we went through that night
again, I might be able to see it, properly, the way I saw all the

other stuff. Things like Toby being born and all the childhood memories. That stuff. I thought if I could see it all as clear as day, then I'd know. I could tell you and the fucking police absolutely, categorically that it was Ray.' She finished her speech, gulping for air, before adding, quietly, 'Then I wouldn't have to endure you looking at me like I'm a fuckwit.'

'Sorry ... *again*!'

'It's fine. I get it.'

'Can I take a guess at what happened when you tried to call him to make another appointment?'

'Go ahead. Treat yourself.'

'You can't get hold of him, can you?'

'No, I fucking can't.' Liv rolled herself a cigarette. Opening the lounge window, she lit it and blew the smoke out into the street. 'I tried a few times yesterday. I couldn't believe it when the number was dead. It worked fine before. That's why I asked to meet with you.'

Hannah watched Liv take her anger out on the small roll up, puff after puff, barely requiring oxygen in between. Once it was a tiny stub, she flicked it out of the window, narrowly missing an old man as he made his way slowly past her building.

Hannah flinched. 'Thank goodness you didn't hit him.'

'Who?' Liv asked.

'Nothing.' She shook her head. 'Listen, just because you can't get hold of Stephen on the phone, it doesn't mean we can't try and find him.'

'Okay.'

'Do you think you could take me to the place where he hypnotised you?'

'Sure. But he won't be there now. It's like 7pm.'

'I know, but if you show me where it is, I can pop back there during the day, tomorrow.'

'Okay. Do you want to grab an Uber?'

'I've got my car outside. I'll drive,' Hannah said.

———

They stood outside a matt grey front door, set back from the street and sandwiched between a deli and a charity shop. There was an ornate light above the door, but the bulb was missing, making it dark and eerie in the doorway. To the right they could just about make out a space on the wall where a plaque had once been attached. Liv ran her finger slowly over the four holes left by the screws. Under her breath, she whispered, 'What the hell?'

'This is the place, huh?'

'Yeah.'

Above the door, on the whitewashed wall, there was an estate agent's sign. Hannah pressed the torch on her phone and held it up to read: *Office to let. One large room and reception area. First floor.* This was followed by a telephone number.

'Looks like I'll be calling them first thing tomorrow,' Hannah said, as she typed the number into her phone.

49

ANNIE, MAY 2022

'WAIT! What? I'm in Ray's will?' Annie asked Jake.

'Yeah. What the fuck? I can't believe it's you.'

'How d'you know?'

'He told me.'

'When was this?' Annie couldn't take it in.

'A couple of years back,' Jake said. 'Christ, I remember the fuss he made. He summoned me to his office, like he was the fucking headmaster. What a dick.'

'Can you tell me what happened?' Annie asked.

'Yeah, sure. I remember going into his study, instantly feeling like I'd done something wrong.'

'Why?'

'You haven't met him. That's just how he makes people feel.'

Annie nodded. It didn't seem the right time to remind Jake that of course she had met his dad, albeit a very long time ago.

'So I kind of lobbed myself sideways into one of the comfy seats. I was trying to keep it light, you know? Anyway, my legs dangled over the edge, and straight away he told me to sit properly. He said I'd break the bloody chair.'

'What did you say?'

'I think I told him to keep his hair on.'

'Right. And ...?'

'He said what he had to tell me was important and I needed to listen carefully. So, I sat round in the chair and I listened. I was a bit worried to be honest. I thought maybe he'd been scrutinising my expenses or that he'd found out about some of my ... umm ... recreational habits.' Jake smiled.

'And had he?'

'No, it was all about the will. He said, *I'll cut to the chase – it's this flammin' virus. All this lockdown stuff has got me spooked.* I told him he'd be okay, that they'd have a vaccine soon. I asked him if he was seriously worried. He said something nauseating, like, *I'm not worried about myself; if I die, I die, there's not much I can do about it.* What a martyr. He was worried about my mother. She's not the strongest of women. Then he said he was also worried about Emily.'

'Emily?'

Jake nodded. 'I know. Pathetic. I told him Emily was twenty-one years old. She'd be fine. It was only old people who were getting stuck on ventilators. They were the ones who were likely to croak.'

'I don't suppose that went down well,' Annie said.

'No. He banged his fist on the desk and told me not to be so disrespectful. He said something like, *Those old people you're talking about have lives, people who love them. This is not a joke.* Like I'd said it was. Then he told me that he knew I'd been out. He didn't think I was sticking to the rules. Stupid twat said I'd been to raves. I was like, *Raves! Jesus, Dad, I'm twenty-five years old. I don't go to raves any more.* He said whatever I wanted to call it, he knew I'd been out.'

'And ...? Had you?'

'The bars were closed. We had to wear masks everywhere. Where the hell did he think I'd been going?'

'So, when did he mention the will?' Annie was becoming

impatient. She liked a good story as much as the next person, and it was interesting to see Jake opening up, but sod it, this was torture.

'I'd had enough, I said that as lovely as it was to chat about lockdown and all that, could he tell me what he actually wanted to speak to me about? That's when he told me he'd written a new will. The previous one was years old. It was written before he had much to leave, apparently. I hoped it was going to be good news; I really needed an injection of cash.'

'And ... was it?'

'He said he was leaving the villa and the contents of his personal accounts to my mum and Emily. A fifty/fifty split. With the proviso that I could live in the villa for as long as I need to. I was like, *What the fuck? Why them?* I think I jumped up out of my chair. I'm not gonna lie – I was furious.'

Annie nodded, 'I can see why.'

'He told me to let him finish. Said I was too hot-headed. Then he said that he'd always taken care of Mum, and he intended to do so long after he was gone.' Jake took a long swig from his bottle, then continued, 'I asked what about me? And he said he was leaving the business to me. Well, of course, I was like, *The business? All of it?* He said, *Not quite all of it, it's another fifty/fifty split.* I thought he meant Mum again, but he said no, it was someone else. He was all mysterious, saying there were reasons behind his decisions. He wanted Emily and Mum to be safe always; he wanted them to have the villa to live in for the rest of their lives. But he also needed to leave the business to someone. He knew I thought he should step down and let me have a crack at it. Well ... he should've, he was already in his seventies for Christ's sake.'

'So why d'you think he didn't step down?'

'I asked him, and he said that I knew why. We just stood there, staring at each other across the desk. Until, eventually, I said, *Why don't we pretend like I don't know, and you just tell me?* He reckoned it was because I would run it into the ground. I tried to protest, but the bastard wouldn't allow me to speak. He raised his hand and carried on, getting louder every second. He told me I didn't have the business acumen; I wouldn't respect the advice Don and Mitch gave me.'

'Don and Mitch?'

'Two fucking minions, who are always trying to lick his arse. He said they had bloody good brains. The pair of them. They knew about finance. They weren't playing at businessmen, like I was. I argued that I worked for the firm, just the same as they did.'

'What did he say?'

'That I swanned into the office late, well at least I did before lockdown, and that I just wandered about. I told him people in that place respected me, and he said, *You're the boss's son, of course they do!* I'd had enough by this point. I said if I was so useless, why leave the business to me?' Jake took another swig of beer. He was clearly agitated.

'Go on.'

'He said that at the end of the day, I was his son and he wanted me to have something to keep me going, a means of making money. But ... there were conditions. Until I turned twenty-eight, even if he died, I'd have no way of making the big decisions. Those would be left to those fucking nodding dogs, Don and Mitch.'

'Jeez, I bet that didn't feel good.'

'I was fuming on the inside. Twenty-eight was nearly three years away then, and in the current climate of fear and uncertainty, it felt like an age. I asked why twenty-eight? It seemed like a strange number.'

'Yeah, I was wondering that, too,' Annie agreed.

'Apparently, that's the age he was when he began to understand proper business, and, in his own words, when he stopped being a little dick. It just kind of clicked into place and he started to get his priorities right and make good investments. He said he was hoping for the same for me. And ... like he'd said, it would be a fifty/fifty split. I'd own half the company, and even after the age of twenty-eight, I'd still need to agree everything with the other person. I was so curious to know who the other person was that I even ignored the fact that he'd blatantly just called me a dick.'

'And ... it was me?' Annie asked.

'Yeah. He said it was a relative of his, called Antoinette Farnley. He said I'd never met her. She was from his past.'

'Well, that's bloody true enough!' Annie fumed.

Jake continued, 'I asked if this Antoinette woman knew about all this, and he said, *No, she will do though, when I die.* I remember saying, great, so, me and this old bird will run the company together, after I'm twenty-eight? He just said only if he was dead. He didn't correct me; he didn't tell me you weren't a decrepit old aunt. He just let me carry on thinking that you were. I asked what made him think Antoinette was going to be any more sensible than I was.'

'And ...?' Annie leant forward in her seat.

'He said, and I had no idea what he meant, that he hoped she would have taken after Susan.'

Annie drew in her breath. 'Cheeky bastard!'

'Anyway, the cleaners witnessed the will, and it was couriered to Dad's solicitor in London. I've known for two years that the company will be mine one day.'

'Ours!' Annie corrected him.

'Yeah, okay. Ours,' Jake mumbled.

50

HANNAH, APRIL 2023

HANNAH WAS DELIGHTED to get through to the letting agents without any problems at 9am the following day. They were able to offer a viewing for later the same day. Dying to see the place, she agreed readily.

A small, round woman was outside the office when Hannah arrived. She introduced herself as Jean. Her vivid purple hair added a hint of bravado to her otherwise prim exterior. She appeared to be in her sixties, and Hannah found it amusing that back in the day the only older women you saw with purple hair were the blue rinse brigade. Nowadays, you saw so many women in their fifties and sixties with deep purple or bright pink hair. It was their way of embracing their autumn years. Jean appeared to be very proud of her vibrant locks. She clearly considered herself a rebel. There was definitely more than a hint of the proud peacock in the way she moved her head and constantly touched her hair. Hannah smiled to herself and decided one day she might go for a similar shade. Jean opened the front door with two separate keys and pushed it open.

The first thing that struck Hannah was the fact that there was not a large pile of unread post on the floor, as one might expect to find in a recently vacated office. It would seem that no one was writing to Mr Stephen Lawson-Ewart.

They were immediately faced with a narrow, carpeted flight of stairs. Hannah indicated she would go last and watched as Jean's sizeable backside jiggled its way up.

They entered a small reception area, which was just large enough for a desk and chair, but not much else. However, there was no furniture. Jean made an unnecessary point of saying that the whole place was for rent unfurnished. She then pushed a door and led them into the main room. It was beautifully decorated in a dusky grey; one wall was papered in the highest quality wallpaper, which featured delightful drawings of birds. Hannah tried to imagine Liv sitting, or lying, she had forgotten to ask, somewhere in this room, and Stephen sitting next to her, somehow placing her into a trance. Could there be some truth in it all? If not, how the hell had he known all about Susan's death?

Jean's voice broke into her thoughts.

'So, what are you planning to use it for?'

'Huh?'

'The office. What business are you thinking of running from here?'

'Oh, right. We have a renovation business. Refurbed furniture, upcycled, repurposed, that kind of thing. We could use it as a showroom.' Hannah shrugged, improvising.

'Good luck getting furniture up those stairs,' Jean scoffed, before clearly remembering she was supposed to be persuading Hannah to rent the place, and adding, 'But it'd be no problem for a youngster like you, I suppose.'

Hannah agreed. 'We'll be fine. We can use it for the smaller pieces, and use the reception area as an office for the paperwork and such.'

'Good idea.' Jean nodded enthusiastically, her fluffy, purple hair dancing in time.

'I mean, just because my friend didn't make a go of it here, doesn't mean I can't, does it?' Hannah said.

'You knew the guy who rented it last?' Jean asked.

Hannah tried to paint herself into the role of a friend of someone called Stephen Lawson-Ewart.

'Yes.'

'Well, then you'll know it's not that he didn't make a go of it. He only wanted it for a short while.'

'Oh yeah. That's what I meant.'

'We don't usually do three month lets. Too short. Not worth the paperwork. But Mr Farnley needed to use it as a short-term office, and he was prepared to pay a very decent monthly rent, so it seemed like a good idea. Now we're left with his decoration. Which is nice, but not to everyone's—'

Hannah's heart was banging in her chest as she interrupted Jean. 'It's funny to hear you call him Mr Farnley. I only ever think of him by his first name. What with us being mates. Odd when that happens, isn't it?' She waited, holding her breath, hoping the gamble would pay off.

Jean was still gazing at the wallpaper. 'I suppose it would be okay for a renovation place. Possibly a little flashy. But who doesn't love birds?'

Hannah tried one more time. 'I never think of him as Mr Farnley.' She raised her voice a little. 'To me he's just ...' She paused. One beat. Two. A tilt of her head, and a cocked eyebrow.

'Toby,' Jean replied.

'Yes, Toby,' Hannah said, exhaling.

51

ANNIE, MAY 2022

'So, now you're just waiting for Ray to die,' Annie said.

Jake laughed. 'Bit harsh!'

'Harsh, but fair?' Annie said. Undeniably, she was surprised at how quickly Jake's true feelings about Ray had come out, but she wasn't surprised to hear that he didn't like his dad much. The way Ray had treated her grandma was so thoughtless and uncaring, she could've guessed he wouldn't be a great parent. 'I mean – he's clearly not going to hand anything over to you while there's still air in his lungs,' she added.

'I must admit, I do sometimes feel like Prince Charles.' Jake laughed again. 'Waiting to take over.'

'You've not waited *that* long.'

'Look, seeing as you've got a bit of a stake in this thing, too, I'll come clean. I turn twenty-eight in January next year, and I need the money that's tied up in his company. Right now, I don't even care how I get it.'

'How's his health?' Annie asked.

'Too fucking good.'

'You've been honest with me, so I'll be honest with you,' she said. 'I didn't have a great relationship with my own dad –

Martin,' she clarified. 'When I was little, things were fine, he had pet names for me and Olivia, he was loving. But, by the time he died, there was a distance between us. In my mum's diary she said he referred to me as the c ... c ...' She hiccupped. 'C ... cuckoo in the ... nes ...' She hiccupped again. 'Nest.'

'That's easy for you to say!' he joked.

She ignored him, pressing on, 'But ... how could he have known that? It's like he sensed the truth. But ... whatever ... I grew up thinking he was my dad, and I was absolutely fine to keep on thinking that. Despite everything, it was a simple fact. Now, it seems that I have a different dad, and I'm angry. I think Ray was told he had a child, and he buggered off. He never once tried to get in touch with me, or my grandma. I know he's your dad, but he's an arsehole.'

'I don't blame you for thinking that.'

'Well, you know him, is he ...?' She hiccupped again. 'Is he an arsehole?'

'Pretty much.'

'What if something were to happen to him? An accident or something,' Annie asked. 'Then you and I would inherit his company.'

'*Jesus!* You're nowhere near as cute and bubbly as you first appear!'

'I'm just saying.' She'd surprised herself. Maybe it was the gin talking.

'Oh yeah, I know exactly what you're *just saying*,' Jake laughed. 'But ... you gotta take me out to dinner before you fuck me, darling.'

'What?' Annie gave her head a shake.

He laughed again, clearly finding this whole conversation hysterical. 'Don't panic! I mean – you went straight in with the *what if something happened to him* line. For all you know I could love my dad dearly and be well offended by that.'

'Do you? I mean – are you?'

'Nah. I'm not offended. Just surprised at how fucking bold you are.'

'So? Answer the question – what if something were to happen to him?'

'It would be impossible. Far too risky.' Jake shook his head.

'Why?'

'Because he's very well known in Marbella. Anything happens to him here, and everyone would know exactly who was involved. There are eyes and ears everywhere.'

'Shame.'

'Are you for real?' Jake said.

'What d'you mean?'

'I mean – is this like some crazy TV show?'

'No!' Annie giggled.

'Are you wearing a wire? Working for the police?' Jake's face suddenly showed a flash of anger.

'Of course not.'

'You're seriously meeting me for the first time, telling me you think you're my sister, and you're also the person mentioned in my dad's will, and, if that's not enough for one fucking day, you're saying you wouldn't mind if *something* happened to him?'

She nodded.

'Wow!'

The pair of them leant back in their seats, both realising, a little too late, that they ought to have kept an eye on the room. They glanced from side to side, checking no one else had entered the bar, and that they weren't being overheard. Luckily, it seemed they weren't.

Annie spoke first. 'If you say it's too risky, then it's too risky. We'll just have to wait for mother nature to take him.'

'You really don't like him, do you?' Jake said.

'He left without a backwards glance. What about you?' Annie asked. 'Do you love him?'

Jake considered the question. 'Would I be a bad person if I said no?'

'I think we've gone beyond judging each other, don't you?'

'My dad always looks out for Emily and my mum; he thinks they're a pair of delicate little flowers who need to be held very, very carefully. But me, no way, he seems to think *I* need tough love.'

'Right.'

'Plus, like I said, he doesn't think I've got two fucking brain cells to rub together. Despite spending a fortune on my education. Imagine thinking those stupid old duffers could run the place better than *I* can.'

'It wouldn't be just *you*. It would be *you* and *me*!' Annie corrected him.

'Yeah, *us*,' Jake said.

'There's a huge difference between being pissed off at him, and wanting him …' Annie ran her finger across her throat, dramatically.

'I know. But I'm telling you, for me it's the latter. I'm sick of him controlling my finances. I'm twenty-seven years old, and he still looks at everything I spend my money on.'

'Technically it's *his* money.'

Jake ignored her comment. 'I've had to become inventive lately. Find other ways of making money. And let's say they don't always pay off.'

'So, you have good reason to want him gone?'

'Yes, I do. And *you*?'

'Yeah. I'm raging. Plus, I could do with some money myself. I've never had anything of my own. My flat's rented. My car's old. Not much to show for a life.'

Annie felt her old foe depression settle on her shoulders.

Jake called the waitress over and, despite Annie's protests, ordered them another round of drinks. Once the waitress had left, Annie said, 'And how dare Ray mention my mum?'

'Your mum?'

'She was Susan.'

Jake nodded. 'Right. Like I said, I did wonder what the old fool was talking about.'

'Fancy saying he hoped I'd taken after her. What did he know about her?'

'Quite a bit, according to her diary,' Jake said. 'You know Susan is Emily's middle name, don't you?'

'No. How would I know?'

'Sorry. I forgot. It's kind of like you're part of the family.'

'He's a bastard for giving Emily my mum's name. If he hadn't slept with his brother's wife, she'd probably still be alive today.'

Their drinks arrived, and despite saying she couldn't manage another one, Annie took a long drink of gin. God, her emotions were all over the place.

Interrupting her thoughts, Jake asked, 'How do you feel about the fact your dad killed your mum?' He swigged his beer. 'That's got to be one big head fuck!'

She took another gulp of gin and lemonade. Her head was swimming; they didn't believe in measures here. 'It ish what it ish,' she slurred. 'I've had decades to realise I can't change it.'

'And it was definitely Martin?'

'He always said it wasn't, but …' She shrugged. 'Several of the neighbours saw him.'

'Conclusive then.'

'Try telling Olivia that?'

'What does *she* think?' Jake asked.

'Olivia has always said she can't believe it was our dad who did it. My brother was asleep, and I was out; she was the only person who could've seen it. She's made her whole life about that fact. She always says she thinks she saw something. But she can never say what. We were all traumatised by it, but she took it the hardest. She has this stupid theory about a stranger coming along and strangling our mum. But the neighbours saw what they saw. They all identified our dad.'

'And he died in prison.'

'Yesh.' She slurred again, shook her head, and concentrated harder on pronouncing her words. 'He was going to appeal. But ... prisons are dangerous places. Stuff happens.'

Nodding, Jake said, 'Shame we can't put Dad in one of them then.'

'Yeah. Too right,' she agreed.

They sat in silence for a minute, their expressions blank, both absorbing the enormity of what they had somehow just agreed upon.

Eventually, Jake said, in a whisper, 'If he died in prison ... there'd be no questions asked. He'd have been extradited to the UK. I could be here. Miles away.'

'True. I guess ...' she suggested, also in a hushed voice, 'the neighbours could well think Ray was Martin if they saw him in the street at night.'

'I guess they could.'

They drank in silence, then Jake said, tentatively, 'Supposing ... hypothetically ... you wanted to set something like that up. Who would you tell?'

'You'd have to go to the police with new evidence.'

'What about your sister?'

'What about her?' Annie yawned.

'Could you convince her that you think it was Ray who did it?'

'Ummm ... I don't see why she'd believe me.'

'It'd be good though, wouldn't it? If she was the one who reported it. Keep it all nice and far away from us.'

'S'pose so.' Her lips were beginning to feel numb.

'And you did say she's always talked about it not being your dad.'

'But how would we convince her it was Ray?'

'What's she like?'

'In what erm ... what way?'

Annie was struggling to keep up with the conversation, and wished she'd switched to Fanta several drinks ago.

'Personality, naivety, that kind of thing. Is she gullible? Does she believe in spiritual stuff?'

'She's pretty flaky.'

'Do you think she could be hypnotised?'

'*Hypnotised?*' Annie giggled. 'Who the hell are you going to get to do that?'

'I know someone,' Jake replied.

52

HANNAH, APRIL 2023

HEADING FOR LIV'S PLACE, Hannah wondered, could she stop for petrol, a drink, a snack, anything to delay delivering the news about Toby? As she drove, she scanned the pavement for a fallen elderly person or a lost child, any valid reason to stop and help, and thus not go to Liv's.

Halfway there, her phone began to ring. Pulling over into a supermarket car park, she checked the screen. Thank God, it wasn't Liv.

'Hi, Lottie.'

'When do you think you'll come back, Han?'

'I don't know. Things have gone decidedly Pete Tong here. You are not going to—'

'Please come back.'

'What's happened?' The hairs on the back of Hannah's neck stood to attention and her palms instantly became sweaty.

'It's Jake ...'

If that playboy has hurt her! 'What's he done?'

'He's not been in touch.'

'Is that all? I've only been gone five minutes.'

'I've messaged him a couple of times and tried to call. His phone's constantly unavailable.'

'I'll be back as soon as I can,' Hannah reassured her friend. 'But I've got stuff to do here first. I expect he's partying somewhere.'

'I've not heard from him since he didn't show up at the tapas place.'

'Lottie, I don't think you should worry. He's old enough to look after himself.'

'I know. But … before, he was contacting me loads.'

'I'll deal with what I need to here and then I'll head back.'

'What was it Liv wanted to talk to you about?'

'I'll tell you when I see you. There could be lots more by then.'

'Oh, okay.' Lottie sounded a little concerned.

'I'll be back as soon as possible.'

'Thanks, Han.'

'Text me if lover boy turns up.'

'He's not my—'

'Just text me.'

'Will do,' Lottie agreed.

———

Liv opened the door before Hannah had the chance to ring the bell.

'Well?'

'Hi. Can I come in?' Hannah swallowed hard.

She'd only been present at the delivery of one agony message during her short career in the police. On that occasion she hadn't had to give the news personally, she was merely there to support. But she remembered the rules; hat on at the door, make sure you remove it once you enter the home. Well, that wasn't an issue today. Make it clear the person has died, never use a confusing euphemism. Refer to the person by name, never *the body*. Again, not an issue today. There was no body. Her news for Liv was not about a death, but a terrible betrayal by a beloved relative. Above all, she knew she must be kind, but not allow herself to become over-emotional.

Clearly sensing the seriousness on Hannah's face, Liv's eyebrows disappeared into her slightly greasy fringe.

'What is it?'

Taking a small step inside the front door, Hannah repeated her request to come in.

'Yes ... erm ... sure.'

She followed Liv into the lounge and gestured towards the armchairs.

Like an obedient dog, Liv took a seat and looked up at Hannah, her eyes already filling with tears, which she was desperately trying to blink away.

'What is it? You're scaring me!'

Hannah took the seat opposite Liv. Immediately, her throat closed up. So much for not getting over-emotional. This was going to break Liv's heart. Hannah remembered the other rule of the agony message: get to the point, don't go all around the houses.

'I got the name of the person who rented the office from the estate agent.' Aware of the rules, she left no pause. 'Liv, I'm really sorry. It's Toby.'

'Toby?'

'Uh huh.'

'*My* Toby?'

'Yes.' Hannah rose from her seat and stepped towards Liv, ready to provide whatever support she could.

'My brother, Toby, rented the place I went to for hypnosis?'

'Yes.'

'Not possible.' Liv gnawed at the little snags of skin next to her right thumbnail, causing tiny droplets of blood to appear.

Hannah wasn't surprised by the denial; she was expecting it.

'I get what you're saying, but the letting woman, Jean, she said it herself – Mr Toby Farnley. Now I don't know why he was doing that or what he was trying to prove by getting someone to convince you Ray killed your mum, but—'

'Toby's dead.'

'I honestly think ...' Hannah did a double take. 'You what?'

'I said he's dead.'

'What? When?'

'Toby died over seven years ago. Autumn 2015.'

'But ... he's paying for all this?'

'Yes. His money pays for everything. But he, sadly, is dead.'

'What happened?'

'Cancer. He dodged the bullet once, but it got him the second time.'

Hannah felt as if all the air had been punched out of her.

'I'm so sorry, Liv. You never ...'

'Never said? No, I suppose I didn't. The fact is, I still talk to him every day, and ... well, I just knew him so well that I often hear his response. He still lives in here.' Liv touched her head. 'And in here.' This time her heart. 'But the horrible truth is, he no longer lives anywhere else.'

'So you *inherited* his money? Was this *his* flat?'

'Yes. He left the flat to me and he arranged for an income to be sent direct to my bank every month. He knew if he left me a lump sum, I'd blow it. He was very blunt about the fact he didn't want me spending it on drink and drugs.'

'Sensible.'

'Yes. He had time to organise everything. We knew he was terminal for a long while. He set it all up. He arranged for enough to come to me so that I could have a good life, but not so much that I would ... go mad.'

'He sounds amazing.'

'He is. I mean ... was. See, I still struggle to accept it.'

'Did he make the same arrangement for your sister?'

'No.' Liv shook her head.

'She was allowed hers as a lump sum?' Hannah said.

'No. Sorry, you misunderstood. She didn't get an inheritance.'

Hannah failed to hide her disapproval. Why?'

'It's like I told Stephen.' Liv paused. 'If that really is his name. Annie separated herself from me and Toby. She never wanted to be a part of us. She left us when we were two broken children, and she never really came back.'

'I see.' Being an only child, Hannah struggled to put herself into either Liv or Annie's shoes. She was dying to ask how Annie could do that, but feared she might upset Liv.

'Toby left her a one-off payment. About £10,000 I think.'

Hannah glanced around the flat.

'So, a fraction of what he gave you?'

'Yes. This place alone cost him a couple of hundred thousand when he bought it years ago.'

'And your sister didn't ... erm ... mind?'

'Who knows? Like I say, we're not close.'

'You don't even follow each other on Facebook or Instagram?'

'I can't stand social media,' Liv replied.

'Right,' Hannah said. 'I'm still trying to get my head around the fact that your brother died.'

'Me too!'

'How did you cope?'

'I didn't. Losing Toby was the most painful thing you can imagine. It was like losing my mum and my dad both in the same second.'

'I guess that's why you still speak to him in your head.'

Liv sighed as she asked, 'Do you have other heartbeats to worry about, Hannah?'

Hannah nodded. 'Yes.'

'Who?'

'Well, umm ... my parents, my best friend, my granny, my employee ... they're the first names that come to mind.'

'That's lovely.' Liv gave a sad smile. 'I have none. The only heartbeat that affects me is my own. Losing Toby was the end of caring about anyone but me. I will never worry about another heartbeat again.'

'I'm sorry.' Hannah knew her condolences were not enough to fix this poor woman who had suffered too many losses and too much heartache to ever heal. Was it any wonder she often turned to drink and drugs? She must want to block out life on a regular basis.

Liv began to cry.

'He fought so bloody hard.' She twirled the rings on her thumbs. 'He didn't want to leave me. *He* was worried about *me*. Can you believe that? He was thirty-one-fucking-years-old, about to die, and *he* was worried about *me*.'

'Not fair.' Hannah stated the obvious.

'No, it wasn't. I wished it could've been me. I wanted to die for him. If I could've swapped ... Toby was clever ... he was so smart. He could've been anything. And he was clean. Clean and pure. I was a waste of space. And *he* died, not me. How does that work?'

'There's no rhyme or reason.'

'After he died, I tried to join him.'

'Oh ...?'

'Not like you're thinking. I didn't attempt anything serious. I just stopped caring. I took everything on offer. I drank like a fish. I didn't care what the consequences were because nothing could ever be as bad as the fear that gripped my body every single day.'

'Fear?'

'Yes, fear.'

'In what way?' Hannah asked.

'The fear that I would never see Toby again. That I was going to have to spend the rest of my life with this gaping hole in my chest. People don't talk about it. When they're bereaved, they say they're fucking heartbroken, they're bloody angry, a swear word salad of emotions. But no one ever says *I'm so frightened because I don't know if I can get over this.*'

Hannah waited for Liv's tears to subside a little, before saying, 'So, it's clearly not Toby who rented the office and arranged for some guy to hypnotise you.'

'Clearly.'

'Who is it then? Can you think of anyone else?'

'No. I don't get it. Why do this to me?' Liv asked.

'I don't know. But I intend to find out,' Hannah replied.

53
ANNIE, MAY 2022

ANNIE LED JAKE into her holiday apartment. Knowing the kind of place he and his family were used to, she felt somewhat ashamed.

Jake looked around; it didn't take long. The only piece of furniture was a double bed in the middle of the room. Along the left-hand wall there was a work surface, which held the microwave and matching red toaster and kettle, a sink and a tiny draining board. Above the draining board there was a small wall cupboard. There was nowhere for Annie to hang her clothes, so they remained in an open suitcase, next to the bed, spilling out on to the floor. A door to their right was slightly ajar; it was unnecessarily labelled *bathroom*. This room contained a WC, a shower and a minuscule sink. It was clear from Jake's face he was not impressed with the apartment one iota. But he mumbled something along the lines of, 'Yeah ... like ... cosy.'

'It was all I could afford,' Annie volunteered, defensively, still struggling a little to get her tongue around her s sounds.

'I wasn't—'

'I told you; I've not got much money.'

'What about your hot shot brother?' Jake asked. 'Can't he lend you some?'

'Sorry. I didn't say – Toby died of cancer. A few years ago.'

'Oh right. Erm … sorry.' Jake shuffled from one foot to the other.

'He left me a tiny bit of money. But most of it went to Olivia.'

'Bummer,' Jake said.

'Yeah.'

'Must've been tough, you know to lose him after your parents.'

'It was. Olivia refuses to accept it to this day.'

'Right … umm.'

'Anyway, like I say, I wasn't going to spend what little Toby left me on a lavish holiday, was I?'

'I didn't—'

Annie continued with her rant. 'We don't all have Daddy's money in our pockets.'

They stood inside the doorway, Jake clearly not sure what to do now that Annie had become a somewhat belligerent drunk. After a second, he said in a steady voice, trying to calm the choppy waters, 'Look, I'm not judging you. I get why you didn't want to spend a lot on a flash apartment. You didn't know what reception you'd get.'

She nodded. 'Exactly. And how was I supposed to know I was in Uncle Ray's will?'

'You couldn't have known.'

'Too right.'

'So,' Jake gently edged her into the room, 'why don't you sit down, and I'll get you a coffee, or something.'

Annie made her way over to the bed and perched on the edge.

'I haven't got any coffee. I only arrived yesterday, and it's not included in this lavish kitchen.' She waved her hand at the tiny work surface. 'Besides, there's no bloody fridge for milk.'

'Water, then?' he asked.

'Yes,' Annie snapped, adding quietly, 'Please.'

Jake opened the wall cupboard, into which the owner had crammed two glasses, two mugs, two bowls and two plates, plus a small amount of mismatched cutlery. He ran the tap for a while and then handed Annie a glass of water. She took it, thanked him, and gulped it down, suddenly aware that she had a headache.

'Can I use your loo?' he asked.

Annie cocked her head in the direction of the door to the right.

Once he was back in the main part of the apartment, there was nowhere else for Jake to go but to also perch on the edge of the bed.

'Right. So ... you wanted to explain about this hypnotising thing?' she said.

'Yeah. I'm sorry we had to come here. It was those people choosing to come and sit right next to us. For Christ's sake, they had the whole place.'

'Twats,' Annie agreed.

'And I can't take you back to mine. We can't risk Dad seeing you if we're going to ...'

'I get it. I know why you're here. So ...?'

'I think it might be possible to convince your sister, under hypnosis, that she saw Ray kill your mum.'

Annie gave a giant guffaw. 'You watch too much TV, mate.'

'I think I can do it.'

'You?'

'Yes.'

'You're the one who's going to hypnotise Olivia?'

'Yes.'

'Are you serious?'

'Absolutely.'

'You can make her think she saw Ray?'

'I don't know. I've never tried anything that ambitious before. But I do think I can get her into a receptive trance.'

Annie raised her eyebrows; the question was obvious.

'I studied psychology at uni. Part of the course was alternative therapy classes. I chose hypnosis. Turns out I'm pretty good.' He gave a broad grin. 'I'm not lying.'

'Go on then.'

'What?'

'Do me!'

'Hypnotise *you*?'

'Yeah, come on Billy Big Bollocks, shhhow me what you're made of,' Annie slurred.

'Look,' Jake sighed. 'It's really not ethical to hypnotise you when you're ... umm.'

'What?'

'Well, you're pretty wasted.'

'Soooo?'

'I'm just saying. I'm not meant to—'

'Are you telling me you've never tried it on some poor unsuspecting pissed woman?'

'I ...'

'Of course you have. Besides, it's just me, we're family. It'll be fine.'

'You're sure?'

'Yesh!'

'Well, okay then.'

'Great!' Annie laughed. 'What do I have to do?'

'Lie down,' Jake said, giving her a tiny push backwards.

He remained balanced on the edge of the bed, and she shuffled in a rather ungainly fashion upwards, until she lay on the hard mattress, awaiting further instructions, unsure what to expect.

Her dress had ridden up to her waist during her manoeuvres.

Jake stood and covered her in the thin quilt. Returning to his perch, he began talking to her in a calm, relaxed voice.

'Can you count down from two hundred, please, Annie?'

'Out loud?'

'Either way.'

'Okay.' She began counting quietly.

Jake said, 'Your eyes are very heavy.'

'Of course they are, I've had about six enormous gins.'

'Shush. You've got to try.'

'Okay. Sorry,' she giggled, and resumed counting.

After a minute, Jake said, 'Your eyes are very heavy.' He pressed on, without a pause, giving her no opportunity to answer with a smart remark. 'And all your muscles feel like they're melting into the bed. You can hear my voice and you will be able to answer my questions.'

Perhaps he was right, she did feel very ... what was the word he'd used ... receptive.

After a few minutes and several references to how relaxed she was, Jake said, 'I'm going to start asking you some questions now, okay?'

'Mmmmmm.'

'Are you ready?'

'Mmmmmm.'

'You'll hear me, and you'll be able to answer straight away. Okay?'

'Mmmmmm.'

'Annie, what did you have for breakfast this morning?'

54

NANCY, JULY 1970

As Derek carried her back to the place she dreaded most, Nancy could think of only one thing to do that might hurt him. Grabbing his hand, she bent her head and placed one of his dirty fingers into her mouth, biting down on it with her sharp little teeth.

Letting out a yell, he dropped her to the floor, shouting, 'You vicious little bitch!'

Nancy tried to scrabble away, but she wasn't able to get back up onto her legs; instead she found herself crawling on all fours, like an animal. All the time Derek was bent over her, making a grab for her legs. She turned onto her back, kicking out at his face, his hands, anything she could make contact with. She couldn't explain it, but she felt suddenly strong, like a magic potion was mixing with her blood.

As Derek managed to get a hold of her ankle, Nancy heard her sister call out, 'Leave her alone!'

Both Derek and Nancy turned to see Patty walking towards them. Behind her back she was dragging the axe that Derek used to cut the logs.

Derek began to laugh.

'You can't lift that, you stupid kid.'

Nancy thought maybe Patty also had the magic potion in her blood, because, although it did indeed look very heavy, Patty gave a loud grunt and swung the axe in the air.

'Put that thing down; you'll hurt someone!' Derek called out.

'Let her go!' Patty instructed.

Derek began pulling Nancy by her ankle towards him. She knew that in a second, he would scoop her up again and she would be destined for the room she hated. She kicked out at him with her bare feet. As her foot made contact with his face, one of her horrible long toenails dug into his eye. It felt disgusting. His eye was squashy. It wasn't her fault; he should have cut their toenails like Mummy used to do after a hot, bubble bath.

Derek instantly let go of her ankle. Screaming in pain, he fell to the floor and rolled onto his back. His hand cupped his eye, and he snarled out some bad words, all about how much he hated the girls, and what he was going to do once he got them back inside.

Nancy focused on her sister. There was a look on her face. The look she used to get when they ran a race, and she was determined to win.

The next second, Patty swung the heavy axe again.

Shouting, 'Move out of the way, Nancy!' Patty aimed her swing at Derek. With a horrible sound, like a pumpkin being carved, the blade of the axe buried itself deep into the side of Derek's neck.

Immediately blood began spurting out of the wound. So much blood. More blood than Nancy could ever have imagined. Derek made a series of gurgling sounds and his eyes rolled around in his head. The blade remained lodged in his neck as Patty let go of the handle.

'Patty!' Nancy cried out. She wasn't sure if she was checking Patty was okay or scolding her sister for doing such a horrendous thing.

'I couldn't let him take you back down there,' Patty said.

In the middle of all the commotion, a neighbour came around the side of the house. The poor woman immediately let out a scream and fell to the floor. Her scream in turn caused more people to arrive. One of them tried to usher the girls away from the man on the ground, telling them that they mustn't look. But not before the girls had the chance to watch him, his face the colour of the porridge he had forced them to eat every day for well over a year, encircled by his own blood, as he drew one last rattly breath.

'You shut your fucking mouth, Derek,' Nancy heard Patty say, as the sound of sirens filled the air.

55

HANNAH, APRIL 2023

SHE'D BEEN UPDATING Dave on the developments as they'd occurred. Now, she sent him a very brief text, 'Toby Farnley's dead. He died nearly eight years ago!' Within five minutes she'd received two replies. The first was a series of shocked face emojis, which Dave *rarely* used, and the words, *Call that an alibi?* This was swiftly followed by an intriguing text, 'Have I got news for you!!!' Dave *never* used exclamation marks.

———

Leaving Liv's place, Hannah made her way over to Dave's flat. This sounded juicy; no way was she hearing it down a phone line. Besides, it would be good to catch up in person.

Dave opened the door eagerly, as soon as she called through the letterbox.

'Thanks for keeping me in the loop, boss. I can't believe Liv was hypnotised. I wish she'd told me. If she'd said all that at the meeting, I'd have given you the heads up that she was a nut job.'

'Don't be harsh. She was ... I don't know ... clutching at straws.'

'Tell me something new. Every desperate soul at those meetings is doing the same.'

Hannah gave Dave's arm a rub. 'Sorry, mate.'

'So ... anyway, why did you charge over here like your arse was on fire and I was the only one with a bucket of water?' He laughed.

'You dangled a carrot, didn't you?' She knew he'd keep her waiting. She wasn't going to beg. He'd get to the juicy news when he was good and ready.

'Yep.' Dave indicated she should follow him into the kitchen. Filling the kettle, he said, 'Pretty shocking that the brother's dead, huh?'

'Yeah. And that someone used his name to rent the hypnosis place.'

'Crafty bastard,' Dave agreed. 'Can't have been easy telling her it was him. I mean, before you knew it wasn't. If you see what I'm saying.'

She nodded. 'I went with the direct approach.'

'I would've come with you.'

'Thanks. But it's only been me and her so far. If I'd have arrived with back up, she'd have *really* freaked out.'

'Well, the offer's always there.'

'Thanks. I did feel like a bitch telling her though.'

'You've had the training, mate. I've no doubt you did it by the book, as you would've done if you were still on the job.'

'Oh yeah, I approached it like a copper.' Hannah paused, then asked, tentatively, 'Anything else you need to say?'

He flicked the kettle on again, tutting at himself for not making the coffee when it had boiled the first time.

Reaching out, she flicked it off. 'Not for me. I just want to know what this news is. Quit stalling, you bugger.'

He had a mischievous look on his face.

'OK. Fair enough. Can I chuck something else into the mix that's going to scramble your little bleached head a bit more?'

'In for a penny – as they say.'

'You know you asked me to research the rest of Ray's family? See what I could dig up.'

'Yeah. Let me guess – Jake's a cokehead?'

'No. Well, yeah. If you say so.'

'He's always got a load of people around him. They're either customers or hangers on. He's definitely up to something. And I'm sure he's been buying and selling large amounts.'

'Actually, what I've got to tell you isn't about Jake,' Dave said.

'Emily?'

'No. I think she is what she seems. A nice girl.'

'So ...?'

'Ray's wife.'

'Uh huh?'

'What do you make of her?'

Hannah answered immediately, 'She's nervous. Almost certainly damaged.'

'You got that right.' Dave chuckled to himself.

'What is it? What did you find out?' Hannah was already sick of her employee's smug expression.

'How about if I told you ...' Dave allowed a ridiculous pause to hang in the air, obviously trying to rack up the tension.

'Come on. You're not announcing the friggin' winner of *Strictly.*'

'Beverley Farnley ...'

'*Yes?*' She could barely refrain from slapping him.

'All right, unclench! I'm getting there.'

'Dave, I will sack you, if I have to. Get there quicker.'

He laughed. 'Her surname used to be Greenwood.'

'*Greenwood.*'

'You've heard of the Greenwood sisters?'

'Naturally,' Hannah said. 'Anyone who grew up near Ayresworth knows their story.'

'She's using a different first name, and obviously her surname would've changed when she married Ray.'

'How do you know this?' Hannah asked.

Dave winked. 'I have my sources.'

She presumed he must've got the intel from an ex-colleague or an old informant. Clearly, he hadn't been cancelled by *all* his contacts over the Barton incident.

As if he read her mind, Dave said, 'Don't stress about who told me. Just trust me, it's legit. It's her.'

'Today is turning into a day of revelations,' Hannah said.

Dave laughed at her. 'Yep, I thought that'd mess with your mind.'

'I remember talking in the playground about the girls.'

'I reckon everyone did,' Dave said. 'It was one of those stories you couldn't stop thinking about.'

'Poor Beverley,' Hannah sighed.

56
ANNIE, MAY 2022

ANNIE WAS awoken by the sun streaming through the window. The curtains were way too small and insufficient to battle against such fierce light. She got up and ran the tap, before gulping down two glasses of water. Her head was banging, and her throat felt parched.

The sound of the running water woke Jake. He also indicated his need for a drink, and she handed him the other glass, filled to the brim. They had slept, fully clothed, on the double bed together. It had all been very above board, not least given the fact that they were more than likely siblings. Thankfully, this morning there was no embarrassment at the ridiculous end to the evening.

Jake asked, 'Do you want to go out and get some breakfast?'

She nodded. 'Yes, please. I feel dreadful.'

'What do you need?'

'Need?'

'I mean … there are some great places around here where you can get oatmeal with fruit and seeds, yoghurt, all that stuff. But—'

Annie interrupted. 'Right, I get you now, what do I *need*? I *need* a proper breakfast.'

'Okay. I know where we can go.'

'You know this place really well, don't you?'

'Yeah.'

'I would've thought you'd hang out in Marbella. It's nicer, isn't it?'

'It's more expensive. But ... I wouldn't say it's nicer. Anyway, there are a couple of blokes I'm trying to avoid at the moment, so I'm more than happy to hang out here in Malaga,' Jake said.

'Right, let me shower and then lead me to this fry up.'

'No worries.'

———

After her shower, Annie was amazed that all Jake needed to freshen up was a splash of cold water on his face and a bit of toothpaste; he declined her offer to share her toothbrush and instead used his index finger. His thick hair, which sat just shy of his shoulders, was more ruffled than it had been when they'd first met, but it kind of suited him. She peaked at him through the open door as he checked out his face in the bathroom mirror. She experienced a moment's pride at her new brother's looks. He was even more handsome than Toby.

———

They sat in another picturesque square, not dissimilar to the one they'd met in the day before. Was that really just a day ago? Jake spoke to the chef directly, cutting out the waiter, and within fifteen minutes a delicious breakfast was placed in front of them. Annie tucked into the ham, eggs, toast and tomatoes as if her very life depended on it.

'So ...' Jake began, cautiously. 'What do you think?'

'About the breakfast?' she said, through a mouthful of ham.

'No, not about the breakfast. Your feelings on that are evident.'

'About ...?'

'The hypnosis,' Jake whispered.

'It's hard to say.'

'Because?'

'You're aware I just fell asleep, aren't you? I wasn't in a responsive mood or whatever you call it.'

'Receptive trance.'

'Yeah. I wasn't so much relaxed, as full on asleep.'

'But ... before that? You were under?'

Annie shrugged. 'I don't know.'

'I think you definitely were.'

'Maybe a bit.'

'How did it feel?'

'I remember feeling a bit cold. Weird, huh? I mean I'm not cold now. This is Spain for God's sake.'

'That's interesting, perhaps the hypnosis made you cold.'

'Does that shit ever work? I mean *really*. Like, someone tells you a load of secret stuff, or says they've been regressed.'

'Yeah. Sometimes.'

'Properly works?'

She cut one of her eggs in half, watching the delicious runny yolk flood her plate.

'To a greater or lesser degree – yeah.'

Mopping up the egg with a piece of sourdough toast, Annie said. 'I reckon Olivia *might* fall for that. Like I say, she's flaky enough.'

'So ...?'

Momentarily pausing the devouring of her breakfast, Annie looked up, meeting his stare for the first time since their food had arrived. '*So?*'

'Are we on?'

'On?'

Jake waited.

'It wasn't real, was it?'

'Wasn't it?' He sipped his coffee.

'No. I mean ... We just ...'

'Wasn't it?' Jake repeated his question.

'I'm not supposed to drink,' Annie explained. 'Alcohol mixes with my meds. Anti-depressants. As if you needed me to tell you that.'

'So?'

'I was nervous about meeting you, I had way too many gins. Bloody hell, I'd had two before you even arrived.'

'Uh huh.' Jake continued to sip his coffee.

'All that stuff we said last night, about Ray, about ...' She lowered her voice. '...framing him for my mum's murder. It was nuts, right? We didn't really mean it. I mean, I would never have said it if I'd not been drunk. We'd have to convince my sister she saw him, and then we'd have to arrange to have him ... you know ... in prison.'

'*I* could do that bit.'

She shook her head. 'No! Jake! We were just chatting, talking crap. It wasn't real.'

'You're sure?'

'Yes.'

'That's how you feel?'

'Yes.'

'Okay.' He picked up his knife and fork and began eating his breakfast.

'I mean ...' Annie said. 'You didn't mean it either, did you?'

He paused. 'Umm ... No. I'd had a couple of joints before I met you. I was a little high. I was kidding, too.'

———

Despite having four more days in Malaga, Annie and Jake didn't meet up again. He was always busy when she messaged him. She spent the time eating frugally and exploring the sights. Somehow it was agreed, although unspoken, that she wouldn't meet the rest of the family. She figured Jake preferred her to be his little secret.

On the last day, he messaged her to say he'd arranged for an Uber on his dad's account to take her to the airport. When the car pulled up outside her apartment block, she was surprised to see Jake in the back seat.

'Hi.' She put her case in the boot and climbed in next to him.

'Thought I'd come and see you off.'

'Make sure I leave without causing trouble,' she corrected him.

He smiled. 'Not at all. I don't think you're going to be any trouble, Antoinette.'

Annie couldn't be sure if it was a threat or a joke.

57

HANNAH, APRIL 2023

ONCE HOME, Hannah flung some fresh clothes into a bag and made a quick call to check in with Lottie.

'Hi. Any news from the missing man?'

Lottie sounded as wretched as before. 'Nope.'

'He'll show up.'

'When are you coming back?'

'I'm looking into a flight. If I can get there tomorrow, I will. Just chill out at the hotel for now.'

'I will. Oh yeah, have you checked on Dixie?'

'I popped in there about an hour ago. She's fine. Mum's making a big fuss of her.'

'My baby. Love her.'

'Grannie Annie was there, too.'

'How's she doing?'

'Not great,' Hannah said. 'A little more forgetful. I swear she still thinks Dixie is her old dog, Winston.'

'Awww. Bless her heart. Might see you tomorrow then,' Lottie said.

'Hopefully, yeah.'

Lottie blew a kiss and hung up.

———

Back in the hotel in Marbella, Hannah watched as Lottie drank her wine.

'A lot to take in, huh?'

'You're not wrong. I see why you waited to tell me. I don't even know where to start. I mean … why the hell would someone use Liv's brother's name to do that?'

Hannah shrugged.

'I get that she still talks to him though. I do that to Mum sometimes,' Lottie said.

'Yeah. But she could've mentioned he was dead.'

'As for Jake's mum. Shiiiiiit!' Lottie threw her hands in the air and pulled an incredulous face. 'D'you think Jake knows? What about Emily?'

'Maybe. Emily's fully aware of how delicate her mum is, that's for sure.'

'So, Liv knows you're here now?' Lottie asked.

'Yep. I told her I'd traced Ray and I wanted to come out and try to get to know him.'

'Did you mention that you'd been here before?'

'Yeah. I did. I told her I was here on a scouting mission whilst she was ill. She was happy for me to come back to Spain. It's fine to put the flights and stuff on expenses. To be honest, she just wants answers now.'

'Does she still think Ray killed her mum?'

'I'm not sure she knows what to think about that.'

'And you?' Lottie asked. D'you think he killed Susan?'

Hannah shook her head emphatically. 'No. I don't think anyone would go to that much trouble to make her believe it, if it was actually true. This whole thing stinks like rotten eggs.'

'I take your point.'

'Someone is seriously fucking with Liv, and I want to know who.'

'And why.'

'Yes,' Hannah agreed. 'Definitely *why*.' She took a long drink from her sparkling water. She was determined to keep her wits about her until she had answers. No glasses of wine for Hannah.

'So, where to first?' Lottie asked.

'You've not heard from Jake at all?'

'No.' Lottie pulled a dramatic face.

'I think we need to get ourselves out of this hotel and over to Malaga and see if he's in any of his usual haunts,' Hannah suggested.

Lottie finished her wine in three gulps. 'Ready!' she said.

———

They sat in the square, outside the bar where they'd first laid eyes on Jake, with the sun beating down on them. Hannah scanned the streets for Jake or one of his friends. She'd already checked inside the bar and seen no one that she recognised. The only other people sitting outside the bar were a group of what were clearly retired local men, who had chosen to sit in the shade of a large palm tree, a few tables away from Hannah and Lottie. They were drinking Cerveza Victoria beer and smoking tiny rolled up cigarettes. Obviously used to the heat, they knew it would still be there tomorrow and the day after that. They had no desire to sit with the sun's rays scorching their skin, which was already brown and leathery. Hannah's eye was caught by the most rotund man in the group. He wore a grey, herringbone flat cap and a white shirt with the sleeves rolled up to his elbows, revealing hairy forearms. He had a small, wrinkled mouth that might or might not have once contained teeth. He and his friends were giving them a look that said *bloody mad English women*.

She didn't care. It was just so nice to feel a bit of heat on her face. Both Hannah and Lottie were in agreement that living in Spain was definitely a goal for later life.

'We could retire out here together,' Lottie suggested.

'Not planning on getting married then?'

'I doubt it.'

'You will. I reckon your beloved Vincenzo will swoop in and take you for his wife.' Hannah smiled.

'Oh shush.' Lottie gave her a shove.

'I'm serious. He's a nice lad.'

'Well, he makes me laugh.'

'He does,' Hannah said.

'And he's very good at accents!' Lottie joked.

They both giggled.

A familiar voice behind them demanded to know, 'How can you two justify sniggering like idiots? It's disgusting.'

Hannah turned around. It was Claudia, on her way into the bar.

'What?' she asked.

'Have some respect.'

About to ask what the bloody hell she was on about, Hannah noted Claudia's attire. She was dressed in black from head to toe, and it was twenty-eight degrees.

'Jake's only been dead for three days, and you're sitting here laughing and drinking. I thought you were his friends.'

Lottie's hand flew to her mouth. 'Dead?'

Hannah instantly placed her arm around Lottie. 'Claudia, sorry, are you saying Jake's dead?'

Claudia dabbed her eyes with a tissue. 'You didn't know?'

'How could we know?' Lottie shouted.

Claudia shrugged. 'I thought everyone knew.'

Lottie jumped off her stool and began pacing around in circles. The locals glanced out from under their palm tree, with little interest.

'That explains why he never picked up his phone. I told you, didn't I, Hannah? I knew it. I knew something was wrong. Oh my God, this is awful. He's so young.'

Hannah also jumped off her stool and halted Lottie in her tracks.

'*Stop!* It's not your fault you didn't know.'

Claudia seemed delighted that she had happened upon two people who were oblivious to Jake's demise. It clearly gave her the opportunity to be the bearer of horrendous news. She dabbed at her eyes and declared, 'It's been hell for those of us who were close to him.'

'How?' Lottie asked.

'How has it been hell? Well, I would've thought that was obvious.'

'No!' Lottie shouted. 'How did he die?'

'And when exactly?' Hannah added.

He died the night we were all waiting for him. The poor darling,' Claudia said. 'We were waiting to shower him with love, and he was …' She paused, dabbing again at her seemingly dry eyes.

'He was what?' Lottie asked, her frustration at the exasperating Claudia barely hidden.

'He was busy falling down the steps at Playa de la Fontanilla.'

'What steps?' Hannah asked.

Claudia gave her a look that said, *You're really not from round here, are you?* Then she replied with, 'The marble steps that lead down to the beach at Marbella. They're very well known.'

'He fell down them?' Lottie asked.

'Yes, and hit his head.' Claudia wept noisily, waving the tissue near her face.

'Oh no!' Lottie cried.

Fearful that she might be thinking of her own dad's death, and the gruesome scene she had unfortunately witnessed, Hannah grabbed her friend in a bear hug. To Claudia, she said, 'Do the police know why he fell? Was it an accident?'

Claudia blinked away more invisible tears.

'I don't think they know. Emily says that according to the coroner he'd had a few drinks and there was cocaine in his blood. Maybe he just tripped.'

'But he was supposed to be in Malaga. What was he doing in Marbella?' Hannah asked.

'I don't know! Who are you, the local policía?' Claudia waved over Hannah's shoulder at a couple of people inside the bar, indicating she'd join them shortly.

'Is Emily okay?' Hannah asked.

Claudia said nothing.

'His mum, his dad?' Lottie said.

'No one is okay. What are you, *stupid*?' Claudia said. 'Jake is *dead*!'

58

ANNIE, SEPTEMBER 2022

SHORTLY AFTER THE death of Queen Elizabeth II, Annie received a message from Jake, the first in the four months since she'd left Malaga. Months of no contact, and then suddenly a two-line message: *So, finally, Charlie gets his turn at the wheel. What about me?*

Although stone cold sober this time, Annie was facing yet another boring, lonely winter in her tiny flat. If she did this, she would be sending Ray to prison. But, in all honesty, what happened to him after that would be on Jake's conscience. It didn't take her long to decide. Within five minutes, she replied: *Maybe it's time. Call me.*

59

HANNAH, APRIL 2023

AFTER CLAUDIA LEFT them to join her friends inside the bar, Hannah tried to comfort Lottie. 'Is there anything I can get you? Brandy?'

'No, thanks. I know it's silly. I didn't really know him at all. We'd barely shared a few kisses. But ...'

'That's not the point,' Hannah said. 'I mean, I never snogged the guy, but I'm still shocked he's dead. What was he – not even thirty?'

'It's awful.' Lottie nodded.

'Yeah. And why the hell did we have to find out from that despicable ghoul, Claudia? Christ, she was milking the grief thing for all she was worth.'

Lottie gave a small smile. 'She is a ghoul, isn't she?'

'I wish we could find out more about how he died. I doubt the local police will tell us anything though.'

'Well, he fell, didn't he?'

Hannah wrinkled her nose. 'It doesn't sit well with me. I mean, yeah, have a few drinks, stumble down a few steps, I get that. But—'

'The steps *are* marble,' Lottie interrupted. 'Claudia said so. I'll bet they're slippery ... and hard.'

'I can't help thinking it had more to do with coke than drink,' Hannah said.

'He did have some cocaine in his system.'

'Oh yeah, I don't doubt it. I reckon he had some in his system most days. But ... I know you don't want to hear this, but I think he was dealing. D'you think he owed someone?'

'You think he was *pushed* down the steps?'

'Probably.'

'By drug dealers?'

'Possibly.'

Lottie shook her head. 'Bloody hell, Han, nothing is ever what it seems with you.'

Hannah gave a dry laugh.

'So, are you going to go to the police and ask them?' Lottie said.

'Nah. They won't tell me diddly-squat. I know I wouldn't if I was in their shoes.'

'So ...?'

Hannah pushed her chair back from the table. 'I think we're going to have to go and give our condolences to Ray and Beverley.'

———

Beverley opened the door. It was hard to tell if she was upset. People in shock are usually pale. But how do you judge the paleness of someone who is always opaque?

She didn't seem surprised at their visit. Judging by the array of blooms that stood in multiple vases in the hallway, they were not the first people to pop over. She stood back and beckoned them in.

Hannah handed her the white orchid they'd chosen on the way over and said, 'We were so sorry to hear about Jake.'

Beverley mumbled her thanks. Absentmindedly placing the orchid on the window ledge next to a vase that was bursting with purple freesias and white roses, she turned on her heels and wafted towards the main lounge.

Hannah and Lottie assumed they were supposed to follow. Not sure what to expect, they made their way down the wide hallway. Would the room be full of mourners, clothed all in black, as Claudia had been?

In fact, the only people in the room were a couple of elderly ladies who Hannah didn't recognise, and Toni, the neighbour.

Beverley waved her hand behind her and said, 'Some more people have come to pay their respects.'

Hannah wondered if she even remembered who they were. She and Lottie duly introduced themselves to everyone. The elderly ladies were apparently local busy bodies, who seemed to vaguely know Beverley and Toni.

Hannah was desperate to find out more about Jake, but to begin with the room was completely silent and she knew it would be utterly inappropriate to start asking questions.

Eventually, after a full minute of silence, Ray joined them from the kitchen, carrying a tray which contained an assortment of teas and coffees. He immediately asked Hannah and Lottie, 'So, how exactly do you know our son?'

He clearly had no memory of Hannah grabbing his arm the other night at the restaurant. Thank God for that.

Hannah waited, allowing Lottie to reply, mainly because, of the two of them, Lottie had been way more friendly with Jake.

'We met him in a bar. He was kind enough to invite us to Emily's birthday do, and to his own meal, that night at the tapas place ...' Lottie tailed off, obviously realising too late that the night she was referencing was the night Jake had died.

Ray nodded. 'Ah ha. I get you. Yes, he's very keen on female company.' He corrected himself. 'He *was.*'

The front door slammed, and within a second Emily appeared in the lounge. 'Oh, hi!' Thankfully, she remembered them.

Hannah gave her an appreciative smile. Without Emily, they could easily have been seen as imposters. 'Hi, Emily. We wanted to say how sorry we were to hear about your brother.'

'Thank you.' Emily gave a faint smile. 'Would you like to go outside? We could sit on the terrace. There's no air in here.'

Hannah begged to differ. The air con was on full blast; Toni and the old ladies were all wearing cardigans and jumpers. But she understood that perhaps Emily was more put off by the atmosphere than the temperature. She and Lottie instantly stood up. Far better to have Emily all to themselves anyway. More chance of asking questions.

———

Once they were comfortable on the terrace with a drink in front of them, a large glass of Rioja for Lottie and sparkling water for Hannah, Emily thanked them again for coming. 'So many people have called in. I guess it's kind. If a little awkward.'

'I can imagine,' Hannah said. 'People obviously want to show they care, but they don't know what to say.'

'Exactly. They say nothing worth saying. They just look sorry for us. Those dreadful old ladies have been here every day. Leeching off our grief.'

'The neighbours?' Lottie asked.

Emily nodded. 'Yeah. So has Toni, and Claudia, come to think of it.'

'Hannah calls Claudia a ghoul,' Lottie said, before placing her hand over her mouth and mumbling, 'Sorry. I shouldn't have said that. She's your friend.'

'Don't worry on my account. She *is* a ghoul. She's awful. All those hangers on are. All the women who used to sponge off him have turned up in tears. Everyone wants in on the angst. Everyone wants to ask questions, but no one dares.'

Hannah swallowed. Was Emily referring to her, too?

Lottie gave a gentle smile. 'I'm so sorry, sweetheart. I know exactly how you're feeling. I've had my share of close losses and it's never easy. If no one comes, you think people don't care, and then when they come in their droves you want them all to bugger off and leave you alone.'

'God, *exactly*! I don't know what I want from people.'

'We can go as soon as you want us to. Just say the word,' Lottie instructed. 'But equally, we're happy to stay if you want us to. Your call entirely.'

'No, no, you two stay. I like you,' Emily said.

'Thank you. We can talk, or we can sit here in silence. It's up to you,' Lottie said, shuffling her chair closer to Emily and placing an arm around her.

Hannah gave Lottie a smile that said, *You're bloody brilliant.*

Emily said, 'I just can't believe it. I mean, this time last week we were all moaning at Jake to sort his life out. Dad was pissed off with him, Mum was ... Mum. Then the police came and told us he'd suffered an acute subdural hematoma.' She said the words carefully, as if she was practising for a presentation. 'And now, here we are, spending our days discussing what his favourite flowers were, like he even had favourite flowers, and trying to decide what to put on a memorial plaque.'

'Sudden death is the worst,' Lottie agreed. 'You just have to take each decision as it comes. One at a time. You will get there.'

'But what do we say? What does a parent put on their child's plaque? What would they put on mine? Here lies Emily Susan Farnley, she wasn't a very good sister. She didn't like her brother much.'

Emily began to cry.

Hannah and Lottie exchanged a look. Ray must've chosen the name Susan because of his sister-in-law. Surely that fact alone was proof enough he didn't kill her.

Lottie stepped in again. Continuing to comfort Emily, she said, 'It's natural to feel guilt when someone dies. You were allowed to not like him when he was alive, you're allowed to not like him now. We have this way of putting people on a pedestal after they die, but, realistically, you have to feel what you feel. Even if what you thought of your brother wasn't entirely good.'

Blowing her nose, Emily said, 'I'm sorry, Lottie, I think I misjudged you before. I thought you were stupidly besotted with Jake, like all the others. But, actually, you're very clever.'

'Hardly,' Lottie smiled. 'I just lost someone very close to me a few years ago, and later I discovered he wasn't a good person at all. I found myself disliking him. Hating him even. It felt wrong, it clashed with the fact I should miss him. But in the end, I just let myself feel what I needed to. It's taken me a long time to realise you can't lie to yourself. You'll learn that, too.'

'How are your parents coping?' Hannah asked Emily.

'I don't think they know what to do. It's shocking. When the police came and told us, we all stared at them. Like they were talking gibberish.'

'When did you find out?'

'The night he didn't show up for the meal. I got home and Jake wasn't here. Mum was asleep in bed, and Dad was in the lounge. He was working on his laptop. I sat down to join him, and we had a little chat. Just stuff. We wondered where Jake was, but I don't think either of us was seriously worried at that point. We talked about the food at the tapas place. Dad was very angry at Jake for not turning up for his own birthday thing. I remember him mentioning the people Jake hung about with. He said they were all dodgy and when Jake came home, he was going to have a serious discussion with him about drug use. In the middle of all that the police arrived and that was it. Game over.'

Hannah asked. 'Who went to wake your mum?'

'Me. I went to the door and the police asked if my mum and dad were in. I told them Mum was asleep and they asked me to wake her. I think both Dad and I knew then it was going to be something serious about Jake. I thought he'd been arrested for dealing or something.'

'*Was* he dealing?' Hannah asked.

'No ... erm ... I don't know. I just meant ... we have no other family here. I have no grandparents, aunts, uncles, cousins, nothing. So, it had to be about Jake, didn't it?'

'I suppose so,' Hannah agreed. It was odd to think that *she* knew Emily's cousin, and Emily didn't. Why had Ray chosen not to mention his family back in Kingshurst?

The last thing she wanted to do was to alienate Emily by coming across as an ex-copper, but she was keen to know as much as possible. So, she tentatively pushed on, 'What do the police think happened?'

'At first, they seemed convinced he'd fallen. Plain and simple. But a witness came forward the next day to say they'd seen an argument taking place at the top of the steps when they'd jogged past. Then the police unlocked Jake's phone and they found text messages from people who are known drug dealers. Now they're not so sure it was an accident. But it must've been, mustn't it? Because if it wasn't an accident that means someone purposely pushed him down those steps, and that's just crazy.'

The patio doors slid open behind them, and Ray appeared. He looked understandably bereft and drained. But Hannah was once again taken by the fact he had a good face. Closing the doors behind him, he pulled up a chair and asked, 'How are you doing out here? You okay for drinks?'

'Yeah, thanks, Dad,' Emily replied.

Lottie and Hannah nodded.

'It's good of you to come,' he said to them. 'It looks like you're being a great support for my daughter.' He placed his hand over Emily's and squeezed. 'She seems a bit brighter.'

'We want to help in any way we can,' Hannah said.

'Being with Emily is help enough. We all need to keep an eye on her.'

'Emily was just telling us what the police are currently thinking,' Hannah said, shocked she was finally talking face to face with Ray Farnley, in a situation where he might not run away.

'They're not thinking anything, are they?' Ray said to Emily.

'Well, they think he might have been pushed, rather than fallen.'

'That's utter rubbish.' Ray shook his head. 'Obviously, he wasn't pushed. This is Marbella.'

'Dad, it *is* what they think. They sat in our lounge two days ago and told us there was a witness to an argument.'

Ray cast a furtive glance in Hannah and Lottie's direction, suggesting to Emily it wasn't something to be discussed outside the family.

'That witness could've been mistaken.'

Suddenly, like an apparition, Beverley appeared on the other side of the patio doors. With her hand to her head, she mouthed that she had a headache. Hannah stared at her face through the glass. Translucent skin, almond-shaped, sad eyes, and a small, reticent mouth.

Ray rose from the table and opened the patio door. 'Okay, my darling. Why don't you take a couple of painkillers and have a lie down?'

Beverley silently drew in her breath. Then, exhaling, she said, 'But the others are still in the lounge. I can't ...'

'That's okay. I'll explain to them you're not well. They're happy enough drinking their tea.' Ray smiled gently. 'You go, darling.'

'Thank you.' Beverley briefly touched his face, and then left, as silently as she had arrived.

There was so much Hannah wanted to say to her. She wanted to run after her, grab her, and tell her she was so incredibly sorry for the horrific start in life she'd had. But she couldn't say anything without acknowledging that she knew who she was. So Hannah remained silent.

They didn't stay long after Beverley went to lie down. Both Emily and Ray were clearly exhausted, and there was only so long Hannah and Lottie could remain before Hannah's inquisitive mind began to raise suspicions.

Ray walked them to the door, once again thanking them for being supportive of his daughter.

'She needs friends around her, people she can talk to. Her other friends have been over, but they're not equipped to deal with something like this. They're so young, and they're too scared to say anything. They're clearly uncomfortable with tears. I saw her outside with you two, and she appeared to be opening up. I'd love it if you could come back some time. Are you local?'

Hannah explained they were on holiday, and only had a week left.

'Shame,' Ray said. 'Well, do try to come back if you can.' He gave them his private mobile number. 'Call me if you'd like to hang out by the pool with Emily. I'll send a car for you.'

'We will,' Hannah assured him.

'How are you getting back to your hotel?'

'We'll grab an Uber,' Lottie said.

'Let me get you one on my account,' he offered. 'Or ... why don't I drive you home?'

Hannah wasn't keen on letting him drive them. Yes, it

would've been a great chance to chat more to him. But he had grey bags under his eyes, and that far away glazed look people get when they're so tired they're not fully present. Letting him drive them could be a dangerous mistake.

'Honestly, we don't want to take you away from your family. But an Uber would be great.'

'I'll sort that now.'

Hannah was delighted she'd finally got the chance to talk to Ray, but she felt more than a little guilty at the circumstances by which it had come about.

60

ANNIE, DECEMBER 2022

ANNIE'S PHONE rang as she was getting out of the shower. Attempting to pull on her bathrobe and answer the phone at the same time, she saw it was Jake calling.

Stabbing at the green button, she put him on loudspeaker and shouted, 'Hi, Jake, I'm here.'

'What you shouting for?' he asked.

'I was just jumping out of the shower. I didn't want to miss you.'

'You didn't. I'm here. So, anyway, did you look around the office?'

Annie wrapped her hair in a towel.

'Yep. But I can't pay the rent. Can you transfer me some money, please? Or pay it direct to them.'

Jake gave a sigh. 'I told you; I'll try to pay it next week.'

'Try?'

'Calm down. I'll get the money to her, and *I'll* rent the place. It's just … fucking hell, you know what he's like, he's always got his eyes on what I'm up to.'

'D'you really think this will work?' Annie made her way to the kitchen and grabbed a bottle of Chardonnay from the fridge.

Wrestling with the bottle top, she said, 'Did you hear me, Jake. Do you think this will work?'

'Yes, of course it'll work. Don't sweat.'

'Okay.' Annie poured herself a large glass of wine and took a gulp. 'And you'll sort the—'

'For fuck's sake,' Jake interrupted. 'I'll pay the money to the rental woman. I'll sort it all.'

'Great. And Jake … don't forget, don't use your own name.'

'Jesus, Annie. I know that! I'll think of a name.'

'Have you been practising?'

'Yeah. I'm getting really good.' Jake sounded smug.

'Not on anyone who knows you?'

'I'm not a total moron. I've practised on girls I've met in bars.'

'God help them.'

'It comes in handy at the end of the night if they're in a receptive trance, if you get what I mean.'

'I don't want to get what you mean.' Annie pulled a face, despite the fact that no one could see her. 'Anyway, rent the place from January, for three months initially. Okay?'

'Yep.' Jake sounded impatient.

'By the way,' Annie added. 'It's not very flashy.'

'Don't worry about that. I found a couple of rolls of dead expensive wallpaper here, left over from Mum's latest decorating spree. There's a nice throw, too. A cashmere thing. She won't miss it. The stupid woman has more throws than she has hot dinners – *literally!*' He laughed again.

Annie wondered how he could be so laid back. Was this all a joke to him?

Before she could voice her concerns, Jake said, 'I'll bring it all with me. It won't take up much room in my luggage.'

'And the rest of the furniture? The sofa? A bed? A chair?'

'We'll hire it all when I'm there.'

'I'm not paying for it all!'

'Jesus Christ, I know! You've already said that. I'm hoping a little deal I'm in the middle of is going to come good. I'll have some cash soon. Stop worrying.'

'What deal? Drugs?' Annie asked.

'Best you don't know,' Jake replied. Changing the subject, he said, 'What about Olivia? All sorted?'

'Yes. I made a leaflet at work. I printed it on some photo-paper. It looked pretty convincing. I put your burner phone number on it and an endorsement from a made-up celebrity, then I posted it through her door.'

'She won't check out the celeb?'

'No. She's not like that.'

'You're sure she'll bite?'

'Absolutely.' Annie took another gulp of wine. 'She's mentioned it to me in one of her texts already. She thought it was just a chance flyer.'

'As if hypnotherapists advertise like that. What an idiot!'

'She's thinking about it, and she can afford it. I just have to nudge her.'

'Don't sound too keen. We don't want her remembering that you encouraged her to go.'

'She won't remember. She's forever forgetting stuff,' Annie reassured him.

'What a stupid bitch.'

Annie remained silent. She didn't like it when Jake spoke about her sister like that, but she knew she was just as guilty of using her, so didn't have a leg to stand on.

After a pause, Jake said, 'Right then, all sorted.'

'Okay. Speak soon. Don't forget to—'

It was too late. Jake had already hung up. He had an annoying habit of not saying goodbye.

61

HANNAH, APRIL 2023

THE NEXT MORNING, Hannah and Lottie stood at the top of the marble steps, looking down. Apart from a small sign, placed there by the policía, which according to Google Translate asked for witnesses to an incident, there was no way of knowing that a few days ago Jake had fallen to his death right here.

The sun shone down from an azure blue sky; tourists and locals poured past them down the steps, towards the picturesque beach. Below them the coconut husk umbrellas blew in a warm, gentle breeze, and attractive people slowly bronzed in the sun or bobbed in the gentle waves. If you didn't know the facts, it presented a sublime image.

Hannah wondered who had found Jake. What was this place like at night? When was it cleaned up? How would this idyllic scene look with the addition of blood splatters? Jeez, once again, she wished she had a badge to flash. If only she could get in with the local police, she might get the answer to some of her questions.

'They're quite solid,' Lottie said, stamping her flipflopped feet on the steps.

'Yep,' Hannah agreed. 'I can see how you could hurt yourself on them. But … *dying*. I still don't get it. I mean, he would have to be really pissed to just fall down, and according to Claudia, the coroner told the parents he only had *some* alcohol in his bloodstream.'

Lottie began making her way downwards, flipflopping with each step. She called back, 'What do you think the witness saw?'

Hannah shrugged. 'Impossible to guess.'

'Come on, Poirot, you must have at least a couple of theories.'

'Of course I do.'

'So?' Lottie stopped, turned, and raised her eyebrows.

'Well, I reckon there are three possibilities,' Hannah said, catching her up. 'Either Jake got really unlucky and somehow tripped down enough of these steps to give himself a fatal head injury. It does happen. Look at your dad; he hit his head just once.'

'Yes. But he was a very heavy man, and the rocks by the stream were really wet.'

'True.'

'Jake falling solo down these steps seems quite unlikely.' Lottie scuffed her feet, testing the slipperiness of the marble. 'Even if they were wet, it's a stretch that he would fall that dramatically.'

Hannah agreed, 'I know. His arms aren't painted on. Why didn't he save himself?'

'So, possibility two is …?' Lottie asked.

'Possibility two is …' Hannah continued making her way down to the beach, her friend shuffling along beside her. 'Jake was involved with some very nasty drug dealers. He was buying and selling coke, and he pissed the dealers off. That would explain why he's been drinking in Malaga for the last few months; perhaps he had good reason to avoid Marbella. They caught up with him here, an argument ensued, and Humpty Dumpty had a great fall.'

'Han!' Lottie said.

Hannah apologised. 'Sorry, sweet cheeks.'

Lottie gave it some consideration. 'Well, it definitely sounds possible. I guess without knowing what sort of argument the witness saw, we can't know if it was a gang of people or just one.'

'Surely if a gang of drug dealers literally threw him down the steps, more than one witness would've seen it?'

'Yeah, I guess so,' Lottie said. 'So, what's possibility three?'

'Possibility three ... is that someone else pushed Jake.'

'Why would they, though?'

Hannah shrugged. 'Who knows? There were a lot of people in his life. Women who wanted him but couldn't have him. Women who wanted him and *could* have him. Women he'd probably had and discarded.'

'Okay, okay.' Lottie grimaced. 'I know I was as daft as the rest of them.'

'Actually, you weren't. What you did was harmless flirting, and I like to think you began doing it to help me. Anyway, I didn't mean to rub it in. I'm just saying, there were lots of women hanging around him, he was bound to piss one of them off. Or one of them could have a disgruntled ex-boyfriend who wasn't happy with our Jakey boy. Not only that, but let's face it, even his own family weren't keen on him.'

'Poor Jake,' Lottie said.

'*Poor Jake* my arse. He wasn't kind to his family. Remember how he moaned about his sister at her birthday thing, and the stuff she told me about the way he treated her and her mum when he was younger? I'll bet he had a lot of opinions about women that we wouldn't agree with. I mean ... being a bully to his mum. What a douche! I don't suppose Ray was proud of him either. Ray strikes me as a decent man, with a good business head on him. He was probably pissed off at how much Jake spent money that wasn't his.'

'Did any one of the people you've mentioned dislike him

enough to arrange to have him pushed down these steps though?' Lottie asked, as they finally reached the bottom and placed their feet on the hot sand. 'Or push him themselves?'

'Possibly.'

'Who?'

'I guess it's down to me to work that one out.'

'You think you can solve this?' Lottie said.

'Yeah. Why not?'

'You think you can do it before the policía?'

'I think I can do it during one of their siestas; I know these people way better than the policía do.'

They stayed on the beach for a couple of hours, soaking up the sun. Lottie was engrossed in her Lisa Jewell novel, drawing in her breath noisily ever so often, whilst Hannah lay on her sunbed, the green canvas grazing her thighs uncomfortably. She closed her eyes and considered every possible alternative regarding Jake's untimely death. Eventually, she hit a brick wall. She needed to know a few facts before she could get any further. Unfortunately, whichever way she looked at it, she needed to talk to Jake's family. She was going to have to try to push them further for answers.

62

ANNIE, JANUARY 2023

'Say that again?' Annie asked.

'I said – we are all systems go!' Jake replied. 'She just called me. Well, she called Stephen.' He laughed. 'I booked her in for the first week in Feb. That'll give me time to get the place set up. Sounds like we pitched the price just right.'

'God! This is really happening,' Annie mumbled.

'Yeah. Sure is.'

'Well ... you'd better get over here as soon as possible.'

'I'm coming. No going back now,' Jake said.

With a hint of nervousness, Annie said, 'Well, if it doesn't work, if she doesn't go under properly, we can still walk away. We can call it quits.'

Jake spoke up immediately. 'No way. It has to work. I need that money. I want control of that fucking company.'

It worried her when he was so determined. But he was right; there was no going back now. 'Do you have the story ready?' she asked.

'Yeah. It's all sorted.'

'You've got it all straight in your head? You don't need a recap?'

No!' Jake barked. 'I don't need a fucking recap; you've told me like fifty times already.'

'Okay, okay.'

'I don't need to hear it all again, Annie. You've told me.'

Annie felt a little annoyed. 'This is my mum's death we're talking about!'

'I know.'

'Right, well, have a bit of respect, please. And just be professional when she comes to you.'

'I will be. I've got the voice all sorted.' This was said in a polite but commanding voice, which sounded quite different to his own. 'I've grown a little beard and I'll have a haircut. I should look a bit older.'

'Can we meet up when you get here?' Annie asked.

Jake tutted. 'We can't risk being seen together. You stay in your flat, and I'll stay in a hotel.'

'You're sure your family think you're going somewhere else? They don't know you're coming to England, do they?'

'Nah. I've told them I'm going to Crete with my mates.'

'What about your lack of a tan when you go home?'

'I live in Marbella, I'm brown as a nut all year round.'

'Lucky you. Anyway, message me as soon as you're here. God, I can't wait for the first session. I wonder what she's got to say about me.'

'I'm going to take it slow. Ease her in. I'm not going to go straight in with stuff about you.'

Annie was disappointment, but she understood.

'Okay.' Then, sensing Jake was about to hang up, she said quickly, 'Before you go – did you make some fake certificates?'

'Yeah. I'm going to get a plaque done for outside, too. I've thought of everything. I might even invent a lovely wife to put her mind at rest.' He hung up.

Annie chewed her fingernails. God, this was stressful.

63
HANNAH, APRIL 2023

AFTER SEVERAL TEXTS between herself and Liv, during which Hannah assured Liv she was getting to know her uncle and the investigation was definitely progressing, and Liv asked several times if she ought to come out there, Hannah put her phone back in her bag and sighed.

'What's up?' Lottie asked, placing her bookmark firmly inside her paperback. She never turned the corners of the pages over; her mother had been appalled by such dreadful behaviour. Yes, Lottie was aware of the irony in that judgement.

'She's desperate to get out here. It's all I can do to stop her jumping on a plane.'

'Oh blimey.'

'Exactly. The last thing we need is her rocking up here, telling Ray he's her uncle and all the other confusing shit that goes with it.'

Lottie asked, 'Have you told her to sit tight?'

'*Yes!* Repeatedly.'

'So, what's next?'

'I think I need to ramp things up; time is against me.'

'Right.' Lottie nodded encouragingly, as if she had the faintest idea what ramping things up entailed.

'I'm going to ask Ray if we can go back to the villa, maybe talk to Emily some more.' Hannah retrieved her phone from her bag. 'Do you think it's too soon? I mean we were only there yesterday.'

'Well ... Ray said he'd like us to call in before we left, and we are only on holiday for one more week. So ... no, I don't think it's too soon.'

'Good. That's the correct answer,' Hannah said, already calling the number.

'Hello. Ray Farnley.'

'Hi, it's Hannah. Emily's friend from yesterday?' There was a question in her voice, as if he was so important, he might have already forgotten her.

'Hello. Nice to hear from you, again.'

'We were wondering how Emily's doing.'

'Thanks for asking. She's about the same.'

'D'you think she'd like another visit from us?'

'I'm sure she would.' Ray seemed to rally a little. 'She's no doubt brooding out by the pool. It doesn't do her good to spend too much time out there alone.'

It was clear to Hannah that Beverley wasn't able to be much support in this situation. 'We could pop over now and hang out with her.'

'Perfect,' he agreed. 'I'm at work, but I'll be buggered if I can concentrate, and everyone I need to speak to has taken off for Easter. I didn't even realise it was Good Friday when I came in. Why don't I swing past your hotel and pick you both up?'

Hannah almost replied that they weren't at their hotel, they were at Playa de la Fontanilla, before realising how utterly crass that would be. Jeez, she'd have to explain why they were there, which would put the cat firmly amongst the pigeons. Not to mention how much it would upset Ray to think about those steps. Instead, she said, 'We're out at the shops, buying sunglasses. We'll pop back to our hotel and meet you there.'

'Perfect. I've got the sports car, but I'm sure you girls will fit.'

Ignoring the reference to them being girls, Hannah gave him the name of their hotel and arranged for him to pick them up in half an hour. To Lottie, she said, 'Quick, let's get back to the hotel and rinse this bloody sand off.'

———

Ray had a gorgeous car. Of course he did!

As he pulled up outside the hotel, Hannah gave an appreciative whistle. *Porsche 911 Sport. Light grey, with the distinct 60 on the doors. Good choice.*

It was polished to perfection. They climbed in. They'd already agreed Hannah would take the front seat. Mainly so she could speak to Ray during the drive, but also because Lottie was the one who had received actual lessons on how to get in and out of a sports car without flashing her pants.

The car smelt of aftershave. It was clearly something upmarket, Prada, Louis Vuitton, something along those lines. Hannah couldn't name it, but she could smell class. The seats were soft leather, and she sank into hers.

Glancing back at her friend, she reached for the lever to pull her seat as far forward as possible. Poor Lottie was so squashed her knees were up by her ears.

As soon as they drove away from the hotel, with a rev of a highly tuned engine, Hannah began the questions. The journey wasn't going to be long enough to beat about the bush, and there was every possibility Ray would leave them alone with Emily once they reached the villa.

'Have you heard anything from the police about Jake's erm … accident?'

'They won't come back to us. There's nothing more to say.'

'But ... the witness ...'

'Just because someone says they saw an argument at the top of the steps, doesn't mean that has anything to do with Jake falling. Christ, we don't even know if the two things happened at the same time. They could've been hours apart.'

'True,' Hannah said. 'But it does seem unlikely that a fit young man like Jake could fall with such terrible consequences.'

'He'd been drinking.' Ray pulled onto the main road, hitting sixty in seconds. 'I think it was an unfortunate accident. And I reckon the police will come to that conclusion, too.'

'You can honestly say you don't think there was any foul play whatsoever?'

Turning to face Hannah, Ray took his eyes off the road for a split second but didn't reduce his speed. 'What's with all the questions?'

'I'm just ... a little curious.'

'Strikes me you're more than *a little*.'

'Come on, Ray. You're a man of the world.'

He seemed surprised by her accidental over-familiarity. 'Listen, my son made some bad choices. He associated himself with lowlife and he took risks. There was a side to him that concerned me a great deal. He reminded me of someone ...'

'Someone you don't see any more?' Hannah guessed.

Ray moved his head slightly and looked at himself in the rear-view mirror. 'Oh, I see him. I see him often.'

Hannah said nothing.

'Don't get me wrong. If there is someone responsible for my son's death, then I want to know who it is. I just don't think we're ever going to get to the truth. If it was any one of those loathsome bastards Jake used to buy cocaine from, then there's no way we'll ever find out. They hide out in the fucking sewers, and the police don't go there.'

'What if someone could help you?'

'Someone?'

'Yes.'

'Like who? You?' he asked, with a smirk.

She ignored the smirk.

Ray said, 'After you left yesterday, I asked Emily what you two do back in the UK, and she told me you refurbish furniture. How exactly does that equip you to help me to find sewer rats?'

Hannah made a decision. 'The truth is, only one of us refurbishes furniture.'

Lottie gave a wave from the backseat.

'*I* used to be in the police force,' Hannah continued.

'As what?'

'A police constable, obviously.'

'*You* were a police officer?'

'Yes. One of Her Majesty's own. Although, I suppose it's His Majesty's now.'

'And how does that help you here in Marbella?'

'I'm good at finding stuff out.'

Ray laughed. 'Have you heard yourself?'

Hannah swallowed hard. She was going to have to go the whole hog. 'Look, I'm a private investigator, and I'm offering to help you get to the bottom of what happened to your son, okay?'

'You're a private investigator.' He laughed again, louder this time.

'Yes. Hannah Sandlin. Google me. There's no g in Sandlin.'

'I'll try to remember that.'

Hannah continued, 'I've had several successful cases.'

'And you're offering to help me?'

'Yes.'

'Let me guess – for an extortionate fee you'll give me the name of the person or persons who you think pushed my son down those steps.' Ray swung off the main road, pulled over to the side, and stopped the car abruptly, creating a shower of gravel.

'No. Not for an extortionate fee. For *no* fee.'

'Why the hell would you do that?'

'I like Emily, and I want to help you and Beverley.'

Ray drew in a deep breath, before asking, 'So this investigation work, you can do it anywhere, I presume?'

'Uh huh.'

'You don't need your smoky office, with its glass door with the letters PI engraved on it, or your deerstalker hat?' He chortled to himself.

'No.' Hannah refused to take the bait.

Performing a neat U turn in the road, he screeched back towards the main road. At the junction he turned the opposite way and began heading back towards their hotel.

'So, you're taking us back? You don't want my help, is that it?' Hannah asked, annoyed at herself for not going slower. *Why did I have to lose my temper with him?*

'I'm taking *you* back,' Ray replied.

'*Me?*'

'Yes. Let's see what you can do. I'll drop you off at your hotel. Lottie can come to the villa with me.'

For one awful moment Hannah thought Lottie was going to be held hostage until she solved the mystery surrounding Jake's death. 'What?'

'She can spend some time with Emily. Emily says she's lovely.' He smiled at Lottie in the rear-view mirror.

'And *me*? What am I going to do at the hotel?'

'You'll have … umm … let's say three hours. I'll send a car for you after that.'

'Right. And in that time?'

'When we next meet, Miss PI, you're going to tell me something about myself. Something you've managed to find out. Something you've investigated,' he mocked. 'And I don't mean financial stuff that you can get from Google. Or, shit like how I won best millionaire's bum, back when that was considered suitable content for the likes of *US Weekly* magazine. I mean something about me that *I* think you don't know. Is three hours enough?'

Hannah wanted to say thirty seconds would do fine. But she didn't. Instead, she pretended to consider, before replying, 'Make it two hours. I'll join you for dinner.' She turned and winked at Lottie.

64

ANNIE, MARCH 2023

As soon as Jake picked up the phone, Annie began to speak, 'Fuck, fuck, fuck, Jake! She's just messaged me. It didn't work!'

'What? Calm down. Start again. In what way didn't it work? She was convinced. You said so yourself. She told *you* it was Ray. That's why I packed up and came home.'

'I think we were too hasty.'

'What are you on about, woman?'

'The police didn't believe her.'

'Shit!'

'But, honestly, how was I supposed to know she wouldn't convince the police? I didn't think she'd come across so ditsy.' Annie chewed her thumbnail.

'Why don't you stop at *I didn't think*? Hit me with a full stop and we're done!' Jake sounded really angry.

'Don't you get shirty with me,' Annie said. 'We both agreed on the plan.'

'Yeah. Well, I played my part. Fucking well, actually.'

'But then you came back too soon.'

She heard Jake sigh. 'I wasn't going to hang around in

England for weeks. It was hammering with rain every day. I needed to get some sun.'

'Well, I still think we shouldn't have packed up so quickly.'

'After she read the transcript from the twenty-first she said she didn't need any more sessions. Exactly what would I have been waiting around for?'

There was a pause, during which Jake said, 'Annie? D'you hear me, what did you want me to wait around for?'

Ignoring his question, Annie said, 'Olivia's just messaged me. She's been to an AA meeting tonight.'

'Never mind her fucking social life, what are we gonna do about her?'

'Just got another message,' Annie said. 'She's only gone and hired a bloody private investigator to help her prove it was Ray. She's meeting with them tomorrow. Yet again, Toby's money saves the day for Olivia! Let's hope they're good, so they can convince the police it was Ray.'

'No. Let's hope they're shit, so they don't rumble us!' Jake hung up.

65

HANNAH, APRIL 2023

HANNAH HAD CHANGED FOR DINNER. She was decidedly hungry. Hopefully, Ray would lay on something tasty. Maybe he'd order in.

She'd been on the phone to Dave, catching up with the latest news. He was also itching to get out to Marbella; in fact if he didn't have Noah with him for Easter, she wouldn't have been able to keep him away.

'Boss, this case keeps getting worse. *Or better!* Who do you think is responsible?'

'Not sure. But I can't help thinking the drug dealers are too obvious.'

'Text me when you know.'

'I will.'

'The exact minute you find out.'

'*I will*, Dave.'

'And be careful, mate. I'm not there to save you this time.'

Hannah laughed. 'You don't have to worry.'

After agreeing with Dave that he would buy Noah the biggest Easter egg he could find and she'd pay him for it when she returned, Hannah hung up.

During the last couple of hours, Liv had texted several times, and Hannah had no choice but to call her and give her an acceptable version of events.

'Are you any closer to finding out who Stephen was?' Liv asked.

'Yes. I'm closer to everything.'

'So …?'

'A lot of loose ends are about to be tied up,' Hannah assured her.

'What do you think of Uncle Ray?'

'I like him. I can't lie. He seems like a good man.'

'Hmmm!'

'Liv,' Hannah said. 'Don't forget – it's highly possible that he didn't have anything to do with your mum's death.'

'I know, I know,' Liv agreed.

'Just try to keep an open mind about those new memories.'

'Okay. I will,' Liv said, grudgingly, before asking, 'Is he married? Does he have kids?'

Hannah paused. 'I promise you; I will update you on everything soon. Did you have a good think about who could've used Toby's name to rent that place, like I asked you to?'

'There's no one. No one would use his name, and no one would want me to think Ray killed my mum.'

'You're absolutely sure?'

'Yes!'

'Have you spoken to anyone about this?'

'There's no one to speak to,' Liv whined.

'What about your sister? Have you spoken to her?'

'I've texted a few times. She's only replied to one of them.'

'What did you say? You didn't tell her about all this did you?'

'Well, I might have already mentioned you.'

'Great! Have you told her about Toby's name being used to rent the place?'

'No. You told me not to tell anyone that bit. Although I don't get why I can't tell *her*.'

'I just think it's best if you wait until we know everything,' Hannah said. 'So, what have you been texting your sister about?'

'The usual. How is she? Is she thinking about Mum? It's getting close to the anniversary, thirty-one years. That's mostly what we talk about.'

'Okay. Well keep it that way.'

Liv said, 'I'm not going to sit here forever, just waiting.'

'I know.'

'Right, well, call me as soon as you're back in the UK, or when you find out who the son of a bitch is who's been messing with my memories.'

'I will. Oh yeah, Liv?'

'Uh huh?'

'What was your grandma called? Ray's mum?'

'Shirley. Why?'

'No reason. I'll call you if I think of anything else. Got to go.' Hannah ended the call as the telephone in her room began to ring. Reception was clearly letting her know her car was here.

———

Ray opened the front door with a smirk on his face. 'Miss Sandlin, I trust you've been working hard?'

'Yes.'

'I did as you asked, I Googled you.'

'And ...?'

'You've got a legitimate website. And as far as I can see there are some reasonable reviews.'

'Like I told you.'

'But this isn't a missing teenager or a lost inheritance. According to you, this could be murder, manslaughter at best. You're sure you're up to it?'

'I think so, yes,' Hannah replied, sarcastically, stepping into the hallway, which, somehow, against the odds, had become an even greater riot of colour than before. More flowers had been added to the ledges. *Jesus, Beverley must've ordered in a truck load of vases.*

'What would you like to do first, Miss Sandlin, disclose all the juicy things you've found out about me, or eat dinner?'

'Well, if it's up to me, I'd like to choose dinner first, please. I've worked up quite an appetite.'

He laughed. 'All right, but I must admit I'm intrigued.'

'You have every right to be.' Hannah smiled. Somehow, despite the reason behind this meeting, they were growing closer. His sarcastic smiles were becoming warm ones. She hoped they would remain that way when she began telling him all she knew to be true.

As suspected, Ray had ordered in from a local restaurant. Much like the ill-fated, belated birthday meal, the food consisted of small plates of delicious food. Surprisingly, Beverley joined them for a while, although she mostly pushed food around her plate. Hannah only saw her place two garlic prawns and a piece of Manchego cheese in her mouth; she then took a tiny bite from a fig and bacon jam crostini.

Hannah remembered when the newspapers had leaked the highly personal information that the Greenwood sisters had been forced to live off mostly porridge and bread for over a year after their parents had died in a car accident, whilst their brother kept them in the basement. Obviously, that had created an unhealthy relationship with food for poor Beverley; she was certainly extremely thin.

Emily ate an assortment of vegetarian dishes and chatted with Lottie a good deal over the meal. It was good to see Lottie with a new friend. She was older and wiser than Emily, and it was clearly doing her a world of good to be able to call on her own terrible experiences to help another person. Lottie ate well, too, happily trying all the veggie dishes suggested to her by Emily. Hannah was starving. It was only now she realised she'd not eaten since breakfast.

She kept an eye on Ray throughout the meal. He seemed to eat well, too; he knew what he liked, and he wasn't afraid to help himself to plenty. He would no doubt pop to his in-house gym later to work it off. But not before he had interviewed her. Every so often she would catch him looking at her, almost with a half-smile. Did he think this was all a joke? What was he expecting her to say? Boy, was he in for a shock! Beverley left the table before the meal was over, drifting silently in her usual manner out of the room. Emily and Lottie made their way to the lounge with a bottle of Rioja, and Ray signalled to Hannah that the time had come.

Hannah gazed around, pretending this was her first visit to Ray's office. She was grateful that he'd made the situation a little less formal by sitting in the armchairs in the bay window, as opposed to the upright chairs with a wide desk between them. She assumed the drawers were all still locked. The air con was switched to full, and Hannah felt the tiny blonde hairs on her arms stand on end. Then, a vague thought struck her that Jake's room was just next door. Perhaps that was partly responsible for the chill that ran through her. Remembering his satin sheets, she found it almost incredulous that he would never again make love in that bed, or even sleep in it. He now slept the eternal rest that we all ponder on. She wondered – did the room still smell of him?

'Fire away, *Ms Sandlin PI.*' Ray interrupted her thoughts. She noted that he was now wearing a supercilious grin.

'Can I ask you to call me Hannah, please? I realise it amused you to call me by my full name, and apparently my job title, but I know sarcasm when I hear it, and I would prefer you not to.'

'Of course, Hannah.'

'Thank you. I'm sure your mother, Shirley, wouldn't appreciate the sarcasm.'

'My mother, *Shirley*. Oh well done. One point to you.'

'Hannah acknowledged the point with a nod.

'Is that it?' Ray paused. 'Two hours for my mother's name?'

'Before I go on, I'd like to ask you something.'

'Okay, but honestly, Hannah, no clues. You have to do this by yourself.' He laughed.

'I don't need any clues. I just need to check – is there any of it that you don't want me to say?'

'Any of it?'

She stared Ray dead in the eye. 'Yes, is there anything I've uncovered about you that you don't want me to say?'

For the first time he appeared concerned. The smile slipped silently from his face.

Not so cocky now! She allowed a smidge of pity to show. 'It's tough. What I'm going to say to you is not easy, and I imagine it's stuff you've not talked about for a long time. If you don't want me to say it, I won't. We can just take it as read.'

After a pause, Ray let out a hearty laugh. 'Bravo!' he clapped his hands. 'You nearly got me there. So you don't have to find out anything about me, other than my mother's first name, and the rest we just *take as read.*' He spread his hands wide as he quoted her. 'Clever girl! No, I'll bite. What else did you find out?' There was a boldness to his voice, but his eyes told a different tale. They were shifting from side to side. He was nowhere near as comfortable as he was trying to suggest.

'Okay. Well, assuming you don't want me to leave any of it out, I think I'll begin with your twin brother, Martin. He was found guilty of killing his wife, Susan. He later died of sepsis whilst incarcerated in Crow's Wall Prison. You have two nieces, Annie and Olivia, and you had a nephew, named Toby. I'm sorry to have to tell you that Toby's dead. You may not know that.'

His face dropped at the final piece of news. 'Poor little Toby. What did he ...?'

'Cancer.'

He rose from his chair and began pacing his office. Rubbing his forehead, he said, 'I didn't expect all that.'

'You set me a challenge, Ray.'

'Two hours!' There was genuine praise in his voice.

Hannah remained silent.

'I try not to think about Martin.'

'And Susan?'

'Yes, I think of her often. We named Emily after her.'

'Yes, I know.' Hannah considered how much further she ought to go. Should she tell him what she knew about Beverley? There was proving her worth, and then there was simply showing off. But she wanted him to let her in, she wanted to try to solve the mystery surrounding Jake's death for him, and the only way to achieve that was to absolutely blow him away with what she knew. So, taking a deep breath, she whispered, 'I also know who your wife was.'

'What?' Ray asked, alarmed.

'The infamous Greenwood sisters. I'm right, aren't I?'

'Y ... yes,' he stuttered. 'Jesus Christ!' He marched over to his chair and slumped into it. Placing his head in his hands, he began mumbling inaudibly.

'You told me to find out all I could.'

'But ... but ... none of this stuff is ... you shouldn't have been able to simply Google all this. It's supposed to be hidden. What if Emily ...?'

Hannah knew she was going to have to tell him the whole truth. She couldn't bear to see him so fraught. He was worried about his daughter, and she couldn't have that.

Placing a reassuring hand on his shoulder, she said, 'It's not all on Google. I promise you. I need to tell you how I know all this, but you have to agree to listen to the end, and you have to let me help you solve how Jake died. Deal?'

Ray nodded. 'I reckon if you can find out all that, it shouldn't take you long to work out what happened to my son. Come on then, how do you know so much?'

'Before I tell you, I need you to look me in the eye and answer one question for me?'

He met her gaze.

She stared at him, checking out the whites of his eyes, as Lottie always said. 'Did you kill Susan Farnley?'

'What?'

'You heard me.'

'No! Of course not. My brother did. You just told me that yourself.'

'One hundred percent, it was Martin and not you?'

'I promise you. I was at home when she died. I made some mistakes. I fell in love with my brother's wife, and I stepped over a line I shouldn't have crossed. But I *did not* kill her.'

'Okay. I believe you.' Hannah took a deep breath.

IT WAS odd realising she was about to tell Ray about Liv and why she had hired Sandlin PI Investigations. Initially the brief had been to prove that he had killed Susan; now, here she was, asking for his help to work out who had tricked his niece. It felt as if not only the brief had changed, but the client had, too. He'd gone from enemy to ally. She could only hope she was right to trust him.

She dived in. 'I was employed as a PI by Olivia Farnley. At our very first meeting she told me *you* killed her mum.

'What? But that's not—'

'Ray, I asked you to hear me out until the end. You only let me get two sentences in.'

He waved his hand. 'Go on then!'

'She told me she had recently remembered exactly what happened, and she had seen it all. My job was to prove you were the one who killed Susan. I guess she was hoping for some kind of posthumous pardon for her dad and retribution for you.'

'What would make her say ...?' Ray stopped talking and waved his hand again.

'Unfortunately, Olivia, or Liv, as she prefers to be called, didn't tell me the whole story. She omitted to mention how she had recently acquired these new memories. She then became ill and was unable to meet me for a while. I took the opportunity to fly to Marbella and check you out for myself.' Hannah could see he was bursting with questions. But she gave him no time to ask them. Pressing on, she said, 'That was when we met Jake and then the rest of the family. I have to say I never got the impression that Liv was right about you. I believed from the start that you were not Susan's killer.'

'Well, thank you for that at least,' Ray blurted out, before pinching his lips again and suggesting she should continue.

'I returned to the UK the other day and met up with Liv. This is when she told me the whole truth. I wish she'd told me this part sooner; her memories came to her via hypnosis. A hypnotherapist named Stephen Lawson-Ewart hypnotised her and somehow convinced her that she saw you killing her mother. Do you have any knowledge of this man?'

Ray pointed at himself. 'Oh, may I speak now?'

'You may.'

'I've never heard of him. And I cannot believe the silly child allowed herself to be convinced about such utter codswallop.'

'She's not a child; she's forty-five years old.'

'Hmm ... I suppose she is.'

'They didn't stand still in time when you left them all. Your mum, your nieces, your nephew, they all kept getting older.'

'Yes. I see that now.'

'Why did you leave them?'

Once again Ray rose from his chair and paced the room.

'I can't justify it to you. I can't justify it to *them*. All I can tell you is ... I had to go. D'you think I don't know what it did to my mum? It was necessary. I'd already met and fallen in love with Beverley by then. She was so delicate. I took her with me. She's remained by my side ever since.'

'That's nice to hear.' Hannah's praise was genuine.

'Anyway, this Stephen Ewart-whatshisname, he convinced Olivia that I killed her mum, and what did she do about it, apart from hire you?'

'She tried to tell the police, but they weren't interested.'

'Naturally. My brother was convicted years ago for the crime. It wasn't me. No one ever thought it was.'

'I think she realises that now. But she was pretty convinced at the time of the hypnosis. Ray, listen, your niece didn't get through all this unscathed. She's an addict, and her addictions have taken her to hell and back. She's not the most stable of women, unfortunately. I think whoever did this to her knew that, and they relied upon it to get you convicted.'

'Well, she needs to think about who recommended this man to her. Whoever put her on to him in the first place is surely as guilty as hell.'

'She can't remember who recommended him. She said she read about him somewhere. It's all very vague. She has memory lapses, she's ... unreliable.'

'Oh, she has memory lapses, does she? Until it comes to remembering me murdering her mother on her own doorstep, then she simply has fake memories.' Ray's face grew steadily puce.

'Instead of being angry at Liv, why not be angry at whoever set this whole thing up? He's the person who actually means you harm.'

'So, this hypnotherapist, he comes to your home, does he? Is it like calling out for a massage or something?'

'No, he had a legit place. A reception and a practice room. I've seen where he worked, although he was long gone from there.'

'A practice room. Like a medical room, you mean?'

'Well, nicer than that. It was an office. Beautifully decorated. Expensive wallpaper. Grey, with images of birds every so often.'

Ray stopped pacing.

'Birds?'

'Yes.'

'British birds?'

'I suppose so.'

'Come with me, please?' Abruptly he left the room and made his way over to the other side of the villa.

Hannah followed.

Knocking gently on a door that Hannah had not made it through during her snoop around the villa, Ray opened it slightly.

'Darling, sorry to bother you. Can I come in, or are you sleeping?'

Beverley's soft voice replied, 'I'm not sleeping. I was thinking about reading or ...' She seemed to lose interest in her sentence halfway through.

'I have Hannah with me. All right if we pop in?'

Although she was clearly confused, Beverley called out her agreement.

Ray entered the room, followed cautiously by Hannah. Walking over to the large floor-to-ceiling windows, he pulled back the curtains, allowing the evening sun to flood in. 'I'm just showing her the décor, darling,' he said.

Hannah gazed at the walls. And there it was, the exact same wallpaper she'd seen in Stephen Lawson-Ewart's room. This time it decorated two walls.

'Is this the kind of thing you were thinking of?' he asked, with fake cheeriness.

'Erm ... yes. That's it. Exactly. Lovely.' She nodded. 'I'm sure Lottie would like it in her room.'

'Good.' He replaced the curtains. 'Sorry to bother you, darling.' He gazed at his wife, lovingly. 'We'll let you get back to erm ...' He glanced at the book that lay on the bed next to his wife. 'Evelyn Waugh.'

Amazed that Beverley didn't seem to find any of this odd, but simply trusted Ray completely, Hannah scurried along behind as he walked out of the room.

67

HANNAH, APRIL 2023

BACK IN THE OFFICE, Ray could barely contain his anger. 'The little shit. What the ...?'

'Are you going to explain?' she asked. 'Or simply rant.'

'That wallpaper is called Flight of Fancy; it's by House of Hackney. It's a couple of hundred quid per roll. We had some left over after we did Beverley's room. If that's the exact wallpaper you saw in the hypnotherapist's office, then there's only one person that Stephen bastard could've been.'

'Jake?' Hannah asked.

'Yes. As soon as you said about the hypnosis, I suspected him. Damn it.' He slammed his right fist into his left palm. 'He learnt some stupid trick at university. Putting people into a trance, as he called it. It never worked on me, load of nonsense. But ...'

'Maybe it would work on someone who was wounded, and lost, and just a little desperate.'

'Yes, maybe it bloody well would!'

She took a second to absorb the news.

'So, if it *was* Jake behind this whole thing, what on earth could have motivated him to do such a thing?'

Blowing all the air out of his cheeks, Ray said, 'I feel physically sick. One minute I'm choking back tears for the boy, the next ... this.'

'I'm so sorry,' Hannah said.

'Don't be. It's the story of my life when it comes to Jake. He disappointed me more times than I care to count. The way he spoke to his mother. The way he treated her with such disregard, after everything she went through.' He shook his head.

'Do the children know exactly what she went through? Who she really is?'

'No. Not all the details. They know, well in Jake's case *knew*, there was trauma in her early years, and that she lost both her parents. But she never wanted them to know her real name. If they looked it up, read the newspaper articles ... She's still ashamed of it all. No matter how many times I tell her not to be. She will never get over how that monstrous brother of hers treated her, and then of course, what her sister did.'

At the mention of Derek Greenwood, Hannah was transported straight back to Dawn Barton's death in the street. It was too shocking. She couldn't bear it. So much blood. You never forget the sight of it. With a shudder, she automatically changed the subject back to Jake. 'So, like I say, what do you think Jake's motive was?'

'Without a shadow of a doubt, it was money.'

'Uh huh.'

'He hated that I was still in charge of the business. He thought an old duffer like me ought to be playing golf every day or sitting by a log fire with a checked blanket over my knees. Jake wanted to take over the business because he wanted to control the money. I think he was trying to make some of his own; I know he was buying and selling that crap he snorts up his nose, erm ... *snorted*. Jesus, it's hard to remember he's dead.'

'Go on. Don't worry about tenses. Just say it.'

'I guess he was hoping I'd get put away for Susan's murder. The next step would've been to suggest I turn everything over to him.'

'Risky!'

'Jake wasn't the sharpest tool in the shed. He probably didn't think much further than persuading Olivia she'd seen me.'

'Would you have given the business over to him? If his plan had worked and you were in prison, would he be your choice to run the company?' Hannah asked.

'He was never really my choice. I have two men who've worked for me for donkey's years. I trust them implicitly. But Jake is over twenty-eight, and for my sins, that was the age I stated he could take over if I died.'

'Not planning on dying just yet, are you?'

'No. But ... in 2020 we all thought we were goners, didn't we?'

'Ah yes. So that was when you put it in writing.'

'Exactly.'

'And Jake knew that?'

'He did.' Ray nodded.

They both stood silently for a second, before Hannah had a thought. 'Hang on a minute though. Stephen's office was rented in Toby's name.'

'What?'

'I spoke to the letting agent. The name used for the short-term rental was Toby Farnley.'

'And he was already dead?'

'Yes, 2015.'

'How would Jake know about Toby?'

'You never told him he had cousins?'

'I never told him anything about Kingshurst.'

Hannah was confused. 'So ... how could he know? Surely, Toby wasn't just a name he plucked from a hat.'

Ray began slowly nodding to himself.

'What?'

The nods became more exaggerated.

'Are you okay?' Hannah asked.

'I've got it. I don't want to believe it, but I've got it.'

'Any chance I could have it, too?'

'He must've been working together with my daughter. No other way possible.'

'Emily? Don't be crazy.'

'Not Emily. My *other* daughter.'

'I didn't know—'

'Antoinette Farnley. She's in the will; she inherits the company with Jake.'

'Antoinette?'

'Yes, Olivia would've referred to her as Annie though.'

Hannah asked, 'She's *your* daughter?'

'Apparently so,' Ray replied. 'If Susan is to be believed.'

———

By the time they joined Lottie and Emily in the lounge the Rioja was all but gone. Ray went to the wine cellar and grabbed another bottle and two more glasses.

Whilst he was gone, Lottie whispered, 'Bloody hell, Han, you look a bit shell shocked. You okay?'

'Yeah. Maybe one too many secrets.'

'Like?'

'Not now,' Hannah whispered back.

Ray arrived in the lounge, pulling the cork from the fresh bottle and saying, 'I don't know about you, Hannah, but I don't have the time to wait for this to breathe.'

'Well ... I'm not supposed to be drinking. I wanted to keep a clear head.'

Pouring a large glass, he said, 'I think you need this.' He then asked the others, 'What about you two, can I top anyone up?'

Both nodded.

'Drink up then, we can't mix the bottles.'

'You've been gone ages,' Emily said. 'What the hell did you find to talk about for so long?' She shot a look at Hannah.

It dawned on Hannah that Emily was worried she might be after Ray. Dear, sweet Emily was worried she was going to steal her dad from Beverley. With a small smile, she said, 'Restoration, soft furnishings, wallpaper ...'

Ray patted his daughter's hand. 'We wanted to give you two time to chat alone. How are you doing, darling?'

'I'm okay. How's Mum?'

'She's not doing too bad. She's reading for now. I don't expect we'll see her again tonight.'

———

They sat in an easy silence. Through one window they watched the lights in the neighbouring villas come on, tiny specks of brightness, each one representing a family, a home, a life. Through the larger window there was an amazing sunset. As the sun made its way majestically into the sea, a combination of orange and red, shimmering and turning the sky violet as it hit the midnight blue of the water, Hannah was desperately trying to digest the fact that Ray was the biological father of Susan's first child. She had asked him if Annie knew, and he had said it was Susan's intention to tell her when she returned home the night she was killed. But Annie had never mentioned it to him, so he suspected there hadn't been time. He said he'd sent a letter to her years later, but again, she had not replied, so he assumed she hadn't received it. He figured the address might have been old.

Hannah sipped her wine. Watching the free show that Mother Nature had kindly laid on for them, she allowed herself to simply breathe. This was the calm before the storm. She was so close to solving this thing, and she couldn't wait to divulge the truth ... and she would do, as soon as she knew it all.

68
HANNAH, APRIL 2023

THE NEXT DAY was one of isolation for Hannah. Instructing Lottie to go and have a good time in the spa, she explained that for her, today was about thinking. There were so many facts circling their way around inside her head.

'I need to call Dave, and there's a couple of things I'd like to check out with Paul at the station.'

'You're sure you'll be okay?'

'Yes,' Hannah assured her. 'I just need to think.'

'The leetle grey cells,' Lottie joked.

'You may mock, Missy, but I'm with Hercule on this one. It's all here in my head; now I need to organise it.'

Lottie began rummaging around in the bottom of the wardrobe.

'I think I might go to the gym. I could do with a few minutes on the treadmill, or the rowing machine. Especially after all that lovely food at Emily's yesterday.'

'Good idea. I might join you later,' Hannah said, absent-mindedly.

Grabbing her trainers, Lottie asked, 'You don't happen to know where my invisible socks are, do you? I can't see them.'

'Are you serious?'

'Huh?'

Hannah smiled. 'Never mind. Sometimes my dad's sense of humour lives in my head.' Casually opening a few drawers, she finally pulled out a tiny pair of trainer socks. 'I'm guessing these are *invisible?*'

'Yep. Thanks.' Lottie put her gym stuff into a bag and headed out the door.

———

Apart from eating the rather good chicken club sandwich that she ordered from room service, Hannah didn't stop all day. She made notes, she took calls, she texted people, and she paced the room.

By six in the evening, Lottie was back. She was even more beautiful than when she'd left, if that was possible.

'Have a good time?' Hannah asked.

'Yes, thanks. The facial was lush. Even the gym this morning wasn't too awful.'

'Good.'

'You didn't come for a run.'

'No, I was too busy.'

'Thinking?'

'Yep.'

'I can fully recommend the hot stones,' Lottie said. 'They might still be able to fit you in.' She checked the time on her phone.

'Hmm ... another time. But I'm glad you had fun.'

'And you? Did you have fun ... thinking?'

'Uh huh.'

'How close are you?'

Hannah held up her index finger and thumb; there was the tiniest gap between them.

Lottie gave an excited squeal. 'I need to know everything.'

'You will, sweetheart.'

'But you wouldn't tell me anything last night.' Lottie pouted.

'It's all coming together. I promise. Not long now.' Hannah's phone vibrated, announcing a text. Checking the screen, she said, 'Ah ha, the final piece. Ray would like to invite us over tomorrow. Easter Sunday lunch.'

'Who'll be there?'

'By the looks of it, everyone who needs to be.' Hannah tapped the side of her head like a true detective.

'The suspects assemble.'

'Yes, Hastings. I believe they do.'

'Hast … Oh I get it, you're Poirot, so I'm—'

'Yes, yes, don't overthink it, love.' Hannah laughed.

———

The next day, they arrived at the villa on time.

Ray answered the door.

'Thanks for coming.' He called out for Emily. 'Hannah and Lottie are here!'

They stepped into the hallway, which was now on par with the Chelsea flower show. The floral smell was almost overwhelming.

'Wow. So many flowers,' Lottie said.

'Mostly from clients. Some of them go back a long way,' Ray replied.

'Is everyone else here?' Hannah asked.

'Yes,' Ray said. 'And I've cooked a roast.'

'Great.' Hannah wasn't sure what else to say. In truth, she found it strange that he could muster up the enthusiasm to cook food so soon after Jake's death.

Somehow reading her mind, he added, 'I want to keep things as normal as possible for Emily and Beverley.'

Caught out, telepathically, Hannah blushed a little. 'Good idea.'

'Pop out to the terrace, everyone's out there.' Ray instructed, heading back towards the kitchen. 'I need to check on the lamb.'

'The only time a house is ever this crowded with flowers is after a death,' Lottie remarked to Hannah as they approached the terrace.

They joined Emily, Claudia, Toni, Thalia and a couple of Emily's friends, whose names they didn't know, but whose fresh faces looked familiar. Hannah was surprised to see that Beverley was also on the terrace. Hannah didn't imagine she was the kind of person to enjoy the heat, and despite being in the shade, the terrace at the Farnley villa was still decidedly warm.

Taking the opportunity to talk to her before she ran back inside like a vampire when the sun comes up, Hannah asked, 'How are you doing, Beverley?'

Beverley gave a small nod. 'I'm okay. Thanks for asking.'

'It's a silly question,' Hannah continued. 'I mean, erm ... no one expects you to be okay. But ...'

Beverley's gaze shifted from Hannah to the other people on the terrace, and then out to the view beyond. Hannah had lost her. *Shit! Rushed it.*

Emily and Thalia were having a discussion about *Bake Off*, which Hannah found amusing but was unable to add anything to, having never seen it. Claudia sat in silence, occasionally sniffing. As before, she was dressed entirely in black. Her outfit was a little over the top, but Hannah had to admit, Claudia wore it well. Toni had also opted for black, wearing a high-necked black floral blouse and linen trousers. Whether she was in mourning or simply looking smart for Easter, Hannah couldn't be sure.

Making an effort to regain Beverley's attention, she said, 'I'm looking forward to lunch. Is Ray a good cook?'

Beverley shrugged. 'I suppose so.'

Ballsed it up again. For goodness' sake, Hannah, she's about as interested in food as you are in Chris Hemsworth. Will you pull yourself together!

Before she had the chance to ask any more stupid questions, Ray appeared at the patio doors. 'Not long now. The leg of lamb is resting.' He immediately apologised to Emily and her friends. 'Sorry, you don't want to hear that. There's something for you girls, too.'

Emily smiled. 'Thanks, Dad. You didn't have to do this?'

'It's Easter. A time for family … and friends.' Ray turned his gaze towards Lottie, who was clearly his favourite.

The next minute, Beverley rose from the table and excused herself. Hannah hoped she would be back.

———

The meal was good. Beverley did indeed return and ate her usual four mouthfuls of food. The talk at the table was interesting and varied. Occasionally someone would mention Jake, and everyone would join in, in the way people do when someone has recently been lost. Memories resurfaced. Stories were told. Some lunch companions laughed, some (Claudia mostly) cried.

After the final dishes were cleared away, Emily's younger friends left, with cries of, 'Thank you for lunch, Mr Farnley.'

Next to say goodbye were Thalia and Claudia. Claudia managed to make a performance of kissing both Beverley and Ray as if they were her closest friends.

'It really is too awful, darling,' she said, as she kissed the air close to Beverley's cheeks.

'Some people protest too much for my liking,' Hannah mumbled.

'What does that mean?' Claudia asked, a pinch of anger on her face.

'Surely I don't have to explain Shakespeare to you,' Hannah replied.

Claudia gave a dismissive shake of her head.

'Well, excuse me for caring.'

'You're excused,' Hannah said.

After this altercation, Claudia swooped out, her redundant tissue still pressed to her face. Thalia followed in her wake, booking an Uber on her phone.

Before she knew it, Hannah found herself in the lounge, with a small audience.

She decided to take the plunge at once. There was no telling how long she would have Beverley's attention for; she already appeared to be itching to get at the dishwasher, and Ray could pop to his study at any minute. It was like herding cats.

69

HANNAH, APRIL 2023

HANNAH CLEARED HER THROAT.

'Ray, you asked me here today, not only to share the delicious lunch you'd made, but because you thought I might be able to help solve the mystery behind Jake's fall the other night.'

Ray nodded.

She wondered if she ought to stand up, or pace the floor. Hmm? No, perhaps not.

'If I can have everyone's undivided attention for the next few minutes, I believe I *can* help you all.'

They placed their coffee cups on the many small tables that were perfectly positioned around the room and turned their gaze towards her. *Good. Finally!*

'As Ray knows, I am not a renovator of furniture. That is a job title held only by my friend, Lottie. I, in fact, used to be a police officer, and I am now a private investigator.'

The room remained silent.

Okay, I had hoped for a little more reaction, but never mind. Hannah pressed on. 'Yesterday, I spoke to an ex-colleague of mine, who is still a serving police officer in the UK, and I can confirm there are several opportunities here in Marbella to buy cocaine. No surprises there. The local police believe Jake may have previously bought large quantities of cocaine from persons who are known to them. Perhaps he didn't always pay up when asked to. Or maybe on occasion he tried to resell it at far more than the usual mark up? Neither of those things would be likely to make the sellers treat him favourably.'

Toni shook her head. 'Silly boy. He ought to have known better.'

Ray agreed. 'I tried to warn him.'

Hannah glanced at Beverley, awaiting a similarly trite comment. None came. Beverley said nothing. Perhaps the things she'd seen at a young age had made her impervious to drama.

Hannah continued, 'My ex-colleague confirmed the local police are pretty confident Jake fell, due to intoxication. Despite the witness who came forward, clearly saying they saw an altercation, I fear misadventure could be the preferred conclusion to all this. I'm concerned Jake's death could easily remain unsolved.'

Beverley leant forward in her seat.

Hannah turned her attention back to her, intrigued as to what she might be about to say.

Disappointingly, Beverley merely reached for her coffee and took a sip.

'I suppose ...' Toni said, 'you can't do much about it. If the local police don't have enough evidence, then ...'

'But remember,' Hannah said, 'there's another person investigating his death. A person who knows more about Jake than the local police.'

'You?' Toni asked.

'Yes, me.'

'Do you think you can trace these dealers?'

'No.'

'Well, what's the point of you saying you're investigating then?' Toni asked with a wrinkled brow.

'I don't need to name the local cocaine dealers. I know who pushed Jake down those steps, and it wasn't a dealer.'

'What?' Ray asked, beginning to rise from his chair.

'Steady. You agreed to let me investigate, and I have. I know everything now,' Hannah assured him.

'So, who pushed him?' Beverley asked in a quiet voice.

Hannah was surprised; finally Beverley had joined the party. 'There were a number of people interested in Jake,' Hannah began. 'We all know that. Any one of whom could've pushed him. I understand he's a good-looking man, he's gregarious, exciting ... to some. As I said to Lottie, there were women who *could* have him, if only for a short while, and there were those who could *never* have him. Several people have mourned him, here in your home and on his social media pages.'

Beverley spoke again; as before, her voice was soft. 'Do you actually know who pushed him?'

'I believe I do, yes. But in order to tell you, I need to go back a bit. I have to divulge some facts that could make you all uncomfortable. Are you all okay with that?'

Everyone stared at her. There was barely contained excitement on Lottie's face. Hannah knew she was proud of her, but she chose to focus on the others. It wouldn't do to get ahead of herself. She continued, 'There were people in Jake's life who were not what they seemed.'

'Such as?' Ray asked.

'Well ... for example ... you yourself,' Hannah replied. 'You said you would welcome my help in getting to the bottom of all this, but in some respects, one could say that you, Ray Farnley, lie like a cheap watch.'

He laughed aloud. 'Pah! I admit, I may have failed to tell people certain facts about my past.'

'Lying by omission,' Hannah said.

'Okay.' Ray gave a small nod of his head. 'I'll give you that. But ... I certainly didn't lie about wanting your help. I honestly

would welcome your thoughts on how our son came to fall
down those steps.'

Hannah gave it a moment's consideration, before saying,
'Yes, I believe you would. You may have kept many secrets from
your loved ones, but I don't think you were complicit in killing
your son.'

With barely a pause, Ray said, 'Look, I'm okay with you
talking about my past if it's going to help.'

'Thank you,' Hannah said. 'I believe it will help enormously.'
She drew in a breath, and then said, 'What some of us in this
room know, but others may not, is that Ray had a twin brother.
An *identical* twin. And therein lies the problem. Ray's brother
Martin committed a crime. A terrible crime. Thirty years ago,
he killed his wife.'

Emily seemed stunned. This was clearly news to her. Hannah
watched astonishment register on her pretty, young face. It was
hard being the bearer of shocking news. Hard, but also the
purpose of her investigations.

Toni asked. 'But how does a thirty-year-old murder relate to
Jake falling down some steps? I don't get it.'

'You will, Toni. I promise you,' Hannah continued. 'Martin
was incarcerated in Crow's Wall Prison. He was guilty, he was
convicted, and he died in prison. That ought to have been the
end of it. But it wasn't. Fast forward to last year, and you find
Jake, desperate for money, and keen to take over his father's
company. Telling him he would inherit it at twenty-eight if you
were dead really was rather rash, Ray.'

Ray shot a look at his wife. 'Sorry, darling. I thought it was
best he knew. It was that damn Covid business messing with my
head.'

Hannah continued, 'Jake devised a plan. A rather stupid one
as it goes. He decided to frame his own father for the murder
that took place over three decades ago. He figured because
Martin and Ray were identical, he could somehow convince the

police Ray had killed Susan Farnley, instead of Martin. But Jake didn't want to get his hands dirty, so he found someone else to report the crime to the police.' She glanced at Beverley, who seemed genuinely intrigued. *At last!* 'Ray has a niece; her name is Olivia. Sadly, she is an addict. She gets confused, she's easily led, and she's emotionally damaged. All these things made her, in Jake's opinion, the ideal stooge. He used hypnosis to persuade her she had seen Ray kill her mum. He did this so convincingly that she employed me to investigate Ray.'

Toni drew in her breath. 'Wait. This is very confusing. How do you *know* Jake did all this?'

Hannah gave a small smile. 'It is confusing, yes, and for that I apologise. How do I know it was Jake who planted fake memories into my client's head? Simple. Yesterday, I sent my client, Olivia, a photo of Jake. One of the selfies Lottie took by the pool with him when we first came here, for Emily's birthday.' She turned to Lottie. 'That's why I asked you to share them with me when you were at the gym.' Back to the room in general, she said, 'Olivia confirmed the good-looking man in the pool was the exact same person who had tricked her. And let me tell you, she is livid!'

Ray rubbed his forehead. 'I'd hoped we were wrong about Jake being the hypnotist.'

'Not wrong, I'm afraid,' Hannah said.

'So ...?' Emily said. 'What you're saying is that Jake tricked your client and she got mad and came over here and pushed him down the steps. Is that right?'

'No,' Hannah said. 'Olivia only knew Jake was her hypnotist yesterday.'

'So ... what then?' Emily said, shaking her head.

'There are two people in Ray's will who are set to inherit the business. I imagine Jake wasn't just planning on getting him sent to prison. What good would that do? He needed to have owner-ship of the company. Perhaps he was planning for a little accident once he got his dad put away. Something similar to Martin's demise.'

Toni tried to ask, 'How did he—'

Hannah interrupted. 'Let's put Martin Farnley's death to one side for now.' She moved an imaginary box to the left. 'What we need to focus on is the fact that there's another person in Ray's will. A woman named Antoinette Farnley. Otherwise known as Annie.' She paused. 'Annie is Olivia's sister. I believe Annie was also in on the fabricated memory plan.'

Beverley placed her hand over her mouth; for the first time she seemed genuinely upset.

'Her own sister?'

'Yes, unimaginable, isn't it, Beverley?' Hannah said. 'I think Annie is the one who pushed your son down the marble steps. When their plan went wrong, I think she confronted him.'

Ray grimaced. 'What? Flew here. Pushed him. And then merrily flew home again, as if nothing had happened?'

'Not exactly,' Hannah said. 'When I sent the selfies to Olivia, she spotted someone else she knew in one of them. Just a glimpse of someone by the pool, but she recognised her.'

All eyes in the room were on Hannah. Time stood still for a second. She felt a moment's exhilaration as she said, 'She spotted her sister, Annie.' Hannah turned her gaze to Toni.

'Did she?' Toni gulped, audibly.

'You know she did, Antoinette?'

'I ...'

'Annie, Toni, both nicknames for Antoinette,' Hannah said. '*Annie* didn't need to fly out here to confront Jake because *Toni* was already here. You came out a couple of weeks ago. You rented a small place, and you wheeled your way into the family. You had no need to stay in Kingshurst; you thought your work there was done.'

'I ...'

'You changed your hair, blonde and curly now, very different. But not enough to fool your own sister. I assume you bought a few expensive items of clothing, and you prepared to settle into Marbella life. Introducing yourself to the family as a neighbour, you were able to see exactly what was going on. But Liv didn't do the job too well, did she? She failed to raise the slightest bit of doubt with the police. The whole thing was a total waste of time. Is that why you pushed Jake?'

'I really don't know wh ... what ...' Toni stammered.

'I know you fought with him. He grabbed you, didn't he?' Hannah rose from her chair and approached Toni. 'May I?' She gestured towards her blouse.

Toni's hand flew to her chest.

'No!'

'If there's nothing there you won't mind showing us,' Hannah said.

After a pause, Toni snorted, 'Fine!' She pulled the top of her blouse down to reveal large yellowing bruises on both sides of her neck.

'You wore a high-necked jumper to the tapas meal. I thought it was odd. It was so hot that night. I guess you didn't think you'd get much wear out of it over here. But I'll bet you were glad you packed it.'

'It was an accident,' Toni said. 'I didn't mean him to fall. I ... look ... *he* was attacking *me*!'

'I can see that,' Hannah said. 'But if it was self-defence, why not tell someone?'

Toni glanced around the room, as if searching for a viable reason.

'There was too much to tell.' She glanced down at her lap.

'Toni?' Hannah asked, 'Or do you prefer Annie?'

'My name is Annie.'

'All right. Annie, can you tell us what happened on the steps, please?'

70

HANNAH, APRIL 2023

'I WANT to start by saying I'm sorry to Ray.' Annie glanced over at him.

He gave not the slightest suggestion that her apology was accepted.

She continued, 'Yes, I was part of the idiotic plan, and I have no excuse. Except to say I've always had nothing, and Jake presented me with an opportunity to have *something* for once in my life.'

Hannah knew Ray was angry. A vein pulsed violently in the side of his head. But apparently, he was also willing to keep listening, perhaps hoping to hear something that would help him to understand.

Annie pressed on. 'You're right. I did come out here a couple of weeks ago. I thought my new life was about to begin, and I was keen to leave Kingshurst. Not that Jake was entirely pleased to see me. I'm sure he would've been happier if I'd stayed put. When Olivia texted and told me she'd been unable to convince the police, I couldn't believe it. It was a huge spanner in the works. Then she told me she was hiring a private investigator. I was surprised, and I must admit I didn't picture *you*. I was already in my little apartment here in Spain when I got the message, and straight away I texted Jake and told him. The next time I saw him was here, at Emily's birthday celebration. He wasn't too impressed; he took me to one side and promised to think of another plan. We were still hopeful at that point that we were going to succeed.' She glanced again at Ray. 'I know how wrong that sounds.'

'Wrong? I'd say *criminal*, but do carry on, Antoinette,' Ray said.

'Jake called me the next day and asked me to meet him at the steps to the beach before the tapas meal. I went along because I thought he had a genuine plan. But his latest idea was even more ridiculous.'

'What was it?' Beverley asked, in an unwavering voice.

'He said ...' Annie paused. 'I'm sorry, Ray, but he said we could get someone to ... you know ... bump you off. He knew it was a risk to do it here, but ... he was desperate.'

'Fucking hell!' Ray spat.

'I said it was crazy. Like something out of a film. But he said he knew people.'

'Right. And ...?' Ray asked, the vein protruding further.

'He had this idea that we should get Olivia out here, and then ...' Annie gazed at her lap, clearly ashamed. 'Then we could frame her for it. He said she was useless, a flake, the police would fall for it. Not only that but the UK police would back it up; they'd say yes, she did come here trying to get her uncle convicted. He thought it was the ideal motive. Crazy ex-junkie has it in for her uncle, thirty years after the death of her mum. Uncle ends up dead. Obvious suspect must be crazy ex-junkie.'

'What a clever boy!' Ray said, his voice dripping with sarcasm. 'I take it you disagreed.'

'Yes. I drew the line at using Olivia that way.'

'Hmm ... shame you didn't draw the line at me!'

'Ray, I'm so sorry. I just got caught up. It ... it just didn't seem real somehow.'

Hannah stepped in, keen to hear the rest. 'I think you should save the apologies for now. You need to tell us what happened on those steps.'

'Okay. Long story short – I said no way was I using my sister like that. We disagreed. It became ridiculous and childish. Then, I said something along the lines of *I'm the eldest of the two of us; if and when Ray dies and we inherit the company, I will make bloody sure you're excluded. You're not fit to run an egg and spoon race, never mind a company.* He was so angry. There was something behind his eyes. A flash, of ferocity.' Annie paused. 'Then he said he would go ahead with the plan to frame Olivia without me. He said he would frame both of us, kill two birds with one stone. I turned; I was ready to leave. The last thing I said to him was that I would speak to Ray at the restaurant. I said I was going to confess everything and let the cards fall where they may. I just wanted it to end by that point.'

'And?' Hannah asked.

'That flash behind his eyes became an explosion. With a brutal energy he grabbed me around the neck and started squeezing. He was shouting for me to keep my mouth shut about everything.' She looked at Ray, her eyes glistening with unshed tears. 'I couldn't get any air in. I was clawing at his fingers, but he was too strong. Each second without oxygen felt like my chest was going to explode. My brain was on fire. I couldn't let it happen again.'

'You're referring to your mum,' Hannah said.

'Yes. She was strangled ... well, she hit her head, but before that, she was almost strangled to death.'

'And you thought you were going to meet the same fate?'

'I honestly did. The pain was intense. I couldn't believe he would do it. I mean ... he knew what happened to my mum! What a total bastard.'

The room remained silent.

'It was so strange to finally know what my mum went through,' Annie continued. 'To see it from this side.'

'*See it?*' Hannah asked.

'Yes.'

'Have you seen it from the other side?'

'Yes ... I ... umm. Yes, I have.'

Gently, Hannah asked, 'Were you there when your mum died, Annie?'

Annie drew in a deep breath but said nothing. The unshed tears finally fell. She reached into her handbag and pulled out a small packet of tissues.

'I think you were,' Hannah said. 'I think you witnessed your mother's killing, and you absolutely wouldn't allow Jake to do the same to you.'

'Once was more than enough,' Annie said. 'I wasn't going to die there on those steps, suffering the way my mum did. That's why I pushed him.' She scanned the room, searching for allies. 'You must understand that I had to do it. I had to get him off me. I couldn't breathe.'

Ray's mouth hung open. Recovering his composure a little, he said, 'You saw Susan die?'

'Yes,' Annie confirmed. 'I did.'

71

HANNAH, APRIL 2023

'IT WOULD REALLY HELP us if you could tell us what you saw the night your mum died,' Hannah said.

Annie nodded, resigned. When she spoke, it was clear she'd thought about this event a thousand times before.

'Trevor was being annoying, *again*. It was nice to be needed, but he was way too confrontational. That boy could start an argument in an empty room. We were in his car, parked up on the downs. I liked it up there, we were never disturbed. But as soon as we'd finished, erm ... what we were there for ...' She gave a small cough of embarrassment. 'Trevor started to irritate me again. He was being bossy. I didn't need that. I asked him to take me home. He didn't seem to want to go, but I just said I had a headache. I reminded him that my mum had asked me to look after my brother and sister earlier whilst she'd gone to do something, and I ought to go home and check if she was back. He was all like, *You don't even like being with the kids though.* Anyway, we drove home, and he dropped me at the end of the road. He always did that, because of the one-way system. I still remember the exhaust on his Polo making an irritating racket as he drove off.'

Everyone in the room listened intently. No one moved.

Annie continued, 'I checked my watch, trying to work out whether my mum would be back yet. I wondered where my dad was. But then I was like, *scrap that!* I didn't care. At that point I thought he was an asshole. The way he spoke to me then was shitty. He was mean, and I didn't like him. When I was little, and it was just me and Olivia, things had been better. Dad looked at me differently, he spoke to me differently. But by the time I was seventeen there was an enormous divide between us, and I didn't know how to close it. Anyway, I was a bit worried that Olivia and Toby might still be alone, so I hurried down the road. As I got to our part of the street and was about to cross over, I spotted two people on our doorstep. They were arguing. I was pretty sure it was my mum and dad. I wondered what the hell they were doing arguing in public. It seemed like Mum wanted to go back inside, but he said no, not in front of the kids! God, I was so embarrassed. If they knew I was there it would only get more awkward. My dad might turn on me.' Annie paused, wiped her nose, and then continued. 'I stood there in the darkness watching them. Then, taking a step backwards, I kind of hid in the bushes. There were twigs pressing into the side of my face. I was waiting for the argument to end, and for my parents to go back inside. A small part of me thought I ought to cross the road and go and back up my mum, but for some reason I didn't move. I was strangely intrigued. What was going to happen next?'

'I know what happened next,' Ray said, his voice full of emotion.

'Yes. I suppose you do,' Annie said. 'All of a sudden, with no warning, Dad grabbed Mum by the throat. I felt sick. It was the most horrific thing I'd ever seen. A voice inside my head told me to go and help her, but my legs refused to move. I guess I was just too shocked. I kept expecting him to stop. He had to. He couldn't keep on doing that. My eyes were fixed on them. I kept thinking, *Why? What had Mum done to make him do this to her?* For a split second, I hoped it wasn't Dad. I even wondered if there was any chance it could be you, Uncle Ray?' Her eyes turned to Ray.

He looked a little shocked to be called Uncle for the first time in so long. Especially by someone he clearly hadn't recognised before.

Annie left no gap. 'I did wonder if that would make more sense. You and my mum didn't get on that well. Or so I thought. Anyway, the next moment, Mum slapped him in the face, and he let go of her. She was gasping for air. Clutching at her throat. Then, she let out a horrible kind of scream. But he grabbed her again. This time he thrust her backwards towards the front wall of our house.' Annie began to cry. 'That house was our home; it was supposed to be our safe place.' Grabbing another tissue, she blew her nose and dabbed at her eyes. 'My mum's head hit the wall with a horrible thud, and she slumped to the floor. I don't think he intended that to happen. I don't think he was in his right mind. He was angry, yes, but he seemed surprised when she fell to the floor. I've never believed he actually wanted her dead.' Annie paused.

Hannah asked, gently, 'And then …?'

'Just as front doors began to open, I took a step forward. Finally, I was able to move. The neighbours started to come out; one was even in her bloody night clothes. Then Dad stepped away from Mum. She was kind of hunched against the house. Dad looked up and down the street, like he was searching for an escape. A couple of the neighbours started running towards him, and he just fled! He crossed the road and ran straight towards where I was standing. Then, he spotted me. We looked at each other, and, just for a second … I was really scared.'

'You're sure it was your dad though?' Hannah asked.

'Yes,' Annie said.

'*It wasn't me then!*' Ray shouted.

'No, it was Dad. As he passed me, he said something that confirmed it for me.'

There was total silence in the room. Everyone waited to hear the words that Martin Farnley had said to his daughter.

'He said, *I'm so sorry, Annie-Panny.*'

72

HANNAH, APRIL 2023

HANNAH SPOTTED an assortment of reactions on the faces in the room. Some, such as Emily, were probably still trying to take in that Ray had a twin; some were possibly focusing on the fact that Toni had been lying to them whilst she'd been in Marbella. It was clear Ray was remembering Susan. He had a melancholy look on his face.

'But you never told anyone what you saw?' Hannah asked Annie.

She shook her head, blankly.

'It wouldn't have changed the outcome. He was caught immediately. Besides, how could I? How could I say all that in front of Olivia and Toby?'

Throughout Annie's revelation, Hannah had watched everyone in turn, paying particular attention to Beverley, who intrigued her. Now, she asked her, 'Beverley, were you aware your husband was a twin?'

'Of course,' she replied.

'You knew all of it?'

'I did. Just as he knew all about me.'

Ray sighed. 'We needed to get away. From my family, from

Beverley's ... well, from everything. I assure you, we had good reason. We'd only recently met, and we knew we had to make a clean start together. It was stay in Kingshurst and suffocate or get out and make a life somewhere else.'

'So,' Hannah asked Ray, 'what happens now? Do you plan to tell the police about Annie?'

He shook his head in confusion. 'I don't know.' Looking at Annie, he said, 'You must know by now that you're more than a niece to me. How am I supposed to throw you under the bus?'

She nodded. 'I read my mum's diaries and Jake told me about the will. I know there's a high possibility that you're my father.'

Hannah heard a small squeak from Emily as she digested the latest revelation. The poor kid was taking some blows tonight.

'I simply don't understand how you could go along with such a cruel plan,' Ray said.

'Like I said, I've never had anything. My mum died, my dad died, my *biological* dad abandoned me ... do I need to go on?'

Ray held up his hand. 'No, you don't.'

Hannah stood. 'I suppose I'll leave this with all of you. Tell the police or let them go with the likely conclusion of misadventure? Decide between yourselves.'

'What an impossible decision,' Ray remarked, his head in his hands.

Hannah paused, before saying, mysteriously, 'I could make it easier for you.'

'How exactly?' Ray asked.

'I could tell you,' Hannah said, 'that according to the police, the witness saw two people on the steps having an argument with Jake.' She dropped her little bomb and waited.

Ray's face displayed total surprise. Whilst everyone else stood speechless, absorbing this latest piece of news, he addressed her directly, 'What are you saying, Hannah?'

'I'm telling you that Annie wasn't alone when she pushed Jake down those steps.'

'Who then?'

'Do you really want me to say who it was, Ray?' Hannah checked.

'Of course,' he replied.

Hannah crossed the room, aware of the enormity of what she was about to say. Feeling awful about it, but recognising the need for total disclosure, she said, 'I think you pushed him too, Beverley.'

One of Beverley's eyebrows shot up.

'It's admirable that Annie was going to take all the blame. But you helped to push Jake down those steps, didn't you?' Hannah said.

Silently, Beverley rose from her chair and brushed past Hannah. She made her way over to Emily, whose eyes were wide and unblinking with shock, her mouth open like a goldfish, firing out the words, 'No, no, no, no, no!'

Beverley instantly took her daughter into her arms, and said, 'I never meant for him to die. I promise you, darling.' Looking towards Ray, she mouthed the words, 'I'm sorry.'

'But ... what? *Why?*' Emily asked, her eyes now darting around her mother's face. Searching for clarity.

'I had no choice. I had to ...' Beverley shook her head, obviously realising she needed to go back a bit. 'I overheard Jake on the phone that day. I've heard him talking to dealers before, but this time it sounded like he was arranging to meet one of them. I decided to follow him. I wanted to see it with my own eyes. I had to know the extent he would go to, and the people he was involved with.'

She sought her husband's gaze, 'Honestly, Ray, I went there to protect Emily. I didn't like what Jake was, and I was scared of what he could do to her. We both know what he was like. No one else knew him, no one outside this family. They all thought he was so charming. But we knew.'

To Emily, she said, 'He had no regard for others; everything was for his own gain, it always was. If he was meeting a cocaine dealer, you could bet your life he was planning on buying the stuff to sell on. Anything for a quick buck. Your father gave him everything he needed; all he ever asked in return was that Jake be straight with him. But transparency wasn't Jake's way. I knew he was getting into something bad, something that might hurt the rest of us. I had to see exactly what he was up to, darling. I didn't want him bringing those dreadful people into our lives in any way, especially not yours.' Beverley paused, before taking a deep breath and continuing. 'But it turned out I was wrong; he wasn't going to the steps to buy cocaine.'

'What you saw was him fighting with Antoinette,' Hannah said.

'Yes, I watched them talking. I was surprised. I had no idea they even knew each other that well. One minute they were talking intently, then arguing, then, suddenly, he was ... strangling her. I didn't know who you really were then, Toni. But I couldn't just stand by and watch my son strangle a woman. He's always been a bully to Emily and me. Verbally, I mean. But never that. Never such violence. I was ... shocked. I thought he was going to kill you.'

'So you stepped in,' Hannah said.

'I walked towards them. I wasn't sure what I was going to do. I hoped seeing his mother would be enough. Although, in reality who was I kidding? But then ...'

'Then?' Hannah prompted.

Beverley sucked in her breath, and her chest protruded. Hannah was surprised to see anger flicker across her pale face. 'I heard him tell Toni to shut her fucking mouth. Just like *he* did. How dare he speak like that? How dare he use those words?' Beverley's fists were clenched.

'And you were triggered, weren't you, Patty?' Hannah said.

'Yes, I was, I ...' Beverley paused. 'You know who I am?'

'I do. You're Patty Greenwood.'

She nodded.

'Jake used the exact same words as my brother did. So disrespectful. So rude, and ... aggressive. He spat them out, like Derek used to.'

'And you had to save Toni. Just as you saved your little sister, Nancy.'

'If he could do that to Toni, he could do it to Emily, and I would not allow that,' Beverley cried, pulling her daughter closer, pleading with her eyes for understanding.

Poor Emily looked even more confused.

'Your brother? Your sister? What the hell ...? Mum, who's Patty Greenwood?'

'*I am!*' Beverley said. 'I'll explain everything. I promise. Neither your dad nor I should've kept our pasts hidden from you for so long, but we wanted you to have a perfect life, here in Marbella. Sadly, I have to say, if you'd grown up in Kingshurst you'd know who Patty Greenwood is. We just didn't want anything from our former lives to ever touch you. But there is a badness in both mine and Dad's families, and through Jake that badness has seeped into our current lives. Jake got hold of some bad genes. It wasn't his fault. But you, you're the best of all of us. I would do anything to protect you.' Turning her attention back to Hannah, Beverley said, 'The intention was only ever to stop him. I had no idea that he had hit his head. You have to believe that. It all happened so quickly, and then we just left. But I wouldn't have left him there if I'd known he was ... I just wouldn't have done that. He was still my son.'

Hannah gave a small nod. Beverley was not a vindictive person, or a heartless one. She knew that much.

To her husband, Beverley said, 'By the time I knew the terrible result of his fall, it was too late. I promise you.'

Ray opened his mouth but seemed unable to think of anything to say.

Beverley asked Hannah, 'How long have you known?'

'Who you really are?'

'Yes.'

'A few days,' Hannah replied. 'And I've wanted to tell you how amazing I think you are ever since I found out. I wanted to say how brave you are.'

'*Brave?*'

'Yes.'

'What for?' Beverley asked.

'For what you did? You know ...?'

'For what I did to my brother, Derek?'

'Yes.'

Beverley shook her head, slowly and purposefully. 'I wasn't brave. I was ... more frightened than I'd ever been before ... or since. But I had to save Nancy, didn't I? Although, in truth I wasn't able to save her. I assume you're aware she took her own life. Yet another reason why Ray and I left Kingshurst.'

'I did know she died, yes. Ray said to me the other day that you would never get over how your brother treated you, or what your sister did. At the time, I wasn't entirely sure what he meant by *what your sister did*. I must confess, I was rather preoccupied thinking about how you both escaped ... the axe, the blood etc. But later, I realised he was referring to Nancy's suicide. I read about it in the newspapers at the time, of course.'

'I suppose everyone did. The parasites at the papers were forever trying keep the story going. To everyone else it was just a little bit more of the tragedy. The next instalment. But for me it was devastating. It took Derek years to kill her, but, make no mistake, it was him who did it. It may have been suicide, but he tied the rope. She just couldn't forget it all.'

'You are incredibly strong to have managed to put it behind you,' Hannah said.

'Oh, it's not behind me. It's right here.' Beverley tapped her forehead. 'It's in the front of my mind every second of every day. It's even in my dreams. My darling Ray has given me a wonderful home and I am eternally grateful to him, but sadly, I will always reside in that basement. I cannot escape it.'

Hannah felt her throat close. What a heart-breaking life. 'Beverley, all you've ever done is protect the people you love. Be that your little sister, Nancy, or your innocent daughter.'

The room grew silent once again.

Ray's eyes were focused entirely on Emily and his wife. Walking over to them he enveloped them both in a hug.

'Can you ever forgive me, darling? Beverley looked up at him.

He nodded silently and kissed the top of her head.

'So, Ray,' Hannah said. 'I think that information may help you to decide what exactly you wish to tell the local police about Jake's fall.'

Ray indicated that he understood.

Hannah continued, 'Obviously, everything that's been said can be denied. There is no actual evidence. It's all anecdotal right now.'

'Whatever happens,' Annie said, 'I would like to thank you, Beverley. I honestly thought I was going to die. When you appeared behind me and pushed him at the exact same time as I did, it was ... fate, or ... karma.'

Burying her head into her mum, Emily mumbled, 'I don't even understand what you've all said.' She looked genuinely dazed.

Lottie seemed a bit embarrassed, as if she'd suddenly found herself in the middle of a Greek tragedy in which she did not belong.

'So ... how about it?' Hannah asked. 'Are you happy to let the police continue down the path they're heading, Ray?'

He replied immediately. 'Certainly, I can't let Beverley take the fall for this.' Realising what he'd said, he shook his head. 'Jesus, what a poor choice of words.'

'Do you think you can forgive *me* as well?' Annie cautiously asked Ray.

'For pushing Jake, yes. I understand why you and Beverley did it. But for planning to frame me? If I'm honest, I don't see how I can.'

Hannah interjected. 'Annie, there's someone else whose forgiveness you need to seek.'

'My sister?'

'Yes, Liv is mad as hell at you, but I can't help thinking, you're all she has. Since she lost Toby, she's been spiralling, maybe you could help her.'

'As if she'd let me.'

'It might be worth a shot,' Hannah suggested.

Ever the businessman, Ray asked, 'So, Hannah, what do we owe you for working all this out?'

'You don't owe me anything,' she replied. 'I already told you that. You were never the client.'

'But ...?'

'Ray, my job was to investigate whether you were a good person or not. I've done that.'

'And?' he asked.

'I believe you are, yes.'

Ray gave a faint smile. 'Remember, Hannah, sometimes good people do bad things for good reasons.'

'I suppose they do,' Hannah agreed, although she wasn't sure if he was referring to Annie or Patty.

73

HANNAH, APRIL 2023

HANNAH THREW herself into the slender aeroplane seat. 'Right, let's get the hell out of dodge.'

Lottie laughed. 'That's enough Marbs for now.'

'Absolutely.'

'Mind you,' Lottie continued. 'I always hate the flight home. It's that horrible bit between the end of a holiday and normal life.'

'This was far from a holiday, Lottie.'

'True.'

After the safety announcement, the cabin crew began passing around their coronation chicken sandwiches. 'I'm not falling for that again,' Lottie said.

'No, me neither. That's why I ate so much paella at that little place in the square,' Hannah said. 'Oh, by the way, I had a text from Liv. Annie's been in touch already.'

'Wow. That must've been a tough conversation. Given everything you told Liv.'

'She's still fuming with Annie. Obviously. But I don't know, I think possibly, in time …' Hannah shrugged. 'Who knows.'

'Could she really forgive that?'

'It's funny ... I was thinking about this. All those years Liv was convinced she saw her mum die, and the chances are she actually didn't. Turns out she probably just sat on the stairs, rooted to the spot. But Annie, she's a different story. She saw it all. But she never told a soul. She kept it from Liv and Toby to protect them from the full horror. She must've struggled to keep that in. I kind of hope Liv cuts her a break. Anyway, Annie is the only other person alive who remembers Toby, unless you count Ray, and I can't see him and Liv becoming buddies just yet. Liv needs to talk about Toby, and she ... she needs more heartbeats to care about.'

'Sorry?' Lottie quizzed.

'Nothing,' Hannah sighed. 'I just think she could do with a sister right now. It sounds like there were a lot of crossed wires between them over the years.'

'So, Annie's coming home to the UK?'

'I think so. It's probably a toss-up between trying to build a relationship with Ray or fixing the messed up one she already has with Liv.'

'Well, I hope they do manage to reconnect. Losing touch with your sister must be utter pants,' Lottie said. 'I can't imagine life without mine.' She gave Hannah a squeeze.

'Aww, bless you, beautiful. We are sisters, aren't we? But by choice, not nature.'

'Yes, we are.'

'I'll pop round to Liv's tomorrow to make sure she completely understands everything. It was tricky to get it all across in a phone call. I'll send her the bill next week.'

'Good plan,' Lottie agreed.

'Then there's Dave, he's so pissed off he missed all this. I had to promise to take him out for a steak lunch and go through it all *again* for him.'

'You'd better treat Paul as well. I mean, he confirmed loads of stuff with the Spanish police for you.'

'Sadly, he didn't confirm a thing.'

'Hold on. Back up a bit – what?'

'They wouldn't tell him shit.'

'You're kidding me?'

'Nope. Fucking Brexit!'

Lottie laughed. 'So… all that, *My colleague has confirmed …?*'

'Bluffing, mate.'

'You said the police had confirmed their verdict and all that.'

'They've already said as much to the family. Like Ray says, they're not going to go after drug dealers when a simple verdict of misadventure is far more likely. I reckon they'd pick their battles.'

'What about the fact there were two people on the steps; who told you that part?'

'No one *told* me. I was watching Beverley when Annie told us about the fight on the steps. Beverley wasn't hearing it for the first time. She was reliving it.'

'How could you tell?'

'Well, if I'm completely honest it was partly a hunch, just a feeling kind of thing. But also, it's like we always say, Lottie, you have to look into the whites of their eyes. The same as we all knew Claudia was fake crying because her eyes were never wet, her nose never ran, she never had to swallow down tears. Beverley's eyes told me she was remembering what she'd seen. Her body language said *I know what you're going to say next.* As soon as I realised she was remembering it, I knew for sure she'd been there. And then it was obvious. I'd always thought it would've been hard for one person, particularly a small woman, to push Jake down those steps. He was a solid bloke. He could've easily stood his ground if Annie had pushed him alone. But Beverley crept up on them. I don't know the exact positioning of them all, but it sounds like she came at them from the side or from behind. Jake was pushed from two different angles; he wasn't able to correct his equilibrium. Their combined energy took him down.'

'You're so clever, Han.' Lottie smiled.

'There was something else about Beverley's eyes,' Hannah continued. 'Something that told me she was involved.'

'What?' Lottie asked, eagerly.

'There was no pain in them. No *fresh* pain, I mean.'

'Fresh pain?'

'Yeah. There's no denying it, Beverley's eyes are incredibly sad. They tell a story of misery, but it's old, it's well-worn.'

'I don't think I—'

'Right, when someone took Dixie, and you thought she might die, you were grief-stricken, beside yourself, yes?'

'Of course I was.'

'Now imagine that was your actual child. Your son of nearly thirty years. And he was really dead, not just taken. That kind of grief shows in a person's eyes. Despite their differences, it was there in Ray's. He was going through hell. But ... it wasn't there in Beverley's. Whatever she felt about Jake, she wasn't grieving for him. I wondered if perhaps she'd just seen too much, witnessed so much horror that she couldn't feel new grief. But once I realised she'd been there, and she'd help to push him, then I understood why there was no fresh pain. He was cruel to her, and she always feared for Emily. She did what she had to do. But she wasn't grieving.'

Lottie said nothing for a moment; she just looked at Hannah in awe, seemingly amazed that she could tell so much from a pair of icy blue eyes. Finally, she said, 'To be honest, I'll be surprised if Ray is able to forgive Annie for plotting against him.'

'Yeah, me too.'

'What d'you think he meant by sometimes good people do bad things?' Lottie asked.

'Not sure,' Hannah said. 'He also said something odd to me when we were leaving.'

'What?'

'Erm ... something about people in glass houses. I didn't know who he was referring to. It could've been Patty or Annie. But we were all completely drained by then, and I didn't want to exhaust him further by asking. Suffice to say, both Annie and Patty were defending themselves.'

'Yeah, they were.'

A different flight attendant walked slowly past, and both Hannah and Lottie declined the sandwiches again.

Once he was out of earshot, Lottie said, 'I can't believe we've actually met Patty Greenwood. I grew up hearing all the stories about her chopping off her brother's head. I was a bit scared of her.'

'Technically she didn't chop it *completely* off.' Hannah pulled a face. 'And ... she's not scary. You know, she seemed so inconsequential, almost invisible, but when the innocent people she loved needed her, she was the strongest person around. She's a bloody hero.'

'Yes, I get that now.'

'And,' Hannah continued, 'I'm sure she really didn't know that Jake was injured when they pushed him. If she'd honestly thought they were leaving him to die—'

Lottie interrupted, 'God, her life is tragic, isn't it?'

Hannah nodded her agreement. 'So,' she asked, trying to lift their spirits, 'D'you think you'll keep in contact with Emily?'

Lottie replied in a second, 'Definitely. There are so many parallels within our families.'

'That's true, there are.'

'Perhaps she'll invite us for a holiday next year.'

'Oh yeah, she's bound to. It's not like we bought a lorry load of chaos to her family this time,' Hannah laughed.

'*You did!* I didn't. Maybe I'll take Chen instead.'

'I'd forgotten about him. When's he back?'

'Very soon.' Lottie gave a cheesy grin.

'Good.'

'I just couldn't believe it when you solved the whole thing,' Lottie said. 'I was like ...' She mimed her mind being blown. 'How did it feel to be the one to reveal everything, Han?'

'Erm ...' Hannah grinned. 'Like I wanted to kick a door down and shout *Let's go girls!* in my best Shania Twain voice. Although, obviously, I'm—'

'Not *a girl*!' Lottie laughed out loud.

———

Current whereabouts of this unopened letter – unknown

Letter addressed to Miss Antoinette Farnley. Flat 42, Fairfield House, Debonair Road, Ayresworth, Kingshurst, Hampshire

Dated August 10th 1996

Envelope stamped – recipient not known at this address; no return address provided.

Dear Annie,

I hope this is still the right address for you. I'm sorry to write to you out of the blue like this. But the problem is, on the night your mum died she was planning to tell you something important, and I have no idea if the poor woman had time. So I figured I ought to be the one to tell you.

On that night, I discovered from Susan that I am more than likely your biological father. I live with the deep-seated guilt that that was the reason for your parents' fight. When I arrived home after meeting with her, I got a call from Martin. He was angry, and he was throwing accusations at me and your mum. I don't know how he worked it all out, but it's my greatest regret that I allowed myself to be drawn into an argument with him. I don't think I said the right thing. I only added fuel to the fire. I'm so sorry.

I only visited your dad once in Crow's Wall. It was when he was first imprisoned there, and he could barely look at me. I don't blame him for being angry. But he said he was going to appeal, and he was sure he would get out. He was a persuasive man. A born salesman. He convinced people for a living. I was worried he might succeed. He told me when he got out, he was coming for me. I understood that. I can take care of myself. But Martin was a violent man. He kept it hidden well, but we all know what he did to poor Susan. I couldn't have him doing that to anyone else. Annie, I simply could not risk him doing to you what he did to your mother.

So, I'm writing to you now because I want you to know that what happened to your dad in prison was necessary. I had no choice; it had to be done to ensure your safety. I'm telling you this even though it's a risk. I can't be sure what you'll do with this information, but I hope you'll understand why I had to arrange it. Just in case, I won't put a return address, so you can't find me. I think that's for the best.

I don't know why I'm telling you this now. Maybe it's because I have a baby son and I finally know how important it is to be a parent. I wish I could've been a better one for you. Had I known before, things would've been different. But there's no point thinking like that. I have my son now, and you no doubt have people in your life who mean a lot to you.

I love you, and I wish with all my heart things could've been different for me and Susan, and for you, Olivia and Toby.

I hope you understand and that you can forgive me.

Love,

Ray
X

ACKNOWLEDGMENTS

Thank you so much to my publishers, Hobeck Books, Rebecca Collins and Adrian Hobart, for their continued support for the Sandlin PI series.

Also, to Sue Davison for her amazing editing powers, and to Jayne Mapp for the beautiful covers she designs for this series.

To Colin for his usual advice and words of wisdom.

Without their help – I am simply a storyteller, with it – I'm a published author.

ABOUT THE AUTHOR

Sue Shepherd began her writing career in 2015, writing contemporary romance. Over the next couple of years, she created three novels with heart, laughs and naughtiness. *Doesn't Everyone Have a Secret?*, *Love Them and Leave Them* and *Can't Get You Out of My Head*.

Realising that one of the parts she enjoyed most about writing was deciding when to let the reader in on the secrets from her characters' past, Sue switched genres and began writing a crime series starting with *Swindled*.

Sue lives on the picturesque Isle of Wight with her family and a standard poodle named Forrest and a Cavachon called Sky. Her passions in life are; her family, writing, the seaside and all the beautiful purple things her sons have bought her over the years. Ask Sue to plan too far in advance and you'll give her the heebie-jeebies and she'd prefer you not to mention Christmas until at least November!

THE SANDLIN PI SERIES

SWINDLED

He's out there somewhere. He's taken everything from me, and ... I hate him!

'...will definitely takes your breath away...an absolute stunner of a thriller...' Surjit's Book Blog
'Loved this book from start to finish' Nicki Williams

COUSIN ASH

'RUN FOR IT!'
Were they also Ash's last words?

'I read this in two sittings' Sarah Leck
'Just finished reading this and I thoroughly enjoyed it!' ThrillerMan

Both books available to buy from Amazon or Hobeck Books.

HOBECK BOOKS – THE HOME OF GREAT STORIES

We hope you've enjoyed reading this novel by the brilliant S.E. Shepherd. To find out more about the author please visit her Facebook page: **www.facebook.com/SueShepherdWrites**.

Hobeck Books offers a number of short stories and novellas, free for subscribers in the compilation *Crime Bites*.

- *Echo Rock* by Robert Daws

- *Old Dogs, Old Tricks* by AB Morgan
- *The Silence of the Rabbit* by Wendy Turbin
- *Never Mind the Baubles: An Anthology of Twisted Winter Tales* by the Hobeck Team (including many of the Hobeck authors and Hobeck's two publishers)
- *The Clarice Cliff Vase* by Linda Huber
- *Here She Lies* by Kerena Swan
- *The Macnab Principle* by R.D. Nixon
- *Fatal Beginnings* by Brian Price
- *A Defining Moment* by Lin Le Versha
- *Saviour* by Jennie Ensor
- *You Can't Trust Anyone These Days* by Maureen Myant

Also please visit the Hobeck Books website for details of our other superb authors and their books, and if you would like to get in touch, we would love to hear from you.

Hobeck Books also presents a weekly podcast, the Hobcast, where founders Adrian Hobart and Rebecca Collins discuss all things book related, key issues from each week, including the ups and downs of running a creative business. Each episode includes an interview with one of the people who make Hobeck possible: the editors, the authors, the cover designers. These are the people who help Hobeck bring great stories to life. Without them, Hobeck wouldn't exist. The Hobcast can be listened to from all the usual platforms but it can also be found on the Hobeck website: **www.hobeck.net/hobcast**.

Finally, if you enjoyed this book, please also leave a review on the site you bought it from and spread the word. Reviews are hugely important to writers and they help other readers also.